Don't Read Between the Lines

A HORDE KINGS VISIONARY STANDALONE

EMMALEIGH WYNTERS

Copyright © 2022 by Emmaleigh Wynters

All rights reserved.

No part of this book may be reproduced in any form or by any electronic or mechanical means, including information storage and retrieval systems, without written permission from the author, except for the use of brief quotations in a book review.

Music Playlist

Breaking Benjamin's "Dance with the devil"
Evanescence's "Bring me back to life"
AViVA "Rabbit Hole"
Written By Wolves "Genius"
Sinead O'Connor's "Nothing Compared To U"
Elise's "Lilith"
This Moment's "Oh Lord"
Rob Zombie's "Pussy Liquor"
Bebe Rexha's "Sacrafice"
Everybody Loves An Outlaw's "Blood On A Rose"
The Calling's "Wherever You Will Go"
SVRCINA's "Battlefield"
Kelsea Ballerini's "Peter Pan"

Songs I listened to while writing.
Karliene's "Become The Beast"
Ruht. B's "Lost Boy"

Corpse, Savage Gasp's "E-Girls Are Running My Life"
Saint Mesa's "Lion"
Boy Epic's "Scars"
Willyecho's "Monster"
Tommee Profitt, Wondra's "I'm Not Afraid"
Sam Tinnesz's "Bloodshot"
Georgi Kay's "Scary People"
Valley Of Wovles "Dangerous Man"
Once monster's "Messed up"
Anson Seabra's "Welcome To Wonderland"
Rain Paris's "Montero"
Slipknot's "Unsainted"
Meg Myers "Make A Shadow"
Sick Puppies "You're Going Down"

Authors Note

Dear Readers,

Here are the facts, Elijah and Adisen's story was nothing like I perceived when I first went into this.

The story that I had in my head, just didn't belong to the voice of Adisen and Elijah.

This is a grueling and semi-realistic tale of a reader, focused more on the real world and real fears and her similarities as to why she concludes to the reason she holds such a strong love for fiction.

I hope you love it nonetheless and enjoy their love story.

It is a beautiful story, one that needed to be told.

It's a difficult process when you're an Author who writes to the voices inside your head and to a trope that is so out of your ballpark, it hurts.

I will always be true to my characters. I will always honor their voice.

However, the story that was originally in my heart will be written in a new novel...

Devoured By The Lines- A Villain King's Visionary.

Another Standalone that will have nothing to do with Adisen and Elijah's story but will hold similarities in a flipped dimension version of the fantasy I had in my heart.

This story will follow the tale of an avid reader who gets sucked into a fantasy world. She will be kick-ass and heroic and will bring her villain king to his knees by force if need be.

She will wield that iron will of hers like a broadsword.

She dreams of a dark fantasy and when she is handed it, she does not disappoint.

So, stay tuned for El and Ezra's story next!

P.S - *As Devoured By The Lines is a new development, a prologue is not yet available.*

*For all of the Adisen's out there.
There is a reality to these words that are written.
So screw them, let's create our own story when the one created
for us just won't do!*

Prologue

"Do you remember me Adisen, Do you remember me now?"

There were things which taunted Elijah Braxton, things which went bump in the night. There were forces at play outside of the betrayal and pretty lies hidden from him within the very walls of his own bedchamber, that he was still yet to uncover. Something wicked, played with the strings of his mind. It created torment, and uncertainty. It created unsettled riots which would become dancing mishaps that would taunt his control. Many things would plague the king, things unseen to those around him. He'd spend his nights wondering if he was going crazy. If the people surrounding him were friends or foes and if he could be trusted to distinguish the difference anymore. One moment deceit was there with a crooked finger beckoning him near. Then poof, it was gone, fading within the distance with an echoing laugh berating on the wind and Elijah began to *wonder… If magic was a kingdom, was the stage within the walls of his mind?*

I toss and turn in the sheets. Sweat clinging to my heating flesh. The scene from the last chapter I read in Elijah's book flashing within my mind, like the strobe lights of a storm as lightning cracks across the earth. All the unknown pieces of his story cut gashes into my fearing soul and I began to wonder if the author has written a danger which could kill my beloved. It's not uncommon that after I finish a book or a chapter it stays in my subconscious. That my mind won't turn off or stop thinking about everything that I have read so far and everything that I expect to happen next.

But this time it's so much more. It's a nightmare.

It's a nightmare that I can't escape.

The face of a monster follows me everywhere I go. It's a terror, as solid as a pill, one I struggle to swallow. My mind races, unable to shut off as my brain creates scenarios, writing chaos of its own before I'm able to pick up the book and read the pages once more.

In order to cope, my mind conjures a faceless foe of my fears.

It gives me an enemy.

Something to fear.

Something I can place as the demon which is after my beloved and here… within the realm of my dream, I find the courage to want to face the darkness for him.

Never trust the demons, created from a nightmare, Adisen.

One

Adisen

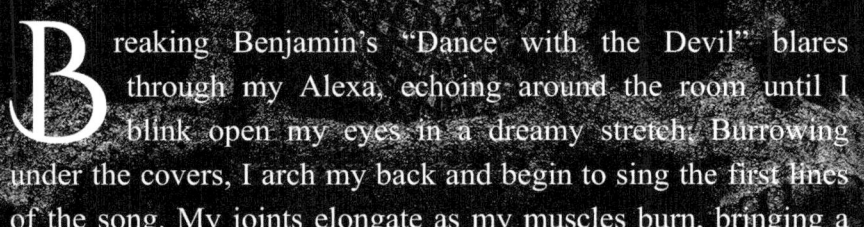

Breaking Benjamin's "Dance with the Devil" blares through my Alexa, echoing around the room until I blink open my eyes in a dreamy stretch. Burrowing under the covers, I arch my back and begin to sing the first lines of the song. My joints elongate as my muscles burn, bringing a smile to my lips. Without my Benjamin in the mornings to take me away to a new reality, I'd never make it out of bed.

Drumming the air, I brush together my thighs as I thrash around within the sheets, allowing the tempo to wake me. My alarm fades and I groan, wishing more than anything that the coffee is already brewed and waiting for my lazy ass to drag myself into the kitchen.

Truth is, I am not a morning person. Never have been, probably never will be.

But fuck it. That's mundane life, rig

"Alexa, repeat alarm," I croak in a hoarse voice as I reach for the book sitting on my bedside table.

It's the same thing I do every morning.

Instinct. Compulsion. Either way, every morning starts with a good book.

Flicking through the pages, just so I can smell the ink and paper as it wafts around me, I reach for the metal bookmark holding my place. Running my fingers over the jewels, I marvel at the beauty of it. It's a unique bookmark, one I had specially made when I started reading this book. — It's shaped like a blade with tribal markings that curve into the head of a beast that closely resembles a wolf. Hanging from one of its canines is a feather imbued with the lightest, pale blue I've ever seen. It's completely majestic and infused with pooling black ink which looks like they entwine together. Dark rubies sit as small gems around the stem. Every time I see it, I think of Elijah Braxton. The leading male character from the book I'm currently devouring.

He's the King of the Horde, which makes it sound like he commands an army. Which he kinda does, but it's one that belongs solely to him. Ruler of the dark ones, *The Accursed* and for some reason, amongst all of my book boyfriends, he's the one that hits differently. I just can't get enough.

I always set my alarm twice in the morning so I have time to read before I head off to work. I can't function without the motivation that bleeds through the words from another world, kicking my ass into gear.

It is not so much a feeling as it is a knowing that Elijah Braxton resides inside, as his eyes roam the crowd within the ballroom, searching through the silken gowns and tailored attire, searching for what calls him near.

He knows with the utmost certainty that this woman who stands out from the rest, like a steel sword against iron, is to be his mate, yet he does not feel it as one should.

There is a numbness inside of him that lingers with no heartfelt emotion but dwells with only the fruit of knowledge.

But it is not Elijah's job to question the fates. So he shall fulfill his duty.

He will become all that she needs him to be, he will take his vow and to his kingdom make this woman his Queen.

Even if it leads him to fall on his sword.

As compelled to do so, Elijah moves through the crowd with the stealth of a beast in the dead of night, circling his prey. The woman lifts her cold eyes, gazing upon him in an awe he has never before seen.

He waits for his beast to growl, to claim this woman who is destined to be theirs, yet the creature remains cautiously silent.

Elijah has not a moment to think, before this woman coils a slender hand around his wrist and beckons him near. A coy smile playing on her ruby red lips as she tucks a loose strand of blonde hair behind her ear.

"I am Jessaleia. It is very nice to meet you, my strong and heroic mate." She steps forward, blanketing his senses and the fog within his mind thickens. The haze is too vast for him to have noticed the look of deviance which had sparked in Jessaleia's chilling blue eyes at his approach, or the side eye, laced with a knowing look, to his brother Bradon who stood observing from the shadows.

"Egh," I scoff, rolling over onto my stomach and bringing the book to lie flat against my pillow debating whether or not I should read another chapter. A quick glance at my phone tells me I'm already running behind and I need to be getting ready for work. If I'm honest with myself, I've had enough of the perfection this character exudes anyway.

I mean, how dare he?

Now I've got to tackle the day with basic-dick, mediocre, egotistical, I couldn't flick the bean and make her scream with a roadmap, assholes that actually exist in *my* world.

I know, right? What a *drag*.

Now I really, *really* need a fucking coffee.

I kiss the paperback in my hands before placing it back on the side table and head into the closet to pick out my outfit for today. Throwing a gray tank and a pair of khaki ripped jeans on the bed, I toss my hair into a bun and sulk toward the kitchen. Sniffling, I pray I'm not getting a cold as I round the corner and head toward the kitchen island only to stop short at the coffee maker beeping that it's ready. I frown, turning to the machine glaring daggers as I wonder if I've finally lost my mind. But that shit is a running joke. Things like this always happen. My mama used to say I have an iron will and if I want something bad enough, it will just happen. I just think I'm not getting enough hours of sleep. I must have set it on a timer or something, even though this particular machine doesn't have one.

Excuses, excuses…

The bad boys that have those kinds of timers are *expensive*.

And rich I am not.

My phone buzzes on the counter and I pick it up, swiping my thumb across the screen and bringing it to my ear.

"Yo, bitch," Maria sings down the line and I frown, pulling it away and shuddering at the mirth in her voice this early in the morning.

"Eh," I grunt, wiping the sleep away from the corner of my eye.

"Oh, good morning to you too, sunshine." She chuckles.

"Dial it down a notch or ten, or I'm hanging up," I warn her as I grab a mug from the dishwasher.

"Okay, okay. Look, the reason for the phone call…" Maria trails off and I glare at the countertop, setting my jaw as I roll my eyes knowing what's coming next.

"You aren't coming, are you?"

"No. Not this weekend, but I promise I'll be there the next." She rushes, as I shake my head in defeat. She lives nearly an hour away, is my only friend in the whole entire world, and I barely see the girl. It makes my heart ache when we have to cancel on each other sometimes.

"That's two weeks away, M. Two." I sigh, pinching the bridge of my nose. "Fine."

"Oh come on, bitch, don't be like that. You know I love you, but I had to pick up this extra shift. If I don't, then I'm up shit creek and will never be able to move closer to you."

I place one of my hands on the side for support and jump when the voltage of a livewire jolts through me. "Motherfucker, dildo cunt sucker!" I hiss, bringing the tips of my burning fingers to my mouth as I kiss away the sting. There's a small puddle of water by the sink that seems to have overflowed across the drain and the charger I keep for my phone out here is laying in it. I yank the cord away quickly and throw down a rag on the liquid. It wasn't enough to cause damage or put me on my ass, but it smarts like a bitch.

"What happened? Are you okay?" Maria panics and I can hear the motorcycles in the distance fall silent as she closes a door and blocks out all other sound.

"I'm fine, just an electric shock is all. Don't worry about this weekend, we can sacrifice a few weekends of being together if it means in the end we'll be closer together, right? Even if you could just move in with me and call it a done deal." Applying pressure to my hand, I wring it out and turn back to the coffee machine, glaring.

Random shit always happens and every time that it does I crave more and more those quiet moments where I can retreat into a small corner with a hot chocolate and a good book.

"I know, I know. But you know my mama made me work for everything. I want to do this properly and besides, it's time I settle my slut ass down and have a kid or two. It's time I stood on my own two feet." I know she wants that more than anything. Maria has always been a party girl, but she's outgrown all of that now and in all the years that I've known her, I never thought that would happen. She's been my best friend since we were kids and our mothers went to school together.

"Okay, if you insist. I'll see you next weekend then?"

"You bet, love." We disconnect the call as I rub the back of my neck, the ache already starting.

Pouring myself a mug, I stare at the black coffee swirling within the bowl and zone out for a moment. Bringing it to my nose and inhaling deeply I take a sip, groaning as the heat seeps onto my tongue. I sigh, my body relaxing as I look out the kitchen window and embrace the woods which circle my property. I got lucky, well, *kinda*. I inherited the house when my parents died so in that sense, it sucks. But I get to keep my family home and remain isolated from half the world. My grandma loved the isolation as well, and the property belonged to my great, great, great grandmother so it's been in the family for generations. Even though there are still houses around us, we sit miles apart on riveting green.

My shoulder throbs as pain spirals around my joints. I can't ignore the ache spreading throughout my body anymore, it's been brewing since I woke up. Moving over to the drawers which hold my medication, I pull out the pills I need for this morning to help me manage the pain of my fibromyalgia as tears prick at the back of my eyes. I guess this is why I lose myself in novels so much. So I can stop feeling like such an utter soul-sucking disappointment for just five fucking minutes.

I'm conditioned to live with my pain.

You wouldn't know how much I suffer just by looking at me. Not unless you're perceptive enough to catch my silent cries or whimpers of agony when they are torn from my throat at my body revolting against me.

I hide it well but it's as brutal as it is draining. I feel pathetic, like this pain will forever control me and I feel ashamed because of it. Ashamed to admit it.

The life I dream of living is limited to the chains of pain that bind me.

There is a fire in my soul. A restlessness. It is one that burns with the need to be reckless and impulsive. I've craved an adrenaline and action filled life since I was a child, with a passion clawing at the cages of my heart that made me thrive with the impulse to do something crazy. To *be* crazy, if only to feel a moment of freedom. When I'm reading, I become captured in a new world, driving fast cars and shooting an arrow into the ass of my enemies. To jump from a cliff and dive headfirst into the unknown because I'm gliding on the wings of a phoenix. That's what I feel when living a life through all kinds of different characters.

Only I'm not free.

No.

I'm not a phoenix that soars.

I'm just a sad little budgie, locked in a prison with no wings at all.

I don't tell many people, and on the days I'm bedbound, I make excuses that I'm too poorly to leave the house. I struggle alone within a bedroom that becomes my own personal Hell.

I've been told I'm not allowed to work, but it's the only thing that I have that's only mine, so I suffer through it.

Brushing off my self-pity at something I can't change, and not one to eat much in the morning, I take the warm mug and head back into my room to get dressed. Slipping on my shit-kicker leather combat boots, I grab my leather jacket and hurry out the door before I'm super late for my shift.

It takes about forty minutes and then I'm pulling into my regular parking space and heading into the diner.

"You're late. Had your head stuck in that book again this morning, have you girl?" Dottie, the white-haired woman who owns this diner, quips as the bell dings above my head. I swing the door open with my hip and strut inside, smirking back at her perpetual frown.

"Of course I have. Like anyone would willingly live in reality," I retort, and she snorts a cackle only an old and wise woman can master. I chuckle and head toward the back to grab my black apron and tie it around my waist.

"I don't know, reality isn't all that bad," she muses and then frowns when a large and greasy-looking man comes to the counter and sends his plate sailing across it until it stops just short of coming off the other side and shattering. There is a dark glint in his eye that speaks of madness, a man unhinged and as soon as he blinks, the wickedness has gone, making me wonder if I saw it at all.

"I ordered triple bacon, layered turkey, pulled pork, and a

roast beef sub. This is a tuna melt with a salad. How could you get an order like that messed up, you senile bitch?" he sneers, narrowing his eyes on her like his large frame will intimidate this four-foot-nothing woman into cowering behind her dishrag. I cock a brow, head coiling back on my shoulders as I stare at the nerve of this rude motherfucker.

"Wishful thinking, my dear. Clearly a man such as yourself would never eat something so nutritious," she snarks, and I bark out a laugh that I don't even try to hide.

Dottie is a touchy one unless you're on her good side. A side I'm not even sure she has. The man makes a noise which I suppose was to be a growl but comes out like an unhealthy-sounding groan instead, and I scrunch up my nose in distaste.

"I've got this one, Dolly. I'll get him his sub," I offer and laugh even harder when she bitches at me that Dolly isn't her name.

I live to piss her off.

"And what will I get for the inconvenience? You owe me something, you old hag," he barks, glaring over my shoulder at Dottie while I make my way to the counter blocking his view.

"You'll get to walk out of here without a fat lip if you keep your mouth shut and stop insulting the boss, who's also probably as old as your granny. The mistake was an accident from the order list. Someone had called in an order and canceled it due to a meeting being moved up." I flick the paper hanging on the rack as I read over this morning's orders. "You got theirs instead of your own," I snap, moving to grab the dish and head back into the kitchen. The man grabs my wrist as I turn to leave. My eyebrows hit my hairline. I glance over my shoulder, glaring at his meaty paws which tighten their hold until I have to bite back a wince. Gently, I place the plate on the counter and slide my hand across to the coffee pot sitting by the register.

"If you were smart, you'd let go. Now," I warn as Dottie gasps and stumbles a step back, no doubt edging toward the bat she keeps hidden in one of the long, rounded counter cupboards.

"I don't like your attitude. I say I eat for free. Come now girl, don't quiver. What are you so afraid of?" the man barks around a shark-like smile which shows me his yellowing teeth.

I grimace, curling my lip in disgust, refusing to admit that he is right. That I am scared. "I say I warned you." I shrug with indifference, throwing the scalding hot coffee into his face, forcing him to break his hold on my wrist. He screams, wincing and stumbling backward falling into the nearest table as the boiling liquid blisters his cheeks.

I pull my arm to my chest, rubbing at the bruises which are already forming. The pain heightened by a million tiny fire ants gnawing through my muscles as the agony bites into my bones. I keep from crying out, at showing just how much that had hurt me and how now, because of it, my entire body is threatening to shut down with the pain shooting through every limb as if my wrist was only acting as a conductor for the rest of my body to feel it.

Why the hell people have to act like indignant fools is beyond me. There is absolutely no reason behind such violence and I guess that's one of the things I hate most about this world.

The complete and utter lack of sense it fucking makes.

"Seriously, asshole? What was the need to act like that? Just get the fuck out and I won't call the chief."

He is still screaming, seriously injured as the boiling water sizzles against his skin. Staggering back to his feet, he blindly searches for the door through clenched eyes as he tries to focus his breathing, but instead ends up sneering through the severe pain.

"You heard her, boy, get," Dottie parrots, moving back to my side with her faded and wood-chipped bat in hand. She screws up her face in a sneer and she reminds me of a pissed-off bulldog. I bite my tongue to stop myself from chuckling, forcing myself to remain fierce despite the fact my heart is beating a million miles a minute and sweat beats along the nape of my neck. My jaw clenches, holding steady as I meet his ugly glare with one of my own.

I'll never cower, but that doesn't mean I'm not human and that this bastard couldn't snap me like a twig. I bite the inside of my cheeks to keep from showing any weakness.

Blinking through hot lashes, he glares before scurrying out the door in a hurry. The diner is still pretty quiet, the dawn before the rotation of businessmen and women alike and busy-ass parents and naughty little kids with sticky fingers come rushing in like the horde is on their heels.

So as usual, no knight in shining armor to save the day.

"Maybe you're onto something there, child. I'm sure fiction holds no such men." Dottie breathes, dropping the bat to her side which stands taller than her waist.

"No, they do. Only in fiction, there is an Alpha to burn the world to protect their women, long after the woman has already removed the balls of any man who dared touch her. That's the thing about fiction, there is no power play at the end of the madness. The couples become equals to nobody but themselves when they realize there is nobody else to calm their demons. Do you get that? The alphas destroy the world but *for* her. And *for* her, they would settle it at her feet as well. There is dominance to an alpha. They take away all of the control and yet at the same time, they give it to you in abundance. Here? These assholes think they know what it is to dominate. That fear, illicit powers. They have no idea how wrong they are," I state, watching the door in case he decides to return and cause more trouble.

"Hmm," she hums, turning to refill the coffee pot, completely oblivious to how much I wish even a small aspect of what I love to read would bleed into reality.

Because with each new book, and each day filled with mundane tasks I can't help but feel like I don't belong here.

Damn, I can't wait until this day is over and I can make my escape. I'll chill out on my back porch with more Elijah Braxton. That will fix everything.

He'll save me from the tedious simplicity of it all. He always does.

Two

Adisen

The constellation shines above, almost as if magical pixie dust itself has been sprinkled upon the lands. Each glistening in the darkened sky reminds Elijah of the captivating depths of his mate. But not the mate he's returning home to. The one whom he has forever dreamed about since being a young beast. His idea of perfection.

The northern star calls to him, beckoning him into a deep memory of where Jessaleia lay so peacefully within his arms. Where her soft skin caresses him like the kiss of a feather, heat trailing in the wake of her touch. He knows he should long for that feeling again.

Not far from his home now, seeing the faint silhouette of his kingdom long lost on the horizon, Elijah welcomed the moment he could return home in victory. Once he slays those on his journey, he and his love would be safe once again. But a part of him *called him away from this place. To something he felt could be a different kind of home.*

Elijah roars, rattling the trees with his war cry as his blade arches high in the air, the silver glow from the moon glistening against the sharpened steel as if the gods and goddess themselves were blessing him for battle. The enemies have grown bolder, their armies surrounding the perimeter of his home. They seek the soon-to-be queen; her death would surely mean the king would fall. His enemies know that if they remove her head, Elijah will have no fight left in him, allowing his enemies to lay siege upon his kingdom, his home, and destroy all that he once knew. That, Elijah will never allow to happen. Not for the sake of his crown and his gold, not for his title or his power, because Elijah would give up all the treasures in the realm for love.

No, Elijah will never allow death to befall her because he would destroy the world and burn it to ash before he allowed anyone to hurt what was his. They made a threat, a threat he would not overlook and for that, they will all die. That is why he and his men are cutting off the head of the snake, striking at the armies who march on his grounds before they have the chance to attack.

He bathes in blood, crying to the moon, elated in the rush, relishing in the bodies which lie at his feet. Limbs scattered throughout the Wolven forests, the beasts howling in the distance, torn apart by the brutal hand of Elijah Braxton, King of the Horde. Controller of The Accursed. The night walkers and all of their creations. Elijah was one and the same, holding every banished beast known to the realm inside of him, blessed with a hound of his own. He is made from them, in blood and bone, fire and ash. He is forged in the strength of his people. The chosen one to lead them into glory. Coiled muscles tense in the dead of night, moving with fluid grace as a shirtless Elijah cuts down the enemy where they stand. "I will not allow them to hurt you, my sweet, sweet Jessaleia," Elijah growls, from deep within his chest. The beast taking over and the raw urge to mutilate those who seek to harm who he believes to be his true love becomes overwhelming. Elijah reaches for his shadows, calling forth the monsters of the night, this is where he obliterates those who oppose him. The darkness rolls in, like the mist coiling close to the water's surface, rising higher until their world is engulfed in black. When the darkness clears, he stands alone in a world of chaos, his enemies dead with broken limbs scattered at his feet.

"Fuck, yes. Elijah," I rasp as the image of him forms within my mind. I can almost see him, I can almost feel him as I lose myself within his world and his devotion. I steady my breathing before glancing back to the page I'm reading, my filthy mind imagining Elijah standing tall and naked consumes me and sets my nerve endings alight in the throes of passion.

"They are gone, my love, slaughtered like vermin. They will never get to you, you're safe. This, I promise," Elijah whispers on a heated breath along the nape of Jessaleia's neck. She stays with her back pressed against his firm chest, embraced within the arms of her beast.

"I never doubted you, my deadly monster. I know you will slay the world for me, we, my divine darkness are unstoppable." He prayed she was right. If he needed to end existence as they knew it and spend the rest of their days alone, he would. He just didn't want to. "They will never stop hunting me, my love, you must strike first. I fear Bradon is in league with our enemies," Jessaleia purrs, her sensual tone blanketing Elijah's ears like wool. He had been told those loyal to the keep seek her head for the injustice of their union. As Jessaleia was a simple maid *hiding a dark secret before she fell into the sights of their beloved king. Many deem her unworthy. He was told of their plans from informants of the soon-to-be-queen. Jessaleia was always the head of the charge. The reason unsuspecting towns were slaughtered. If only he knew she was having an affair with his brother, her true mate and together they strived for the kingdom which rightly belonged to him.*

"Ergh, lying bitch," I snap to the chilled night, like the stars would reply to my heated disagreement with a fictional character. I sit on my patio, a throw draped over my shoulders. As I long to trade places and hide myself within the arms of the beast, consumed within the ink of the pages. My mind can't make sense of this bitch. Why would anyone ruin something so perfect with a man so great?

"He is my brother, Jessaleia. He would never." Apparently, Jessaleia was done speaking as she turns into his hold and places claim to his lips. He growls hungrily, charging forth, holding firmly to her waist until he pushes her flush against the wall. His brain told him he needs her, craves her unlike anything he has ever craved. Without thought or pause, his rough hand reaches out and snatches the clothes which do her flawless body little justice. He's engulfed in the fever's harsh and scorching vise, lost to all else but the need to have her. Elijah tears the clothes from his body next, standing naked before his would-be queen as he parts her succulent thighs and readies his soldier to go to war on her glorious pussy. She moans in satisfaction. Having a firm grip on his neck aids Jessaleia as he hoists her into the air and drives his largely endowed cock into her slick entrance. Elijah's wide and tightly roped hips thrust forward, pounding into his woman without mercy, the sound of wet flesh connecting as his balls clash against her ass makes him groan.

Silent pain echoes within the depths of Jessaleia's pale-blue eyes as she becomes intimate with the beast that drives the rhythm of his hips, too weak to handle his dominance. Yet Elijah remains oblivious. Despite being this deep within her, he isn't deep enough. Elijah always craved more when within the arms of his mate, he just never understood why.

"Oh, Elijah," I whimper in unbridled pleasure, my book discarded onto my side table, my feet lazily hanging over the arms of my seat as my powerful, and slender vibrator slips beneath the silken surface of my panties, which I wore under my lounge pants. I tease the length of my slit before the rippled surface finds my clit. I see Elijah, my version of him anyway, so perfect within my mind's eye as the orgasm builds. My wrist is trained to hold the pressure as I target my clit, rough and precise circles have me bucking my hips and writhing against my hand as my fingers rhythmically pound my tight folds, craving the penetration. I ungracefully sail into the precipice, lost in exquisite rapture. I gaze at the night sky, the stars above glistening more than what is considered natural, as if each one is winking at me in their knowing approval. My cheeks flame scarlet as I whisper into the universe, "I wish Elijah Braxton was a real man. They don't exist in my reality." I blink in confusion, my heart twists within my chest as ravens take flight within the core of my stomach. The aftershocks of my orgasm tears through me until I quiver and risk falling from my seat.

I sit in silent awe as the stars begin to fall. I straighten in shock, watching as the heavens descend. An explosion of silver light detonates in the center of the greenery of my backyard. Metallic silver billows like smoke, cascading into the dead of night. I watch with bated breath as the cold air parts, the smoke clears, and a naked man straightens himself within the shadows.

Unfurling to his seven-foot-two height. Dark curls dust his long lashes, a scar marring the corner of his right eye curls like a crescent moon, pearl white and throbbing with beauty staring back at me. Death and power, unlike anything I have ever seen before exuding from the depths of his liquid-silver complexities, submerged into a pool of obsidian, looking like disturbed waters as it appears the glow of the moon fades from him.

Did the moon bring him here?

Shadows break into the night, curling themselves around him. Menacing violence as he tilts his head to the side and studies me closely. My heart stutters, seizing under the power thickening in the air. Holy fucking shit.

Elijah Braxton, the fictional beast from the paranormal romance novel I was reading, is now standing in my backyard, and he looks like he wants to tear my head from my shoulders and beat me with it.

He's exactly as I envisioned him.

Exactly as I wished for. Kinda.

That look has my heart racing and my senses rioting. I rise on shaky legs, subtly righting my wet panties, but I'm not subtle enough. His head snaps down, eyes following as he focuses on my apex, drenched in desire while he scents the air. Sniffing it as if he can actually smell my arousal from where he is standing.

Fuck, fuck, double fuckety fucks.

Looking out into the once largely open space, now shriveled in size, engulfed by the presence in what is surely my hallucination, the gray fleece falls from my shoulders, gathering around the backs of my legs as I take a step toward the man who radiates the promise of death.

Shit.

'Stop! Adisen, how stupid can you be?' the voice inside my

mind shrieks, falling on deaf ears as I continue my heavily entranced stroll toward the unknown. Elijah's glorious head is hung heavy, the shades of his eyes obscured by the wild curls feathering across his forehead and falling over his deadly gaze. His shoulders are drawn high to the skies, tense and ready to attack. I can hear the feral snarl escape his full lips, bounce off the trees and ruffle the leaves as they crack and whistle more ferociously than mother nature's harshest riot could ever create.

He's inhuman, animalistic… *'Yes, beast, remember?'* the voice exclaims, fear speaking volumes within my subconscious but apparently not registering within my mind. My gaze falls, and I stall my pursuit for one moment as my mind adjusts to the hardened cock pointing in my direction. I gasp into the night, only to have the chill of the air bite back against my chest, and scrape against my throat. Okay, his cock definitely looks human and isn't *totally* the length of an entire arm like I'm imagining, but that bad boy definitely is larger than the male population here on shitty old earth. A husky smile curls at my lips as I bite down seductively and continue on my way. I'm still dreaming, in subspace with an orgasm that has rocked me to my core. This can't be real, so the danger is not registering even though Elijah freaking Braxton looks anything but friendly right now. He's everything like I dreamed about and absolutely nothing like I dreamed about. He's a fantasy come to life, towering above me with defined and hard ridged abs that I itch to caress. He's a dark cloud shaped like a man that chills the air with a wicked warning. Even the tattoo of his ink doesn't look real. It's shiny and onyx and is slick on him, like glistening liquid. My heart races as it tightens in my chest. My tummy flutters and my mind becomes blank.

There is no way this can be real.

"What kind of sorcery is this, witch? Where am I and where is my mate? Answer with the truth and I may kill you quickly!" The deep timber of his voice echoes like thunder, kissing against my flesh in warning.

I clamp my mouth shut, contorting in disdain at his mention of that bitch. Clearly, I've hit my head and the universe didn't really grace me with such a wonderful gift. I close my eyes tightly, expecting him to be gone when I open them again, only he is now five steps closer, leering over me like a tower, blocking out the moon's light and engulfing me into an abyss. He growls and my pussy weeps, I'm racked with a violent urge to be filled by him, my breath catches, and my heart catapults into my throat. What the fuck is this? "I'll kill you if you have hurt her," he roars, then he lunges.

Apparently, that is the moment the danger radar kicks in and I take off on a quick sprint, winding my way through the forest in my backyard. Fear stabs at the surface of my skin, as I'm pushed with a rabid need to survive.

I don't think I have ever run so fast, I didn't even know I *could* run.

Working out is *not* my thing. Hurts like a bitch.

The wind whispers threats of death as it settles upon my shoulders, heavy like a cloud of dust as it wafts over my being and seeps into my pores with the sense of fear. The earth rattles, the winds roar, and the trees echo from his feral growl. I could feel the moment something changed. Something unnatural and not of this world is now hot on my heels.

I can't see the shift, but I can feel it like the cold barrel of a gun, pressing down upon me, with a promise.

It's thick like the veil of shadows that surround me.

I'm being hunted by a beast, a hound from the darkness.

Excerpts from his story filter through my mind as the panic increases.

The beast savages throughout the night.

Again, the monstrous beast wins victory in slaughtering the unkillable.

Rabid and untamed, the night beast tears through a village and claims again the souls of the wicked, banishing them as The Accursed.

Larger than the Fae's Lizard and deadlier than the Coral Hounds, Elijah's beast outpowers them all.

The roar which reaches the moon and beyond confirms my deepest fears that I am now the prey to Elijah Braxton, a man of nightmares and fiction combined. How do you run from a man who is not real? More importantly, how did you convince him you're not the enemy and his mate is a two-timing whore who, oh yeah, doesn't exist either?

I crouch in the shadows, hidden behind a tree trunk which is larger than any man, yet I know it still won't be wide enough to keep me hidden from the beast who seeks me. There is a thrill that shivers down my spine and electrifies my blood. My feet run from him, but my stupid heart? Calls to him.

Maybe there is some wicked witchyness afoot here. Because I'm tripping balls.

Fog crawls along the ground, kissing every molecule of earth that surrounds it. My shoulder burns as I scrape it along the harsh bark, running faster and further away from my cover as the howl calls to the night, asking it for assistance. The growl of the beast gnaws at my bones, threatening my stance as my mind screams to cower and fall like an impulse. Like it is a sound made to immobilize. But my fight or flight is hollering at me to haul ass as far away as I possibly can. Rain falls hard and heavy, the heavens open and threaten to drown me in their wrath. Branches crack under foot, leaves ruffle and the earth shakes. The hard air bites at my chest, scratches at my throat, and tightens at my bones as I push off from the ground once more and hurry forward. I feel like I'm running along a terrain super-charged in dark magic, like I'm no longer just a woman running wild in the woods. But a woman running amidst power.

There is another howl, this one rings out closer. Tripping over a tree stump, I crash to the ground. Hands digging into the soil as I fight for balance, crawling my way to be standing back upright again. A sharp pain feathers up my ankle, but I can't see. I shake uncontrollably trying to break free from whatever has me captive. Yanked from my feet, I'm pulled along the ground. As I'm dragged further away by a few feet, my back chafing along the detritus, I scream to the sky, my cries unfurling around me. My foot kicks out on its own accord as I break free of the vicious hold. I scramble to my knees and take off again, deeper into the woods and way beyond the limits of my house, panicking. I feel hysterical and on the verge of irrationality as I flee for my life without any idea as to what exactly is chasing me.

"Think, think, Adisen. What do I do? What would they do in the damn book?" Everything is spiraling around me. The faint whisper of the pitter patter on the water's surface, drifting through the air as the rain lands, breaking through the stormy sounds as it hits the lake up ahead. I hang onto that sound with all that I have, knowing that maybe, just maybe, if I get to that lake, I can submerge myself in the chilly depths and cover my scent. I'm not sure what kind of beast is on my heels. A wolf or some other kind of hound? Or even something else altogether but trying to hide my scent is the only option I have right now.

Elijah isn't supposed to be real, so how real is the information I've read about him?

I just have to hope that what I have read so far will be enough to save me from his wrath.

I twist and twirl through the trees, fabric is torn from my flesh as it catches on the branches. Blood pounds against my ear drums, my skin tingles with intensity and every nerve ending in my body seems to be alive as it sends tingles shooting through me as if I'm standing on an electrical current. It pushes me on with the urgency to not be maimed in the one place I find my peace.

The woods.

The sound of wild teeth snapping down in the air echoes around me. Dark mist coils around my frame searching through the night. Just before the darkness can capture me in a bone-shattering grip, I leap from my feet, jumping into the air and hurling myself into the lake. Thundering down into an icy grave, I gasp, sucking in mouthfuls of water until my lungs burn from the intensity. I thrash under the restrictions of the liquid blanket, desperately trying to find my feet. I'm swirling in a watery tornado after I lose my footing. I spin frantically after my jump, which is slowly but surely dragging me deeper into the mouth of death. The depths of this lake aren't even that deep, my feet should be able to reach the bottom but, in my panic, I'm struggling against rational thought.

Something razor sharp bites into the flesh of my hip, clamping down and jolting me back and forth, the resistance of the water moving me in slow motion. I cry into the lake, gaining myself another mouthful of muddy water before I'm dragged from the cool depths. A snarling beast hovers over me, a dark silhouette without features. I struggle to make sense of it, to see past the shadows which conceal him from me. The darkness is enormous in height, prowling closer until it is on top of me. My hair stirs in the windful breath of the monster.

I'm frozen, willing my mind to work, hoping my adrenaline will kick back in, but something happens, in that moment, something changes. I tilt my head to the sky, no longer afraid as I surrender to my terror, accepting my fate.

The air shifts, weaving in and out of existence. Spiked furs shrink back into normal, butter-soft skin. The massively coiled frame moves up along my body, gliding against my flesh as naked as the day he was born or in Elijah Braxton's case *hatched* or *created* or *plucked out of thin air* who the fuck knows? Golden eyes drill into mine. No longer silver and black. Confusion and awe stare back at me with the bitter edge of anger hardening the border of his gaze. His face tenses, and wet tendrils of curls feather across his forehead. High cheekbones clench in frustration. My gaze zeros in on his lips, slick with moisture from the glistening lake. He looks like he just stepped out of the cover of a fitness magazine and all of a sudden, I'm robbed of all coherent thought.

We still for a moment, both frozen in time and lost in each other's complexities. Vines of darkness circle us, interweaving between our close bodies. I barely notice it at first, the fact that he is inching closer and closer until his lips hover just above mine. His golden eyes shift, changing completely. Obsidian bleeds within, before bursting with orbs of silver until it looks like he has absorbed the moon in his depths. The heavens screech, lightning cracks across the skies. Vivid orbs of blue surround us, striking against the earth in its unbridled assault. Hot white fire burns around me, scorching the ground by my head as lightning bolts thunder all around us.

He looks down at me before his head drops to stare at the bite mark on my hip. I don't even feel it, completely numb and a slave to the shock and outright disbelief. His eyes widen, uncertainty filtering across his hard features before his body vibrates from the tension.

I gawk mutely as he shakes his head like a feral dog, teeth descending into the fangs of a wolf as he growls and snaps that menacing glare back toward me, and before I know what is happening, his jaw unhinges and he bites into the curve of my throat. I scream, the sound tempering into a lustful whimper as the pain races through me but blazing in its trail is arousal, unlike anything I have ever known. I arch my back, pushing my chest into his as I moan.

He pulls back, mouth bloody and eyes now fully black as his crimson lips crash down on mine. The livewire which jerks through my body has me mewling while the copper scent bleeds through my sensitive taste buds. It tastes like the world's greatest delicacy and I crave to have more of it.

My own blood tastes like heaven when on the lips of the devil.

"What have you done to me, witch?" he growls and the anger is so potent it burns in my veins making me recoil.

He hates me.

The man of my dreams is finally here and he fucking hates me.

That is the last thought that flickers throughout my mind before darkness consumes me.

Three

Elijah

Something happened.

I couldn't control the beast or the man. I sank my teeth into that vile witch while my cock ached to feel the toxic little minx clench around me, drawing blood from my skin as she savaged me. It makes me livid, my temperature rising in disgust as I relive that moment in my mind.

One moment, I was balls deep in Jessaleia, chasing a high that for some reason - no matter how good she feels - she could never sate.

Then a blinding light consumed me.

It stole my senses and erupted into my world until I found myself in a strange land. Staring at a strange woman, who speaks tales of utter beauty unrendered.

Her brown hair has golden streaks running through the smallest part of her golden strands, framing her face. Dark green eyes shine under the moonlight, twinkling with curious sparks that remind me of the stars that also seem so strange in this world.

She must be a femme fatale.

An evil seductress.

Anger burns in my veins, slithering under the surface until the urge to hunt down a little witch becomes too much to ignore. She ran and everything inside of me yipped to join in on the chase.

My skin gave way to fur, my thoughts gave way to chaos and my agony gave way to grievously tormented howls. Until I felt her flesh in my teeth, her blood on my tongue. It was enough for me to fight for control. I didn't want to hurt the witch before she undid whatever wicked sorcery she conjured. But then I lost control of the man as well and did the unthinkable…I bit her.

I don't know why. It was an impulse. An insidious need that lived like poison inside of me.

Everything about her drew me in like a foolish moth drawn to a damning flame. My skin burned, my cock hardened with the scent of her on the wind and it was enough to send me wild, wishing I could bottle it up and keep it with me forever. It made me bloodthirsty and the thoughts of her being with other suitors had me murderous.

It's a disgrace. The way she looks, the way I'm all of a sudden feeling. These emotions are drawn from me, brutally, unnaturally.

It should be like pulling blood from a stone, instead it's like watching the water fall as you tip the glass full of liquid, not expecting it to arch and hit the ground so quickly.

I have no place for having such toxic thoughts but they

plagued me with scenes of slaughtered demise all the same. Of a battlefield, filled with the dead as I ravished her on their corpses.

My mind was hazy, and I knew nothing other than the need to strike.

She blacked out and I fell on my ass violently. Something unsettled tore apart my gut as I stared down at her, so meek and vulnerable.

I've never even had the urge to bite Jessaleia.

Why?

Now, I'm lost. My gaze was unable to fall away from her still face, or the subtle flicker of her long lashes which feather across her cheekbones. I find myself drawn to her breathing, making sure she is still drawing air into her lungs. I hate myself for the thought. I long to wrap my hand around her throat and squeeze until those pretty emeralds bulge.

But I know that I need her. I tried to teleport, to use my magic to carry me back home.

It failed as the world glowed a wild blood-red kind of blue and knocked me on my ass.

Something is keeping me here and I think it's the little witch laying at my feet.

I shake my head, fighting through the muggy waters and with a savage growl, pull her into my arms and make my way back to her quarters, following the steps of the chase which has my mouth watering and my beast howling.

Nothing feels right in my world anymore and I'm beginning to think it's because I'm not in my world.

Here, the skies are black. Utterly black without purple hues. The stars are scattered across the sky instead of consuming it within its liquid silver, demanding my Kingdom's attention.

This definitely doesn't feel like home.

When this little witch wakes, she'll tell me everything. Even if I have to tarnish her beauty with saltful tears to get the answers I so desire. I'll play with her silken skin that beckons me, by painting it with a sheen of glorious crimson and covering all those delicate features of beauty that have ravens warring within my core.

I'll make her talk as I toy with her air, becoming her God as I make her surrender, giving me all that I demand.

After all, I am the King of the Horde.

She's never met a monster like me.

I stalk through the towering trees and back into the clearing out the back of her house. It's different from the ones in my realm, built oddly. I glance around and notice there are no stables for the hounds or pounds for the creatures. I can't see any towers and the air of magic only fizzles to attention in my proximity. The rest feels dull and non-existent. No monsters fly overhead and the dragon's fire doesn't crack throughout the earth as I walk, licking against me in praise of the king that I am. In my land, I'm recognized and revered everywhere I go.

I frown, prowling the wooden steps. Kicking open the back door I walk inside only to come to an abrupt halt as I take the place in. The kitchen is tiny. Nothing like the one in my palace. Strange appliances sit along the counter and I find myself repositioning the woman to my chest so I can reach out and touch one in curiosity. Turning the dial to a free-standing, oval- chalice looking thing, an outrageous roar echoes through the tiny space making me growl and retaliate. Ferocious blades twist and twirl in a brutal rotation as I pump the air with two fingers, ripping it from the wall and sending it sailing through the open space and shattering against the other side. Lifting my nose in the air, I edge toward it with caution making sure the witch's pet is dead.

It lies on the ground in a heap. Weird, metallic silver parts littered around the floor torn limb from limb. I grunt, hugging the woman to me tighter with the urge to throttle that slender neck of hers as I turn and continue my way through her quirky accommodations.

How dare she think her pet stood a chance against me.

No throne room, ballroom, grand hall, or anything like it. The tiny home is barren. Don't get me wrong, my realm has houses for our people. Small cottages built upon hot coals and rocky mountains, surrounded by the crystal-blue waters of health. Without your daily shot, you become easy prey for consumption. The creatures of evil will possess you and feast on your bones from the inside out, leaving you a hollow husk of the being you once were until you wither to ash and float home on the wind thanks to such parasites.

Does this woman not care for her safety? Or does she not have to worry about such things in this foreign land?

Finding a room with a bed, I lay her in the center of it. Taking a lingering moment to drown within her effortless beauty. I tuck a loose strand of silken brown hair behind her ear before I shake my head and dispel such traitorous thoughts in my weakness. Gathering her thick strands, I push them away from her shoulder and tilt her chin to bare her throat to me. I choke on a snarl that burns like hellfire as my creature growls for me to lick it better.

What the fuck is wrong with you? The witch is the enemy. I snarl internally, and my hound just turns up his nose, huffing at my ignorance.

Probing the wound with my fingers, deranged pride blooms within my chest at the jagged marks and torn flesh as blood seeps from her open punctures. I line my lip, drawing the digits into my mouth and swirling my tongue around her life's essence with a feral moan. My head hangs heavy and I close my eyes against the sensation.

I'll kill her for this.

For these sinful, wonderous urges this witch has implanted within me. I'll never be unfaithful to my mate. I'd die before I ever became that kind of husband. I haven't even married Jessaleia yet. The bond hasn't even been fully coiled and knowing she's alone, in a kingdom rising against us, eats away at the protective side of my murderous nature.

Tensing, anger rides my muscles like a wave until I notice how fucking hard I am right now. How my body aches for this witch's heat as I find my hand wrapped around my angry shaft unbidden as it burns hot in my palm.

I growl, yanking my hand away and clicking my fingers, conjuring some pants in frustration. Clenching my eyes once more, I snap them open and notice I've wrapped my hand around the woman's throat. She stirs as I apply more pressure with my rage and she flutters her drowsy eyes open and stares at me with rounded globes of wicked green orbs filled with utter confusion and bewilderment.

I sneer, my lips curling back until I flex my fingers tighter and lean down, putting my nose to hers and growling, "Time's up witch. Time to undo whatever spell it is you put on me."

Four

Adisen

I fight through the darkness, trying to find my way back to the light but something within me howls at how wrong that is. To turn around and fling myself into the abyss. My body heats, my veins igniting into a furious fire which melts my being and makes everything - even coherent thought - impossible.

The fire spreads, coiling around my throat and putting pressure that sits heavy on my chest.

So. Much. Pressure.

I can't breathe.

My ears pop. My mind fills with air and I feel like I'm about to explode through the starvation of whatever I'm being denied. My eyes fly open, black wells stare down at me. So much anger and hostility hardening his already sharp features. My heart tells me to cower but my brain just can't process the fact that any of this is real.

That *he's* real.

I claw at his wrists, panic making my mind hazy. My eyes fall heavy as oblivion calls to me. But I refuse to close them, to look away from such dark magnificence even if it means my death. I grit my teeth, noting if this is a dream I'll be fine come morning anyway so why not give into my desires?

Why not allow this fictional man to use me in a way which sends electricity zinging through my veins?

Shadows peel from the walls, darkening the edges of the room first before encroaching around us. I glance to the ceiling, noticing the shadow dome above our heads appears like storm clouds.

I'm helpless, at the mercy of a man who is the embodiment of dark and dreadful power.

Maybe the orgasm I had on the porch took me to subspace or some shit and I'm still coming down from the high?

Because I'm definitely fucking high.

It's the growl which snaps me back into this warped reality. Because it is otherworldly.

So far from human, everything within me riots to retreat and cower from the threat that's lingering near at the ominous and layered sound.

Elijah grits his jaw, grinding his teeth as a prominent tick makes his jawline twitch. Leaning down, he inhales deeply, smelling my hair before pulling back just a fraction so those black eyes meet mine and hold me captive. "You smell so sweet, witch. Real juicy. Good enough for a nightmare like me to devour."

A shiver runs down my spine and I arch my back, my chest

pushing into his making him frown and glare at my hardened nipples that pebble through the thin fabric. I'm fading fast, he isn't letting up on the vicious hold he has around my throat making floating dots splotch my vision. I can feel the bruises as they form along my neck, blood vessels popping under my skin.

"We can do this the easy way, and you can right the wrong you have caused. *Or*, we do this the hard way. Where I make you." His breathing is heavy but controlled. A soft and sensual rasp that hides the threat to his tone. But I hear it, I hear it like I hear the echo of my heart as it pounds for freedom within my ears. I shake my head, unable to speak to even attempt a response to something so utterly ridiculous.

I don't know why he's here, but I know I had nothing to do with it…

Right?

"Answer me," he demands, and I widen my eyes and ungracefully thrash my head back and forth in a *hey, dude. I can't with your meat hooks crushing my windpipes* kind of way.

Tilting his head, his eyes fall to his hand and he relinquishes me as I slump back into the sheets, panting like a fish dying under the sun, begging for the ocean. Moisture wells in my gaze at the agony throbbing under the surface, my eyes bulging as they become veined with bloodshot tears. I catch the odd look on his face when he catches me struggle, doubled over heaving for every breath willing myself to not freak the fuck out right now, but still not fully understanding just how much danger I'm in.

Because none of this can be fucking *real*.

"What the fuck is happening?" I wheeze, rolling to my side and bringing my knees into my chest as I try to regain some kind of control.

"You tell me? Why have you brought me here… and I *swear*,

if you have hurt my family, I'll hang you from the palace walls by your bowels as a warning to all those who dare stand against me."

I blink, my watery eyes finding his as I let those words settle into my bones. My first reaction is to run from this meth head serial killer, then when my pussy clenches, I remember he is a fictional beast and disembowelment is common practice and my sick and twisted mind finds threats like that hotter than a volcano about to go boom.

"What? Are you a *mugel*? Speak!" he roars, lunging forward and gripping my upper arms as he yanks me to a sitting position inches away from him and his heaving chest. My eyes trace the runes gracing his body and for a moment, I lose myself again. "What is this? What have you done?"

"What am I? A magic-8 ball? I don't know why you're here," I utter distractedly, my eyes swirling with the runes themself as they slither under his skin and a beast, larger than a wolf and scarier than a hellhound, takes form within the smooth expanse of flesh on his right pec. I swear to Satan, it's…*Preening?* Nose high in the air as the beast prowls back and forth with an air of arrogance that screams, *look at me.*

Burly fingers snap in front of my face and I draw back with a start, eyes snapping to Elijah's who looks at his chest and huffs a grunt of disapproval before turning back to face me, dismissing the moving entity, and becoming more angry as the seconds pass.

I shriek, legs flying skyward as I bounce from the bed only to fall back into the mattress with a heavy thud as some kind of vines slither from the tip of my toes, over my feet, around my shins and up my thighs until they pin me in place. My wild thrashing and colorful words, futile as the invisible restraints prick and caress my waist in equal parts pleasure and pain, while they coil around my stomach and flatten my chest to the bed, gripping my throat in warning.

I still, frantic eyes glaring murder at this man now standing on his feet, looming above me.

"You will tell me everything, or I'll show you why my powers are much stronger than your own, witch. As of right now, you're my hostage and I am your *worst* nightmare," he muses, a cocky smirk hiking his lips a little higher to the left, cold eyes narrowing as he tames his prey.

I can think of uglier kidnappers, but I can't seem to think of any more terrifying.

"I don't have powers. I'm not a witch and I don't know why you're here," I start, rushing through my words with a flare of irritation as a front for my spiraling fear. "You know, you're turning into a really bad wet dream. Where's my countless orgasms while you praise me for being a good girl and squirting in your mouth?" My sarcasm is a front for not wanting to believe in my delusions.

Elijah's face falls slack as round eyes watch me in shock. I chuckle, loving that in my dreams, I can be as brazen as I want.

"I'd never be unfaithful to Jessaleia," he snaps, affronted I'd even suggest such a thing while his eyes fall down my curvy frame, burning with heat.

I run my hands through my hair, pulling savagely at the strands as my mind revolts. I laugh inconceivably because this shit is just un-fucking-conceivable. "This shit isn't real. I don't know what the fuck is happening, this can't be happening," I mutter before scowling at him, lips turning down in distaste. "Hey, if this *is* my wet dream, then that bitch's name is banned here, okay? She's the one fucking Bradon and getting you high off that damn love potion."

He closes the distance between us swiftly, almost miserable as his fingers replace my own, tightening within my hair as he pulls my head back to face him, cupping me at the nape. His nostrils flaring as he presses his nose against mine as he sneers, "What the fuck did you just say, witch? They would never betray me in such a way. What you're saying... it's impossible and I'd watch what lies spew from those pretty lips, less I turn them black." The air becomes stifling under his rage, and I start to feel sorry he's so certain of that fact. It's like I've just spoken in a foreign tongue and he can't decipher the strange language. I should be horrified right now, but something about the savage hold he has on me - my body pressing against his as his lips hover above mine - has my skin heating.

My lungs seize as I fight for air while I struggle against the vines. My mind is short circuiting when beads of blood cut through my clothes and seep from my skin. "*Adisen.*" Falls unbidden from my lips and as soon as it does. I no longer remember if I said it at all.

"Dammit! Are you trying to hurt yourself?" he howls, and I shrink in on myself, wondering how my dream is taking such a dark turn. He relinquishes his grip in my hair, hands moving to my side, ripping my shirt from my body, and exposing my lacy-clad chest, making me gasp. "I'm glad I didn't threaten you with the poisonous ones," he mutters under his breath but I catch it, wondering what the fuck he's talking about.

A fever takes root at the base of my spine, like a wave coursing through my body as my limbs begin to ache and I become slightly more sluggish. Everything feels heavy as my arms fall to my sides like a deadweight. It's becoming hard to hear him at all through the wind swirling within my mind, drowning everything else out.

"One moment, you were in between the lines of a dark and delicious, epic fantasy romance novel and then you were standing in front of me. I was angry you were sleeping with Jessaleia, when she had just drugged your wine that evening with the love potion before the army surrounded the lands and you went to war. I was turned on at how hot that was and how I would give anything for you to be here... With me. Then, you were. I don't know how. I don't understand what's happening. Why is this happening?" I'm rambling, working through the muddled thoughts sinking into the murky waters of my numbing mind. My eyes are falling heavy. I close them for a moment before forcing them open again. "I-I don't know if you're real anymore. Am *I* real?" I feel delirious. Slowly shutting down as the pain I live with daily becomes unbearable. I feel as though my soul has become a deadweight, fighting for freedom from the confinements of my body.

"What's wrong with you? You're slurring," he asks around a grunt of annoyance as he leans forward, laying me back on the bed. His eyes are igniting with a glorious kind of fury that's quite magnificent. "If this is a trick, witch… What you're saying doesn't make sense. Why would they betray me?" It's like he's talking to himself while I struggle to hear him at all.

I feel him, his confusion and rage licking against me like a warm flame. "I'll cut those pretty lips of poison from your face for daring to tell me such a li-" His ranting drifts around me, dying off and so does his rage as I feel it dissipate from the room. I don't know if he finished his sentence or if he stopped abruptly but the next thing I know the pressure falls away from my body and I'm pulled into his arms.

My eyes close and my head drops limply on my shoulders.

"Hey, hey, witch. Wake up. Open those dark eyes for me," he insists, demanding. A rough hand chafing against my cheek as he slaps me to attention but I feel too weak. I'm standing in the flames of an inferno and it's burning me alive. I can't breathe. Sweat beads along my brow, dripping into my eyes causing an unbearable sting. He jostles me again, and I bounce on his lap as I try to open my eyes.

When did he pull me onto his lap? Wait...

I manage to peer through narrow slits, staring at the vanity table mirror across from the bed. My small and frail frame is draped over his ginormous one, infused with such power it charges the air and whispers around me like the kiss of a promise.

I roll in his hold, no longer having any use or function of my own body. My head drops, exposing the wounds in my throat, which make my heart want to leap from my chest. The wound is brutal, savage and does strange things of warm intimacy to my insides as the marks wink crimson tears from the column of my neck. I shudder, only to realize it was my soul that reacted, not my now lifeless body, compliant in his arms. I lose the battle and my eyes close again, only to open once more with a burst of energy when something zings in my veins, making me gasp in the open air and arch my back in the hold of the man whose frantic grip is bruising. With no will of my own, the current burning like a live wire inside of me takes over.

My gaze zeros in on the mirror, where the wound in my throat begins to glow an ethereal blue, veined with the essence of a pearl-white shimmer. First, it's subtle until the brightness becomes blinding and explodes throughout the room, raining down some kind of pixie dust around us.

"*Fuck*!" Is the last thing I hear bellowed through the room with a roar before blacking out…

Or is it blueing out?... Whiting out?

Because damn.

My eyes burn.

Five

Elijah

"**F**uck!" The room is engulfed in a blinding, bluish-white light which kisses against my flesh in such a heated caress, it feels like coming home.

What the fuck is that?

I used my powers on her. I wanted to know her name without her knowing I *needed* to know her name.

Adisen.

It whispers into my mind, a velvety caress which has my heart racing and my skin tingling, as I cradle her to my chest wondering what the fuck do I do next?

It's better when I call her witch, it keeps the distance between us. It keeps my rage current. I can't subside this unnatural worry I have for her that is forming inside of me as she thrashes back and forth. I can't give in.

I'll fight this spell of attraction with everything I have, but when the little vixen begins to convulse in my arms, panic seizes my chest and my rage is unable to ward it off.

My beast howls and it's the most grievous sound I've ever heard ring within the channel of my ears, which resounds to the hollow depths of my bottomless soul and if I wasn't sitting on the bed, it would bring me to my knees.

Her throat is exposed, the marks on her neck shimmering from something that looks like the crystal waters inside a moon-pool. The wound glows with the strangest kind of blue in the crevices of the hollow puncture. Sick pride is there, riding my core hard and I find happiness in the fact she's wearing our mark. It leaves me confused and I'm never confused.

Not about anything.

Ever.

The confusion has anger gathering inside of me like a demonic creature of possession.

"What the fuck?" I growl. Having no fucking idea what the hell is happening right now.

Why the fuck I'm here or why the fuck this woman is dancing in my hold like I've zapped her. I didn't use my powers for ill intent. Nothing should have harmed her.

Nothing.

Yet here she is fighting off something that is plaguing her body like an unseeable foe.

My temperature rises as does my fury at the unknown, crackling beneath the surface like the shock of lightning.

I shake her, willing her to keep her eyes open.

If she dies, I'm stuck here.

With no way home.

That is all that I can think about. Self-preservation with a need so deep-seated it feels more like a necessity than an instinct. I have to keep the witch alive. I have to do everything that I can to get back to my kingdom. Back to the world, I have always known.

No matter the consequence.

No matter the allure in this witch's pretty emerald eyes.

I have to return home and I need this enchantress to do it.

Through the darkness clouding my mind, I fight for a steady breath. To keep my monsters at bay. This isn't my world. I don't know what will happen if I unleash the monsters that I hold. Nothing is safe here. Not from me and not from my demons. If I allow them free, everything will burn within the black flames of hell and I can't allow that.

Not until I have answers.

When I used my magic I had thought that I had summoned it from the vines from the Dead Lands back in my realm. Thought that was what I had bound her to the bed with.

Now I'm wondering if I can even draw magic from my realm at all or if everything I think I'm pulling is just a manifestation of my memory. A conjured scene. The vines pricked at her skin but they can't be the cause as to why she's now seizing, head arched, eyes white as she jerks back and forth in my arms. I didn't use the ones laced in Dead Man's blood.

They *shouldn't* have harmed her. I just keep repeating everything in my head. Like the knowledge that I didn't do this intentionally will make me feel any less of a cunt for whatever it is that is trying to kill her.

I have no room for weakness, no room for kindness.

If I have to pretend, if I have to allow myself to run with these strange feelings, even only for my survival, then I will.

As long as I remember… She means nothing. The witch means nothing, and she's my only way home.

Something hard and brutal pounds against the walls of my mind. It echoes, the beat of a warrior's heart as I feel like my darkest recesses are trying to warn me of something.

To make me remember.

A distant memory hides behind a billowing veil and I just can't reach it.

Oh, little howler. When your skin becomes ablaze, dance within the fire. Don't run from it. Nothing will ever feel more glorious than having her in your arms.

An old and ancient voice echoes in my mind, a harrowing sound which has me shaking my head to stop my ears from ringing and for the pain to stop tearing me apart as it pulsates in my skull.

It blindsides me, and as soon as the words are heard, my ears once again become deaf and the feeling fades. I try to hold onto it, I try to fight the memory which is already running from me but I can't. It's like I know that it's there but I'm being forced to overlook it.

For now at least.

Placing Adisen on her back, I roll her to her side. My hand hovers over her forehead, heat radiates from her like the molten fields of fire and I curse under my breath. An emerald glow, entwines around my fingers, feathering across her skin and seeping into her forehead until the green glow turns into a sapphire spark that lights up her eyelids. Emerald orbs, eerily chilling, stare back at me, unseeing.

But my powers don't break her fever.

They only stop her from convulsing, but she still refuses to wake.

Once I stabilize her, I lurch from the bed with a bellow of fury reverberating from the cages of The Accursed that I house within.

When I ache, they ache and when I'm enraged, they roar to slaughter and maim.

I call forth my shadows. They gather around me like the soft storm of a lover and darken the room until the only thing to be seen - like a beacon drawn to the damned - is the woman in front of me. The darkness parts like a curtain. A silken sheen surrounding the witch and heightening her to my menacing scrutiny.

I can feel it as my body changes, my eyes consumed within the abyss as the monsters peek out and the sneer plays a torment on my lips, gathering within my throat.

Adisen shines, like a dark allure which beckons me near, so blissfully unaware of the monster towering over her. I take a heavy breath and hold it, blowing it out through my nose, as I take a step closer to my prey. Clenching my fists, I come to a halt and spin, giving the sleeping beauty of dark seduction my back and storming from the room.

I tear apart her strange little home, looking for any spells or incantations that can better tell me how to undo whatever it is she's done. There is no being more powerful than me. That I know for a fact. I don't know what kind of power is at play, what kind of trickery is afoot, but I will find it. And if I can't, I'll have to have fun with my little witch while I force her to tell me everything that she hides.

It isn't about how smart the battle plan is from your enemies. It's about how smart you navigate the war brought to your door.

Right now, there's nothing.

No indication of witchcraft at all, and if it is, it's none I've ever seen before.

No smoldering cauldron or cursed potion bottles.

No Fae wings, crushed into shadow dust and no vocal cords torn from a Banshee.

There's also a shit ton of items I've never seen and have no knowledge of.

It's nothing like my kingdom and it's unsettling. I can't distinguish what's her wicked witchery and her normal, mundane appliances.

The unfamiliarity of it all makes a shudder run down my spine as I growl, knowing that if I ever want to find out the truth behind her insidiously spoken words about my mate, or the truth as to why I'm here and just who exactly this little witch is, I have to nurse her back to health. I can't deny that anger is finding a way to control me. That it is clouding my judgment as I fight the war inside of me, but at the same time, I also can't deny that I feel more coherent and clear-headed. More in control of my own thoughts even though my control itself with everything else is slipping from my grasp.

Now I'm away from Jessaleia's firm embrace, I feel as though the heavy waters have parted and I can finally breathe. Something feels wrong, a niggling awareness to hunt for answers no matter the cost.

Almost as if the lines in the script have changed and I'm running my fingers through the pooling ink, with a need to do something with the silken liquid but unsure as to what, mesmerized.

I go back out into the clearing, wondering if there are any answers there, but find nothing. Taking a deep breath, I center myself as I try to calm my racing heart and burning anger.

My eyes search beyond the lines of trees which surround the property. A dark head of hair and a familiar stoic face stares back at me, with cold, calculating eyes as the air shimmers and I run forward, with a speed of power, my feet pound along the terrain.

"Bradon? Bradon?" I roar, coming to a halt at the spot I had just seen my brother standing in, finding nothing but an emptiness around me.

I heave a heavy breath, kneading the tight skin of my forehead from the ache beating against me.

Am I going crazy?

I tell myself that I will get to the bottom of this. That I will find out the root of this witch's sorcery and that I'll make her pay for her treachery.

I turn around and stalk back the way I came with a heaviness in my chest. On my way back up the steps, to check on the witch, I see a book discarded by the entrance of the door. I lean down, retrieve it, and turn it over within my hands. I see my face on the cover and frown. My beast at my side, a million shadow demons at my back and a war within my eyes as I charge toward my kingdom.

It's from the battle before I ended up here.

I flip through some of the pages at the back of the book, all of which are blank and my frown deepens as my brows knit together in confusion. I'm halfway through the empty pages when a low whimper reaches my ears and I charge through the halls like a witch drawn to the moonstone, unable to help myself but to answer her whispering call.

The man snarls.

The beast yips.

Loving the idea of being close to her once again.

What the fuck has this witch done to me?

Six

Adisen

I dance in the flames, under the stars, within my new dreamscape.

I have no idea where I am, walking through a foreign land, vined with frightful beauty. The trees surrounding me are withered and bare, the sky darkened above us, as I make my way through the scene of a horror movie.

Only I'm not afraid.

A feeling of utter rapture pulls my soul from my body as it writhes within the blood-red clouds of content. It's brewing a storm of demise and I half expect bodies to fall from the heavens, but it looks like I'm staring up at the bowels of Hell. Angry and wild, it billows and wars, meeting together in tiny tornados that whiz past my head.

AViVA's "Rabbit Hole" is echoing all around me, giving me the feeling that I'm floating as if I was on hallucinogens.

I feel like I'm in the land of twisted dreams, whirling within the endless possibilities of a dark and depraved kind of happiness, candyfloss, and cock... I'm suddenly running with the blue bunnies, my bare toes curling within the sapphire sands.

Candy?

What the hell is happening to me? What kind of fucked-up, morally gray dream is this?

And of course that's the only part that seems strange to me, the only part that echoes within my head telling me that none of this is real. That it can't be real and not the little bluish-gray gremlins devouring onyx mushrooms right in front of me.

Everything here depicts a picture of broken sanity. It's warped and menacing but I find myself smiling at the sight. Almost as if I'm shrouded in protection and bone aching desire.

Welcome to Wonderland, Adisen, babe. I've been waiting for you.

I've been drugged. Must have been. It's the only thing that can explain the absurdity of all of this.

My toes disappear within the sapphire sands as I dance under burgundy skies. I throw my hands in the air, my long fingers caressing the skin of my arms as I laugh without a care.

A huge silver and black beast, with hellfire lava streaked through its fur, comes barrelling toward me. He's metallic and ethereal and looks utterly out of this world as his rugged hair glows and shines under the pale moonlight bleeding through the crimson clouds. I laugh even louder, a whimsical sound which drifts on the cotton candy breeze like a sweet tooth's guilty pleasure and I find myself licking the air, surprised when it tastes just like cotton candy.

The beast laps at my hand and I giggle as monsters descend from the molten sky.

The clouds brew into a wild storm and it's nothing if not beautiful.

Twisted but fucking beautiful.

So many volatile emotions spin around me and gather into a hurricane as the monsters whiz and whirl overhead. Demonic creatures cackling, conforming into a shiver which feathers against my goose bumped skin.

I feel a rush of adrenaline. A tsunami of protection and deep-seated content. I feel like I'm living in the warmth of a mate, forever guarded despite the creatures that shriek around us. That I'm seeing the monsters that the one you love often tries to hide from you, but you see and adore them anyway.

I know that I'm seeing someone's demons and fighting with the urge to make them my own. I can *feel* it. Like when you can feel the presence of somebody close by. Like when you know you're being watched but can't find the eyes leering at you through a crowd of chaos.

I can feel the change in energy.

It may be my dream, but this isn't my world.

Led further through the harrowing trees, the bloody skies darken still as they turn into a brooding gray-storm. Soul-withering screeches tear through the night, banshees crying in the wind as I stop dead, head tilted as I listen to their cries. I'm pulled toward them, my heart seeking a forbidden touch of what I can only imagine will be my damnation. As I walk, the deeper I'm drawn, the darkness begins to fall. A foggy mist, which matches the skies, makes it impossible to see what surrounds me. The wails get louder, piercing through the drums of my ears right as I feel the stroke of a phantom grabbing at my arms.

One hand turns into the hands of a thousand as I'm pawed at and caressed by the same gray shadows which now form entities of monstrously-shaped silhouettes. High frequencies bellow to the void around me, desperation echoes with the force of a broken speaker as they all welcome me with hands as unforgiving as the beast who brought me here. The hound trots at my side, butting my hand with his head as I run my long fingers through his rough fur. Looking around, I notice the silhouettes come by the millions. That I'm almost looking at rows of prison cells, towered above one another as the creatures reach through the iron bars trying to reach me in their haste.

But I can't tell if that's true or not.

All I can see is gray bleeding from gray, pulling me closer. Me needing their acceptance but not knowing why. It reminds me of how I've always envisioned purgatory. The one depicted in Elijah's book. He holds a dimension for The Accursed. Creatures that have trespassed against his laws or become too grotesque and vicious for his realm. Once he's consumed them, they became bonded with him. A sacrifice that fuses with some kind of black blood if I remember rightly. It's a horde. His own personal army which makes him undefeatable within his realm.

The scene within the book runs through my mind and as quickly as it comes, I'm once again lost in my dreamscape.

Elijah houses a Labyrinth Of Torment. The king is the keeper of a purgatory dimension that dwells within the bottomless pit of his chest. When the laws are broken and the creatures become too hazardous for his realm, he consumes them and their power. Encapturing their essence within the walls of his purgatory prison that imprisons the horde of The Accursed.

He stands tall above a creature destined to become one of The Accursed now.

One he has to punish for his crimes against the world.

Here, Elijah would never allow the innocent to be feasted upon.

The second he touches the beast, the air around him changes and you know that whatever is next to transpire, will be a fate cemented in all-of-time. Once he consumes him, the demon, - which has no place within this kingdom - he will become bound to Elijah by the lining of the Blood Of The Black. This is an ancient essence that runs within his veins- that dwells within the terrain, running beneath the realm and comes with a soul-tethering loyalty.

If Elijah ever becomes untamed and you can hear The Accursed cry, know… You have been marked for death and there will be no escape.

I'm dizzy, coming to kneel in front of the beast who lays down beside me. I nestle closer, hiding within his rugged fur and closing my eyes in complete, soul settling ecstasy, right in the middle of the rows and rows of shadow creatures. They still stroke the air around me.

I'm worshiped by them all.

Rolling to my back, leaning against my own creature, who licks at my ear, I stare to the wrathful-like sky as it tilts and warbles like a broken illusion. My soul takes another hit at feeling utterly out of this world, high on a drug that could never have taken me down such a rabbit hole if it had came from earth.

Sound dissipates, moving further away as I dwell at the bottom of an endless chasm. There is a heady pressure around me, weighing me down. It's like when you swim to the bottom of the ocean. The further down you dive, the more the real world fades away and your oxygen becomes limited. My ears ring, and I ride the wave of my euphoria like a pro-surfer, refusing to let it go. To let that tide pass me by.

I burrow deeper, refusing to leave, as the sky falls like a blanket of fire and heats me in an inferno I melt within. I smile at the bunnies, bluish-gray gremlins, and wild creatures overhead, all running free in this warped kind of wonderland.

I want to keep them all with me, take them home and have them at my side. I want the souls too. I want them to continue their caress of mine so I no longer know the meaning of the words pain or anguish. That I will no longer feel the wrath of torment and regret.

All luring me into the pretty delusion of whacky illusions and a better kind of reality.

Considering how any other person would find this land terrifying, it speaks volumes on how I would favor this dark paradise over life. My life, who I am... I am now slowly realizing it is filled with something.

Something toxic and dangerous. Something that is the biggest killer of humans.

Depression.

I'm depressed and I just hadn't known it until my heart found this content kind of peace.

Each creature speaks of a promise of imperfection. They're grotesque and gnarly. At first glance, a normal person would scurry and hide to remain off their radar. But when I look beyond the perception of ugly, I see a creature unlike any other with a twisted smile on their face just living their best little freaky and demented life.

It's peaceful. They answer to no one. Without any need to be perfect or normal.

They're free. Unbound. True to nobody but themselves.

It's so fucking empowering, running wild among monsters with the feeling of being untouchable.

Here, I'm the danger. I just don't understand why.

I close my eyes once more, refusing to come back to my horrible, tedious, mundane reality.

You may wonder why this darkness is my friend?

Why do I favor the void over the light?

It's because the darkness *is* the allure. It bears no judgment, only content. In the abyss, in the expected badness of it all, your heart and soul are just quiet. You don't have to be perfect. You don't have to be fine and you don't have to worry. You can close your eyes in peace, knowing that nobody can touch your vulnerabilities here.

That you are fighting for nobody's expectations other than your own.

That's why I love the darkness and the beasts I read about.

Why I love the written word of menace, the broken and twisted beauty of an alpha.

It's why I love the thorns of a rose.

Because the beauty that makes you bleed is often the truest.

Just as I'm about to drift off, a man's voice whispers into my mind.

Come on, little witch. Wake up. Come back to me, I'm not done with you yet.

Seven

Adisen

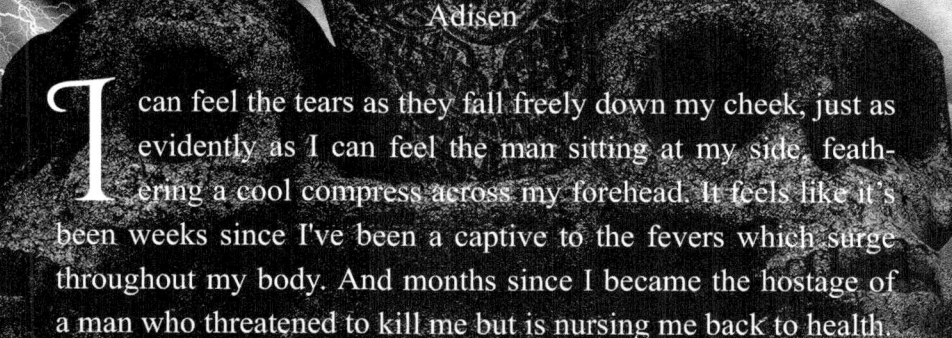

I can feel the tears as they fall freely down my cheek, just as evidently as I can feel the man sitting at my side, feathering a cool compress across my forehead. It feels like it's been weeks since I've been a captive to the fevers which surge throughout my body. And months since I became the hostage of a man who threatened to kill me but is nursing me back to health.

The heat of the fever no longer bothers me but when Elijah moves from my side, it brings an unexplainable agony. It must have been his power's effects. None of this is supposed to be possible so maybe he just didn't understand the consequences of using his ability on a human.

What am I even thinking?

I cackle internally, thinking myself insane for even having such a crazy thought.

I must have the head flu or somethi—

The tears that fall are for a whole other reason now. At first, I cried from being stolen from the dreamland which holds my heart. Now I'm crying because of the pain that is seizing my body.

It isn't the fever or whatever kind of parasite which makes me seize causing this brutal kind of hurt. It's the familiar ache within my bones that tells me so. The pain I'm used to, even now in the midst of something so unthinkable and somewhat wonderful and without explanation, I'm still a victim to my human agony. I'm still a victim to my disabilities that find me even in another world.

I don't tell him I'm awake, I just lay in silence as he hums a tune that isn't in English or any language I'm familiar with in fact. The deep rumble of his voice reverberates within my chest and my next breath is a deep one as I let it escape past my lips on a sigh. The smoothness of his sinful tone wraps around me like a lullaby as I become a child cradled within the ancient lyrics.

"I know you're awake," he muses, using his thumb to push away a moist strand of hair which has clung to my temple. "Is the pain bad? Is that why you're crying? I don't know how to help you, Adisen. I don't know what's causing this." There is a desperation in his voice, like he isn't used to not holding all the answers. I'm so out of it, that I almost think I dreamt it. It brings a soft smile to my lips as I keep my eyes closed, unable to face him and share with him my weakness.

He helps turn my head, bringing a heated spoon of some kind of soup to my mouth, taking me by surprise. The taste seeps onto my tongue, an explosion of earthy ingredients that taste out of this world and has my confused mind salivating. There is an awareness that creeps into my heart, cocooned within a warmness at the kindness of his actions. It leaves butterflies warring with the strength of ravens in my core. I feel like a little girl again, being cared for by the one person who seems larger than life in my innocent little eyes. Even after he threatened me, he still has the foresight to care for me and something about that moves me on a deeper level.

I can't remember the last time I ever considered myself innocent, though. But around him I feel as such. Like I just don't understand the ways of the world and I have the suspicion that it's because even though I'm in my world, at the same time, I'm also very, very far from it.

Because being next to him, is to be consumed by him, and to be consumed by him is to be consumed by a power that I know just doesn't exist.

He may only be a dream, a fantasy to see me through these dark times, but still, I find myself not wanting him to see me as anything less than perfect.

The only explanation for all of this is that it has to be a dream. Maybe the altercation back at the diner had escalated more than I had thought.

Became violent and I suffered a bump on my head.

Excuses, excuses. Something mockingly whispers into my ear making me frown with narrowed eyes. Elijah places the bowl on the side after feeding me a few spoonfuls. It warms my heart that his beastly mind was considerate enough to feed me while I'm in such a state.

"It isn't the fever. It feels almost peaceful when you're by my side. The heat brings sweet dreams of illusions that I find myself craving. My tears are for something else, Elijah," I whisper under my breath, turning my head away from the sound of his voice and whimpering at the strain of it in my neck. A gentle finger brings my face back to his.

"Open your eyes. Tell me what's wrong," he pleads on a gentle rasp, and like a compulsion, unable to deny his request, I do as he asks. The concern which still wars with uncertainty is enough to beat against my chest like a wave beating against the shore. He caresses the side of my cheek and I almost think I see a hint of vulnerability in his golden gaze.

"I'm human. Isn't that enough?" It's barely audible but he still hears me, narrowing his eyes and canting his head like he doesn't understand. The contemplative look, softening the features of his brooding face as he studies me and the meaning behind my words. "I don't know why you're here. I don't know if I'm dying or dreaming but even now, I can't escape my reality. The pain, I'm used to it."

"My magic works on you, I can help. I just can't remove the fever." Running his hands through my hair, his hand glows and the ache within my body recedes while I gasp, shuddering out a chilling breath at how refreshing it feels. The retreating waves of pain leave me with a feeling that this could become an addiction. One moment, where nothing hurts, is a moment even the strong will crave and even the iron willed will succumb to.

I reach out a shaky hand to caress his cheek, marveling at the awe of this creature and how powerful he is. He pulls back like I've burned him, like my touch is poison despite the fact his golden eyes tell me differently. The fact that even in his rage at me, he can't hide the gleam of concern which stares back at me. It's enough that it makes my heart flutter and twinge in pain all at once. I'm still a little delirious, the words running away from my lips, my mind not catching up to the rejection. As those eyes of concern turn lethal with his sneer. "Your eyes, they're golden again. Bright and rich like honey. I want to bathe in them." I breathe, as he catches my wrist in his hold. His jaw's tight as the tension coils within his body, having him straining above me. The conflict of wanting to embrace my touch and push it away all at the same time is written in the hard planes of his face.

Everything about this man is hostile and scary and I find that I don't mind it all that much. That even though the war within him could land me on the side of a personality he holds which wishes to snap my neck. There is nothing soft about this man. Nothing gentle and yet I'm helpless to stop myself from pushing. He's a contradiction, as his hold on my wrist tightens and flexes as he tries to hold himself back. It makes me wonder what game is running wicked through his mind right now as he stares at me after making sure my feverish body was cared for and fed.

"What do you desire, Adisen?" he asks slowly, peering into my eyes like they're the gateway to my soul.

I'm still half high, so I don't even think of the answer as it falls from my lips. "To be special. To be loved. To be anyone other than who I am. To find one moment of peace where my demons can't find me." My words seem to confuse him even more, if not anger him slightly. His jaw hammers, teeth grit as he glances away from me for a moment, before glaring down at me once again.

"Your fever changes nothing, witch. I'm simply nursing you back to health so you can return me home. I do not trust you had no part in this and you need to trust that whatever spell it is you put on me, I will not succumb to," he grinds out the words like they pain him, twitching like there is something in his core fighting against him as he speaks such hated words. He lets go of my wrist harshly, it jolts my arm as my hand lands against my chest with some aggression. I wince, narrowing my eyes at him, as trepidation whispers against my skin.

"I guess we'll have to work on that. I'm no witch but how

cool it would be to be one," I smile, a deflection at the worry taking root in my heart. His frown deepens and an awkward chuckle escapes me. "I guess since you think I'm at fault and that we are clearly stuck here, I better prove my innocence and show you the ways of my world." I can feel my skin as it heats again, clouding my mind. "I mean, that would only be fair, right? I don't want you to smite me in my sleep without having all the facts. What a shame it would be to die at the hands of my beloved." I bite my lip, eyes fluttering closed as I think. Not even noticing how I just declared that I love this fictional man. Later, I'm sure that I'll be grateful I missed the confused disgust in his eyes. "Let's start with a movie, shall we?"

He pulls back, looking at me through a scrunched-up nose and narrowed eyes. "A what?" he asks, clearly not knowing what a movie is. I'm sure his reasoning behind not refusing such an offer is because he feels like he needs me to get back home. That much is clear by the endless amount of times he asked me to do as such by returning him.

Even though I have no idea how to do such a thing.

I chuckle whispering, "A different reality."

Eight

Adisen

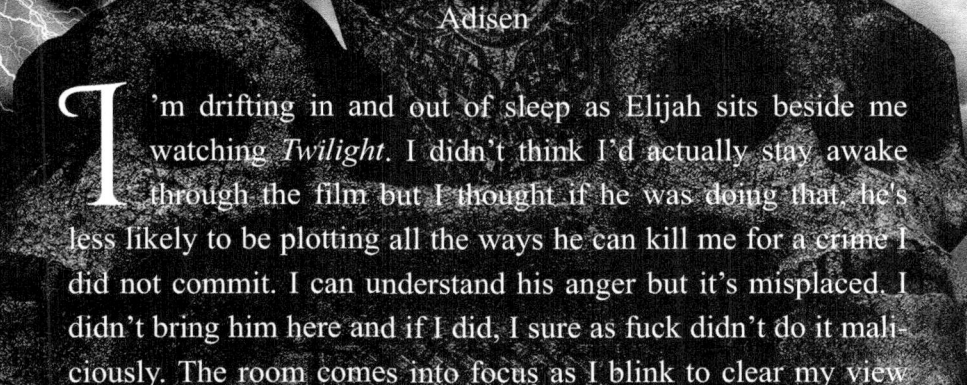

I'm drifting in and out of sleep as Elijah sits beside me watching *Twilight*. I didn't think I'd actually stay awake through the film but I thought if he was doing that, he's less likely to be plotting all the ways he can kill me for a crime I did not commit. I can understand his anger but it's misplaced. I didn't bring him here and if I did, I sure as fuck didn't do it maliciously. The room comes into focus as I blink to clear my view of the figure sitting on the end of my bed.

"He looks like a mermaid's pearl," Elijah mutters and the absurdity of it has me rising from my slumber rather quickly.

"What?" I croak, blinking open my eyes as he finally comes into view. Shirtless and leaning forward on his knees to get closer to the screen in my bedroom. The TV is mounted to the wall, directly in front of my bed. Edward Cullen is standing in the woods trying to scare the love of his life away, glittering like some sparkling lamp and trying to act like the big bad vampire.

Elijah turns to me distractedly, uttering, "You know. When a mermaid is ready to breed she omits this shining essence each moon. Then they become vicious fuckers. Sooner take off your hand than accept the food it offers. Proper beastly." For one single moment, his guard is down. A man in awe and not in rage.

I blink again, trying to work through that in my mind and the only conclusion has me batting my eyes like an owl in shock, and a little in warped curiosity, "You mean to tell me Edward Cullen, a teens wet fantasy, looks like a mermaid's... *period?*"

"Exactly so," he confirms and I can't hold back the riot of laughter that racks through my weak body, making my shoulders quiver. However long I've been in and out of my dreamscape, the promise of such dreams taunting me, the more I want to go back.

But that world, the one belonging to my fever, has nothing to do with the dream I've woken to.

To this man that fell from the sky and landed so gracefully dark at my feet.

I don't want this to be a dream. That much I can feel cemented within my bones.

To stay in this easy existence between us.

This man and everything he stands for fascinates me. The stories of his realm intrigue me and my Alice heart wants it all. To understand it all. I want to become a part of everything he's ever known and experienced and I can't understand why. I can't pinpoint what it is about him that makes me sad that I haven't been there through it all. That there are memories and emotions in his heart that will never be mine.

I don't know why I have a fever, but I know that it feels like it's changing something inside of me. Each time the skies change and I find myself in a different land within this dreamscape full of such underrated wonder, the more my heart grows fierce. I've traveled to many lands for however long the fever has had me. I'm starting to feel more open-minded. More at peace with any and all unanswered questions. And as a human, I have a shit ton.

Like what's the fucking point of life at all?

It all fades away when I'm somewhere other than here.

When I have no option but to surrender to the calmness of it all.

Like maybe the possibility of all of this may not be so far out of my reach and maybe, just maybe, I'll be taken to a place far more welcoming than the one I was born into.

An escape from reality, so I can fly away and never have the burden of mundane pain and sadness.

The pain of my disability, the sadness of missing my family, the hollowness that comes from forever feeling so alone despite being surrounded by so many people.

Most days, I don't want to get out of bed at all. Lying there staring at the ceiling until my tired eyes find the strength to once again make sense of the words on the pages and as soon as I'm able, I'm right back to it. Living another life, through another character.

I spent my childhood alone, isolated because I was forced to grow up too fast due to the spoils of life. My family wasn't lucky in wealth and we sure as fuck weren't lucky in health. I spent years as a kid in and out of hospitals. Years with bad attendance in school and dealing with fallouts from *'friends'* because I was never around. Because I wasn't the one they were forced to be with every day, so on the days I finally did return to school, whatever drama they would get themselves in would somehow be my fault. I was bed bound and clinging to my mother's chest terrified that I was going to die because I was too young to understand why I was in pain all of the time. Why my body was so weak and determined to work against me. I was too young to be too wise and familiar with the presence of death. It felt like every year I was burying someone I loved and eventually they all left, and my biggest fear finally happened.

I wasn't feeling alone, I was *actually* alone, without the people who ever mattered to me. All I have now is Maria, but even she lives too far away to meet regularly when she is saving like hell to uproot her life and move here.

For me.

Running his hand up my thigh, to my neck, Elijah presses the back of his hand to my forehead and a small smile cracks across his devilishly handsome face. "Your fever is lessening." Then the smile fades and his hand retreats.

"Hmm." To look into this man's eyes, means to look into something akin to hope. They transport me to such a different actuality and I find myself drowning within them. "Tell me more," I asked, transfixed. "About your home." Because there is a craving within me that goes deeper beyond the description on a page. I need to know about him as a man, as the person who was written so well within the lines of a book that he captured my heart from chapter one.

There is a moment here, a small window where his guard is down and my own inhibitions are gone. We're bathed in a calmness, gracing ourselves with the lightweight feeling of floating in still waters. I don't want to lose it. I don't want to lose the Elijah that lays this close beside me with gentle intrigue in his alluring eyes.

Turning, he moves to my side and hovers above me. His lips are so close to mine as he studies my face that I can feel the heat from his breath caress my smooth skin. I want him so badly to close that distance. To fuse those sinful lips with mine, my instead the darkness that lives inside of him gathers within his storm-riddled eyes. "Want to know all of my secrets so you can use them against me, Witch?" Running his thumb along my jawline, my lips part as I arch my back mewling into his touch. He grips my jaw bruisingly, but not in a way that hurts, but in a way where his hold speaks of a demand, taking root inside of me. The dominance, feathering throughout my body bringing a riot of emotions. "I won't make my downfall easy on you. That I can promise." The brooding look in his gaze, chased by the vines of evil that leave no question in my mind as to how dangerous this man can be, stares back at me.

But again… My mind just doesn't seem to care.

"I don't want you to fall," I whisper, in quiet confusion, even though my tone speaks of a declaration. " I have never wanted that for you. Just one moment where you're unburdened from duty and responsibility. Just one moment where you're free. That is all that I long for," I add wholeheartedly, feeling it from the depths of my very core. All he's ever known is the king who would take on the world alone, a sacrifice to save his people. He deserves to know the man. The man who is coveted for who he is and not what he can do.

Lightening the mood I muse, "Although, I don't think it helped my case by making you watch *Twilight*. A witch could surely not sit through something so painful without casting a spell or two." A soft smile plays on my lips and then darkness kisses against my slumbering mind once more, his growl of annoyance reverberating through my chest.

Nine

Adisen

"So, what other tricks can you do?" I groan, rolling to my side and bringing my knees to my chest as I rouse from the fever. I inhale a deep breath before rolling to my back again and trying to ease myself into a sitting position. Elijah reaches out quickly, catching me by the shoulders and helping me rest against the velvet headboard with a grunt.

I'm not in pain anymore and the fever is nothing more than a warmth to keep me toasty but my body still aches like a bitch. I'm stiff, needing to loosen my joints.

"Did you miss the part of you being my hostage? I think I'm the one who should be asking the questions." He stares at me like I should take it as a warning to keep my mouth shut.

I stare at him blankly before blinking, shrugging my shoulders with indifference and asking again. "So, what other tricks can you do?"

"I'm not sure what you mean," he states solemnly, with a face that gives nothing away and a tone that brokers no question in regards to his irritation.

"I mean…" Huffing, I stop to think about what I did actually mean and come up empty. "*Fuck,* I don't even know." I chuckle breathlessly, clutching my side as a stitch causes me to wheeze. "None of this can be real, right? So what good are empty questions."

"You keep saying that…Yet you seem pretty real to me, witch."

"Back to that, huh? Nursing me back to health didn't soften that heart of stone and make you rethink this whole witch thing then?" It was a long shot. But as it stands at the moment, this wet dream is a sour dud and doing nothing for my libido. Okay, well… That's a lie. Just looking at his sinfully hard edges and hearing that dark brooding timber in his voice hits me in the feels. The pussy-clenching - this bitch just doesn't understand the depravity - feels.

"Only did what I needed to do in order to get back to my people," he utters gruffly and without emotion, causing me to narrow my darkening green eyes around a frown. "So now you can undo whatever it is you did and send me back before I make you understand just why you never should have conjured me in the first place."

"Had nothing to do with the fact it was your fault I became sick?" I bite back, folding my arms across my chest like a petulant child. The truth to his words are barbed, the fact that even my fantasy doesn't want to be around me stings, forcing me to trace the wound on my throat absently as I process that.

"I had nothing to do with your fever, Adisen. It was probably one of your parlor tricks. The vines I used are not harmful and I would know if my powers had hurt you." The growl in his voice knocks me back for a second, but only a second because my annoyance bleeds through rather quickly at the nerve of him.

"Of course you would, just like you would know the truth about what has been happening in your world. It's easier to blame me than yourself right? Easier to pretend it's me that's the lie." I'm not sure why I'm getting so angry, but now the fever has broken and I'm more coherent, I find myself pissed as fuck at the entire situation.

"I'm in the middle of a war, witch. I don't have time for your games. I have-" He sneers, causing me to sit a little straighter, my eyes drawn to the turbulence in his golden gaze.

"-You have what? You're a part of a war that is plaguing your kingdom for the wrong damn reason, Elijah." I sigh, closing my eyes for a moment as I really consider my sanity.

I'm arguing with a fantasy. *Is this really happening right now?* Maybe I still have a fever...

I had formed some kind of insane and foolish connection to the man in the book. I had read between the lines and fell in some kind of moronic love with the man the author had created. I had thought my dreams would have made him perfect, my version of perfect at the very least. But instead, I'm faced with a walking, talking, brute of a man that wants to make me the villain in his story.

Not fucking likely.

Life's hard enough without my dreams turning into my nightmares.

"I need coffee," I moan, throwing my legs over the edge of the bed and steadying myself before rising to my feet. The familiar tingling sensation circles my ankles before spreading out across my calves. I bite my tongue, refusing to acknowledge the ache churning within my bones. I go light-headed and catch myself on the windowpane as I pass. I can feel the inferno which burns through my body at the intensity of Elijah's scrutiny as he blocks my path, staring at me with wrathful eyes and an indignant expression as if he can't believe how brazen I am.

"Where do you think you're going?" he growls, towering in height as he looms over me.

"To. Get. Coffee," I reiterate, refusing to cower.

Screw him, I'm mad at his sinfully gorgeous ass anyway and I refuse to show him any more of my weaknesses. He's seen enough of them and if he wants to make me the bad guy, he can go whistle. Because it fucking hurts. The thought of that for whatever reason he is here and he is staring at me like I'm worse than the plague fucking hurts.

I stumble through the room and out into the hallway, sensing that he's following closely behind. I stop short at the mirror hanging there, as my eye catches the bite mark in my throat.

"Holy fuck in the baptized waters! You bit me! You and your goodman beast!" The events leading up to the fever assault my mind in a torrent so forceful, it makes me sway on my feet as I remember. As the memories flash like a brutal strike of lightning in my head. I don't know if I'm fuming, or if it makes me feel some strange sense of pride.

I literally don't know anything anymore, the more coherent I become, the more I can see the confusion clouding my mind.

"Is that going to scar?" I realize I'm still in nothing but my bra as I gaze down at the violent bite on my hip, inches deep with blood-red bruising.

The crazy is finally starting to come back to me now that I'm back on my feet.

"I don't know what came over me," he grunts, avoiding

making eye contact as he bores a hole into the wound on my tender flesh, deep into my side. "I'd never have touched you if I was in the right frame of mind."

I spin on him, not sure if I'm furious, aroused or still so fucking confused this is happening at all, "Heal it! You bit it, you fix it. And next time, take a girl to dinner first. *Jeez Louise*."

"I can't. My powers work on you, but they won't allow me to remove the mark. Or allow me to return home. Here, everything is muted."

"Why?"

"I don't know. Some things are strange in this world. Things I don't understand."

"Fan-fucking-tastic. Well, at least I can say I'm the damn chew toy of the sexiest mutt to ever exist in fiction," I grouse, and his eyes flicker to obsidian. I suddenly have the feeling it isn't Elijah staring back at me, but his beast. That I've pushed him too far and the predator has finally consumed the man. Or maybe it's even the horde of The Accursed that is staring back at me because there is something soulful in his abyss.

I shiver, thighs clenching tight as I rub them for friction. My body is a sick riot of unease and burning arousal at the beast staring back at me. Everything in me screams to remain still, not to anger the monsters who I can sense are salivating for another taste of my blood. But I can also see Elijah there, lingering behind the surface. I have the instinct to bear my throat to him, but my stubbornness turns it into an uncontrollable twitch instead.

Shaking it off, I give the beast my back which in hindsight is a dumb fucking move. Something hard plasters itself to me, thickly coiled as muscular arms wrap around my waist and lift me off my feet, slamming me back into his unrelenting chest as one of his fierce hands wraps around my throat and presses curious fingers against my pulse.

I grunt, the air leaving me in a rush as he embeds his nose into the curve of my neck and inhales deeply, drawing the scent of my skin into his lungs as the tip feathers across the tender scar which aches so beautifully under his touch.

I freeze, trying my hardest to keep from trembling, but still find my ass grinding against his groin as I circle my hips from the intensity of the situation and it prickles against my sensitive skin. I'm aflame. Magic licking against me with the warmth of a wildfire, making me burn. His unseen powers thicken within the air.

"Careful, woman. Hold very fucking still, if I snap this pretty neck before the time is right, we'll both be fucked," Elijah growls in an inhuman voice that sounds like grinding gravel. It's like he's speaking with the voice of two men. Two very dangerous men. "You fascinate my beast and I find myself warring against the creature I have always been one with. Never turn your back on the hunter." He places a soft kiss on the curve of my neck. His cool lips caress my smoothness as a small whimper leaves me and my eyes flutter closed.

Elijah seems to find some sense of control and wretches himself away from me quickly, dropping me back to my feet and putting space between us. I gulp, clearing my throat, and cautiously step toward the kitchen, still facing away from him on unsteady feet. A Gray tank materializes on my body, covering me from him and I gasp, shivering at the strange feeling his powers elicit. I clench my eyes, not willing to believe it.

Just as I'm about to turn to the kitchen, I hear a low growl from behind me stopping me in my tracks as my entire body tenses with the warning wondering if he'll touch me again, if those lips will touch me again "Your witch's pet is dead. I hope you weren't too attached," he utters thickly, and when I glance over my shoulder it's to see him a foot away with his arms folded and a grizzly frown on his thick lips as they curve downwards in his grouchiness.

I don't have a pet, so with a frown of my own, I anxiously cross the threshold and look around, expecting to see a dead cat hanging from my ceiling rafters or something.

Instead, everything looks normal, all until I round the kitchen island and see my blender in absolute tatters on the ground before me.

"You destroyed my fucking blender?" I spin to face him, fury boiling in my veins in utter disbelief.

"It attacked me," he states blandly, and I widen my eyes questioning if he's actually serious or not.

A dry chuckle leaves me in a hurry and I'm helpless to do anything but to shrug, "Of course it did. Elijah Braxton, King of the Horde."

"Are you…" He unfolds his arms, straightening to his full height as he takes a menacing step into the room, narrowing his obsidian eyes on me. "Are you mocking me, witch?" His growl of perplexity sends tingles down my spine and I shrug again, biting my lip to avoid a coy smirk at ruffling his feathers.

"Of course not, I wouldn't dream of it," I reply with a snort as I head over to the coffee machine and flick it on. Elijah tenses, lunging into the room when it offers a resounding beep and as if by instinct, my hand is already in the air to stall his attack before my brain has even registered he has moved at all. Elijah ground to a halt, my hand a fraction away from his heaving chest. My eyes are drawn to the movement of his erratic breathing, the urge to close the small distance and feel his skin under mine an itch I have to fight to scratch.

I pant shallowly as I whisper, "It's just a coffee machine. Try not to break it, okay?"

He leans down, lips a fraction away from brushing against mine as I still, watching as those dark eyes of his narrow further. Canting his head, he peeks over my shoulder as the machine starts dispensing the dark liquid into the mug sitting under it. Clearing his throat, he backs away and kicks the metal pieces of my blender on the ground before waving his hand and making it all disappear. I blink and he looks back over at me with accusation in his gaze.

"Stop looking at me like that, what you just did is not normal!" I breathe, before taking a deep breath and addressing the way he frowns at me. " It makes smoothies. Another form of drink and now, thanks to you, I won't get my nutrients in the morning," I grouse, with little to no heat. Because it's kind of funny as shit when I think about it. When I really...*really* think about it and not how insane all of this is.

Witch's pet? Ha!

I scratch the back of my neck and pull the mug from its stand offering it to him. "Try it," I urge, as he takes the mug from my hands and the muscles in his shoulders ripple while I gaze at them like somebody who gazes upon the moon.

In awe and utter longing.

Coughing to cover the sound of me clearing my own throat, I turn back to make myself one when a large hand clasps my shoulder and turns me back to face him. "I know what coffee and smoothies are, witch. Don't patronize me. We just don't need these things to make them." He waves his hand at the appliances and growls, throwing the contents of the mug into the sink. "I won't allow you to poison me."

My eyes widen and I chuckle mockingly.

"If I wanted to poison you, I wouldn't do it by being the one to offer it to you, now would I? Overlooking how rude that is, how do you make them then, *Einstein*?"

"With magic," he retorts, using his free hand to snap his fingers making a new steaming hot mug appear in the palm of his hand. I swallow nervously, eyes widening as my brain begins to hurt at watching the air around me distort and something materializing from nothing, into something as solid as a freaking mug. Running my hands through my hair, I massage the ache away by kneading the scalp, but still, I can't seem to force myself into looking away.

"And I'm the witch, huh?" I utter, still blinking at the spot in his hand as if looking for the illusion to break and reveal all of his secrets.

He clenches his jaw and flicks a brow at me. "I'm the Horde King. Power runs in my veins. But I'm no witch, I'm a thing made of shadows and nightmares. When the air changes and the spirits scream, it's my name they wail." Deep and rough, the timber in his voice tickles against my heated skin like a vibrator. There is something wicked and full of lustful depravity in the darkness of his tone and it does immoral things to the molten lava rushing through me and heating me from the inside out. Of course, something so ominous should chafe against the raw instincts of my fight or flight, but naturally my deviant and smutty reader's mind is A-okay with the threat that lingers there. I know most of this, I've read about it in his book. I don't know everything, obviously, the fucker fell from the sky before I got to all the kicks and twists. But

I know most of it. "And I much prefer the mocha sands as opposed to the dark beans." Quirking a brow, the smug bastard smirks at me and at first I'm confused until I remember a scene from his novel about dark beans being coffee and mocha sands being hot chocolate. Like, the drink is made from *actual* sands of chocolate.

It sounded fucking awesome.

I turn back to the coffee pot, brows drawing together as I turn back to him and think why the heck not? Offering him my hand, I ask for one. "I want to try the mocha sands. Make me one." When he stares at me in amusement, I belatedly add a please onto my demand.

"Thought magic wasn't real, witch? Thought *I* wasn't real?" The mirth in his now amber eyes has me wanting to kick the smugness right out of him. But he's right, and I still don't believe it. I'm just deciding to run with it.

How do his eyes change color like that?

My heart stops, only to pick up speed again in my chest. The blood pounding within the drums of my ears, echo like the voice of the tiny devil on my shoulder that urges me to sell my soul to the man standing before me. My lips part, as I suck in a quick breath at the dangerous beauty that lingers there. I forget everything else and with weak knees, I suddenly feel overwhelmed. Losing my focus as I try to answer.

"You're becoming a pain in my dreamscape ass, Elijah. I might as well make good use out of you until I wake up."

"We don't have time for these games, witch. When are you going to fix what you have done to me? To my kingdom? Me being here leaves them unprotected. I need you to send me home." Gone. In a cloud of smoke, the man I spend my nights dreaming of disappears in a heartbeat and in his place is this misguided and rage filled king.

Like a light shattering around the heated shards of glass, the lightness of the moment fades when he shoves a hot mug in my hands and turns to walk away. There's a pain in my heart at the urgency in his need to return home, to a kingdom where I don't belong, and the more I feel the uncertainty which leaves behind nothing but sorrow, the more I begin to accept that maybe this isn't a dream at all.

Only real life can hurt like this.

"My patience is wearing thin. You went through a fever. Probably a side effect to whatever kind of magic you used. Isn't that right? A little witch out of her depth. But you aren't suffering from the fever now and I want answers. So start talking."

I bow my head, shoulders curling over my chest as I angle my body away from him in slight humiliation. My skin tightens as my ribs squeeze painfully in my sides. I turn toward the back patio doors and reach out to unlock them, then attempt to pull them open in the hopes of a breeze. Some fresh air to clear my desperate mind. But when I try to pull the door open, they ignite like the flames of a fire and zap my hand. I jolt backward, clutching my aching hand to my chest as I turn back to face Elijah who is now standing nose to nose with me. He walks forward, forcing me back until I hit the door and become caged in, trapped within his engulfing presence. Thankfully whatever zapped me is now dormant while I'm not trying to open the door.

I swallow thickly, losing focus rapidly as darkness creeps from the corners of the room and encloses around us so the only thing I can see is those golden eyes that seem to glow.

"What part of you being my hostage do you not understand, witch? You aren't the queen here and this is not your fairy tale. You took a very bad man from a very dark place. I don't know much but it is evident that whatever dimension you hold me in, you're not ready for the hell I can unleash. I can promise you, it's coming. This rageful wrath will burn you where you stand. I am no longer playing games. If I don't get answers soon, I'd sooner destroy us both than dwell in this miserable limbo you have forced us in. I will fight this magic, this pull I have toward you." He grips my jaw, sinful fingers prying my mouth open as his thumb teases my lips before dipping inside. I shudder, my core aching as my traitorous panties dampen. "With everything that I have. Do you understand that?" I nod, entranced at the demand of my submission he exudes. "You can't leave this house until I allow you too."

I bite around his thumb, making him groan before he pulls it savagely from my lips. "You'll never believe a word I'll say," I whisper quietly, staring into those wicked eyes begging him to believe me. "You'll have to see it for yourself and then maybe you'll be able to figure out what happened because it isn't me with the powers, Elijah. I didn't do this. I'm a nobody. In every world." Lifting my head, I gaze toward the backyard, remembering. "You need to read the book."

"The book I found on the ground? It's empty. I placed it beside your bed," he offers, his brooding gaze watching me closely with a fixed stare as his body turns rigid, thick arms crossing over his wide chest as he steps back. He clears his throat pressing his lips together. Elijah's face tightens like a pissed off Pitbull and for the first time since meeting him, something uncomfortable sits heavy in my chest.

I allow myself a moment to just stare at him, to try to make all of this make sense within my mind but the longer I stare at him, the more I feel for something which should never have become a reality in the first place. The more I lose myself.

The time flashing in neon green numbers on the microwave catches my attention and I turn to take them in fully.

"How long was I out?" I ask, no longer able to keep staring at him. It suddenly hurts too much. I turn toward the door, knowing he'll follow as I make my way back to my room.

"Two days." He grunts.

"I've got to work tomorrow night, so whatever this is, you better figure it out fast," I snap, a little irritated as the stress from everything happening causes my body to hurt so much more than it already is as it all begins to catch up to me. "I'm not keeping you here. So if you can't find what you're looking for, feel free to leave. There is nothing I can do to stop you." It hurts to say that. To push him away. But I'm helpless for any other outcome if it's not me he's looking for. If it's not me he wants. I'm a hostage to a demon and not one who will please me with wicked sins kissed upon my skin.

"I fucking tried. I told you, my magic won't allow that while I'm here. I don't know why but I feel like it has your name written all over it!" he sneers, and I ignore him.

Walking over to my bedside table, I see the book lying on top but before I touch it, I grab the medication from the drawer and pop a few pills. I keep them laying around the house, because sometimes when my body locks up, I can't travel from one room to the other.

Placing them in my mouth, I wash them down with the hot chocolate and moan unexpectedly when the flavors seep onto my tongue and rush through me.

Holy bat out of Hell, crackman! That tastes so fucking good.

I steady myself on the side of the unit as a mini orgasm rockets through my body, making me sway on my heels. I guess magical choco is a hell of a lot different from our stuff. "That's some good shit," I muse, placing down the mug and replacing it with the book as I pick it up from the side. It takes me a moment to right myself after something so succulent. I turn at the waist but keep my eyes glued to the cover, refusing to look at him. I'm too captivated by the man standing amidst a battle that had my stomach in knots. I remember how I felt reading this scene and exactly how I felt with the war of emotions that came during that exact moment as well. It's like I'm reliving it all over again.

"What are those for?" Elijah asks, closer than I was expecting him to be as he nods to the drawer with my meds.

"They help with the pain." Is all that I offer as I still stare at the cover and turn at the hip to face him, holding it up so he can see it for himself. "Can you deny that this is you?"

"No, but that means little. Magic works in mysterious ways," he retorts, folding his arms across his chest causing every muscle within his body to dance under the tension.

I rub together my thighs, looking away as that familiar feeling in my core begins to heat with the action.

"Right, well you would know that better than I would," I remark, flicking through the front of the book, noticing first the ink scribbled on the pages. I frown, looking back at him. " I thought you said it was empty?"

"It was." Moving to my side, he settles his hands on my hips as he pulls me back into his hard chest so he can look over my shoulder. Once I get to the middle of the book, it just ends.

Nothing. Blank page after blank page.

"You're no longer in the book. It must have erased your ending," I whisper in awe, as I think out loud. Blinking rapidly as if the pages would correct themselves but they don't.

"So now what?" he asks, irritated. Hands flexing on my hips. The domineering hold is bruising. I shudder, curving my spine back into him and I bite my lip stifling the moan which wants to slip free. Something feels different behind me as I feel a pull, so I glance over my shoulder, noticing Elijah staring into space, glaring out into the hall as if he expects someone to pop around the corner and say hello. The air settles, feeling utterly normal and I frown at his reaction.

"Are you okay?" I ask, snapping him out of it as his eyes flicker back to mine.

"Fine. Now what?" he grunts, clearing his throat and refusing to show me any other emotion.

"Now, I read you your own story. So you can see firsthand I'm not the bitch you make me out to be."

Ten

Elijah

"Look, this is from when you... I don't know? Popped out to say hello?" Adisen explains, looking off into the distance and squinting like she's trying to find the right words to describe whatever the fuck this is as the book sits open on her lap.

The woman is crazy. Faced with the beast, she just fucking smiles like I'm cute. She jokes and laughs even though I can smell her fear mixed with her arousal. I wonder if she knows that. Knows just how much she is exposing to me without so much as uttering a word.

We've moved from her bedroom to what she calls the lounge. She sits beside me, curled into a high back, charcoal gray, quilted couch that engulfs the pair of us. I have no idea why she requires seats so big when she's so small. The thought distracts me as I gaze at her, wondering who else dwells in her quarters and if it is truly her and her alone. For some reason, the thought of another man being here, around her, has a growl building in the back of my throat before I can stop it. I can't be this possessive. It's turning me into a man I never want to be.

A man, no matter how powerful, should never treat a woman with anything less than respect. My parents taught me that. Through all of the violence, blood, and power. A real man never lays his hands on a woman. We use that unyielding dominance and immense power to destroy our enemies but never our females.

But right now, as I gaze at her, respecting that tight and lithe little body is the last thing on my mind. That breeds an anger so potent, the lights above us flicker and hiss, shifting us in between light and dark. I knew that I had to nurse her back to health, that I would have to force her hand to return me home. Everything I have done is with the motivation to return to my land and my people. That is what I was created for, the king I was born to be and I never knew anything else.

Not until her.

I can't deny that the lines are blurring and it angers me that I don't know how to stop it or why it's happening. For the last two days, I've watched her slumber. Murmuring absurdities and mewling in content. I got to do nothing but watch, relax, and observe. I had no kingdom to contend with. No war to fight and no creature to slay. I was left with nothing but these strange feelings and this sleeping beauty. For the first time in my life, I was left with nothing but myself and the strange voice of the man I had not given much notice to before right now.

"What are you looking at?" she asks, a knitted throw draped over her shoulders as she burrows down like a nesting mate and resumes drinking her cocoa. It makes me frown in unease as I war between wanting to be her warmth and tossing her witchy ass out in the cold.

It's fascinating how we call cocoa different things. *She's fascinating.* This whole realm is fascinating, if not a little warped, with its stupidity and without an ounce of forethought. I mean not having a dungeon to burn those who wrong you, forcing them to flame within the depths of their fire, never dying, only ever suffering from the sweet torture of the inferno over and over again from a dragon's eternal torch is mind-blowing. Or not having a Pegasus compound on your property to transport you from one place to the next if you do not harbor the power of teleportation? ... like I said, stupid.

The hot liquid meets her silken lips and she moans, pushing her ass into the couch as she takes another greedy sip. "This is seriously the best shit ever."

"Will you focus?" I snap, gritting my jaw as I can feel the obsidian bleeding into my gaze. The beast within me marches on its confinements, a warning to watch my tone. I have no idea why he is so pulled toward her. Why I am so pulled toward her. It isn't making sense and things that don't make sense make me edgy. Needy. Violent. Yet I don't fucking understand why.

There is warmth in my chest, and an ache in my groin and I find myself feeling things I've never felt before.

I know anger. I know war and violence. I know pleasure, which I had thought was the precipice and now I find myself wondering if it was even the basics of sweet, tormenting rapture. I don't know anything anymore and it makes me pissed as fuck. Because I'm feeling things around her I've never felt before and my body doesn't know how to handle it. I don't know how to handle it.

'Focus now, my beast.' My mother's soft voice caresses my

mind as she walks around me, coming to stand at my front with a soft purse of her lips. 'You need to focus. In war, the mind will be your biggest tool. There is a lot a weapon can do. Unimaginable pain it can cause. But the mind? It can both end the war and begin one. It needs to be a force impenetrable. Something only you control. So again, do not let me in, Elijah. You are the key, now turn the lock and dispel me. Become the keeper. Do not let my will change your perspective. Do not let me allow you to forget.'

A searing pain rushes through my head at the memory and I growl, shaking my head and clenching my eyes tightly. I fight for understanding. To remember the lesson. I hardly remember my parents, and now I'm having memories that I had long forgotten. The last two days, the more these memories fight to the surface, the more questions I end up with. I can feel Adisen's eyes on me, but I don't want her to know. Not if she's the one blocking my memories. "You need to concentrate," I demand, running my fingers along my brows to smooth out the pain there.

She narrows her emerald eyes at me but lets the shift in me pass. "Why? This is only a dream. Granted a fucked-up kind of dream quest, but it's fucked with my dream quest. So it can wait for me to charge into the adventure which awaits us with a war cry so my fine ass can become the hero I've always dreamed of being, then I can finally wake the fuck up. I'm drinking my cocoa first though, so *hush*."

"I was kidnapped by a mad woman," I huff in exacerbation, throwing my arms out wide in frustration.

"Ditto. I was tied to my bed and made sick by a mad man also. Guess this dream has a theme."

"Enough already!"

"What? Hey, that rhymes!" she shouts cheerily. "If you're in such a rush, feel free to read ahead without me." She shrugs carelessly, taking another sip which causes her to mewl like a cat getting the cream. She's fucking insane. Like, actually insane.

My resistance to her dwindles, but my temper rises as does my body heat. I scratch the side of my neck, glaring my best daggers at the little witch who is holding me under her spell.

"I can't. I cannot read your language," I admit lowly, around another growl at having to admit that out loud.

"But you can talk it?" she asks with a little twitch to her button nose and her brown speckled green eyes widen like an owl and blink at me with a look that says I'm a fool.

"Apparently so," I grit, flexing my fists as I reclaim my seat beside her.

"Huh, the author wrote in English. In your world, you read from the ancient language of the old ones. I guess it's a built-in effect?" she muses, looking me over like something will pop out of me and fill in the blanks.

"I'm not a build-a-beast, Adisen. Nobody created me," I snap, trying my hardest to keep my temper in check.

I settle a little in shock when I raise my head, locking eyes with the witch as her whole demeanor changes and she exudes her own annoyance, taking me off guard.

"Build-a-beast? Dude, stay the fuck out of my head," she barks, snapping her teeth with each word and I find myself stifling a smile at how cute she actually looks while she is pissed. *Fucking focus, Elijah.* "And clearly, somebody did, asshole. Somebody - namely an *author* that goes by…E.M Liddion." She wiggles her legs, causing the book to bounce on her thighs and draw my attention. All while she refuses to let go of her damn hot cocoa.

"What are you talking about?" I sneer, trying to hold onto my anger. Because it's the only way I can remotely even think straight. The only way I won't reach out and make her mine, with a claim laid upon her lips, is to remember how toxic she is. She's the one who stole me from my life. The only world I've ever known. I don't know what's happening, not truly. Such thoughts feel like a betrayal. Like acid in my veins. Thoughts I've never felt so impulsively before. I'm disgusted that I feel them, furious that I do.

"Don't play dumb with me, pretty boy. Build-a-beast isn't exactly in your terminology now, is it?"

"Again. What the fuck are you talking about?"

"Eh! You're so frustrating. I'm... I'm," she becomes mute in her fury, looking a little lost as she stares at me like she's confused before leaning back in her seat and gazing at me in accusation. "Strange. That wasn't *my* temper," she utters, staring at me like she's looking for the trip wire before her dainty little ass goes up in smoke. "I'm not mad. I'm not even annoyed."

I groan, rubbing my temples because I'm about to beg her to put me out of my misery. I think I'd prefer the mad hatter to torture me instead of whatever the fuck this is.

"Adisen..." I breathe, pinching the bridge of my nose in annoyance, before turning ready to descend on her. My hand itches for her throat. Whether because the threat is needed to kick her ass into gear or because I have the impulse to touch her, I can't answer. But before I have the chance, she places her hands out in front of her.

"Okay, okay. You big baby. Buckle up buttercup because I'm about to rock the world you once knew." She giggles, before frowning. "Well, technically it's this E.M Liddion chick, but I'm reading it. And I'm good at sucking you right in."

My gaze instantly falls to her plump and parted lips,

wondering just how hard she can really suck. Snarling, I grit my teeth, grinding bone at where that thought had taken me. Glaring at the mug she places on the side, I refuse to look back at her anymore.

I hang on to her every word when she begins to speak, using that as my anchor as I fight the lust taking hold in my core.

"Something called to Elijah as he pumped with vigor into the mate beneath him. Slowly, things began to change and consciousness began to seep in. Every time he was with Jessaleia, she was faceless. He hadn't realized that until now. Breaking free from the claws of need and blinking his way through the fog of naivety, Elijah pulled back from their connection and stumbled backward, leaving Jessaleia cold, and panting on the chilling ground where she fell slack without his domineering grip. He canted his head, staring down at her without rose-filtered glasses and began to question how he ended up here at all. Something called to Elijah again… The voice of a siren. It echoed through space and time. A voice that sung sweeter than the angelic angels of harmony. It beckoned him near.

Elijah, Elijah… Oh Elijah.

A soft whisper on the wind.

"Oh shit! I did not see that coming! About fucking time." Adisen breathes, with energized enthusiasm. Shifting her position on the couch, the throw becomes discarded as she curves into the seat and brings her knees to her chest, gripping the book with both hands like she's fully invested in this tale. "Bitch is about to get a wake-up call. I hope you hang the slut from the rafters once you find out what she did!" She's so heated, so drawn into the words on the page that I find myself more focused on her reaction, her investment, and passion for the written words than I am on the words themselves... Words about *my* life.

When she reads, there is a light in her eyes, unlike anything I've ever seen. Happiness to her aura that draws me in and refuses to let me go. Her cheeks are stained with a deep blush, flaming bright as it feathers down her neck and across her chest. I had conjured her a tank shirt, now wishing I hadn't so I could see how far that blush had traveled. She dances in place and wiggles her shoulder in rhythm with every word she speaks. Appreciation radiates throughout her body.

The story she speaks, is one I now find I vaguely remember. These are my memories, moments of my life. If this was magic how could she possibly know any of this?

"Fuck, this better be worth it! You have broken my heart over and over again, Elijah. You have no idea just how much. You deserve someone who loves you, who truly loves you like she never can!" Adisen's talking heatedly down at the pages as she stares intently at the book, lost in thoughts as her cheeks become even more heated at the passion in her fierce and devoted tone.

My heart sinks, tumbling down into my core that riots with the wings of dragons as it pounds harshly against my ribs. Something strange happens, as my chest heats and I realize I don't think I've ever had someone care so deeply about me before that I break out in a cold sweat. Unease crawling down my body at not knowing what it is I'm feeling right now.

I clear my throat, utterly at a loss as to what the fuck is happening and how to show that I'm still unaffected. Still indifferent and still in control.

It takes everything within me not to show weakness, to not lose my head.

Her gaze flickers to mine quickly before flying back to me

completely startled. "You deserve so much better!" She wiggles the book at me in her declaration. "So much better than what she can give you. You need to see that. Please say you'll see that," she implores. "Now where was I?"

"Elijah, Elijah! Oh yes Elijah! The chant entranced him, distracting him as the world around him changed and the stars began to fall from the sky, bleeding through the ceiling of the castle and capturing him in one of their orbs. Carrying him away to a land where his visionary awaited him.

"What the fuck is a visionary?" we both ask at the same time.

I move closer, my hip melding to hers as we both stare down at the pages before us, not that I can make any sense of the blobbed ink staring back at me. The connection has electricity zinging through my body, sending a full-body shiver to rack through me and cause me to sit up straighter, refusing to move away and show any effect.

Jessaleia stared, mouth agape as the key to the kingdom disappeared in a cloud of smoke. The soft planes of her once beautiful face turned cold and ugly as they distorted with her rage. Struggling to her feet, she began to bellow the name of her true mate while removing the taste of her fake one from her poisonous lips.

'Bradon, Bradon!"

The door to the king's quarters bursted open as Bradon hurried to the distress of his beloved, wielding his sword like a knight ready to defend.

"My love? What is it, what happened? Where is my brother?" he asked frantically, as he searched the open space finding only her, naked and scrubbing her ruby-red lips raw.

"I do not know. Something happened, one moment, we were

painstaking together," she hissed, lips curling in distaste, *"the next, an orb took him from us. Magic, unlike anything I have ever seen. I no longer sense him in our realm,"* she sneered, her claw-like fingernails untangling the strands within her matted blonde hair. *"We did not come this far for him to escape us now. The love potion made him believe he was truly in love with me in the first place. Hiding how we are together around him. Keeping him blind to our love. Having his hands on me, touching me. Sending him to slaughter against the enemies that would rise against us. Using him to command this kingdom while gaining his confidence. We played him. He did all that we had asked. We were so close, Bradon. So close. We need Elijah Braxton dead, we need him dead so we can claim the throne. The realm will revolt if we don't."*

"How do we do that now that he's gone?" Bradon asked, sheathing his blade as he pulled his love into his awaiting arms, kissing her softly. *"My brother must die. But how? How, when we do not know how to find him?"*

"We wait. We wait until we can sense his presence again and when we do, we'll end him with the tool we have spent countless moons creating!"

In that moment, a weakness arose. The traitorous couple felt the ripple in the air, both adorning wickedly cruel and sadistic smiles as they felt the power, the key to their quest, finally paving the way to their victory.

I can barely hear the words through the buzzing in my ears. A whirlwind gathers a tornado in my head as my heart rate runs wild with my fury.

How *dare* they!

My beloved. My trusted. My *brother*!

They have all betrayed me.

The more I think of life before here, before I found myself in a strange land, confronted by a strange woman, the more I find I don't really remember *them* at all.

I know my land, my kingdom. I know my people and I know I had a mate and a brother and I can see the memories within my mind. But they all seem displaced, as if I'm watching from the outside. The memories of another flashing like a slideshow burning behind my eyes and yet I feel no emotional connection to any of them. Through all of this uncertain rage and confusion that is filling me, I direct it at her because I don't want to face my own truth. The truth that what feels most wrong isn't the land I find myself in, or the witch sitting at my side. But that *I'm* what's wrong.

I feel like I've just woken from a bad dream, my consciousness only now just catching up in my haze.

Another life. One that no longer feels like mine, is written within those pages and now I feel like I'm only just remembering it.

I'm growling, snarling with the voice of the beast. It drops an octave, coming out layered and in different frequencies. Adisen slumps back, eyebrow cocking as she watches me.

My magic fills the room, thick and potent. I'm about to explode. All until I'm hit aside the head with the damn book.

I blink, turning to Adisen who has my life in the palm of her hand, risen above her head as if she intends to wield it as a weapon and club me with it.

"Don't shift, you'll molt on the couch," she jests with a wicked smirk, the corner of her lips lifting in her mischievous humor. "Are you okay? That bitch makes my blood boil. How could you ever have believed a word she said? I mean, I know you were drugged and all so maybe I'm expecting a little too much from you." She shrugs and I blink amazed at how easily she can shift her attention. "But... really, are you okay? You never deserved any of that."

"No? What did I deserve?"

"Everything. You always charged headfirst with this unyielding devotion. It didn't matter the reason, only that it was the right one. No matter how much anger, power, or wicked wrath you housed, no matter how misguided and hurting, you always put the innocent first. You always used the darkness for the right reasons."

She's drunk from the balloon of hallucinations, down by the well of wishes, because this woman has lost her damn mind.

She must have been to my realm. *Must* have. She's too... mystical *not* to have.

I've never been described in that way before. Appreciated for my efforts.

It was always a given, but this woman... this witch, she seems to see me in a way I've never before seen myself.

Ever since I fell from the sky, I was convinced that I would keep seeing Bradon. He's like an aspiration that appears in my turmoil and now I wonder if maybe my consciousness hasn't always known something was wrong. I felt him in the hallway and as I charged through the woods, but by the time I searched his presence out, he was gone.

I rub at the sore spot on my head, my heart calming as I turn to face the lethal little witch, who looks like a frenzied beast I would've had to have tamed not so long ago when the little devils escaped the keep back home. "I don't know how to be fine," I admit. "I know how to be angry. That's all that I have right now. I also don't think that's how it works in trying to wake from a dream. Aren't you supposed to pinch *yourself?*"

"Right, yes!" she squeaks, pinching her arm. "Ow! Shit. Fuck. Why did I do that? More importantly, how did you *know* about doing that? Do you have the same ways in your realm?"

I frown, thinking about it. "No, actually. We don't."

"Curiouser and curiouser," she muses, tilting her head as she studies me with narrowed eyes.

"Alice In Wonderland?"

"Damn right, fucking creepy! It's my favorite film." She gasps, jumping from the couch and pacing around the lounge as she cradles the arm she pinched. "How did you know that? Reading minds again?"

"I don't read minds."

"This is nuts. Impossible, even! I'm done. My head hurts and there are not enough pills in the world to take away the pain of this stress. Your mate is a hussy, Elijah. She declared war on your kingdom and she wants to eradicate you from existence. Yet here you sit. Right in front of me. Driving me insane! Mad at me, for something I didn't do!"

"Then tell me how to fix this, witch!" I growl, rising to my feet and stalking her until she stumbles backward with wide, shock-filled eyes.

Her nostrils flare and she looks affronted before she plants her feet and sticks out her ample chest. "I don't fucking know how to fix this! Because. I'm. Not. A. Goddamn. Witch! And this is not some backwater, shittily made ol' movie! We aren't going to find witchdoctors in back alleys and ancient oracles in the yellow pages! I don't know how to fix this or to get answers! I don't! But I really, *really* wish I did!" she screeches, flinging her hands in the air, then wincing with what I assume must be an ache. She's still weak, slightly warm and her getting fired up and ready to make my ass implode isn't going to help anyone. The wound in her neck is a gnarly eye, blinking its crimson tear at me. The outline curls, brittle and welted with red and blues that have an uneasy feeling sloshing around my core.

I hate that I hurt her. That I showed her violence and gave in to brutality. That I marked her. That was not how my parents raised me, so it leaves me confused as to why such a heinous act leaves me feeling a pride I've never felt before.

"Calm down, Adisen," I sooth warily, like I would when taming the Dragon's Queen. She breathes scorching fire too. Every time one of her young steps out of line, she goes red in the face to remind them who's boss, and right now, I'm pretty sure my little witch wants to be the boss too.

It must be the wrong thing to say because she pulls back, scoffing as she stares at me with a demented gleam in her emerald gaze.

"Calm down? Did you just tell me to *calm down*? What the fuck, Elijah? If this shit is real, you're supposed to always say the right thing and that is very much the *wrong* thing to say!"

"Clearly. I just want-"

"Don't even think about saying answers because I want answers too!" she seethes as the noise is sucked from the room. It returns with a pop, causing me to tilt my head and wring out my ears.

"What the fuck?" I growl.

"What in the fuckery, indeed." My voice resounds back to me causing me to spin on my heels and come face to face with… myself.

A British, hellish, and scruffier version of…myself.

Adisen screams, jumping backward as I reach out to grab her quickly, pulling her into my arms. This version of me that stands before us in ripped black jeans and a black wife beater which molds to his muscular frame causing every inch of him to ripple, is arrogant as fuck. He smirks, eyes glistening as he gazes at the woman in my arms. The likeness is uncanny, even with the detailed ink of my tattoos. "Hey there, beautiful," he rasps, the British accent thick in his tone.

Adisen lets out a low purr, her fear fading as she assesses the intruder, going slack in my arms. "Now, *that's* more of a wet dream," she muses dreamily, staring at him like she is in some kind of trance. I growl, pulling her behind me and growing into my full height.

The very fibers of my being vibrate with the urge to protect her, to save her.

Even if it is from myself.

The fucking irony.

My eyes bleed to obsidian, the beast and every creature I house within the horde coming to the forefront. Shadows bleed from my flesh, coiling around the room and enclosing around his tall frame, darkening him within the veil of a silken black essence that carries a warning of evident and pain-filled perish.

She *purred* for him?

She purrs for *nobody* but *me*...

Fuck, where did that come from?

Who the fuck cares.

It's there... written within the pages. I have unknown enemies, and a war I still need to fight. But it changes nothing in regards to this pull in my core.

My beast and I are finally in full agreement.

The little witch is ours...

"Touch her, and I'll set a fire so scorching to your bones that you'll feel the inferno long after you spend an eternity in the bowels of Hell."

Eleven

Adisen

"Holy fuck balls on a unicorn bat man. There are two of you?" I shriek, my gaze flying between the lethal and uptight Elijah and the ruggish, lethal and damn right perfected Elijah once the reality comes rushing back. I don't understand what's going on from one moment to the next, my head spinning with so much information and impossibilities.

What the fuck?

The threat of the Elijah who cradles me in an iron hold sits teasingly in my core as the words replay within my mind. I blink up at him, losing myself to the lust and danger burning within his golden eyes. The room remains bathed in shadows and I find myself wanting to weave and dance within them, my heart and soul finding them familiar but just not understanding why.

They call to me, a softness to lay my head upon like a cloud of content. A darkness to protect me from rejection.

Reflection? My senses spin around me and I find myself a little dizzy.

"You called?" Elijah number two grumbles with a smug smirk on his lips as he crosses his arms against his chest and leans his hip against my couch. My nose burns as it twitches at the smell of something earthy and potent that wraps around the smell of diesel. It takes me a moment to take note of all the undertones. The strangeness of the mixing scents, then I realize it smells like marijuana and burnt matches.

Holy smokes that voice! Those eyes! That outfit... and is that a nose ring I see?

I'm about to melt into a puddle with no fucks given. Because Satan just lit a fire up in here.

I've totally lost my train of thought when the grumpy Elijah grunts, glaring at me, as his hold bites into my skin. "Not a witch huh? What do you call summoning my clone then?"

I scoff, stepping back as I throw my arms out wide and then hiss with the ache that follows, "Dude, I did not *summon* him. And I am not a damn witch. Jesus, all the time I spent fantasizing about being one, I never foresaw the damn aggro it would bring."

"I assume your use of 'aggro' is a mundane version of the word aggravation and the aggravation you're referring to is what? Being burned at the stake?" he questions with mirth in his dark eyes and a quirk to his brow as those sinful lips twitch in the corners.

Is he... is he laughing at me?

"Don't smart mouth me, Elijah Braxton!" I spin, stepping

closer to the new Elijah and the old one matches me step for step. "Tell him I'm not a witch!"

"Oh, like he'll argue your case!"

"She isn't a witch," the British stud states.

"Ha!" I retort with too much arrogance.

"And I'm not your clone."

"Double Ha!"

"Oh, like I'll believe the witch's pet," Elijah grunts, reaching out and pulling me back into him again, making me frown. "Stay away from that asshole."

"You mean stay away from yourself?" I tease, my sanity finally fleeing like a thief in the night. What else can happen? I'm already arguing with fiction.

"That isn't me!"

"We'll it sure as fuck isn't me!"

"Actually, I am you," Mr. Rugged states, smirking wider as we both spin to glare at him.

"What now?" I ask in a high-pitched tone I've never heard myself use before.

"Yeah, come again?" Elijah parrots.

"Well, if mommy and daddy stop fighting for five minutes, I'll be able to give you the answers you're quarreling over. Well, most of them anyway. You two are worse than an old married couple." He winks and I rock on my heels, belatedly steadied by the man behind me as he rocks back on his own as well. The snipe comments have our mouths snapping shut as we stare at him wide-eyed.

"Finally… Adisen, I'm your conscience, babe."

"My conscious? How is *he*… I mean *you*, my conscience?"

"Your consciousness is your desire, Adisen. And since you desire *him*, you created *me*."

"Right. Okay. Awkward." I give Elijah the side eye as my head spins. "This is all too much. None of this is real. It can't be real. It's creepier than all hell… That's how unreal!" I ramble as I pace back and forth, a headache which is surely trying to see me in the grave before the night's end begins to throb in the back of my head. A pressure formed on the bones of my brows.

"You're a woman who dreams of multiple realities. How many nights have you laid awake in bed and dreamt of a moment like this after reading another book that has stolen your heart?" he asks, throwing himself over the couch to lay across it, kicking his feet up on the arm.

"Too many to count," I whisper.

"And why do you read?" he questions.

"Reading frees me from the limitations of real life and the things I can't do, Elijah. When I live through a character, I get the experiences I could only ever dream of having here, in the real world. I read because to read is to dream, and to dream, is to never lose hope in the darkness." The words leave me smoothly as if they had longed to be spoken. I look back at him, sorrow in my eyes. "Did I do this? Did I bring him here? Did I take him from his life?"

"You already know the answer to that."

"How?" Tears fill my eyes, threatening to fall at the new reality slamming into me.

I was so certain I didn't do this. How could I have gotten it so wrong?

Elijah was always my dream. Somebody I spent my nights fantasizing about, wishing more than anything that he could be real. That I could have someone so great in my life. I've always wanted this. Maybe not exactly like this, but all of this magic and wonder? I've always wanted that.

So why is there hesitation and fear plaguing my heart?

To Elijah, I must be a true monster. A monster who has taken him from everything he has ever known. The hostility he has toward me settles like acid in the back of my throat, now I know he has every right to that anger.

I have conjured the man of my dreams, plucked him right from the ink within the pages.

This should be all that any woman wants right?

Any reader?

But there's a lingering fear encased in dejection within the back of my mind.

One I can't acknowledge it because once I do, there's no going back.

"You're a visionary, Adisen. You have an iron will and when you want something bad enough, it tends to happen. A little like the coffee this morning."

"I am a witch?" I ask quietly, going a little lax in Elijah's hold as I try to absorb the information. His arms tighten around me as if to offer me silent comfort but I know that's just my mind breeding more delusions.

"No, you're most certainly human. I guess you could put it this way. You have extremely good luck. A visionary is someone so passionate, so avid in all that they love, that their passion could move mountains if required. A visionary is a soul so beautiful, so loyal, that whenever it craves something with desperation, the universe answers." He looks at Elijah with disinterest, almost unbelievably as if he has some kind of anger toward him for not knowing that whatever it is I have done, that it didn't come from a place of evil. But a place of desperation when I hadn't known just how lonely I truly was.

It's sad. Pathetic and I close my eyes, unable to face either of them. "Only you'll live as a human and you'll die as a human." He turns to his side, resting his head in his hand as he watches me intently. "You know, unless the ink dries on the page first," he states nonchalantly, shrugging his shoulder as he winks at me while I blink at him mutely.

"What does that mean?" the Elijah holding me questions, squeezing me tighter when I feel like I'm about to fall apart. I whimper, the pain in my body intensifying as I begin to feel stupid at how weak and human I am around men made from nothing but power. Elijah growls, the vines of darkness wrapping around the neck of my consciousness but he just smirks like the devil, without an ounce of fear. "She won't die! I won't allow it!"

"That would be telling now, wouldn't it, mate? This is real life, you don't get all the answers handed to you, here. But I will tell you this, sometimes the things we convince ourselves are delusions are more often the utter-fucking truth. Remember that. And if you want to go home, help convince a woman who didn't think that magic would choose her, that it finally did," Taking a moment just to stare at Elijah, he allows that to settle in. I have no idea what they are talking about, but the look in Elijah's eye tells me that he does. "You fell from the sky, in the backyard. Maybe try there? And just to recap though, not a witch. Totally a visionary. Your novel is true and you're being a bitch ass punk about it, dude. Man up a little. Gotta go." With one long lasting and knowing look, he fades from existence on a cloud of black and electric-blue smoke. The air warbles and my head suddenly feels seasick as I fall a little from my feet, more into his unwavering arms.

"No, wait! What happens next! How do we fix it?" Elijah shouts, lunging forward to grasp at the fading smoke as I become unsteady in his hold, even though he never let me go, his grip tightening as he anchors me to him.

I swallow thickly, moving myself away from Elijah, untangling myself from him thinking maybe the Brit was my conscience after all. Because he just saved me from facing my biggest, most mundane fear.

Never being good enough.

Not even for my Fantasy.

Twelve

Elijah

Those words penetrate and I find myself wondering if I really have been seeing Bradon. Is he really here? And if he is, how does Adisen's conscious know about it? Or was he being a vague pompous ass on purpose and referring to myself and Adisen in general?

There are still so many questions. None being answered.

Something in Adisen changes, she withdraws and retreats to the other side of the room. Folding her arms around her waist, she curls in on herself and completely shuts me out. It almost scares me seeing this side of her, a hollow husk of the brightness she radiates.

It's wrong. So fucking wrong.

My light in the darkness dwindles until I'm left alone in my abyss. It's a big enough wake up call to knock some sense into me. Link together all of these bizarre feelings and everything this fake Elijah has just said, and some of this anger dissipates toward her.

Some.

It takes me a moment to allow all of the pieces to settle. For my new reality to mellow out without some of the harshness of my temper.

I was right, she did do this.

She brought me here, but the more all of this unfolds, the more I realize she hasn't done this with malicious intent and I wish I could say that takes away my anger and resentment but that would be a lie. I'm still burning with a raw rage, flaming from the inside out and it's all because I've never felt so disconnected. So fucking wrong in my own skin. I'm not even angry at her, I'm angry at the fact that all this time, I've been someone else's puppet.

Entertainment for a race I had no idea even existed.

That everything inside of me is wrong and jittery. Unnatural and foreign in my own flesh.

All I've ever held close to me was the realness that hardens my core and sets the pace of my entire life - Loyalty. Family. Honor. Those are what I knew, what had been written in ink on the very stretch of my bones. Because even if I had nothing, I had that. And now I'm left wondering, am I even really like that? That is how I've been written. But given the choice, would I hold the same values?

It's why Adisen scares me so much, even though I'm loath to admit it.

I hurt her, my beast hurt her and I feel absolutely no remorse for it.

Why?

Who am I turning into now the ink is chipping away and the man is finally free?

My world and everything within it is fabricated fiction, created from the whimsical mind of a mundane woman sitting alone in her home office.

The only reason I'm here at all, a real man with real intent, is because this dainty little witch wanted me so badly she breathed me into existence. Bringing me *literally* to life, with an iron will, because to her, I was worth the stars that would fall down upon her head and rain like a wildfire all around her. I was worth the darkness and the wrath I'd carry with me.

But to her, I'm a risk. I'm a risk to the only woman who read between the lines and fell in love with the beast in between the pages anyway. She called for me and through all of my harshness, she hasn't pushed me away.

The monsters I've always kept hidden from Jessaleia, I find myself wanting to play with alongside Adisen are bellowing inside of me.

It stirs so many emotions in me, they sit heavy on my chest and thicken my airways as I try to navigate the unnatural waters I'm sinking within. I've always had control, but here, around her, I'm spiraling into the darkness, blacker than I've ever seen before.

I don't know what I want and it's because, for the first time, I'm given the option to actually choose. She gave me that. This little mundane I've been nothing but cruel too… She's given me a choice and for the first time in this odd existence, I find myself uncertain of what I'll choose.

Seeing her like this, completely shutting me out assaults me to my very core and for some reason makes me murderous. It slithers like something vile along my skin and I have to fight the urge to itch at the wrongness of it all.

I want to go to war, to fight the enemy and come out the victor. Just to see her look at me the way she did when I fell from the sky.

That is what I know. To heck with the rest of it in this very moment.

I glare a hole into the wall, frustrated there's nothing around me I can take my wrath out on. Staring at her, taking in the delicate lines of her curves, I'm drawn to the sheen of tears within her eyes. I move toward her, arm encircling her waist as I turn her into me, using my finger to lift her chin, and force her eyes to meet mine as I fight for a calm I don't truly feel.

Everything rebels inside of me, touching her like this, holding her so tenderly.

I'm poison to her innocence.

But I hold her anyway, because as hard as I fight to hold onto this upset and rage, I can't bear the look of anguish within her gaze. It's so wrong when she looks at me with those innocent eyes.

"What's wrong? What happened?" I breathe, the rawness to my tone coming out as a husky croak. "I'm trying here, Adisen. But I don't understand any of this, I'm trying but I just don't understand."

"Neither do I, but I'll do my best to send you home, okay? I'll try and send you back to her. I don't know what I am and I don't know how to control it, but I'll try okay? For you, I'll try." Something about that doesn't sit right. It sours my tongue and clenches my muscles as I go rigid with tension. I don't want to go back to *her*. I might question if all of this is really true or not, but I do know that the numbness around Jessaleia is nothing like the torrent of emotion I feel around Adisen. It's enough to convince me that at the very least, everything regarding Jessaleia and my brother is correct.

They betrayed me.

And that is not a slight I will allow to go unpunished.

She tries to pull away, slipping free from my arms but I refuse to allow the space to grow between us. Not this time.

"We need to know what we're dealing with first, before we can make a war plan, witch." I smirk, trying to lighten the mood but her eyes darken. "Maybe you can bring back Mr. Know-it-all," I offer belatedly, trying to offer some reassurance at the defeat staring back at me.

"I don't know how." There's resignation in her voice, a mellow sadness that burns at my chest.

"You will, when the time's right you'll figure it out," I assure her, finding that I want to keep her calm and settled because the look of sadness on her angelic face is like a broadsword to my senses.

It fucks me up and spins me around. It's not a feeling I like nor wish to ever feel again.

"So, now, what do we do?"

"I guess you teach me about life as mundane and I'll teach you all the ways of a realm, that I guess, really doesn't exist." I shrug, grunting to clear my throat around that bitter pill to swallow. Once she gets us home, I'm sure everything else will fall into place. I just have to help her get us there.

I don't believe in being the most powerful thing in the room yet feeling so powerless all at the same time. I can feel the magic in the air, a live wire that sparks all around me. I can feel it running like hot lava, wild and free in my veins.

How can any of that be fake?

How can I be anything but real?

But I'm here all the same, with a woman who is as enchanting as she is frustrating and I find myself wanting the truth, even if it keeps me here for longer, preparing me for a war back home I never even knew was brewing.

Because if Jessaleia thinks I'll allow my kingdom to fall, or my brother to keep his head, they don't know the man who houses The Accursed at all.

Thirteen

Adisen

"I can't do this, Elijah. I don't know how," I groan in frustration, kicking the ground with the heels of my feet in a tantrum as I huff, throwing myself onto my back from my sitting position and glancing up at the sky above me, focusing on the patterns of the soaring clouds.

We've been out here for hours, and I've done nothing.

Zilch. Nada.

I'm beginning to think my consciousness is a crock of shit.

"Yes, you can. You just have to focus," he insists, pacing above me.

"Do you think this is one of those things, you know? Like now that I know about it, my mind will think it can't do it? Like when the little soldier gets anxiety and struggles to perform?" I ask, throwing out ideas as to why I'm being such a dud right now. My question brews silence as I roll my head to the side, finding him staring at me blankly. "What?"

"Little soldier?"

"You know… A penis that can't get hard?"

He bulks, head drawing back on his shoulders as his face screws up in disgust. "That is absurd. Does such a thing happen in this world?" His frown deepens as he waits for my answer.

I shrug, turning back to cloud watching. "That's what I'm told, Batman. Guess you are written to be perfect."

"You're a peculiar little witch," he murmurs and I pout at him, hurt in my teasing eyes.

"Ouch. Why are you back to being Mr. Mean Elijah?" My lower lip quivers and his eyes widen in his head in discomfort. I burst out laughing, closing my eyes, and heaving a deep breath. "Relax."

"Relax?" he parrots.

"Yep. It's something you do when you want to… you know, relax?"

"Woman," he growls, and I laugh again. Opening my eyes, I roll to my side and offer him my hand. He takes it with caution, staring at me like I'm about to sear his flesh like a hot iron before he comes to kneel on the ground beside me.

"Lay on your back," I demand, and he growls again. "Please."

"Fine."

"Good." We lay side by side, staring up at the darkening sky as the white clouds move overhead. So many different patterns float on by.

"What are we-"

"What do you think that is?" I ask, pointing to a cloud a little to the left of us.

He narrows his eyes, before turning his head and following my direction. He squints even harder, turning back to face me before looking once again. "Kind of looks like a fleet of doves."

"Huh, I thought they looked more like the harrowing wings of a pissed off phoenix." I purse my lips and concede to the fact we see things differently.

"Is everything you see laced with some kind of magic?"

I think about that for a moment as we fall into a comfortable kind of silence. I trace the clouds, and when I see magic in all of them, I turn back to him with a frown. "I guess I do. Don't you?"

"No," he answers immediately, staring into my eyes. "My world is full of magic, Adisen. Sometimes, it's nice to know that it exists without actually existing ,you know?"

"No, I don't know."

It's his turn to think now. He breathes deeply, flicking his eyes toward the sky before they land back on mine again. "With you, I'm shown this different kind of reality. A wild kind of magic without any power. You show me imagination, and idealism. You show me what it's like to dream and in the middle of all these revelations, you have time to process it. The world isn't going to end. At the end of the night, you get to lay your head down and sleep in a world where you know that you have to be strong for nobody but yourself. That when you aren't, that when you slumber or fall apart, the sun will still rise when you do. I don't have that luxury."

My heart pains in my chest when I think about that and about everything I'm learning about this man who carries the entire weight of a kingdom on his shoulders. "I guess it's kind of lonely for you too, huh?"

"I never knew that either, until I met you."

"Guess you can start thanking me now instead of hating me then?" I ask hopefully and he glares, trying to hide the smirk pulling at his lips.

"Don't push it, witch." I sigh in defeat and turn back to the sky. " I can show you, ya' know?" he adds after a moment.

"Show me?"

"My realm. I can show you everything you have forever dreamed about. You can come back with me."

"I can?" I ask, bolting upright to hover over him. The quickness of the action has my side cramping and I fall forward, my hand falling to land beside his head, my face a hair's breadth away from his as my breathing becomes harsh.

"You can," he whispers, tucking a loose strand of hair behind my ear. "If you learn how to get us there, that is." The smirk he graces me with is one of the first I've seen that seems genuine, a kindness warring with the wickedness he wears so beautifully. "What do you want right now? More than anything?" I smirk, my heavy heart lightening but it fades in an instance when he switches our positions and lays me back to the ground, blocking out all the light and he peers down at me. "And it can't be me. I'm too dark for your light, Adisen. You deserve better than an abyss."

His words are barbing, even though I know he holds no menace behind them. Only a conviction he perceives to be true. That is more saddening than the pain I feel at that statement. But if anybody knows what it's like to feel unworthy, I certainly do. I know that he won't welcome my tenderness right now, that if I make any move to comfort him, a man who still believes he can hold no room for himself, only his kingdom, he will retreat again.

I smirk, batting my eyelashes at him as I answer, "A banana

split." He stares down at me in utter confusion. "A big, fat, girthy, nine-inch banana split with an abundance of cream and a riot of toppings."

"What the fuck is that?" he asks, making me laugh like a schoolgirl. I want desperately to show him. To show him everything that he misses out on when hiding behind that heavy crown. He deserves to live like a peasant and feast like the starved. In this world, I guess we take for granted the small and little things.

He grunts, stilling above me and tensing like he's balancing a wrecking-ball on his back, "What the fuck just landed on me?" he asks in shock?

"What?"

"My back, Adisen. Something just fell onto my back."

I peer around him, ducking under his arm as I run my hands all over him starting at the base of his spine, before knocking against something heavy sitting on the back of his shoulders.

"What in Satan's red dick is that?" I gasp, taking it in my hand and maneuvering it to the side and off his shoulders so he can move.

I sit up, holding the banana split in my hands. "Fuck me, I did it!" I ungracefully hurry to my feet, shoving the ice cream at his chest. "I did it, I fucking did it!"

"This is a banana split?" he asks with furrowed brows.

"Yep. It's ice cream. Taste it."

"You didn't conjure spoons." My excitement must fade instantly because he looks back down at the sundae and two spoons appear. "You sure this is good? I'm not in the habit of putting thick and long things in my mouth," he growls, and I bark out laughing, having to double over as it becomes a physical pain in my core.

"Well, Mr. Growly, we have to change that!"

We eat the sundae, and I suddenly feel lighter. Wondering what it would really be like actually going into a world I've only ever dreamed about. The man beside me is offering me all of my heart's desires and yet I just can't seem to get it to work. After we eat, we take a walk deeper into the forest, coming to a stop by the lake. The night that I brought him here flashes in my mind and my hand flies to my throat, tracing the scar. Elijah catches the action and doesn't seem too happy about it and it makes me frown. But I'm too lost in those flashing memories for me to question it. He looks uncomfortable and uneasy, shifting on his feet before he walks away, circling the lake and coming to a stop on the other side.

I stare at the still waters, wondering if I could do what he did. If I could make them rise and twirl like an angry entity, but the waters remain calm and still. More hours pass and nothing else happens, I can't make anything else work and as night falls, I find myself even more angry than I can't do it at all.

"You're getting too worked up. It won't work if you're angry," Elijah states, tossing pebbles into the water beside me and making my reflection ripple.

"How do you know that? How do you know anger isn't my trigger? We have been at this for hours and nothing, Elijah... We have searched for any hidden portals and nothing!" I argue, folding my arms over my chest and spinning to face him.

"You weren't angry earlier. What were you feeling then?"

I narrow my eyes, looking back up at the darkening sky, blowing out a cold and frustrating breath, "Honestly? I don't know anymore." I felt something like desperation but if I tell him that, if I admit that, I'm not sure on what methods he'd applying when trying to help me.

"Then let's take a break. Conjuring one thing is better than conjuring nothing, lets head back."

I drop like a lead weight, plonking on my ass and crossing my legs. "I don't want to. Not yet. What do you love the most about where you come from?" I ask him, gazing up at him, hoping that he would tell me.

He narrows his eyes slightly, annoyed before he relents and sits beside me. "How different it is. Here, everything is black or blue. There? It's a riot of color, and a hurricane of a warped and strange kind of beauty. You don't need to be perfect, just free. It's kind of easy, I guess."

"I thought you felt burdened there?" I ask, he looks at me like he can't believe I made that conclusion.

"I did. I drew those conclusions from watching my people. They never seemed to have any worries."

"That's because they didn't. They weren't written to know the struggle of life. Unfortunately, you were written to know it all. Painfully."

"Huh, I guess that I was."

"Come on then, witch," he says as he stands to his feet and dusts off his palms before offering me his hand. "I showed you mine, now you can show me yours. Show me why this world is better than mine."

I bark out a laugh, taking him surprise as I take his offered hand. "Who the *fuck* said my world is *better*? "

Fourteen

Adisen

"You asked for it," I sing song, outright laughing at the discomfort on Elijah's face.

We're surrounded by a crowd at the bowling alley, and the sneer on his lips at the people milling too close to him makes my tummy tight with joy. He wants to see my world and I can't think of anything more fun and grueling than a close proximity nightmare for a king surrounded by the peasants.

The thought makes me chuckle.

"Where the fuck are we?" he asks with distaste, lip curling as he looks at those around him like everyone surrounding us is riddled with the plague or something. The air around him darkens in the already bleak space and the hustle and bustle of a busy crowd zings in the air.

I step closer to him, pressing my chest against his as I take his hand in mine and squeeze tightly, drawing his attention.

"Remember what I said. This world doesn't have magic, Elijah. You can't use it here." I remind him in a fierce whisper, glancing around like we're sharing our own little conspiracy.

He quirks a naughty brow at me and pulls me into his hold, hands on my hips as I stare up at him wide eyed at his quick change in demeanor. He smirks, forgetting everyone around us as he cocks his head and I swear to all the big dicks in the factory the fucker is laughing at me. "It's magic, Adisen love. I can make them all forget," he whispers on a husky purr against my ear as he leans down and brushes his lip against the shell.

"You can?" I ask in awe.

"Who knows?" He laughs darkly, pressing his lips firmer to the side of my ear as he whispers, "But wouldn't it be fun to find out?"

I shudder, shivering in his hold is making him chuckle in a tone used by the sinfully demented. "I don't know? Is a strait-jacket fun?" I ask with a broken chuckle. Fuck me, this is a turn of events. I can't keep up with his emotional whiplash but I can't lie and say that I'm not enjoying this flirtatious side of him.

"Alright, Jekyll. Let's go get our shoes." I breathe, breathless from his close proximity as I pull away from him. His musky scent of cedar wood and bonfire is so thick and heady as it wafts around me, that it has me licking away the drool which pools along the seam of my lips. I clear my throat and give him my back, allowing him to follow me through the crowd. I approach the counter, stopping short to stare at the tiny ass blonde behind the desk openly ogling an oblivious Elijah as he stops at my side, still taking everything in. Those amber eyes of his roam over the heads of everyone pottering around us as he assesses them. Thankfully the low lights darken his eyes enough to pass for normal in the shadows and fluorescent lighting. His shoulder bumps mine with a saucy smirk and I realize it was stupid of me to think the woman's attention had gone over his head.

He is a man that sees everything after all.

I lean on the counter, chin in my palm as I wait for her to notice he isn't alone. To buckle up and do her job without the open display of lust dancing within her dull brown gaze. I purse my lips, an irritated sneer, teasing the back of my throat. Elijah chuckles broodingly again. I can feel his eyes drilling a hole into the back of my head as if my reaction is cute to him.

I clear my throat, breaking her lingering stare and finally gaining her attention. The flirty smile fades in an instant and in its place is a deep glare and a sour ass frown as she turns to regard me.

"How may I help you today?" she asks, in a bored tone, huffing and flexing her fingers in front of her as she stares down at her lime green nails.

"Alley for two, if you can handle that?"

She freezes, stilling in her movements as her eyes flicker toward mine. "Sure can. But not for another hour, we're fully booked." She smirks, smugly. Sticking out a hip and placing a dainty hand upon it as she reaches the other hand across the desk to run up Elijah's arm, which I'm sure she'll pass off as harmless comfort.

You know, like when someone places a hand on your back to point you in the right direction?

I guess this place has a 'sorry, we're all booked' hands on policy.

Note the sarcasm and cue the motherfucking eye roll.

I can feel Elijah shift, and I can almost see the frown on his lips as he readies himself to argue that there are three empty lanes as he pulls his hand away sharply like her touch had harmed him. Instead of arguing, I return her smirk with a shit eating grin of my own.

I mean, there's always one right? An arrogant, entitled bitch who has to throw down some kind of claim when it comes to another woman's man. Not that Elijah is my man but fuck it. My ass brought him here, I may as well enjoy it before he poofs away from me and back into his own reality. The thought leaves a sour taste on my tongue as I force myself to shake off the unwelcome feeling. I want to become a part of everything he's ever known and experienced. I do. So fucking badly, I do. I want to escape this reality and be queen in a world that appreciates his dark beauty, even though he doesn't seem to think I deserve somebody shrouded in such darkness. I wish he knew that this world has darkness too. We just call it depression. I just don't know what's holding me back. What is blocking me from being able to take him back and keeps us bound here?

"That's fine, you can book us in for then," I tell her simply if not a little sickly sweet. "Names Adisen, he's Elijah. Be a love and jot it into the system?" Then I turn to him, a huge smile on my face as I take his hand in mine and start to lead him away with a pep in my step like some love-struck teen, throwing over my shoulder, "You can win me a teddy while we wait handsome!" Because if she wants to be petty, my ass can be petty too as I make her watch him win all the goodies for me and me alone.

I catch her narrowed eyes and chuckle. Elijah shakes his head, his grip on my hand tightening as he pulls me into him. Stopping us in the middle of the crowd as he towers over me and catches me off guard. No fucks given that we're smack dab in the middle of everyone trying to pass. His brows furrow and release as he gazes at me with intense focus. Tilting his head to the side as a slow smile builds. One hand snakes around my waist, sitting firmly on my lower back as he pulls me closer into him and curves my body to the contours of his. He threads his fingers through the thick strands of my hair, holding me to him.

I gasp, eyes narrowing as I question him. "Are you playing with me right now?" I demand, in shock that he's still flirting with me, while at the same time being afraid it's all some big joke to him. This morning he was ready to tear my head from my shoulders just so he could return home. Now he wants to take it one day at a time? I can't believe that everything the conscious Elijah has said is enough to break through to him.

No amount of time with Elijah Braxton would be enough, I know that now. Even through his mood swings, the need to be around him is more fierce than my need to be cautious of him.

The man with the power to hurt me with nothing but the heat of harshly spoken words.

My heart can't handle another rejection. But if he's open to growth, then I guess I should be too?

"So what if I was?" he retorts, his sinfully wicked smirk growing wider and it's almost like those pearly whites fucking wink at me. "What would you say?"

"I'd say I'd get my payback by kicking your ass at bowling and forcing you to win me a small farm of animals." I smirk at him with a wink, leaning into his hold as I flirtingly run my hand over the hard planes of his chest.

I'm fighting the smile pulling at my lips. My guard is finally dropping, my acceptance that this man is real, or as real as he's going to get, finally settling the anxiety that came with the thought that I was going crazy. He pulls back, staring at me with a raised brow and amusement dancing in his quizzical gaze and then something changes.

It's like something flickers inside his head and then he remembers himself, stepping back and away from me as he clears his throat and looks around at the machines.

The douse of the hot and cold waters has something lodged in the back of my throat, pain and embarrassment mixing in my core at the brush-off during our flirting.

I try to banish the feeling, a smile spreading across my lips which feels devastatingly sad so how it looks to him when he stares back at me is beyond me. He's already said that he's not the one for me. I just wished I believed that to be true. It would hurt less.

Rubbing my arms together, I avoid eye contact for a moment while I try to gain my bearings again.

He nods in the direction of nothing. Literally just nods his head as if he's in search of something to fill the awkward silence while he tries to make light of the mood and convince me everything is still fine. "I thought you were going to murder that woman back there." He huffs a laugh, the sound feathering past his lips.

Glancing over his shoulder at the petite bitch still gawking at us, I parrot the sound. "I thought I'd change my tone and be all sweet to you while I ask you to use your powers and turn that bitch into a frog or some shit," I drawl, my tone alluring as I flutter my lashes up at him jokingly.

He straightens above me, amber eyes darkening as they become swirled within silken black vines that bleed through his irises as he turns to regard her. She sticks out her chest and offers him a sultry smile in return.

My heart quickens at the thought of him finding anyone else attractive and I twitch, hating the feeling growing in my chest and warring within my core.

My eyes snap back to him when he whispers something with a low and dark timber. The ancient words in a foreign tongue slip past his lips with the sweetness of deluxe honey. I find myself leaning in, mesmerized. The chant is so low, I hardly hear it but somehow, it engulfs the space around me and cocoons me within its sinful darkness. Something about it is chilling. It caresses me in a way that begs for my surrender as the aged words whisper around me, kissing me with the softest lips of a tender lover.

Slowly I turn back to face the woman at the counter with a tightness in my ribs as my eyes bug out of my head.

One side of her face is warped and blistered with some gnarly looking warts and blackheads. Her skin has caved around the sides of her eyes, white scarring and crisscrossing like those who suffer from really bad acne and have the welts to prove it, long after it turns their face into a crater. I'm almost horrified at how bad she looks, how sore and painful it must be but she doesn't even seem to have noticed the change in the texture of her skin.

"It will heal, next cycle of the moon. Are you happy now?" he rasps, hands flexing back on the curve of my hip as he turns to look back down at me with such intensity. I think I stop breathing altogether. Lost to the contrast of his behavior. He removes his hand and places it into the front pocket of his jeans.

I nod mutely, turning back to drown within those compelling complexities that burn like the sun. "You did that for me?"

He looks back at me with such fierceness in his eyes, it constricts within my throat and makes my heart thump loudly within my chest. My palms sweat as I feel like the only person in the world with how deeply he is gazing at me.

"Of course I did," he declares.

Trying not to sink within the moment, to not allow myself to feel any more for the man who is destined to leave me when I already hold so much love for him on the pages, I nod and offer him a small smile before turning away and leading him over to one of the machines that has multiple giant animal teddies inside with a huge claw dangling above them.

Even if he does go back to his realm and he does take me with him, happily ever afters scarcely exist. I have to keep telling myself that.

I pull out a quarter and insert it into the slot before stepping back and staring at him expectedly. He stares back blankly, looking at me for a clue and I laugh.

"Sorry," I utter, biting my lower lip drawing his attention. "Just to clarify though, this is *not* another witch's pet so please don't blow it up."

He growls at me and I smile back at him with amusement.

"Calm down, don't shit out a pup," I joke, with a smile and laugh hard when I think about how fucking random we are as humans. How we must look to him, the King of the Horde, but random shit coming out of our mouths that makes no sense is just how we're made,

"Thinking that our machines can turn into monsters happens to the best of us. You should see the stigma around self-driving cars." I wiggle my brows tauntingly at him, finally relaxing within myself at being so close to him, surrounded by so many strangers. It almost feels normal.

"Are self-driving cars new or something?" he asks.

Tilting his head as his gaze roams all over me, he makes my skin prickle in heated awareness. I get the feeling he's more interested in my reaction to him than he is about learning something new at this point.

When he bites his lip in thought, I have to squeeze my thighs together in arousal, fighting to stay on track.

"Kinda. People don't believe in putting their trust in machinery. But I don't think we're quite at the era of the metallic invasion just yet," I comment, with a cheeky smirk at the questions I know he must have. Nodding back at the game, I explain how we play it. "You use this to move the metal claw back and forth and when you think it's in the right place to grab a teddy, you press the button." I demonstrate the move, although he doesn't watch what I'm doing, instead opting to watch me acutely so he completely misses the fact I don't end up with a teddy at the end of it.

"Sounds easy enough," he grunts, turning to face the machine he towers a good few feet over. "And I wouldn't shit out a pup. I'd shit out a harrowing beast bigger than anything this land has ever seen and utterly deadly. It'd pillage and destroy leaving nothing but corpses and bones in its wake, with the soils of this godforsaken earth bathed in the essence of their victims' blood," he deadpans with eerie foreboding. But I almost get the sense he's catching on quickly with the witty and unsophisticated humor of us mere mortals.

His huge hand engulfs the tiny joystick and moves it back and forth with a heavy fist.

I gape at him, mouth falling slack and my eyes widen in horror. Instinctively falling to the rounded globes of his ass as that image pops into my head. "No way?" I ask like a moron, making his lip twitch as he tries to not outright laugh at me. "No fair! You promised to tell me about your land. The truth would be nice. After all, how am I supposed to know what's real?" I chastise around a really fucked off huff.

He smirks, glancing at me quickly before turning back to the swinging claw. "So I did," he muses. The chain jerks on its runner, before stuttering to a stop over a huge octopus.

"Go for the wolf!" I direct, finding that one the most beautiful and worth the shit ton of space it will take up in my house, so easily distracted when a massive, jet black one with hues of red catches my eye.

He grunts a short laugh before he moves the claw again, smacking the button and shaking the machine with the brute force of it. Turning to fold his arms over his chest with a smug smile as if he just won. The claw misses, knocking against the bear beside it before coiling back to the starting position.

"Easy enough, right?" I throw his words back at him with a saucy smirk. "So where's my wolf?"

"What?" He turns back to face the machine, searching the hole it should have fallen inside had he won. "What the fuck? Where is it?" He rocks it back and forth and I pull him back by his shirt, cackling before he sets off the alarms.

"You lost."

He stares at me deadpan, before blinking slowly. "I never lose."

"Just did, welcome to the shitty, irritating things in the mundane world, my friend.

Machines like this are as annoying as that bitch over there still glaring at us."

He pays the blonde no mind before taking another turn. He loses again and again and with each loss, grows more increasingly frustrated as I start to fear for the machine's safety.

"This is outrageous," he roars, the tense muscles in his arms dancing under the strain drawing my eye at the sheer strength he wields within those humongous arms.

The joystick cracks under his unforgiving hold and my eyes widen as I angle my body to shield him like we're naughty children about to be chastised for breaking school property or something. "Fuck this," he growls, punching through the glass and pulling out the massive wolf, lion, and black unicorn that all stand to size at my hip. I gasp, pulling back in shock at how the glass shimmers like a pool of metallic water, flickering with darker hues as it remains unbroken while he retrieves the teddies. I look around frantically, hoping nobody saw. I glance at the blonde, thankfully she's occupied with another family giving us a reprieve from her scrutiny for a hot minute.

Visiting the nut house is not on my list of things to do before I die.

"There, here's your damn farm of animals," Elijah grunts, stacking them against the machine. "You want, you get. I will never lose." He preens, shoulders back as he glares at me, daring me to argue.

"Look mama! Look at what they won. Can we play? Please, please," a little girl with braided pigtails begs as she pulls on her mother's jean-clad leg.

"Honey, they must have spent a fortune!" the mother utters with sadness around her aging eyes, staring at the amount of teddies we have before glancing back down at her daughter.

"Here, have a unicorn." I gulp, shuffling it toward the little girl in a frenzied hurry. She gushes brightly before I throw the lion at Elijah and clutch my wolf to my chest as I hobble away due to the weight of it.

The mother smiles at me softly offering a heartfelt, "Thank you." Before I turn away from her completely.

Moving us as far away from the machine as possible still in shock, I look back at the glass, expecting it to be otherworldly but instead it's exactly as we found it. Not a shard to be seen on the ground. Sweat beads along my skin, stroking my nape and making me shudder.

"What? What did I do?" he questions, following close behind me growling with annoyance.

"Nothing dude, that shits totally normal. Nobody will lock us up and throw away the key if they saw that. Nope. No. *Totally normal*," I waffle, heading back over to the bowling counter. I glance around hurriedly, like someone will pop out of nowhere and start the witch trials.

He grabs for me, holding me by my wrist as he glances down at me with awe in his eyes. "You wanted a farm. Why give it away?" he questions, and my heart flutters, my body relaxing at the rightness of his touch.

"Powers don't exist here, we fight tooth and nail for everything we have and half the time, it comes with breaking the bank using money we don't have. All that woman wanted to do was give that kid a good day, and those machines are rigged as fuck. She never would have won. And besides, she'd get more use out of it than I would, and I'm more than happy with what I have. I appreciate it because it came from you." He hums, nodding his head like he understands but there are still lingering questions in his gaze.

I take a deep breath and square my shoulders, taking in the people around us.

The profoundness of how I'm a single person in a sea of humans, slowly spinning in a circle and watching their every move and yet not a single one notices me. It hits me with the weight of a comet... Not a single one can even garner the thoughts twirling within my mind.

Because I'm a vessel and my intentions are mine alone. When I really think about that, about how nobody will ever know what I'm thinking unless I make it known, is terrifying.

Never expecting to find a monster next to us.

"Today was about having fun. I wanted to take your mind off everything you learned last night. And the stress of today. But if you want a real lesson about this world, look around you, Elijah. Tell me what you see."

He does as I ask, watching every single person and their companion with an acute awareness gleaming in his golden eyes. He furrows his brow and wrinkles his nose, "I see people," he observes, following the trail of my wandering feet as we continue to turn in a circle together. "I see happiness, boredom, annoyance…" He squints, his gaze intensifying. "I even see some anxiety," he notes, staring at a few of the people that stand around wringing their hands and shifting uneasily on their feet. Their eyes flitter back and forth without really taking anything in. "I see upset, and frustration." Parents and their misbehaving children. "What do you see?" he questions, peering down at me.

"Strangers. Disconnect. Not one single person is aware of the next or the people surrounding them," I comment, sighing heavily. "I see a hell of a lot of loneliness in a world filled with so much emotion, that the goings on around us seems to take a back seat. I see sadness and the fucked-up thing is not everyone notices it until they're struck with a moment of soul sucking clarity." That got deep and dark really fast.

I don't know why I'm pointing this out. Why I need to show him the difference. I think maybe it's so he can have some understanding.

Hell, maybe it's because *I* want some understanding.

At times, when you take a step back and really pay attention, this world can be miserable.

I guess I don't want to suffer that fate alone anymore.

I want to bring him into my world.

Into the good, the bad and the ugly.

I clear my throat and shake off the tension which is riding me hard. I want today to be fun for both of us. Smiling, I shrug it off and head back over to the bowling section. I can feel the intense stare boring into my back as Elijah stares at me with a newfound intensity that probes my soul and promises to uncover all of my secrets.

Back at the counter, I watch him from the corner of my eye.

Bowling with a supernatural? Well, this should be fun…

Fifteen

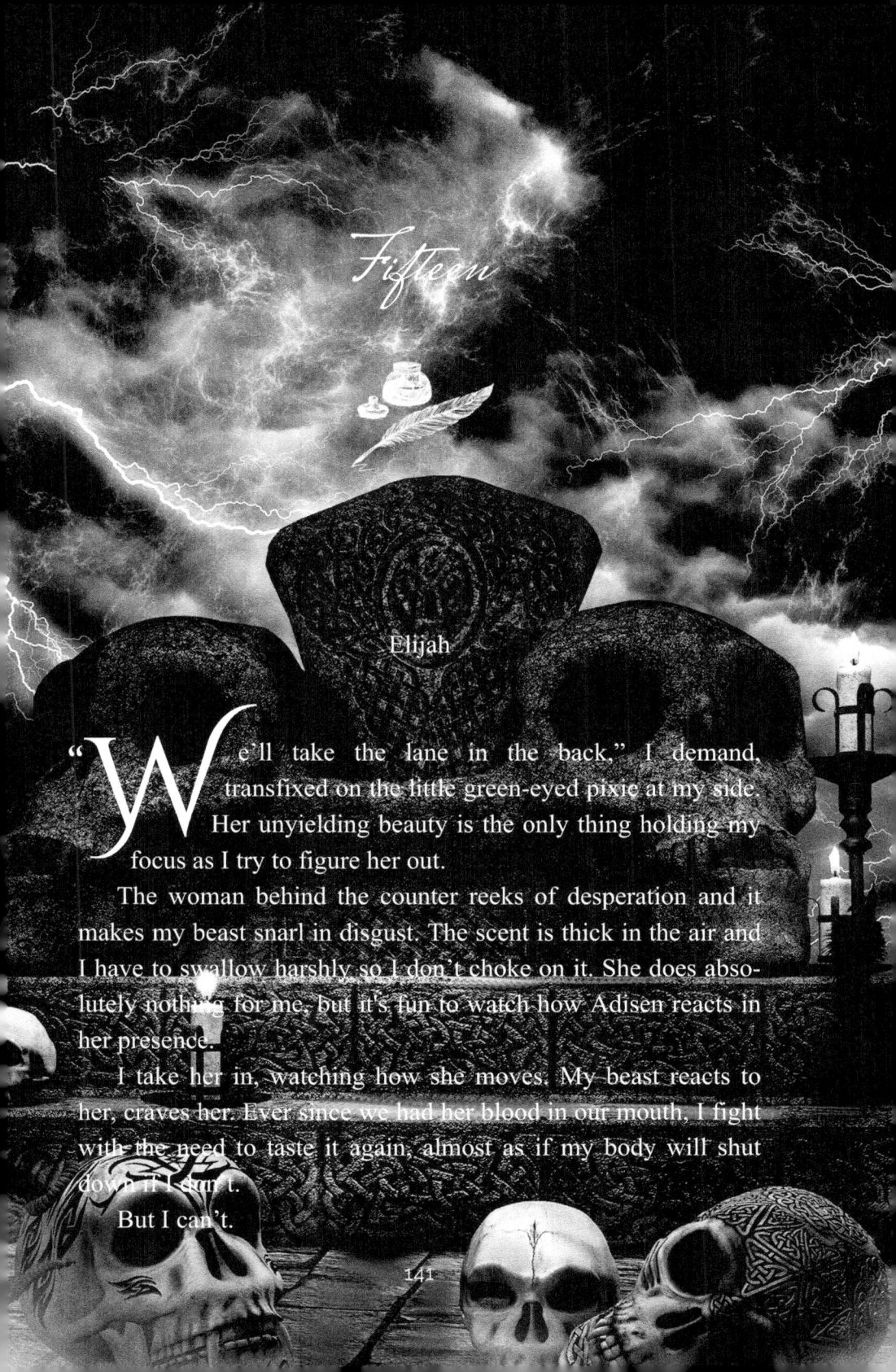

Elijah

"We'll take the lane in the back." I demand, transfixed on the little green-eyed pixie at my side. Her unyielding beauty is the only thing holding my focus as I try to figure her out.

The woman behind the counter reeks of desperation and it makes my beast snarl in disgust. The scent is thick in the air and I have to swallow harshly so I don't choke on it. She does absolutely nothing for me, but it's fun to watch how Adisen reacts in her presence.

I take her in, watching how she moves. My beast reacts to her, craves her. Ever since we had her blood in our mouth, I fight with the need to taste it again, almost as if my body will shut down if I don't.

But I can't.

She can never be mine. I come from a world of brutality. Even in this world, I struggle with that. With being soft, and tender, not the alpha that lives within my skin. Not the darkness which consumes the earth. In my realm, everyone knows who I am.

Here. I'm almost a nobody.

It's taking everything within me to act like I'm in control around her. But I also can't deny that the closer I become to her, the more things begin to make sense. The more my memories seem to come flooding back. As I learn her, I somehow begin to learn myself as well. Whatever this bond is, I fear it's the key to unlocking all of my questions and finally finding answers.

I just hope we don't have to reply on that.

I have no delusions that I understand this world, but I sure as fuck make no such statements that I even remotely understand Adisen at all. She's so complex, a riddle inside a mystery I crave to unravel. She acted with kindness today, gifting her winnings to that little girl. She showed me what being selfless looks like. It was the first time I had ever really noticed that I wasn't so familiar with that before tonight.

The air around her is bright, happy yet is tinged with something sad and dark I just can't work it out yet. There is a resentment in her seemingly joyous eyes and I can see it around the lines of her sweet, angelic smile. I just don't understand where it stems from.

What in this world has darkened the way she perceives it?

I see no monsters here. No creatures coming to attack. Maybe there are hidden dangers here and it makes me wonder if in some ways they may be worse than the dangers I'm used to.

She moves with grace, but I often catch in the corner of my

eye acheful frowns and subtle winces. She's clearly hurting, but she never asks to slow down. Never complains. She never stops.

I thought I knew what strength was until I saw her fight through another day, even when the fevers held her captive. She never gave up. She never gave in.

It confuses me, as to why she even hurts at all, now the fever has broken.

But I have a feeling if I ask, just like every other time, she won't tell me the truth anyway.

So I'm left to my observations.

I'm not used to close quarters, being so close to all these people has me on high alert, my gaze firm on the woman at my side as I wait for the threats to rear their ugly heads. Because that is what I'm used to. This is what I know.

Surely they will in a place where everyone is so crammed, touching shoulder to shoulder. I almost look forward to seeing what an altercation in this realm looks like. I'm sure it's very different from my own and leaves me with a hint of excitement.

Going by what my little witch says, smiting is frowned upon here.

"Sure thing sir, I can do that for you. Is there anything else I can do for you tonight? Anything at all?" she asks as she pouts thick lips that remind me of the Harlequin Jester Demons back in my realm. She flutters her eyes, but unlike when Adisen does it, it holds no effect over me.

"Yeah, actually there is," I reply, watching as Adisen scowls beside me. "You can take your desperation elsewhere. It reeks and I find it irritates the beast within me."

Her face flames pink as she stumbles back a step with wide eyes. Adisen chuckles, shaking her head as she places her hands out in front of herself to steady them on the counter. "He means the beast of his annoyance. Don't worry, he isn't a serial killer or anything. Not unless I ask him to become one." She snorts, wiping stray tears away from under her eye causing me to smirk down at her.

"Names are on the screen. You have ten frames. Shoe size?" the woman snaps, recovering rather quickly as she taps away at the keys on the board in front of her and leans over the counter to better see the screen making sure our names actually appear like she has said they would.

After Adisen gives me a once over, she throws out a random number and a pair of the ugliest looking shoes I have ever seen are placed in front of me.

"I am not wearing those, I'm a king for fuck's sake. They're awful," I snarl, lips curling at the hideous sight before me.

"Sure you are," the woman drawls. "Rules and regulations. Wear them or leave."

I turn to Adisen. "Are we required to wear these monstrosities?" I ask.

She shrugs. "Yes, unless we bring our own and we-"

Running my hand down the thick muscles of my thighs, I hide them behind the counter before conjuring two pairs of what they call bowling shoes. Black, with midnight blue embellishments that shine and shimmer under the fluorescent lights. I drop them down on the counter and raise a brow at the woman testing my patience. "Like these?"

"Er- yeah?" she stutters, pulling one closer to her so she can assess the sole. She jolts up on her tippy toes, trying to see where I pulled them from in confusion.

"Great! Now that's sorted, let's bowl!" Adisen offers, grabbing the shoes and pushing me toward the three little steps to our right leading up to the lanes. "Dude. Seriously, I don't want to be kidnapped and dissected because you can't be discreet," she hisses at my back.

"Why? It's not like anyone would hurt you. I'd kill them if they did. And if I ever lost you, I'd use my powers to find you again. My witch to torment, remember?" I wink at her as she stares at me dumbfounded.

"Yeah and knowing my naive and shit-as-fuck luck that will be around the time we discover the government is more educated than we believe and all the magic that used to live in this world now lives as hostages in their basements with anti-magic counteractions in place," She utters and I spin to stare at her.

"You think? I thought this world didn't have magic."

"Well, it doesn't." She sighs, stopping to stare up at me. "But what the fuck do I know anymore? You just punched through glass *without* breaking the damn glass."

"Never say never I guess, you did rip me from my world with as little as a thought," I agree, and she narrows those shimmering emeralds at me.

"Yeah, lest I ever bloody forget," she grits, turning to run her hands over the balls in the runner. "Anyway, bowling. This is how we play-" she starts, but I cut her off.

"Now this, I know how to play. Only we use heads from the slayed demons in the realm and the winner wins a feast at the hall of souls. An ancient ground of ruins that allowed the spirits long since passed to wait on you in the debris with the melody of harrowing wails and lights of dancing essences."

"Come again?" she asks as she just blinks at me blandly.

"It's like our realm's finest dining hall. It takes many rotations of our realm's golden moon to even make a reservation. It's greatly priced and mostly only the privileged can dine there. It's located under the Icelandic stars. The most brightly lit ones within our skies."

"Skies as plural?" she questions.

"Yes. And after the meal is complete, the souls gather overhead and put on a show as they flicker with a silver flame coming together as one to celebrate the lives they have just catered too."

"You mean like stars?"

I shrug. "Not even close. In a way yes, but there is nothing as awe inspiring or as reflected as one's soul. It truly is a sight."

"I wish I could see it." She frowns, taking a seat by a small table. She deflates, shoulders slumping as she looks back up at me. "Golden moon?"

"It only comes around once every fifty white moons."

"Wow," she breathes out, eyes lighter than I've ever seen them.

The screen flickers with a timer warning, and my name appears in thick block-blue letters. I move to the runner and find the heaviest ball. It's not a screeching head but it will do. I take my place at the starting line and wind my shoulder before pulling back and bending at the knee. With precise aim, I coil high before forming a rapid circle, and letting the ball fly with the momentum as it takes off rolling down the waxed, wooden lane.

It's strange doing something light and carefree. I never expected myself to be intrigued by another land. I've always been so consumed with my own that I never had any time to look beyond that. But now that I'm with Adisen, I find myself wanting those little sparks of wonder in her gaze when I tell her about my home. It leaves me wondering if maybe that same gleam shines in mine when I look back at her as she shows me everything about hers.

A shrilling, ear bleeding scream pierces the air making Adisen and I turn fluidly toward the sound. My hackles rising as a growl builds in my throat. It dies off when I see the blonde bent over, running her hands all over her face as she gazes into the small mirror strip running through the shelves of packages that was behind the counter holding snacks. Her screaming is cut off abruptly when the grounds beneath our feet shake and a huge boom echoes, rippling through the bowling alley drawing my attention back to my lane where my ball has shot a hole through the wall, breaking brick and coughing up dust.

"Two for two." I smirk like an arrogant ass, turning to wink at Adisen who has her mouth hanging open. "Told you I will never lose. Your turn."

"I should have gone through the rules!" She chokes, covering her mouth with her hands. "Are you familiar with the saying tuck tail and run?"

"The run part." I glance behind me nonchalantly as I add, "But my tail isn't out."

"So many fucking questions!" she bellows around a startled laugh as she takes my hand and together we begin to run from the bowling alley, like the mutts from the viper-tongued hounds are burning hard on our heels.

Sixteen

Adisen

"Oh fuck! I can't breathe," I wheeze, doubled over as my very soul tries to strangle the fucking life out of me. "You broke the bloody wall!" I recount through the burning in my throat. We ran from the alley, not wanting to face the questions and demands of an explanation as to how the fuck he is that strong. I mean, *nobody* is that strong.

My mind is still trying to catch up with the events of the last four days. It's information overload and I have to fight to stay awake from the shock that pushes me to want to sink back into that whacky dreamscape I was in when I had the fever.

My muscles smart, and I bend at an angle that relieves some of the tension in my back.

"How was I supposed to know that wasn't part of the game? In my realm, the goal is to throw the head hard enough that the friction causes the head to burst into Elijah huffs, not even having broken a sweat despite the fact we just ran half a mile to the beach.

Night has fallen, the stars scatter across the sky, somehow brighter tonight as they glitter and gleam above us. My heels sink into the sand and the full moon sits in the center of the ocean, casting a pathway of bewildering light that reflects off the water's surface. The whole night is enchanting and I take a moment to take it all in. My eyes naturally flickering back to Elijah, stunned silent at how the shadows fall across his chiseled face and how the moonlight makes his amber eyes almost 3D orbs that glow like a cats in the dark.

The breeze gathers, picking up around us and somehow bringing us closer together. I'm breathless, less than a foot away from a gaze that burns right through me. My lips part as my hands tremble, finding ourselves locked here, within one another's thrall. I'm suddenly extremely aware of the rhythm of my heart as it beats a pattern into my chest.

The sexual tension like electricity that cracks through the night.

Elijah's golden eyes dilate and almost shimmer like parted waters as he steps closer to me, inhaling deeply as his breathing grows rapidly, "Now what will you show me, witch?" he utters thickly, the brooding husk to his tone sending a shiver down my spine.

He reaches up, brushing a caramel strand of hair from the curve of my cheek bone and gently tucking it behind my ear. My skin flames, supercharged in the wake of his touch.

"I think I've shown you enough of my world for one day," I whisper. My entire body longing to arch into him. "I think it's your turn." The mood changes, charged with sensual energy that I can taste on the tip of my tongue.

The anticipation, the sensation, all coiling into one ball of trepidation as the torment from the last few days catches up. I'm wild with a need for him with the craving to taste him, just once, overcoming me like a glass consumed within water. I'm an adrift buoy, drowning under the waves.

"I think you're right," he breathes out.

Removing his hand from my cheek, he trails it down my neck, shoulder, and arm until he takes a hold of my wrist leading me over to the rocks stacked tall within the shallowness of the ocean boarding the shoreline. I follow him, unsettled with how right my hand feels in his as he kneels just in front of the retreating waves. Pulling me down beside him, he turns us until we are better angled to see how the rocks part and some of the crashing waves filter through like a waterfall. Dropping his eyes to the waves at our feet, he hovers his hands above them. Obsidian infused blue rocks grow from the sandbanks, peering just an inch above the water's surface, occupied by two blue infused, glowing crystals. The once calm waters begin to circle around the stone, growing higher still until a small tornado forms and the color of the dark ocean drains into the palest, neon blue I have ever seen.

My fingers instantly trace the bite wound on my neck, for some reason drawn to do so.

"This is what your throat looked like before the fever set in," Elijah states, catching my movements. "It's the first thing that ever really unsettled me. Not knowing what the hell was happening to you or why your throat had turned into the color of a moonpool, shimmering in a color exactly like this." He holds the tiny little structure, on the surface of the ocean as he speaks and I can't rip my eyes away from the otherworldly beauty of it. "There was something there, in the back of my mind forcing me to remember, I just haven't yet. I'm not sure how or what it means."

"Maybe you will soon?" I offer, helpless to give him any other kind of reassurance.

He looks at me from the corner of his eye, before glancing back at the ocean. "Maybe. I don't understand any of this, Adisen. I don't know how to process what's happening or the fact that I was created and not born. That I'm not real and that my loved ones have betrayed me," he admits, his tone turning so dark, the hairs on the back of my neck rise.

"One day at a time, just like you told me. You may not have existed in this world until my dumb ass ripped you from the pages, but you existed. You existed enough for me to want you, even if I knew I could never have you. You existed to those you serve to protect in your kingdom and I'll get you back somehow I swear," I offer my own truth, stepping closer to the ocean until the waves kiss against the toes of my bowling shoes. We left our regular shoes back at the alley.

A moment of comfortable silence falls between us. "You wanted to see something special right? Something magical from my world?" he asks, the smooth tone of his voice fitting the calm mood surrounding us perfectly.

I nod, watching him as he smirks at me wickedly. Stepping back, he throws those lethal arms of his up in the air and the entire world tilts as I fall on my side, vibrating under the shaking sands. The whole world quakes so much, the pain is lost amidst the rattling of my bones. I watch in surprise as those two tiny rocks thicken and grow, shooting from the ocean to form a small castle the size of a tiny house right before me. A harsh pain stabs the back of my neck and down into my shoulders from the fall but my shock is almost enough for me to not notice it. Staggering back to my feet, I dust myself off as I stare, bewildered at the ocean palace he just created with nothing but magic, with the aid from nothing but air.

"Back home, when the ruling became too much, I had a small palace on water's paradise. It's a small island surrounded by waters as blue as the ones I've just shown you. If I could be anywhere within my realm, it would be there. It's my home away from home. The only place I ever truly felt happy and at peace. The only place I ever remember feeling something other than nothing at all. I'm always fighting a war in my world. Always having to destroy something. Here, everything was just calm and gentle and my mind could rest," he grumbles, seemingly lost in thought as he gazes intently at his creation. "I've never shown anyone this. Never took anyone there either."

Something in my heart fractures, and I swallow thickly. None of this was mentioned in the book. He's going off script, remembering things that were hidden within the lines, and the fact he is growing, and changing, has unease and pride dueling with each other inside of me. I shiver, wrapping my arms around my waist to starve away the cold, and the stunning castle before me crashes with roaring thunder back into the ocean, shattering the seas and creating a massive wave that towers thirty feet above us. My heart leaps into my throat, my breathing stalled within my lungs as I see death salute me like the fucker that it is.

Elijah turns into me in one fluid motion. His grip on my arm gains momentum as he spins me into him. His other hand clasps firmly on the back of my neck, burying my face into his shoulder before the whole world goes dark.

Seventeen

Adisen

The darkness recedes and in its place is the warm glow of the lights in my lounge. I went from a darkened beach to being back home, all without moving my feet. The entire room spins and my mind leaves my skull to drift off into space. I blink open my sick swimming eyes, finding myself standing in the middle of silken black tendrils that entwine around me. I reach out tender fingers, caressing the darkness in my haze. A feral growl resounds beside me, echoing within my pulsating ears. "Keep stroking me like that, woman, and this night will end a hell of a lot differently than either of us planned."

"You?" I ask numbly. Lost in a daze so thick, it's a comfort I don't wish to wake from.

"I am the darkness, witch. And every time you caress it, *I* can feel it." He rasps, sending a shiver racing down my spine. I can feel him pressing against me, hands resting bruisingly on my hips while he holds me close, reminding me that even though I can hardly see, he's still here.

The hardness that is tenting his jeans, is firm against my stomach. I blush, hoping the shadows hide the tinge of scarlet in my cheeks.

It takes a while for his words to sink in, so I don't hurry myself in stopping, needing to feel the satin like texture under my palm lest I never find myself again in the thrall of something so wonderful.

I can feel it when he shudders against me and a small smile filters across my face.

"What happened?" I ask quietly, uneasy in myself as a vile bout of sickness churns in my stomach. The world slowly settles, falling back into place as it stops spinning like the rotation of the planets around me.

"I transported us," he whispers, and I freeze, feeling his lips a hairbreadth away from mine. I can almost feel the promise of them against me. A phantom touch, I find myself leaning into. I can't see him, he's nothing but the very same shadows that engulf me.

The air stalls in my lungs, trapping a small whimper in the back of my throat that is fighting to be freed.

I don't dare breathe, I refuse to even move, held hostage by the moment of intimacy which captures us in this unsuspecting moment.

He steps closer, backing me into a wall and I gasp at the quickness of it. His thick thigh presses between mine as a low growl burns throughout his chest. A snarl that has a rough undertone brewing deep within the brutal sound as his golden eyes fade to a shiny onyx while the beast joins in on his panty-sizzling, you-best-heed-my-warning, warning.

Maybe a sane person would fear a sound like that, but something within me splinters at the seams and makes room for it within the hollow depths of my soul almost as if it belongs there, deep, deep inside of me like a warm comfort. Like some of the missing pieces of my being, reformed and meld back together.

He steps back with a growl and I jerk forward, gripping his wrist and refusing to let him go. To allow him to back away from this, from me... from us. "No, no! Don't do that. Don't you dare do that! Stop pulling away from me, Elijah. I know you want this, so why? Why do you keep refusing to touch me?" I swore I'd never beg a man to love me, to want me, and here I am, ready to lay it all on the line. Elijah has been hot and cold since he dropped into my life and I can't handle the pain anymore. The anguish which comes from swimming through freezing oceans only to find myself in the water surrounded by a freshly erupted volcano.

Either way, the temperature burns.

I've never felt desperation as hard as the one riding me right now, whispering to me just how unworthy a woman like me is of a man like that. But still. I need this. I need him.

I'm a pawn in his game, a means to an end and his only ticket home.

I don't want to believe it, to believe that I'm lying to myself. But as the words slip out, I find myself holding my breath in preparation for his response.

"Do you know why I don't touch you? Why I don't *want* to touch you?" he explodes, turning back to me and stalking me like a seasoned hunter about to torment his prey. His eyes darkened to the gleam of the devil as he cages me against the wall. "Because you're poison to my very existence, Adisen. A pretty kiss away from rewriting the fates. From rewriting *me*, and... because if I did. I know I won't stop. I won't stop until I've destroyed you." A rough hand coils around my throat collaring me, firm pressure which brings a moan from my lips instead of a frightful whimper. I square my shoulders. Meeting him eye for eye, refusing to cower. He doesn't hurt me, he's trying to warn me. " Until I took you to places even your precious books couldn't explore. I won't stop until you become the fire that burns within my core and I, the arousal running in your veins. I won't stop until I own you, until I've used you. Not until I became the first and last thing you ever need, pretty girl. Not until the light in your eyes dims and my very own darkness stares back at me because I've enveloped you so completely, you know nothing else other than me. *Elijah Fucking Braxton.* I don't touch you because I don't want to break you. Because I have *never* craved someone so fucking much, that I can't be sure that I would never hurt you. Even though I need to get back home, I still want you. I should feel bad about that, shouldn't I? I should think about the kingdom I have left behind without my reign. But I don't. I couldn't care less if the price is that I get to taste you and that infuriates me. " His voice fractures and I suck in a broken breath. Clarity staring me dead in the eye and I wonder how I ever missed it when I see the conflict sparked within his golden, heartfelt eyes. "I can't hurt you," he whispers, resting his forehead against mine, our breathing entwining as we share every breath. The pain in his words is a barb in my heart. "That is why I refuse to touch you. Because there would be no going back. Because to be with the king of darkness, baby girl, you'd need to look good in black."

Elijah threads the thickness of his fingers through my dark strands and cups the back of my head, pulling firmly until my head is tilted backward and away from the wall, and I'm forced to stare up at him. The shadows fall across his face, highlighting his most sinful features, that leaves me dry within the mouth. There is a savagery to his gaze, a tightness in his jaw as it hammers away in his restraint. "You do such things to me, woman. Things I no longer find myself wanting to fight to understand." He misses nothing, his stare so probing I can feel it like a live entity that crawls against my sensitive skin. "Only feel, because the feeling of you curved against me is enough to make a very bad man go mad. You don't want to see me mad, Adisen. Rabid with my need for you."

"This woman is fairing no better at you being so close to me. The feel of you, the smell of you, I can't breathe, Elijah. I don't need to breathe. I only need you here, beside me and nothing else seems to matter." I whisper into the otherwise silent room. The sound of our ragged breathing is the only thing to be heard at all. "Black has been the color of my soul for years, Elijah. All you'd be doing is bringing it back to life."

"I still don't trust you," he growls, the tick in his jaw feathering out to flutter into his cheekbones as he grinds his teeth.

"And I still don't believe any of this is real," I reply.

How can I?

The perfect man, carved from the stone of the gods, chiseled to wickedly scandalous temptation, coated with immoral sin is standing right before me, telling me he wants me. That it's a need so brutal, it's set him alight and has taken away his impulse to fight such an alluring sensation. And believe me, the things I want him to do to me, to submerge my body within, are very fucking immoral.

Men like this, so domineering and commanding in a way that isn't forced or cringeworthy, just don't exist and if they do, I sure as fuck have never met them.

I'm aching for this man, with a desire that is choking. It

settles heavily in my limbs, making my entire body tingle with a hunger that has me salivating at the mouth. I feel like I'm standing in the center of the sun, with the pressure of being stolen by the moon weighing heavy on my chest. Like I'm running out of time, and once the darkness kisses me, I'll be forever changed.

Evanescence's "Bring Me to Life" Begins to whisper around us and he smirks, making me wonder if it was my will that has conjured the music from thin air.

"I can feel your need for me, woman. It burns down here," he gravels, hand trailing down my ribs, pulling a shivering shudder from me as he brings his palm to hover over the center of my apex. He is no longer touching me, only teasing me with the promise of it.

My body flushes, heating under the statement and it almost feels like my pussy erupts into a raging wildfire at the promise of his attention to a part of me that is demanding it like a Kardashian who demands the world bows at their feet.

The entitled little hussy clenches with a need so raw, that I squirm from his close proximity and rub my thighs together without an ounce of shame. I'm too drunk on lust to make sense of what he just said, or to question how he can feel me so intimately. He hadn't stated that he can sense it, smell it, or even make an assumption as to how I may even feel that way.

No.

He stated he could *feel* it, like my need for him is seeping from my body and settling into the very pores of his own.

Either way, I find my hips jutting out without pause, pressing my core into his palm until he curves his fingers and cups my heated desire within his firm hand. The heat somehow turns into a small explosion as the feeling of him against me has my entire body jolting like I've been electrocuted. I dance beneath him as he closes the distance and flattens me to the wall, covering my dainty frame beneath his hugely muscular one.

A large hand falls to my thigh, lifting my leg until it wraps around his waist and he grinds into me, the hand still holding my pussy a barrier between us. He looks at me in a way that is almost feral. The air twirls into a small hurricane and I can see the ripple within the breeze his mood alone creates.

My hair billows around me like I'm standing in front of a fan and golden eyes flash from honey to onyx like the flickering of a light switch. The darkness of his tanned skin within the shadows, blinks from muscular shoulders, to a hunched silhouette as he flashes between the man and the beast.

"I can't," he growls. The word rumbling out of him like the purr of an engine as the sound continues long after the word has been spoken. "I can't fight this."

I reach out a shaky hand, cupping his cheek as I try to gain a steady breath. But it's no use. I can't breathe at all, stolen to the choppy waters as I surrender to the current. "Then don't," I whisper.

That's all the encouragement he needs as he lunges forward, hand wrapping around my throat, tight like a collar as the hand keeping his hard length away from me is removed. Rough lips land on mine, demanding I open to him as his tongue slips past the seam of my mouth and explores my own. I moan into the kiss and he growls into me, giving into the frenzy that is consuming him from the inside out.

My resistance to him, to this, breaks like a dam as the floodgates open and my pussy gushes. I throw myself into him, tearing at his clothes but the second my trembling fingers grasp onto the fabric they flame under my hand. I gasp, pulling back as the clothes he conjured melt away from his body exposing the flawlessness of his defined frame and mouth-watering abs. I trace the divots, wanting to explore them with my tongue as I lick, stealing a taste of him. I can only imagine it tastes as good as his smell.

Tribal markings cover most of the smooth expanse of his skin, angelic strokes that have created art so divine you can't look away. That same beast that preened on his chest three days ago, that I thought was a part of my delusions, moves again, howling at the invisible moon before he shifts, changing directions until he grows in size and morphs so it's nothing but his head that I can see. The beast earnestly studies me through a dark and hungry expression, growing bigger still as if he wishes to tear from his confinements and get closer to me. The atmosphere darkens with the intensity of that very gaze making the shadows enclose around us.

I suddenly feel so small, so insignificant under the ruinous scrutiny.

A gazelle about to be devoured by the wolf on the hunt. Ready to consume his prey.

Instinctively I bare my throat to the image, arching my back and pressing my ample breasts into Elijah's hard chest and a roar echoes throughout the room. "Good girl," he praises and I whimper at the proud tone he uses. I suddenly feel weak, unable to stand on my shaky legs and a sharp panic stabs at my chest. If I'm ready to crumble from his nearness, scent and promise of wicked pleasure already, how the hell am I going to handle it when he begins to actually touch me? Just as I'm about to slump to the ground he catches me, pinning me with his grip around my throat once more. "Not yet, beautiful. I'm not even remotely close to being finished with you."

Stepping back, he extends his arm, keeping me in place as he puts distance between us. Licking his lips, he takes on this deliciously dark and probing stare which burns through me, creating an inferno with the starvation I see there consuming his ombre shifting eyes. He looks me up and down, appreciative, assessing and bites his lower lip with furrowing brows.

Humming deeply, his gaze flickers to mine quickly before flying back to my body at the same exact second a cool breeze licks against my bare skin and my pinkened nipples harden under the taunting sensation which sends awareness running toward my clit.

Glancing down, the clothes are torn from my body. But they don't burn away as they did from him. Instead they're suctioned from me like the quick removal of a tablecloth and flutter toward the hearth of my fireplace - which was drier than the Sahara a moment before the fire combusts into orange flames - and sends my clothes up into smoke right alongside them. The burst of heat whispers against my already searing flesh.

"That's better," he rasps. "I like you this way. Bare and exposed to me. Utterly fucking beautiful."

"Oh, fuck me," I groan, my head rolling on my shoulders as my hand darts toward my core and my deft fingers circle my throbbing clit. Rough hands smack mine away and my eyes snap open to glare down at the wondrous man who stares back at me with an unrelenting smugness that leaves behind a teasing side smirk on his kiss-swollen lips.

"No, baby girl. The only one who gets to enjoy this body is me. The reason behind those lust filled moans will be *me*," he growls savagely, riding the waves of the husky desire in his voice. "You'll come for nobody but *me*."

"Fuck, Elijah!" I lean into the wall, hoping it will hold me up but the effort is too much on my sensitive body. "I can't. I can't stand anymore."

"Who said you had too?" he replies, and in a movement quicker than the kiss of wind that gathers at the action, both hands cup my ass and hike me into the air until the backs of my thighs are sitting on his shoulders and my legs are crossing at the ankles, settling around his head. I'm pushed up into the wall, heated breath fanning my wanton desire as I clench at the need of being filled by him, right here and right the fuck now, before I'm the next thing to combust.

A soft kiss graces the top of my thigh, gliding downwards until he's feathering kisses to the top of my knees and back up again. Hot warmth follows his gentle mouth as he licks away the sweat beading along my skin, in such sensuality I'm panting on the verge of passing out.

My eyes fall closed when his attention is redirected to my pussy. Masterfully stroking through my folds making me gasp, rocking my hips forward until I'm pushing myself right into his face with the pressure of my shoulders flattened against the wall.

Something cool, breaking through the heat slithers around my throat, teasing the hardened peaks on my breasts and running all across my body has me jolting forward, eyes wide as I stare down at Elijah and see him, pulled back, sitting on his haunches, eyes glued on my fluttering sex. He's moved us down the wall, so he's on his knees, but I'm still wrapped around his head. His gaze is zeroed in on my slick heat, watching my pussy's sweet liquor weeping for him, coaxing my cream from me with nothing but his powers.

I heave in a deep breath, startled at the fact he is not touching me at all. But the black tendrils from when he transported me here were. The very same essence that started all of this in the first place, is the sybaritic fingers brushing against me, edging me toward an orgasm I don't think I'll survive. He's so focused on my core, that my heart stops beating within the brittle cage of my chest, when those utterly black and devious eyes snap toward mine.

Then all of a sudden, I'm thrown into a hypersensitive whirlwind that sweeps me off my feet and kills me dead five times over.

The black tendrils are everywhere, all at once. Coiling around my puckered buds, applying a pinching pressure which is just enough of a warning, without bordering the line of pain. The same tendrils enter me with vineful thrusts that feather against the parts of me I didn't know existed. Other tendrils simultaneously stroke my sides, tickling my sensitive skin until my whole entire body feels the rush, my soul chasing the high. Everything is raw, brutal and I writhe under the intensity. Almost convulsing from the uncompromising sensitivity that has tears welling in my eyes, and a pain to come undone, stabbing me within my core.

The tip of one of those damn tendrils, circles my clit teasingly, a growl follows, tearing from Elijah's throat. "Fuck, those sounds are everything," he rasps. "You're going to come for me, Adisen. Just like a good girl and when you do, you're going to remember that while your body is plagued with the entity of your desires that I *allow* you to feel… I also feel *everything* you do."

I don't know why being called a good girl sends me wild, panting like those words are the very air that feeds my starving lungs.

Maybe it's because I want to be good for him. To be wholly desired and wanted in a way that my reaction to him alone, is enough of a turn on that he, like myself, has no control over the need tearing through him at the seams.

Because that's a power unlike any other right?

Being a woman who is craved enough to drive a carnal man untamed and feral with his desire.

I want to be the center of his arousal. His good girl.

And every time he utters those words, I cream for him a little bit more.

"Will you give yourself to me, Adisen?" he asks, sounding a little bit closer now. "Will you allow me to use you in any way that I wish?"

I can't speak, I can't move. I'm a hostage to his assault, fighting for my life, hanging on by a thread as the darkness closes in all around me.

"Answer me sweetheart, before I stop making you feel so damn good," He groans, and I nod weakly. Trying desperately to grapple with my slack mouth to form even the most simplest of words.

"Ye," is all that slips free. "Ya." I try again and fail.

He chuckles darkly, the sound booming around me like the explosion of a bomb as it shakes the walls from his evident, amused filled lust. "Good enough, sweet girl. Now come for me!"

At his command, everything within me tightens. The tendrils turn brutal, and unrelenting. Closing their vine-like fingers around their hold on me. Clamping down around my clit, nipples, and pricking into my sides, fucking me hard with an ungraceful rhythm.

I open my mouth, ready to scream but no sound comes out. My soul is sucked from my body as a torrent of arousal causes the jetstream of my orgasm to pour from my tender pussy in waves. I'm drenched and it doesn't seem to be stopping.

I'm helpless. Boneless. And completely at his mercy. Just where I want to be.

I'm lifted in the air, suspended in time as my legs unwrap themselves from around his head through no will off my own.

I blink open my eyes, watching blurry and black monsters dancing around us in the shadows.

Varying distorted faces, rioting in joy, almost in victory of Elijah's conquest.

Like his shadows are just as sated as he is. Familiar shadows that have a soft smile playing on my lips. The faces are as monstrous as you could imagine.

Rough hands entwine themselves through the strands of my hair and grip tightly, yanking my head back until thick ropes of something warm and liquefied paints my mouth, and glides down my throat.

I gulp, swallowing quickly so I can keep my breathing even and prevent it from choking me. The action which commands my full submission is enough to make the walls of my pussy flutter and gush some more. I'm so sensitive, every ounce of pleasure turns into a soul-torturing agony that has a gasp torn from my throat. I'm elated, sated and honestly?

I think I'm a little unalived.

The shadows part like a veil, retreating a little but not fully, allowing only a speckle of light to shine through. It's enough for me to make out the silhouette of a thick and fucking glorious cock hovering above me, shooting its load all over my lips.

Elijah strokes my hair, shushing me from my trembling limbs and erratic breathing as he praises, "That's it. My good girl, just breathe. You're so pretty painted white, Adisen. Has anyone ever told you that before? I sure hope not, it's no way to spend my time murdering all those who have touched you when I could be here, making you feel this great all over again." Panic rockets through me and my eyes must widen in fear because there is no fucking way I can go through that again. He chuckles, stroking my cheek. "Soon, sweet girl. Rest for now."

He reads my body cues better than I do because in the next moment, my body has betrayed me as my breathing mellows and I pass the fuck out.

Darkness welcoming me with another warm embrace.

Eighteen

Elijah

Bring *her to me.*
 I silently command my darkness, *The Accursed,* watching as they heed me and bring her close, floating her within the air. I take her into my arms, cradling her tight toward my chest as I move through the house and back into her bedroom. I tried to resist her and in the end, she wouldn't let me. My body is more alive than it has been in my thousands of years within those pages of a book I'd only just discovered. Maybe giving her a taste of the dark side will be worth it if we all get what we want. If it helps me unlock more of my memories.
 I wonder how old I'll be in her world?
 Ha. Such a mundane thought.
 I glance down at the little witch and smile. Everything that is natural inside of me says I belong in a land of power. But I have to admit that the rest I'm finding with my mind and soul in not

having to constantly fight is soothing in a way I hadn't known I longed for.

It's almost peaceful.

I've never fucked anyone into oblivion before without actually fucking them. My darkness is my essence so I feel things even more acutely than I would through a simple touch alone and fuck me if I didn't feel her like a livewire that coursed through my veins, entwining with my darkness and dancing across every nerve ending I have.

She was so responsive, so raw that she had me twitching with a sensitivity unlike anything I've ever felt before. I was preoccupied with her heavenly scent. In watching the way her body came undone. Adisen's legs parted, those pretty and pink folds throbbing with a desire so thick, the mere evidence of that desire shined brightly for me.

I was mesmerized.

I couldn't look away from her glistening, slick perfection and when I did, when I gazed into those hooded and lust-riddled green eyes of hers, any and all restraint that I had broke and caved.

I became a man with a weakness and I've never been a man with a weakness.

I couldn't fight the war drum that beat a rhythm into my chest anymore. It was a drum to wage a war on her body and my own. The battle had been too hard to resist with her around me, consuming my senses. The need to feel her, to be inside of her was too great.

A lesser man would have given in a lot sooner. But I'm not a lesser man.

I wasn't just fighting my attraction to her, I was fighting the beast inside of me.

His obsession with the little witch only grows, and after my moment of weakness, it's grown into something so much more than even I can understand. He's never been so vocal within the walls of my mind. Never yearned to sink those rigged teeth into something so soft and keep her so close like his very own comfort blanket, tucking her into the folds of his ginormous body.

I can't allow him to bleed through, to hurt her any more than he has by sinking his teeth into her throat. It's one war I don't know how to end.

I fucked up when I was afraid that I would hurt her. But I proved to myself that I could show restraint. It's why I haven't taken her yet. Why I didn't consume her, filling her with the cock that craved her. Because I was heated, because I was cruel and she still wanted me.

I had called her poison and she had bared her throat to me.

I had rejected her and she still gave me her glorious body.

But she didn't plead and beg. She demanded. Adisen wanted me and she wouldn't take no for an answer. She knew her worth and that to me was the biggest turn on I could ever experience.

But at the end of the night, I just couldn't rest again without having tasted her.

There is still something there, lingering deep within the back of my mind. It's a deep awareness. Like my consciousness already knows but I can't formulate such a feeling into words or emotions. I have no way of explaining the way I feel around her or why I even feel that way at all. She's the sun and I'm the storm yet I'm willing to sacrifice her innocence just to keep myself well-stocked with the addiction of her taste. Returning home almost pales in comparison to such a feeling.

I've never felt this way before, never been one controlled by my emotions. Yet around her, I can't even think straight. I don't want to think straight because the whispers of my darkness no longer feel roaming, utterly lost when she is beside me.

They dance and wither with a content I've never known.

Tonight, I projected for the first time since the very night that I discovered I could. I can call the creatures from the purgatory within my chest near when I'm in aid of their brutal assistance. I can call forth their shadowy essence to build an impenetrable army around me. A shield of the damned and the demented.

A billowing smoke of the insidious horde.

The vile and the feared.

But tonight, I didn't summon them at all.

She did.

I became overwhelmed in such rapture, everything I held within me bled to the surface to enjoy the sensations.

I saw a different side to her tonight. She laughed and smiled more than she had since I'd met her.

Light and carefree. The change in her was noticeable as some of her guard dropped and she became somewhat more open to me being real. The unease at me using my powers in public was endearing. Watching how those emerald eyes fluttered and those rounded cheeks tinted red. She showed kindness to that young child and spoke with such profoundness that it startled me. I hadn't noticed her observations about the loneliness in this realm until she really had me look.

When I did, it shocked me to see how right she was.

I had been so caught up in her, in my need to tease and taunt her. To touch her. That I had overlooked almost everything else, the way those people milling around had overlooked us.

I guess the same can be said from my realm now that I think about it.

Loneliness isn't biased. It's a skilled tormenter with the capability to sometimes make you not even realize you're lonely at all.

I was a different man back home. Numb. Following the same routine not really knowing or seeing anything other than the single-minded focus that had driven me.

War. Strife. Fight for my kingdom and my woman.

My woman.

Even the thought of it leaves a bitter taste in my mouth. I grunt, clearing my throat as that same bitter taste turns fucking sour.

I had always known something wasn't right with Jessaleia, but just like right now, when I know there is a memory calling to me, it had been suppressed with a cold nothingness that hid behind a veil of forbidden truths. I still can't be sure that any of this is true, but I do know the longer that I'm here, the more I'm starting to think for myself.

Adisen stirs in her slumber, burrowing her nose into the crook of my neck and this strange kind of warmness courses through me. My hold on her involuntarily tightens as I feel this overwhelming urge to hug her closer and protect her from any unseen dangers.

I'm struck when I look around and realize that everything within this house is an unseen danger.

I'm not familiar with it and that needs to change. Since I've been here, she's shown me so much. She holds such a sadness and such a strength it's a contradiction that has me thinking of questions and seeking for answers.

Entering the bedroom, I lay her in the center of the bed. She whimpers, a small frown pulling at her lips as she furrows her brows in annoyance at the loss of contact.

I chuckle, brushing the strand of hair that has fallen into her eyes behind her ear, and retracing my retreat to then glide across the softness of her cheekbone, marveling at how soul-suckingly stunning she is.

I never intended for tonight to happen, but I don't regret it. I gave her a small part of myself tonight on that place she called a beach.

When I showed her the castle that I've only ever kept to myself.

She showed me her world, and I want so badly want to show her mine.

The perplexed and awestruck look that gleamed within her curious eyes had settled the beast. Seeing that bewilderment was a wondrous sight, better than any magic could have ever conjured. I don't know how I fit into this world, but while I'm here, I may enjoy the things that call to me most.

Her.

It's been her since the moment I fell from the sky and was captured by her dark emeralds.

I can't help myself when I lean down and steal a kiss, pulling back to hover my hand above her forehead. I have no idea why she takes those pills or why she's always in pain, but after what we just did, I know she'll wake in agony. I don't need to tell her I helped her, that it pains me to see her struggle, just as long as when she blinks open those beautiful eyes she still looks at me how she always has.

Like when I fell from the sky, I brought with me the stars.

And her body has a reprieve from whatever it is that plagues her.

The thought has an idea forming in my mind, one I'll have to wait till tomorrow night to accomplish. I smile, proud and now somewhat excited for the night to bleed into the day. Only to be stolen once more by the night.

I kiss her again. The feel of her soft satin lips soft against mine is nowhere near enough to dull the craving ache clawing at my chest.

I pull back nonetheless and step back toward the door. "Sleep well, sweetheart," I whisper, just as another small whimper falls from her glorious lips. She rolls onto her side, shifting the pillow beside her to bring it into her chest and hug it like a full body. With one last glance over my shoulder, I head back into the sitting room.

She wants a taste of my world, it's only fair I give her one.

'A mate, my boy, is the woman who finally makes everything that once never make sense, finally fall into place,' that same male voice ...

That same male voice whispers into my mind, and I fight to remember who that voice belongs too.

Nineteen

Adisen

I wake before my alarm - the one I only set on the days I have to work - to firm and hard arms bound around me, pulling me back into a hard chest. I feel nauseated, blinking open my sleep riddled eyes. It's a fight just not to fall back into the slumber I had roused from. I can't remember the last time I had slept this well, but everything inside of me longs for another undisturbed night like this again.

My eyes aren't even fully open yet but I go lightheaded, a feeling of euphoria chasing away the dizziness.

'Oh fuck. Am I seasick?' My mind panics.

'Need to be on a boat for that, moron,' my internal bitch retorts.

I jiggle a shoulder, trying to find some room in order to move and turn, but Elijah is holding me too tight like he fell asleep afraid that come morning, I wouldn't be.

I sigh, deciding that I don't need to see his devastatingly handsome face in order to sink into the warmth that surrounds me. I burrow myself a little deeper, pushing my back into his hardened groin and shift my hand so I can feel the teeth marks along the curve of my neck. It's become a silent comfort. When I feel the thickness of his cock, sitting comfortably against my ass, my eyes widen as the night before comes rushing back to me.

He had murdered me dead with pleasure.

Fucked, teased, and tortured me into oblivion with the vines of his darkness.

My cheeks flame pink and my pussy clenches in remembrance. My entire body comes alive, buzzing with an awareness that has my sensitive clit, pulsating to the point of pain, demanding some attention.

Fuck nut on a buttercup.

That cannot be good. I can't crave something so badly it leaves behind a physical ache.

That just won't do.

Although if I focus on my raging pussy, it may distract me from the pain that riddles my body daily.

Come to think of it though, my pain isn't as strong today.

It's official. I died in the hands of unfathomable passion.

"I can smell your desire for me, woman," Elijah growls in my ear, startling me from my thoughts. I gasp, shuddering when his warm breath feathers across the shell of my ear. "If you wish to wake to the new day boneless and utterly sated, screaming my name, just ask darling."

"I-" The words die in my throat when Alexa starts blaring Breaking Benjamin.

Elijah shifts, pinning me to the bed with one arm before it quickly retreats and I'm caged in with a black, transparent bubble that looks like a huge ball of gum. I blink in shock when I try to sit up, only to have the bubble growl at me in return. It's then that I notice those same monstrous shadows from last night, *are* the damn bubble.

A demon-like entity with the face of many that is stretched taut like latex with distorted, harrowing expressions screeching back at me. Despite it looking gut-wrenchingly terrifying, it's almost like they're rabid with their need to protect me instead of eat me and that has me canting my head in curiosity.

My mind short circuits, and I'm struck stupid until something explodes and Ben is cut of mid-lyric. I turn my head, drawn toward the sound of something shattering and glare the daggers of death at Elijah's back when I see a bolt of blue firefly across the room and blow up my alarm. The tension seems to drain from his rigid shoulders when he sees the remnants of my Alexa on the ground and slumps forward, turning back to me with a sheepish look on his hard face. "Another blender?" he questions.

"No, another Alexa," I hiss, my arms folding over my chest as I huff out an annoyed breath. But despite all of that, I can't help the soft smile that plays on my lips.

I can't be mad at this man.

The utterly perfect man who ravished me with nothing but my pleasure in mind. He spoke harsh words, words that stung like acid against my skin but he kissed away the wounds with a burn of passion that has left my heart full this morning.

He chose me.

Above the fear, and above the hatred and rage, he chose me, then when I fell unconscious, passed out from the bliss, he proceeded to take care of me. Staying at my side and cocooning me within the protection and warmth of his arms.

"Something you can live without?" he asks hopefully, and I

roll my eyes at him, regardless of the fact he looks damn cute right about now, actually showing me concern and remorse.

I don't know what I expected this morning, but I had thought it would more than likely be a regretful and burly Elijah.

Did I mention he's topless?

Holy smokes on the balls that choke Batman!

It takes me a moment to compose myself and stop ogling to reply. "Nope, I need it like I need a gallon of coffee."

He turns back to the Alexa on the ground and throws out a large arm, flicking his wrist. The destruction of my Alexa gathers and reconnects, flying back across the room as it settles back together and on my side untouched.

"Holy fuck, you can turn back time?" I exclaim, jolting forwards as my nose bumps against one of the stretched demons and I squeak, falling back into the mattress. The shadows retreat and before I have time to draw in an unhindered breath, Elijah is above me.

"When it comes to destruction of property or a being, yes. But not time in general," he tells me, eyes flickering back and forth between mine searching for something. "Are you okay? Did I scare you?" he asks, a hint of desperation in his deep and brooding tone that grinds like wheels churning on gravel.

My heart flutters and my stomach bottoms out on the wings of a butterfly. I shake my head, gazing up at him in unfiltered appreciation, "Surprisingly, no," I admit, breathlessly. "All you do, Elijah, is fascinate me."

"Is that a good thing?" He smirks, settling himself between my open thighs.

I don't answer directly, opting to make a vague statement instead. "Oh how easily you could become an obsession, Elijah

Braxton," I whisper, staring into those golden eyes that dance with silver specs, like he holds the constellations within them.

He stares at me, his expression unreadable. "How are you feeling?" Dark eyes roam all over my face, assessing and exploring, as he checks for something that may be out of place.

"Fine, more than fine. I'm great. I thought for sure you'd killed me." I chuckle slightly, glancing away as my neck flushes and a blush runs toward my cheeks.

"I can't kill you. I need you, remember, witch?"

For a moment my heart stops, then I look back at him and the smoldering fire that billows within his gaze has me questioning his meaning. Something happened when I accidentally summoned the other Elijah. I thought I would have been the subject to his rage when he discovered everything he knew had been a lie. That I am in fact to blame for the misery he has discovered in a new land. But since that moment, something seemed to have softened him and his beast and I don't know if I can trust it.

The thought that all of this might all be a ploy to get him back home, back to Jessaleia, has bile rising in the back of my throat and my heart clenching agonizingly within my chest.

Because it's a massive contradiction isn't it? To want something so badly and then to be faced with all of the ways it can be taken from you if you were to ever have it.

What kind of way is that to live? In constant fear of the ground giving way and you falling to the bottom of a pit you'll never escape.

Rock bottom is real and it's a killer.

What does it even mean to fear a future that I cannot see or even begin to understand?

I'd be miserable living for the what ifs. Instead, I want to live for the right now.

I can't see a world where he can ever forgive Jessaleia. But then again, I have no idea what will happen if he once again steps onto the page and seeps between the ink.

Will he forget? Will everything that he has learned here become nothing but waste?

Will he revert back to the beast without a mind?

I have so many questions and not even one answer to calm my raging anxiety. I want to go back with him, to see the land that he calls home.

Not to live in constant fear of betrayal and not being good enough in a world that holds very little room for imperfection due to the fierce demand for everything to be so effortlessly perfect. Because in a world like mine, you're always waiting for the Cinderella slipper to shatter into a million pieces and slice you with it.

"Hey, where did you go?" His golden gaze captures mine, and I realize that I became lost in my thoughts.

That happens way too much since I've long since favored alternate realities instead of facing my problems or worries head on. Instead of facing something that scares me, I fake it until it goes away. I bottle it up so tightly, it waits in a vault ready to explode at unsuspecting moments because I distract myself with novels and fictional men that feed the part in me that just wants to be loved.

To be wanted and kept safe.

It's not uncommon for my anxiety to take over sometimes, for me to drift away and lose all sense of my surroundings, but I've also never had something so easily bring me back before.

His voice is so rough, sensual and it's a feather to my nerve endings making me shiver. I blink, fighting away the negative thoughts and decide to not worry about something I can't control.

After all, I conjured him to be perfect, right?

"Nowhere. I just zone out sometimes," I tell him, shifting so I can settle the strain in my neck. "Did you sleep well?" I blurt.

What kind of question is that? But I'm hot and bothered and suddenly feeling awkward as this Adonis looms over me.

"Like a dream, yourself?" he rasps, those eyes of his burning in a sultry fire.

"Same."

"You passed out on me last night, right before we got to the good part." His growl rides the waves of lust and douses me with the infliction.

My hips lift, as I try to keep myself still and not act like a schoolgirl twirling her hair in front of her crush. "Yeah-er, sorry about that. But that wasn't the good part? My soul damn-well left my body."

"Why apologize? Watching you come undone like that, watching you swallowing my come like such a good girl, without a hint of hesitation, only beautiful fucking greed? It was the best damn thing I'd ever seen. My darkness has never reacted to someone like that before. I have never felt anybody as viscerally as I felt you, baby, purring to life inside of me. It was a damn good night." His lips twitch, eyes darkening as he leans down slowly and tastes the seam of my lips.

I arch my back, moaning into his mouth as my hands fly toward his head, tangling my fingers within his hair and pulling him into me. My leg lifts, settling on his hip as my blood burns from the inside out. The passion riding him last night made me light-headed, but this morning he's soft and exploratory. Not rough and ragged ready to fuck me into a hot mess I'll never recover from. Yet this is somehow still explosive, very fucking explosive. Rocking me from the very core of my foundation. I feel like I've stepped on a livewire, a display of fireworks lighting up the sky as I internally dance within the ruins.

"Elijah!" I groan, rolling my hips into the hardness of his thick cock, throbbing between my thighs.

"You moan my name so beautifully." He pulls back, golden eyes mingling with obsidian as he fights for his restraint. Peering into my widened eyes, his narrow.

My heart stutters in my chest, as my lungs constrict and rob me of the tiniest bit of air I had left. I gulp, hope soaring in my veins that he's a man true to his word. That I'm a woman he'd destroy the nation for. The words caress my skin, settling in my chest like a current that wishes to pull me under and never let me go. I bite my lip, trying to fight the smile pulling at my mouth as I lose myself in those everchanging eyes of his.

My thighs part, falling wider at my sides as a clear invitation for him to move that little bit closer. Close enough in a way, we'll become one in the most intimate of senses.

I've been through a lot in my young life, experienced many darknesses and tragedies that have made me who I am today. I suffered the death of my loved ones, the murder of my uncle. The bullying from my peers, and I learned early on that in a world so cruel, it was always better to watch out for yourself.

To go through the day to day but to never go out of your way in engaging with a world that is bound to hurt you. So I never got to experience one of the biggest moments in a woman's life.

Losing her virginity.

I've never wanted to. I preferred pleasing myself. I knew no other person could know the cues of my body like I could. I knew that I could surrender myself without anything holding me back and keeping my mind hostage. I wanted to keep this part of myself hidden until I found someone deserving and as the years passed and I became older and wiser, I began to doubt that I ever would.

But I have no doubts now.

It finally all makes sense as to why my life has led me here, to this man who I know will protect me.

I want to give them all to him, all of my firsts and all of my lasts. I want him to consume me and I want Elijah to know that I'll forever be his. Even if he does leave. I want him to know he has already tattooed his name onto my soul.

I feel like I should tell him, warn him of my virginity.

But no words come out. Instead, I reach forward, holding his head to mine as I kiss him with a passion that filters through the hollowness of my body and supercharges my senses.

He moves softly, his body gliding against the curves of mine as his large hands roam all over me, exploring and appreciative as he worships me while he goes.

Heat coils in my core, and unlike last night, everything is slow and sensual as he feels me.

Soft lips press to the curve of my throat as he kisses my pulse, licking it with his tongue. The head of his thick cock strokes through my folds and butts against my clit making me gasp and arch into him, pushing my shoulders down into the mattress and raising my hips so I can grind against him as he slips through my folds again and again. Gods, I've never been so wet. So slick. I'm a mess and he glides through it with sensual ease.

The anticipation drives me wild, and impulse burns in my blood as I chase that high. I become impatient for anything else as I move against him, hands stroking through his curls as the pleasure has me pulling at the roots, roughly.

"I want this, Elijah. I want you, I've only ever wanted you!" My eyes are clenched tightly, the words a sultry declaration whispering past my lips.

"You need to be careful, Adisen. A man like me, would devour a pretty thing like you."

My eyes fly open when something wet and warm encloses around the bud of my hardened nipple. I groan, panting heavily as he pumps against me, leaving teeth marks in my tender flesh. I whimper, the pain shooting an arrow to my clit which stabs me with the knife of arousal.

"Do it," I plead, legs coiling around his waist as I pull him into me. The darkness closes in on us, a black cloud fluttering down from the ceiling as it falls around us like a blanket. "Make me yours."

Elijah growls, teeth biting into the swelling flesh of my lower lip as he pulls away with a pop. The flat side of his tongue running across my mouth as he licks me from chin to cheek, kissing away the sting before sucking on his lower lip to taste the flavors of my skin and for some reason, the wild look that burns in his eyes, showing me just how brittle that leash of restraint is, has me salivating at the mouth to taste him as well.

Sinking my teeth into his throat, his hips buck and suddenly, I feel stretched full with the girth of two of his long fingers pumping into me. He doesn't push them in all the way, instead twisting them just inside of me and using the pad of his thumb to circle my clit.

A wicked and cruel tease to my burning flesh.

After a few thrusts, he pulls them out and brings them to my lips, tracing the seam of my mouth before pushing them into me and forcing me to taste them. My eyes dilate as I suck them hungrily clean, panting and whimpering with desire.

I've never given much thought to how I had imagined I would taste.

But this would surpass anything I could have imagined. The sweetness of my pussy and the frenzied aggression on Elijah's face is enough to make me feel the pressure of my impending orgasm, sitting heavy within my core.

I purr, the vibrations tickling against my lips as I bite around the digit in my mouth. Elijah growls, grunting into my ear when he falls forwards to bite into my neck, licking the scars along my throat, while he throat fucks me with those thick and unrelenting fingers of his.

There is something about it, something wicked and untamed as he pulls back, staring at me with those dark and sinful eyes watching with keen interest as he ruins me.

Something forlorn passes within his returning golden eyes and I suddenly feel like I'm losing him while he defiles me in the best possible way.

Clasping his face within my hands, I bring his attention back to me, placing soft kisses along the line of his clenching jaw, easing away the tension as he slowly softens under my touch.

"Goddamn, woman. Do you taste that? The sweetness you make me so addicted to?" he sneers with raw emotion, and I smile softly, my eyes filling with joy as I finally have him return to me.

"Suck my fingers, love. Suck them while I fuck you raw and imprint my name like a leash around your throat." A rough hand wraps around my neck, squeezing until my air becomes tedious and at the mercy of a man who has already explained that he wants to see the light in my eyes fade, replaced with a darkness he is kin too.

I want that too, I need that as badly as I need him inside of me.

Right. The. Fuck. Now.

"Elijah," I wheeze, eyes fluttering closed and rolling into the back of my head as the need to feel more than the head of his cock glide against me becomes a desperation in my bones.

"Right now, beautiful. I'm not going to use my shadows. I'm not going to use any magic at all. Because I want to feel you, just the woman and the man. I want to feel it all. Savor it all, and show you just how much you ruin me," Elijah whispers into my ear, no longer teasing and taunting.

He enters me in one quick and brutal thrust, burying himself to the hilt as I scream. My back lurching from the bed, my nails raking bloody gouges into his back as I'm assaulted with violent pain and euphoric pleasure. I never thought that something that hurt could feel so damn good. That when the pain stabs into me, I breathe easier instead of breathing harder. Unplagued and utterly content as he tears through my barriers, leaving an ache in my lower abdomen.

Maybe it's different for me because I'm always in pain. Maybe I find it arousing because any new pain is refreshing instead of a burden. Either way, the air gets caught in my lungs and I find myself rocking against him whispering a "fuck yes," into the room. Elijah stills above me, going eerily still much to my frustration. He may not be touching me with his powers, but he's definitely using them, the room darkening completely until he is the only thing I can see. Golden eyes bore into mine and all the air in my lungs seize, my chest constricting at the look on his face as he stares down at me.

"Are you a virgin, pretty girl? Is this pussy pure and untouched for me?" The possessive growl in his voice sends shivers racing down my spine. Everything snaps taunt, my body calling to him like he's my temple and I'm overdue a sinful worship. Something feral passes in his gaze and a wicked smirk pulls at his lips. "You have no idea what that does for me. How fucking aroused it makes me, but guess what, love?" He brings his tormenting lips to my ear, whispering, "Do you remember how I told you I can fix all that I break?" He rears back, slipping free of my aching pussy as it clenches around his absence, begging for him to come back. Then he surges forward again, filling me completely and pulling a scream which tears from my throat like the screech of the devil bellowing his triumph to his followers. I dig my nails in deeper, riding him harder as he breaks through my barrier over and over again, taking me for the first time with each retreat, seizing me with that wondrous sensation, again and again. He smirks and whispers, "That includes your innocence too, pretty girl. Mine to worship, mine to own and most definitely mine to break. I'll always be your first, sweetheart. Your last, and when those moments pass, and you think the sensation will fade so you're left to nothing but a memory, I'll give it all back to you. I'll make you fucking remember who was here, writing his name with the seed of his cock into the fluttering hold of your tight cunt. I'll make you remember who possessed you, honored you and made you feel this damn good. It would be criminal to forget something so wicked, love. So I'll never let us. Now be a good girl and scream for me while you bleed on my cock and show me who you belong too."

"Fuck, yes, Elijah. Harder, fuck me harder," I don't know what comes over me, but my skin feels like it's on fire and my soul feels like it's on a spacewalk. The filthy words slipping from my lips are unlike anything I have ever spoken before but I can't stop them. I need to voice the urgency in me, I need to feel as dirty as the acts of sin I'm committing.

The filthier the better. I want him to ruin me. To consume me.

But I need more.

"Fill me full of your thick cock. Own me, Elijah. Fucking destroy me. I need it to hurt!"

I can feel the heat which exudes from his flexing body. Muscles coiled tight as he holds himself above me and then in the next instant, he flips us and lays flat on his back while I ride him like a queen. "Anything for you, pretty girl."

"I'm so fucking full, it hurts, Elijah, it hurts," I whimper, unable to keep myself from moving. I find a rhythm, back and forth, up and down as I wind my hips in a figure eight. One of his hands toys with my breast, flicking my nipple and sending me into a new wave of chaos as the other pinches my clit and I cry out, nails clawing at his firm and glistening chest. I'm fixated on the way he moves, the ripple in his frame and the bunching of his muscles as I lick my lips. Leaning forward, I lick the beast, watching it shudder under my tongue, inked on his skin.

"He wants you, sweet girl, more than he has ever wanted anything."

"I want him too," I admit, stroking the tip of my nose against him.

"No, you don't. You wouldn't be so sweet if he got a hold of you, love." There is strain in his voice, hands firm as they bite into my hips as if he's trying to hold himself back.

"Then maybe I should show you just how wrong you are. After all, a kiss from the devil is also sweet and believe me,

Satan can more than handle himself in the ruins," I whisper, slowing my movements as I tease him, allowing the sultry tone of my voice to feather against his skin as I do something I've never done before. Something that feels natural. I clench my pussy walls as I lift myself up, holding him inside of me, I suction him and pull a feral growl from his throat as his eyes darken still.

"Is that right? You think you can handle us both, pretty girl? We'll see." His grip tightens on my hips, his fingers bruising into my skin and he launches his hips from the bed, hovering in the air as he pumps into me with abandon. He tears me apart, filling me so completely, that it borders on uncomfortable when he seems to grow, thickening as he watches me with a wickedness in his eyes that sends my pulse racing. I bounce on top of him, my tits bounce with me and I can't help but squeeze them, twisting the puckered buds between my fingers.

"You're so beautiful, Adisen. So perfect, now if you want to be rewarded like the good girl I know you can be, you'll take it all. You'll take all of me without protest because you know this is where I belong. What do you think? Can you do that baby? Can you take all of me?"

His hand wraps around my throat and I claw at his wrists, bouncing on him harder and faster as the globes of my ass smack against his balls as he meets me thrust for thrust. He hikes a brow, challenging my answer and a smile wider than the Cheshire cat's spreads across my face.

This is exactly what I want, my beast without restraint.

Unbound, carnal, and fucking raw.

"Yes! Yes, no fuck me! Harder, faster. Be brutal, Elijah. Show me that you want me. That you need me. Take it all away."

"Take what away, love?" The grunts, eyes of intent boring into my mind adding to the flames of my passion.

"Reality!"

A wicked smile filters across his handsomely chiseled face as everything within me tightens. "Genius" by Written By Wolves fills the room, the base pumping through me, widening my eyes as the course of my hips takes on a new path. I dance and grind on top of him, moving in ways I didn't think possible and then before I know it, we are flipped again and I'm on my knees. Elijah is pounding into me from behind and that's when my eyes darken, the pleasure taking me to the precipice once more.

"So. Fucking. Delectable. So fucking perfect," Elijah grits before he moves in a cloud of smoke, dematerializing before reappearing before me. Using his powers, he repositions me to sit on his lap, legs wrapped around his waist as his fingers thread through my hair, "Together, love. We finish together because my needs will never be more important than yours. And I can't finish without having you look into my eyes." He stares into my awe-stricken gaze, so much emotion stirring within his amber depths that tears fill my eyes and threaten to choke me. I swallow them back, refusing to disrupt the intimate moment as everything slows and together, we come undone and for the first time in the history of my life, I feel the first spurt of come as it paints the inside of my walls and I can't help the strange sense of pride that filters throughout my chest.

"So, beautiful. So perfect," he whispers once again.

I've never felt loved, seen, or wanted.

I had never felt beautiful or more coveted than the finest gold.

Never... Not until Elijah Braxton, my possessive beast, fell from the sky and ruined me.

Laying me flat on my back, he conjures a basin of warm soapy water and a rag, cleaning me softly before applying some kind of cream to my pussy and thighs. Once he smooths it into my skin I feel instant relief from the fire running across my flesh that I hadn't even noticed until it had been chased away with the coolness of the salve. He pulls me into his side and onto his chest, wrapping me tightly in his arms as he tickles my sides.

"Elijah?" I whisper cautiously, my heart rate beginning to show my anxiety as it pounds away within my chest.

"Yes, love?"

"How do you feel?" The question falls from my lips and I hurry to add context as I turn into him. "I mean, all of this is crazy right? How you ended up here, how I feel this insane connection toward you. The power that you wield. I'm struggling. So I can't even begin to imagine how you feel after finding out what you have. Are you sure you're okay?"

He falls silent for a moment, and my heart stutters. I want him to be okay, I want him to be happy. I love talking about his world and the look he has in his eyes when he does, but there is also some deeply rooted sinking feeling inside of me that comes when he talks about it as well. Almost like I'm afraid of it and I don't know why.

"To put how I feel into words would mean that I understand how I'm feeling, and I don't. Not even a little bit. I thought I had seen everything, and yet I had no idea a person like you could exist. A human with more power than the gods, if only you knew how to use it," he rumbles into the quiet room, holding tight onto me like he is afraid I'll fade away. "That I thought my life was great only to learn I never really had a life at all. You gave me your first, Adisen and I gave you mine. Whatever was written within those pages, it wasn't me. And as much as I want to go back, as much as I feel like I should, there is something anchoring me here just as forcefully too."

"There is?" I whisper, so softly, I don't think I've said anything at all. "What?"

"You." If my heart had a face, it'd smile like a love-struck fool. " I now believe that maybe the fates know a lot more than we do and that everything is happening as it should. All we're doing is letting it."

"You really believe I can do it? That I can send you back?" I ask, shifting to ease the ache in my shoulder.

"I know you can. Rest now, there is always tomorrow." He kisses the side of my neck, sending warmth coursing through me, putting us both back into a deep sleep. The sweat of our bodies, slick against one another as we both let out a breath, just letting it all go and savoring nothing other than us and this moment of firsts.

Twenty

Adisen

"What in the flames of hell is that burning?" I ask, sitting up in bed as the smell of something burnt wafts under my nose, waking me. It twitches as I look beside me noticing that Elijah is gone.

Turning back toward the bedroom door, he hurries in carrying a tray exuding steam and a tall glass holding an array of bleeding hearts. Vibrant colors of black, blue and a silken looking gray hang over the rim and my heart soars at the beauty of the bouquet of flowers.

"What did you do?" I ask, chucking and he comes in looking all disheveled and even more handsome than the night before. My body aches in remembrance and I smile wider.

"Made breakfast," he utters dryly, looking at the tray like it's the bane of his existence.

"You made breakfast? The human way?" I ask dumbfounded as my brows furrow. He looks back at me with a pissed off expression and I laugh, expecting a tale of how making breakfast in this realm is so hard.

"Yes. I did," he mutters. Defiance in his eyes as they narrow at me and I clock on instantly.

"And that's what on the plates?" I lean forward as he places the tray on the end of the bed, and my mouth waters at the mountain of perfect-looking golden waffles staring back at me.

"No, that's what's in the trash. This is what I conjured after I set the kitchen on fire," he growls and I draw back staring at him with eyes that could rival an owl.

"You set my kitchen on fire?"

"Yes. And then I used my powers to extinguish it. Why this realm is powerless is beyond me. Magic makes everything so easy," He huffs, and I smirk.

"Does it? Or does it make everything a hell of a lot harder?" I tease, raising a delicate brow as his head snaps back toward me.

"How the hell do you figure that?"

"Well, I already know that in your realm not everybody holds the same powers. That your villagers also do mundane tasks somewhat. Yet, here you are. The King of the Horde, with a weakness. Unable to make something as simple as breakfast." He blinks at me like I've lost my damn mind and I chuckle. "Not that I'm complaining because these waffles are making me drool. Thank you, Elijah."

His chest rumbles as his eyes narrow and he conjures me a fork, handing it to me as he utters, "You always have such a peculiar way of looking at things."

"Maybe so. But I think it's good to have every tool in your arsenal y'know? It makes you even more powerful when nothing can take you by surprise," I mutter around a mouthful of sweet, succulent batter. I groan, savoring the taste.

"You'd make a good war-queen, you know that?" he adds, using his finger fuelled with power as he hovers his waffle in the air and brings it to his awaiting mouth, then chomps down on it.

"You think?"

"I know. A good queen has the strength needed to lead, the fortitude to withstand the anguish and the heart to care for her people. It's hard sometimes, you know? When you're the king of it all and how very quickly all you become familiar with is war. It hardens your heart and sometimes, it makes you a shit king when you can no longer resonate with your people. When you can no longer give them your heart and understand their quarrels because you're too busy planning another war to save them. Everything else becomes tedious."

I freeze, staring back at him with a mouthful of food as I think about that. Huh, I guess he's right. I never really saw the other side of it before now, before him. But I guess that is what ying and yang is, right? The hard and the easy. The good and the bad. The other half to your souls that carries the perspective when you need it and you carry the reassurance when they do.

"You showed me the other side of it. Back at that alley? When you gave the girl that unicorn? It made me remember how I used to be. How I want to be again."

My heart warms at that as I glance to the side of the bed and face my wolf and lion with butterflies in my tummy. We eat the rest of our food in a comfortable silence and I appreciate this man a whole lot more. Falling so much harder as he shows me new things too. He changes my perspective and makes me rethink about all the things that I thought I knew and wanted. All the things that I once thought were so black and white.

After we finish, he waves his hand and all of the dishes and tray disappear. The glass of flowers, hovering to sit on my side table.

I smile, thinking how quickly these will become my new favorites.

"Guess I should shower. Try and ease the ache in my back. Do you need anything?" I ask, standing from the bed and just before I'm about to step into the hallway, I stop short, mouth agape as I stare wide eyed at the scene before me.

Rapidly I blink, thinking this is it. The moment my sanity left me.

Glancing over my shoulder, I take stock of my room. My eyes roaming over every inch of it and finding it exactly how it has been for the majority of my adulthood. Standard, somewhat dull and practical. I never put much effort into decorating it because what's the point? I'm the only one who sleeps in here, and after long hours at work, dealing with my pain and fighting with my anxiety to allow me any kind of semblance of a life, I find it grueling enough without adding decorating the place into the mix.

But back to the point of my ungraceful mouth-slacking shock.

When the fuck did I move into Neverland?

Tuning back to the hallway, I stare down at my feet watching the calm surface of ocean blue waters burrowing into the floor. In what appears to be shallow depths, consuming my hallway and looking like a long stretch of a puddle.

Down in the deep depths, past the shimmering waters is an entire underworld of waterful magic. Ancient ruins withered and worn, lay broken against the sapphire sandbanks. Tropical and totally otherworldly fishes, gliding past in explosive colors of various shades which look heightened by majestic powers.

Illuminous corals glowing in the light and darkened hues of the ocean. Distorting as the waters waver.

I gasp, stepping back startled when the pointed fin of a shark swims on by. A shark with a mutilated eye, deep tar-like purple skin and spikes sticking out of its gills that inflate and deflate with each vicious breath it takes. The thing also has damn spikes running down the length of its back. Like some punk rocker shark with good taste in music.

I jolt backward into a hard chest, when strong arms wrap around me and walk me forward, so I have no choice but to stand on the threshold. My toes brushing the line of the door frame separating me from the alluring waters.

I squeal when a hand coils around my ankle. Looking down with broken breathing I take in the steel-coloured hair. Wet and slicked back to the body of the mermaid tempting me close. Or is she a siren?

Parts of her silken strands are braided. Others are entwined with gems and jewels, forming a crown atop her head. She's utterly pale. Skin bright and almost translucent with the sheen of porcelain glass. Her thin eyebrows, brood over deeply piercing emeralds that glow, consuming her irises, nothing but unnatural orbs blinking back at me as I become dazed. Tilting my head slowly, I watch her through curious eyes, utterly entranced and under her thrall. Her own eyes are dark, painted like a Viking as black streaks smear under her eyes and down across her cheeks, glistening with obsidian glitter that become moist like tears of twistedly beautiful tar.

The silken texture of her arms are two-tone, milky white

bleeding into metallic gray, that become see through between her webbed fingers that tighten around my ankles.

"You wanted a taste of my world, beautiful. You've given me yours, now here's mine," a raw and sensual voice rasps in my ear, sending shivers racing down my spine in a war to see which can make me shudder first.

I tremble, unable to contain my body's reaction to him. Elijah's arms tighten around me and for a fraction of a second, cool wind whispers against my chilled skin as he replaces my sleepwear with a two-piece bathing suit.

Hardened, golden seashells form over my chest, covering my heavy breasts. Gleaming blue pearls wrap around my neck as golden leaves cover my apex, those same pearls holding them to my waist, sitting in threes across my hips. My tanned skin shimmering under golden glitter as I look over my shoulder to face the man behind me.

"Are you ready to experience all the things I love about my realm right alongside me, witch?" The rasp in his rough voice is a caress to my overwhelmed senses. I don't even find the mind to correct him for calling me a witch anymore.

I'm too lost to the devastating beauty of him.

I focus my breathing, calming myself enough to respond, "How-" I'm cut off when his lips close around mine.

He pulls me into him, hands gripping my rounded globes and he kneads the cheeks of my ass, grinding against me as the memories of our bodies colliding not even a few hours before flicker through my haze filled mind. The fever starts, my skin heating as he sets me aflame with a passion that was made to shatter innocent women. Make them helpless, a victim to his will, laying ourselves bare and at his mercy if only it means I can feel that good again.

I'd do anything. *Be* anything, just to have him love on my body the way he did.

He pulls back, awe and trepidation clouding his golden eyes. "Now you can breathe underwater, love. Welcome to my illusion," he utters, breathlessly.

"Did you have to kiss me for that to work?" I whisper, staring at those full lips like they're my lifeline, wanting so desperately to taste them again. I never want to stop tasting them.

With curious eyes, I search his for deception, still uncertain even with how close we have become, how intimate. I feel like it's the breakthrough of all breakthroughs and I don't want it to fall apart. I don't want to go back to the contempt and the rage. I guess I fear it because nothing in my world ever lasts.

"No. Not at all," he growls, looking me over once more before turning me back toward the devious mermaid who looks like she's calling me home with a siren's song.

She's a cross between utterly stunning and slightly unnerving.

Both feelings together render her weirdly magnificent. A tragic beauty.

"Are you ready to take the plunge? Do you trust me enough to keep you safe?"

Very good questions.

Ones that echo around my mind with a resounding warning.

There is a very good chance I'm living within a fairy tale. That one day soon, I'll wake to find myself utterly alone again. But until that day, I'm going to *carpe diem* the hell out of this glorious man and everything he has to offer.

I glance back down at the freakishly beautiful mermaid whose midnight blue and golden tail swooshes in and out of the water. She thrashes her hips, bobbing over the surface and I notice there is no tail line around her waist like you would see in a mermaid show or read about in a fairy tale book. The midnight blue and golden scales are in a sense her actual flesh, feathering up to her waistline and then thinning out around her stomach like she's had each scale sewn into her skin. The end arches wide like the quill of angel wings and then narrows, layering over one another to take the shape of the ruffled end of a satin black dress. Those same two-tone scales trailing down the center. I'm still in awe of the dark beauty of it all, but she studies me with a cock of her head and whatever she sees in my eyes is enough. Because in the next instance, she's yanked my ankle and I'm torn from Elijah's arms being dragged into the bottom of the otherworld sea, drawing in a frantic breath before the waters consume me. A chuckling Elijah follows.

Twenty-One

Adisen

I sink further and further into the bottomless depths of an unimaginable ocean. Panic seizing my heart as I wiggle and writhe in my haste for air. It doesn't occur to me to do anything other than hold the air trapped within my lungs hostage as instinct warns me that if I don't, I'll drown.

It's human nature.

Common *fucking* sense.

But even in my gut-wrenching terror all I can hear is the dark chuckle of that sinful man encompass me like my own taunting lullaby. It calms me in equal parts as much as it irritates me. I begin to spin, sinking further still as the water gathers around me like an oceanic tornado making my head swim. *Literally.* The damn mermaid crocodile twirls me for shits and giggles while my lungs burn and my mind riots against me in fear.

Fear shouldn't bring elation. It should bring terror.

But the fear coursing through my veins at this very moment is like a drug I know I'll beg more of as soon as the erratic beat of my heart settles. It's what I feel like I've been missing all of my life, always having to play it safe because of my pain. Always having to hide behind my confinements.

When the bubbles clear, and the taunting shrilling-cackle of the mermaid-siren creature dwindles, I notice the huge crystals, bleeding translucent blue in their center descending from the sapphire sandbanks, similar to the ones that Elijah showed me on the beach.

They are massive, bigger than an average building and sit in clusters at the bottom of this fantasy ocean.

Enormous Orca whales, deep burgundy and rose gold in color instead of their normal black and white, circle the rocks serenading the ocean with their famous melodious symphonies that echo the underbelly of dreams and hallucinations with their hauntingly beautiful tunes that sound absolutely nothing like they do in my world.

It's more harrowing and settles in the lining of your soul. More impactful, leaving you with a heart full of tears, weakened at their beauty.

The mere sight of it is enough to strike me dumb and I forget myself for a moment, gasping deeply only to begin spluttering with muscle memory that at this point, I should be drowning.

Only I'm not.

I'm completely fine. Then I remember that Elijah said I would be seconds before that bitch hauled my ass into a watery grave. I just forgot it in my panic. And now I look like a unicorn's twat-waffle, thrashing around like a baby seal throwing a tantrum.

Large hands clasp the sides of my face in his hold, bringing my gaze to focus on him as he ushers me to calm down and my heart rate to lower. The look in his eye is imploring, and I've never felt more protected than I do at this moment. Never felt so utterly certain of my safety in the eyes of another being before.

I blink, stilling in the deep depths of water and allow myself to float, looking around and taking everything in, winding my arms and then kicking my legs when the bitch mermaid lets go and swims off somewhere with a teasing smile which looks villainous.

Elijah is behind me now, hands settling on my hips pulling me back into him as I steel myself to be this close to him once again. To be consumed by his mere presence alone.

I get caught up in everything going on around me, that at the time, it's all that I can focus on.

But then he touches me, surrounding me.

Kisses me.

Stares at me longingly.

Utterly *destroying* me.

I'm hyper aware of him.

More aware of him than I have been aware of anything in my entire life.

He closes in around me and it all falls away.

Everything and anything that has ever plagued me, leaving me hollow inside disappears.

I'm left with nothing but him.

The feel of him, the thought of him.

It captures me so completely, I lose myself for a moment. But that's okay, I've never been all that fascinating anyway.

Not like him.

My King of the Horde.

My beastly nightmare with abs for days.

Every time his body brushes against mine, it's like the first.

And every time he moves away, I wish that he'd stay.

I'm sucked into another word. An unheard of reality.

Everything is so surreal and I find myself in the center of the one thing I've dreamed about since I was a little girl.

Something magical and completely out of this world.

There is nothing toxic here.

Nothing that makes my heart hurt as I'm surrounded by such unpolluted beauty, I can feel the pureness of it in my veins. I can feel the magic as it kisses against my skin and seeps into my being.

In fruitful colors and mind-boggling creations. In sea creatures made from the innocent dreams of a little girl who used to wish for a beautiful life. I'm swimming in the depths of a foreign ocean, gliding with the mermaids and being graced with the songs of wild Orcas. My heart shouldn't hurt here and yet for some reason…

It does.

It beats with the hammer of agony at how I wished all of this would be real. How the real world could be this beautiful without fault. Without pollution. Before Elijah fell from the sky, I kind of went through life without much thought or feeling. I took each day as it came, which in hindsight I think we all do. But now he's showing me another world, it truly dawns on me just how dark and withering mine really is.

"I can feel your sorrow, sweet girl. Why are you sad?"

I don't even jump when the sensual rasp of Elijah's voice echoes within my head. He told me he can't read minds and poke around inside my head like a mole poking holes in a hilltop. But he said nothing about not being able to project his voice into my mind. I don't know if I can do the same, but I try anyway. A little withdrawn.

"You can feel it?"

"I can feel it."

"How?" I ask, staring at the underwater realm before me in awe and a little forlorning sadness. Everything here is just so perfect. I notice the mermaid who dragged me down under, sitting on the smaller crystalized rock along the sandbanks with others of her kind. Hundreds of others who sit braiding each other's hair and bellowing a siren's song that bounces back and forth between the Orcas that have swam so far into the distance, it's nothing but a lingering response.

I find myself wondering what issues they actually have down here?

No worries. No stress. Only magic.

"I don't know. I've been able to feel some of your mood changes since you woke from the fever. Why are you sad?" he asks again, a demand for the truth riding his tone hard.

"Everything just seems easier here," I reply as he turns me in his hold and I spin with little protest with the help of the water. He pulls me into him, legs winding around his waist as he threads his fingers into my hair and tilts back my head until I'm staring up at him. The both of us just float here with ease.

My heart picks up the pace as it gallops in my chest at the attention.

"Easier, how?"

"Easier in a way I wouldn't even be able to explain," I answer, losing myself within his golden eyes. *"Thank you for bringing me here. I spend all my time reading about magical*

things that I never really considered how breathtaking it would be to actually see it before me. To feel like I'm a part of it."

"*Maybe beauty isn't something that is shown to us. Maybe beauty is something we create. When we chose to overlook the flaws and find the one perfect thing it hides. Surely everything hides something pretty?"* He raises a brow, daring me to counter that with something that would disprove his theory.

But I can't.

Because he is right.

Maybe humans do spend so much time hating on the bad that we never see the good.

But then again, that's easier said than believed.

Because I've lived in that world. I've felt the misery and the heartache that comes with loss and belittlement in a world that enjoys to suck the life right out of you.

In grief and in discontent.

I clear my mind, shaking away all of the unwanted thoughts. He has done this amazing thing for me and I'm letting my mundane world take it for granted. I don't want to worry about how much better this world is, I just want to enjoy it while I can. "*I'm sorry. You didn't bring me here to compare it to my world and put a downer on things, did you?"*

"No, witch. I brought you here to show you that if what my arrogant British ass said was true, then this doesn't have to be a dream," he growls with heat in his eyes that skates across my entire body. He shudders, eyes drawn to the hardened shells covering my breasts as he looks to be fighting for some self-control. It's a moment before his eyes meet mine again, flickering between obsidian and golden. *"You can come back to my realm and see everything for real. Not just illusions I can create. But the real thing, Adisen. You can have the real thing with me."*

I've dreamed about a world like his for so long that I wish I knew what was holding me back.

That I knew how to be brave and face my fears, saying to heck with the rest of it.

I *want* this.

Don't I?

He's shown me something he knew my heart has forever desired, probably thinking that maybe I'd be more willing to work at this. To push myself until we got back home to his kingdom.

All those sweet and wicked words and possessive sin-coated vows were all designed to help me get rid of whatever fucking wall is standing in between what we both want and stopping us from getting it. I make a decision here and now to let it all go. To take whatever part of him he is willing to give me without worrying about what can go wrong if I hand him my heart. I don't know how to go back to being without him, to be alone in a world that swallows me whole. I want this depression to fade away so I'm only left with this man and the way he is staring at me now.

He's my magic and he can give me everything I've dreamed about that has helped me chase away all of my nightmares all of my life.

Elijah narrows his eyes, studying my change in mood and I move things forward quickly so I don't have to answer any questions.

I untangle myself from his arms and kick my feet, swimming away from him with a laugh echoing in my mind. He follows me, kicking his thick thighs to catch up but I'm like the ocean's fastest sea creature.

Whatever the hell that is.

He grabs for me and I twist and turn, making it harder for him to capture me.

"Fine, you win. I'll try to bring the hotter you back after my shift tonight, kay?" I chuckle, making snow angels. Or should I call them water angels?

I want to learn how to control my will desperately. I want to make him happy and give him all of the happiness he is giving to me, and to do that, I need to just try harder than I am.

I push myself and I'm not intentionally fucking all of this up, but I'm also not pushing myself to uncover why I'm so afraid either.

Because I know that has to be what keeps us here. Fear. Fear I don't want to give a face to.

Elijah stills, staring at me with darkening eyes that make my pulse thunder harder beneath my skin. *"The hotter me?"* he queries as the entire underbelly of the ocean is plunged into darkness. Those silken tendrils of his are bleeding from his body like coiling snakes as they gather around me, gripping me anywhere they can tighten.

I writhe back and forth, thrashing within their unrelenting confinements, trying to get free, chuckling even harder. Golden eyes shine through the bleak abyss, and that's the only sign I have that he's coming for me. Watching those golden orbs bob up and down as they draw closer. The anticipation has my stomach fluttering and I gulp, trying to settle my breathing. My entire body coming alive under the prospect of what could follow.

I'm flipped upside down when Elijah grips my hips and then I'm sandbank-face-down and watching as the specs of sapphire sands glisten through the cracks in the darkness.

The mermaids retreat into the caves just as the darkness

reaches them. I gasp from the action, looking up and damn well near having a heart attack.

I forgot about the punk rocker shark.

How the fuck could I forget about the shark?

I begin to panic, thrashing harder as my mind short circuits and terror plagues me. The purple, scary-looking fucker is swimming right toward us with a wink in his mangled eye just as the darkness closes in.

But it isn't closing in fast enough and even if it does, can it keep the big monstrous thing away?

"Elijah! Elijah!" I panic, the shock burning throughout my chest like acid.

"Yes, sweetness?" he rumbles back.

"Don't let me get eaten!" I plead in a tone that is more *if you do let me get eaten, I'll beat you to death with the very same fin of the fucker who gobbled me up* other than an *okay, save my life and I'll give it to you freely* kinda tone.

"Can't make that promise, sweet girl," he replies smoothly and I swear my heart gives out and I am taken to the lands of magic and dicks.

Maybe I even blacked out? Did I black out?

"Well, at least not by anything other than me," he adds.

At that moment, the darkness closes around us and the shark is left on the other side of it. A slight thunk the only indication that it in fact can't get through his shadows and my savagely brutal heart begins its slow descent into a casual jog instead of a full fucking sprint.

"There will never be anyone hotter than me, Adisen. Nobody better. Nobody similar and nobody that can make you feel like this. Now be a good girl and heed the lesson."

A kaleidoscope of colors, tinier than the grains of sands under us, break through the darkness and flitter around our heads like tiny explosions. It looks like the rare colors you find in the center of old corals and I'm left with the feeling only a person high off narcotics could explain, drifting in a dreamscape that makes me mindless.

This beast is mine.

I lean forward, kissing him with every ounce of emotion I'm feeling at this moment. I want everything that he wants. I want to make him scream in ecstasy and give him the feeling that I make his world a better place.

I want desperately to take him home and have him be proud of me for being able to do it.

I breathe deeply, then a white light detonates around us and we gasp, pulling away from one another enough but still holding each other close to see what in-the-whitelighter just happened.

And then suddenly, this no longer feels like an illusion and I can no longer breathe.

Fuck! Elijah bellows into my mind as my lungs burn. He wraps me in his arms and uses some kind of super-sonic speed and in the next instant, my head is breaking through the surface and I'm gasping for clean air.

"Holy fuck-cunt what the hell was that?" We bob in the water, kicking my legs wide as I try to get my soul back into my body and not go back under.

Elijah looks around, water curling along his lashes as the glistening beads draw my focus. He snaps his head back and forth, spitting a mouthful of ocean water back into the magical pool swarming us.

"You've done it. I think you may have actually done it. I'm home," he utters in shock.

"Say what now?" I exclaim, finally opening my eyes and taking in my surroundings.

First thing I notice?

The plural fucking skies.

"Oh yeah, we aren't in Kansas anymore."

Twenty-Two

Elijah

Fuck me, she did it. Adisen actually did it.

I gaze around, taking in my surroundings and instantly feel the familiarity as it circles me.

We're in the ocean of seduction, the hue of red and purple waters lapping against us as I peer up, looking at the multiple skies above us. Blue starlight borders the realm as the purple starlight feathers across the skies in the center of it. Different planets are large and evident in the skies, rotating slowly as the realm circles on its axis. Various colors pop throughout the galaxies, as stars shoot from the skies and look like long white lights being hung from the heavens as they descend toward us. A riot of all different kinds of moons shimmer in the night sky, winking down at us as they fade from translucent to all kinds of colors like blue, red, white, green, and so on.

I forgot just how beautiful it is here.

Then I look back down at Adisen in awe and remember why. "I knew you could do this," I tell her, pulling her into me as I hold onto her waist, wanting to ease her struggle as she fights to stay above the water's surface. "You brought us home."

"How?" she whispers, something like fear lacing her voice.

I narrow my eyes. "You believed."

She huffs out a breath and turns drowsy eyes on me. "Elijah. I'm feeling really strange. Carnal almost. Hot. I'm struggling to breathe." I chuckle darkly, bringing her close to my chest, enveloping her deeply.

"These oceans are a little hard to handle if you're unsuspecting. We can always return to them later, love. I have so much I want to show you."

"Aren't you going home? Back to the palace?" she asks as her breathing becomes shallow and her skin tinges pink. She grinds against me, lost in her struggle to notice what it is the warm waters are actually making her feel.

"Later. I have time to be king later. I want to show you the world you longed for first. Besides, sweet revenge that has rivers running red was never won in a day. I have to find out how deep the poison in this realm runs. I have to make Jessaleia and my brother pay for what they have done to me. To this realm." I'm not sure at what point it changed and at what point I wanted to return to this world more for her sake and wanting to be the one to give her all she has ever dreamed about. When it became more than a need for me to actually return here and become king once again for myself.

But it did.

It changed.

And I have much to do before I can announce my presence. I need to know what I'm dealing with first. I need to know how deep the lies run when it comes to Jessaleia and Bradon. How accurate the tales of their treachery are. The Accursed screech inside my head as the beast howls. All entities salivating for the blood of our enemies. I can already feel myself changing. The darkness creeping back in and silencing everything else. As who I was slowly consumes who I've become.

I hold the girl in my arms and get ready to show her my wicked realm.

The good, the bad and the ugly.

Jessaleia slams her taloned hands down on the war table. No closer to locating Elijah now, than she was weeks ago. Bradon does little to comfort his mate. She's too lost to her wrath. The underlying subordination she feels at the inferior emotions that torment her, forcing her to become a different version of her usually composed self.

A more insane and unmanageable version of herself, in fact.

She's becoming undone, losing her composure and slowly exposing her true nature.

Vile and insidious.

Bradon sighs, at a loss once again when he opens his eyes and finds his mate staring back at him expectantly.

"Well? Could you find him? He is blood of your blood. Did the astral projection work?"

"Not this time, my love. It isn't like the select few times I have been able to locate him before. Now, he's just gone." *That irritates Bradon to no end. Knowing that he is helpless to offer his mate the one thing he knows she wants. That even now, he is living in the shadow of his brother, the king of it all.*

Jessaleia screams ungracefully, her blonde hair falling in untamed waves around her face as they fall in front, the pins of her glistening crown falling out while she clears off the table of various maps from the kingdom.

The air shifts and a dark and menacing power filters through the land. It comes with a warning, eyes that watch them from where they stand as they hide beyond the walls of the palace.

Jessaleia and Bradon share a look and together they know…

The king has returned home.

"Tell me, pretty girl, when you fantasized about being here, how did you see yourself?" I ask as I teleport us onto dry land. We're in the Land of Bones, where the dead can bring your dreams to life. It's a land of illusion here in my realm, one that those who are longing for a subspace kind of high travel too, seeking a different reality themselves. In that, our lands do not differ. She bites her lips coyly, avoiding meeting my eyes. "Tell me, Adisen." I want to give her everything. She held a book in her hands, ones filled with nothing other than ink. Meaningless words scribed onto a page and yet to her, they mean everything.

To her, they moved her enough for her to conjure me from the pages themselves. If I can give her this, make what she once dreamed about so beautiful, then I will.

"Empowered. Dressed in a seductive black outfit which bespokes of danger and magic." Glancing down, she looks away from me as her eyes gaze over the barren lands filled with bone-made structures. "I don't know, Elijah. It's hard to explain. I see myself as the female warrior within the books I read. It's silly, I know."

"That isn't silly, love. It just means you want to be the person you have denied yourself in being for so long. Does an outfit like this work? I want you to experience it all."

I use my powers to redress her. A black billowing skirt gathers around her waist, split down the center as thinner strips of fabric coils around her legs and arms. The design looks like a lethal harness as it melds to her slender frame. A bralette that shines a silky black onyx covers her breasts. A black headdress wraps around her head, obsidian and midnight blue gems dangling down her forehead as they glisten under the blue moon as black makeup circles her eyes and turns her into a witch of wickedness that bewitches me still. I narrow my eyes when an inky black essence swarms around her, almost bleeding from her like tendrils of smoke the same way my darkness bleeds from me.

A sharp pain shoots across my brow bone, making me clench my eyes tightly shut to ward off the assault.

They're the mirror of you, my love. Their soul, it doesn't recognize one that is familiar like the stories depict. It doesn't even find its missing half, like the tales that are whispered into the night say. No, when you find her... the one, her soul won't be finding its kin. It will be returning home. It will flame like a twin, a reflection of everything it has ever held deep within and it will smile because that one soul can finally see itself mirrored back at them. Only the one, will ever shine like a beacon in the darkness my boy. That is when you will know.

I blink rapidly, the headache making it hard to concentrate as an angelic face appears in front of me, a picture of concern. I stand stoic and idle for a moment, the words of my mother fading into the distance as I stare at the woman looking back at me with worry.

"Elijah? Elijah, are you okay?" She hurries to my side, taking my hands in hers as I glare at them in a strange kind of unease.

It takes me a moment to shake off the odd feeling, my mind

finally catching up as I place the deceitful beauty before me. I smile at Adisen, squeezing her hand in mine as I pull her into me and try to ease her worry. "I'm fine. Why wouldn't I be?"

"You zoned out for a moment. You were looking at me like you didn't even recognise me. Are you sure you're okay?" I hate the fear in her voice, it takes away from the excitement I want to hear. But I can't deny that she's right. That for a moment, I forgot where I was and who I was with.

"That's absurd, I could never forget you. Now tell me, pretty girl, do you like the dress?"

She still doesn't look convinced but a soft smile plays at her lips nonetheless. "I love it. It's beautiful Elijah. It's perfect. It's everything I ever envisioned."

"It's not even close to being perfect, love." Nothing will ever come close to being perfect, not when it is compared to her. Adisen will always be the queen of flawlessness.

"This land, it's as creepy as it is beautiful. I don't remember it in the book." She turns in a circle, walking deep into the graveyard until she finds a bed of skulls that is shaped like a large throne. With trepidation, she stalks closer, running her hands over them in turn before she cautiously takes a seat and peers back up at me with a nervous smile lighting up her emerald eyes.

"It's creepy, so expectations are lost. It's the only way the magic works," I tell her, coming to loom above her as I step to her side.

"Magic?"

"Magic. Tell me love, what would you love to see? Beyond everything else. Think of it and it will appear. It will make you feel high though." I smirk at her wickedly.

"It will?" she asks, slowly.

"It will." I smirk, hiking a brow and wondering what she'll conjure. Wonder what drifts unbidden through her glorious mind.

The back of my spine prickles with awareness, the new memory from my mother still not making any sense. In every memory, they talk about a woman. A woman who easily reminds me of Adisen. I just don't understand why. I just can't fathom her importance? Or why these memories are so important.

The fact I came out of it and struggled to place where I was, leaves me unsteady in my core. I never want to feel like that again. I never want to feel like my will is being taken from me.

Something glows a pale, baby-blue from the darkness behind Adisen and then tiny little dragons appear, flapping their infant wings and landing on her shoulder making her gasp.

She's a sight to behold. A wicked beauty that has my cold heart racing.

This is where I want to be, in a land where the magic isn't just around us, but a part of us. I want to see that look in her eye. The one that sparks in a way you can't even begin to describe. Adisen is a looking glass, and to watch her experience my realm for the first time is like me experiencing it for the first time all over again.

A woman with hair as black as a raven's and as long as a veil flies over head, circling us with black wings frail and spiked. She spots us from a great distance and circles back, her black clothes coiling around her waist similar to Adisen's but looks more like a corset with missing fabric as her skirt hangs from her hips in shreds. She lands gracefully, followed by another that bleeds from the shadows as they step closer to Adisen. They gather around her, picking up the strands of her dark hair and weaving them through their fingers in awe.

Adisen's eyes widen as she stares back and me and I chuckle

darkly, offering her some insight. "They're the dark Fae. They're drawn to darkness, Adisen. They find it rather beautiful."

I narrow my eyes and smirk, as I finally begin to see her in a way that her realm had forbidden me too. There is a darkness inside of her, one that shines like an onyx and is kin to my own. My darkness exudes power, hers exudes untold amounts of strength. That is why she is dark. That is what she hides. She had once told me that in her realm, there is a sickness called depression. It's what has pushed her so deeply into other worlds. I now wonder if that depression was protecting her. Keeping her safe until I arrived. I hadn't realized how alike we were until this very moment. Until my realm had stripped the veil that had divided us, standing first like an abyss too wide for either of us to cross. Darkness is subjective, how dark you see it all depends on how you wield it. She may have been depressed but she was a survivor. She woke up every morning and fought the day like a warrior. She just doesn't give herself enough credit for it. I may have always been drawn to this darkness inside of her without knowing why or where it stems from, but she has this lightness too. This peace. It's something we both crave and in her world, she taught me to become okay with the silence.

"You think I'm dark?" she asks, her attention half drawn to me and half to watching the fae as they surround her, pawing at her like she's a shiny new jewel.

"Pitch black, love. But don't worry, you'll need that darkness to survive this world. After all, you know how wicked it can get. Are you ready to see the illusions this Land of Bones can offer?"

Yeah , my woman has a light inside of her. But she has a darkness too and it's one I think she'll need to survive this world. If only she learned to stop being afraid of it.

Twenty-Three

Adisen

It's beautiful. It's beyond beautiful.

It's tragic.

And I never thought that I would find tragedy so utterly stunning.

I would rather be damned, a soul that blooms within the darkness than a flower that wilts under the light.

His world is magnificent and is absolutely everything that I dreamed it would be. *More* than what I dreamed it could be. We can imagine the greatest of magics, but in reality they don't exist. It takes a special kind of mind to see beyond the veil and into a new world. To see a wonder that just isn't there. Those who can are the lucky ones. Whenever I read a book, I can almost picture the scenes within my mind like a TV show. And now here I am, playing a character on the big screen.

I know that I'm passed out, draped over the throne of skulls as my mind leaves me to float into oblivion. I'm in the upside down. Walking along the tiled floor of dominos as I step off the board, only to be sucked right back in a loop, like I'm a hamster on a wheel. Playing cards larger than doors gather in a cluster around me, varying faces of warped looking demons staring back at me as they shuffle and flicker between themselves. The red skies riot, flashing blood lighting that cracks along the marbled ground and has me giggling. Shadows bleed from beyond the soles of my feet, looking like laughing faces. The feet I'm peering up at as the long strands of my hairbrush against the clouds under me as I stand there, upside down. My dress billows like tendrils around me. The coiled lacy straps covering my apex in boy shorts.

The angelic dark faes chuckle around us, spinning and dancing as Elijah prowls closer to me. He takes me in his arms as he spins us and that brooding, sinful laugh of his is a caress to my senses. "Thank you," I whisper.

"Don't thank me. Just tell me that for one single moment, you're unburdened from whatever it is you have been running from," he replies as I rest my head on his shoulder while we dance in wonderland. Everything else fades away and I'm left with only him.

I wish that I could. I wish that I could explain this unease inside of me, but I can't. I no longer know what it is that I'm running from but I know, there is a trepidation that is feathering down my spine and making me tingle in a foreboding kind of awareness. I know that something is wrong, a warning that shuts down everything else and chases away my will.

Something dark and sinister lingers, swirling around us in the air and leaving me wondering how well my sanity is faring after all of this. I just can't put that into words.

I don't know how.

So instead, I just smile and keep my unease to myself. "How can I run from anything when you're at my side?"

"Hmm, you know I can feel you, right?" he asks, skeptical.

"You know I can feel you too, right?" I retort, raising a brow at him as I dare him to argue.

I have felt something off about him since he conjured this beautiful outfit for me. He stumbled where he stood, with some kind of headache and the way he looked at me is a way I never want him to look at me again. It was like he was staring straight through me. Like he had no idea who I was or every moment we have shared.

Through all of the uncertainty that is what terrified me most.

"I'm fine, Adisen. It was just another memory I didn't understand, is all. I've been having them for a while. They just don't make sense to me."

I'm about to speak, to tell him that maybe if he spoke about them with me I could help put them into perspective but he keeps talking.

"We have more to see. Come, I want you to meet my people."

His people?

My heart sinks and a new kind of panic seeps in. It's one thing to want to be a warrior-queen, to dream about charging into battle and wielding a power that can raze the lands.

It's another to be one. It's another to be thrown into a world you have longed for with no idea if you'll actually be worthy of it.

I don't know if I'll be cut out for such a role and all of the possibilities in trying to find out has me terrified.

It's one thing to want to be an experienced cliff diver.

It's another to jump from the ledge and land in the choppy waters without breaking your goddamn neck.

I smile nervously, allowing him to take my hand and teleport me somewhere else in this magnificent realm of dark and twisted fantasies.

Jessaleia stood within the walls of the palace, in the room of glass as she peered into its reflection watching as the peculiar woman wanders through a village.

She looks up, peering into the shadows and the air stalls within Jessaleia's poisonous lungs. Something dark and twisted sparked in those emerald eyes making Jessaleia feel something akin to the tendrils of fear spiral within her cold heart. Who is this woman and where is the beast that she hides? Then, like a cloud of smoke, she was gone. Hidden from her sights. The demonic entity coils along the cold ground, twisting higher until the crimson smoke hovers before her.

"Find her. You know what to do."

Yes, Mistress.

And then the demonic entity vanishes, searching the land for the key to the kingdom.

"They can't see us. We have to keep hidden until I get back to the palace and see what damage has been done. It will be beneficial to know what my people are feeling at the moment," Elijah whispers into my ear and I nod in understanding.

I stare bewildered at the mountain that cracks and bleeds glowing lava. Hundreds of tiny cottages sit rows upon rows. It's so breathtaking. That's what it looks like from down here, walking through one of the forests that border along the kingdom. Passing through the Goblin Woods, tiny little creatures potter about, and it strikes me at the simple mundane tasks they're doing. The females wash their laundry in the tiny lakes.

The men chop firewood and stack it into piles. It amazes me at how simple it all looks.

I hold in a yelp when one of the gnarly face goblins turns on me. His face is shaped like an oval, facial features far apart as the ears on top of his head curve back and point outwards. Orange eyes blaze as he shuffles forward on his short legs.

"Hey, rass what are ye staring at? It's rude to stare, don't ye know?" he grits and I blink, stepping back as I turn to Elijah.

"Rass?"

"It's another word for female," he informs me.

I chuckle anxiously at thinking these beastly little goblins are fictional Scots. And rass is just their version of lass. "I'm so sorry. I didn't mean to offend you. I just haven't seen one of your kind before." I turn back to Elijah and frown. "I thought you said they can't see us?"

"I meant they can't see me." He laughs darkly and I balk, my face turning stern as I glare at him.

"Wee rass, talking to de shadows. Eh, crazy," the goblin mutters as he storms off.

I punch Elijah in the arm and he chuckles. "That was so not fair!"

"It was cute though. Watching you get all flustered. I want you to experience everything, even if I have to keep myself hidden."

Pulling me into his arms he teleports us into one of the villages within the mountain. A purple moon shines overhead as a small bridge curves over cobblestones and golden lights light up the night.

It's so peaceful. So beautiful.

"It just doesn't sit right, you know? Where is he? The king is always here, at hand and now he's just what?" a woman sitting at the kitchen table within one of the cottages says, her withered old voice drifts through the open windows as we creep within the shadows.

"To war," another softer voice replies.

"What war? He disappears and now we're to just accept the reign of this blonde-haired bitch? King Elijah could have done better than that common woman. Something about her does not sit right. How is she worthy of a mate like him? Like our king? It's ghastly. Unthinkable," the older voice adds and it reminds me of an old mothers meeting. Her grouchy voice has tears welling in my eyes as it reminds me of my late grandmother.

"*Mana*! Keep your voice down, you know you will be stricken if her generals were to hear you speak badly about her."

My head draws back as I turn up my nose and turn toward Elijah, apparently needing a translator in the realm. "Mana is a term for a grandmother who has raised you since birth. Her birth mother must have died," he tells me and my heart breaks as I hear the devotion in their tone as they address one another.

"Bosh," the older woman dismisses. "Let's see if they can smite an old mite like me. I survived the cursed ones, remember? I'm practically a part of this land. All I'm saying is, something is rotten smelling here and that King Elijah deserves a mate with a tender heart. Not one hardened by the diamonds that it seeks. Jewels are not the consumer of love my dear. There is no room for it within a rotten ruby."

"It's what happens beyond the palace walls I worry about, Mana."

Elijah and I share a knowing look as we continue on our way, spying on a kingdom which I'm sure has more eyes that we can see. Elijah glares into the darkness and my heart stops, something whispers against my skin and then I suddenly feel like I'm standing inside a bubble.

Before I get to question it, I gasp. Something cold is infusing my chest as I feel like a storm cloud is coursing throughout my body. Everything becomes chilling, cold to the touch and numb as my very being entwines with another entity. A demonic and evil entity that has terror seizing my heart. I try to panic, to reach out and grab Elijah for comfort but my body is no longer my own. Everything inside of me feels dizzy, like it's wobbling back and forth like a drunken sailor as I fight for stability. I scream, the sound echoing around the walls of my captive mind and resounding back to me. I screech, I cry, I bang against the walls of my very soul for freedom, but none of it translates into action.

Instead, my head cants to the side as I stare at Elijah, through curious eyes that appear sinister as they gaze upon him.

What the fuck is happening? What is happening? What is living inside of me stealing my very will?

"*Elijah!*" I bellow, but no sound comes out. "*Elijah!*"

My feet turn, carrying me away from the man who is currently shouting my name and deeper into the kingdom, on the yellow-brick road toward the palace. "Adisen? Adisen?"

Something controls me as I walk further and further away, a wild screech resounds in my mind as my soul collapses, fighting against the rioting racket within my mind as it shuts down all of my senses as I lose the fight. Do you know how terrifying it is to lose your voice?

To be acutely aware of your surroundings, but forced to feel whatever the fates plague you with?

Firm hands grip my shoulders and I'm spun around into Elijah's vicious hold, as he stares at me through narrowed and accusatory eyes. "The waters of health," he utters as if he is only now just realizing a vital piece of information from a serious equation. I thrash and wail, fighting against the demonic power that holds me captive. "A possession demon. Get out of her now, before you meet an end unfathomable!" he growls and the world around me rattles as do the bones confined within the walls of my skin.

I can see everything - sense everything - but I'm a shut in. A hostage and the feeling is a vile invasion of my nervous system. It's defiling and sickening as it burns like acid against my organs. It hurts, it fucking hurts as every ounce of my control is stolen from me.

Elijah pulls me into him, hand firm around my throat in warning but not tight enough to harm me. His eyes burn with dark red light as everything evil within him coils into a ball of destruction ready to explode.

"I. Said. Now!" he bellows with the flames of fury riding his growl that reaches me to the depths of my quivering soul. The earth around us quakes, power detonates like a tidal wave and everything around us becomes uprooted as my back arches and my head is thrown back. My mouth opens, throat raw as it burns like a wildfire as a torrent of a demonic benevolence gushes out of me like a jetstream and dissipates within a cloud of ominous red smoke.

I collapse, shattering within Elijah's arms as I slump to the ground.

He saved me.

But it was too late... My fear had already betrayed me.

"Adisen." His dark voice reaches me in the darkness. "Come on, pretty girl, open those dark eyes. Look at me." A gentle slap against my cheek has me opening my eyes, blinking back at him in trepidation. I don't want to give a face to the violation I just felt. To the horror.

I don't want to give it a name. To give it a voice.

"Are you okay?" he asks, but I'm so far from okay.

I'm so far from being okay as tears fall freely down my cheeks. I wasn't ready. I wasn't ready for the power that was brought to my trivial little mundane world and it breaks something frail inside of me.

"W-where are we?" I ask, clinging to his chest with a fear that is paralyzing, not wanting to look at my surroundings.

"Back on earth love, you took us back to your house."

I gasp, drawing back as I look around frantically. I find ourselves laid across the floor in my kitchen. The sorrow drowning me even more as I feel like such a failure.

"You got afraid and you took us back to the place you felt the most safe. I'm just sorry it wasn't with me, love."

Twenty-Four

Elijah

I never thought that another woman would steal away the numbness that has been with me for longer than I can remember. I had thought this was just how I was supposed to be.

An unfeeling king, motivated by what I knew I should be doing and how I should be acting, opposed to being driven by emotion, by thoughts unhindered.

With Jessaleia, I was performing a masterful art.

I get that now, that part of my life that finally makes sense.

I was a slave to somebody else's will.

But how am I to make sense of a woman who stirs a hurricane inside my chest and a riot in my core?

That takes every emotion known to man and racks my body thoroughly with it, forcing me to endure more than one, all at once?

I thought that being ripped from my kingdom again would have unnerved me. Set me back and maybe even angered me. But it hasn't. I know she can get us there and that is all that matters. I'm more concerned about her and her mental state.

That possession demon terrified her in a way I've never seen anyone become so afraid before.

I'm a creature made of nightmares and a devil that deals in trade, yet I've never felt it so internally before last night. We returned home and she shut down. I know why, I can feel it.

The anger, worry and disappointment. The rage she feels at herself. All I can do for now is stand at her side and try to help her through her fear.

It's one thing to want to be consumed with power, it's another thing when you have no power to defend yourself against it.

I know that now as new memories and unwritten things in my past come to light, I still have much to learn. I felt Jessaleia watching us back in that village. I had to cloak Adisen from sight, not realizing that she would even pop up on her radar. It was a stupid, naive mistake.

My realm is something she has always dreamed of, so it was my realm that I wanted to give her.

How could I not anticipate that she'd see the insidious side of it?

That spark in her eye? I want to be the reason it glistens. But maybe it was selfish of me to be so narrow minded.

I watch her as she potters around the kitchen in her sweats, hair wet and wavy as it falls down her back still damp from her shower. She seems so jittery now, so on edge and I hate it.

I'm not used to taking into account another person's emotions, I find myself uneasy with the lack of knowledge in how to console her.

Sinead O'Connor's "Nothing Compared To U" plays lowly in the background. At first I didn't notice it. Not until some of the words started echoing through my ears as soulful whispers which resonated in my chest. Some of the lyrics remind me of Jessaleia and I sneer down at the countertop. I'm free from the thumb which so intently pinned me beneath and now I find myself so infuriated I was even pinned there at all. Being back in my realm, feeling her toxins brush against me. Hearing those women talk, back in the cottage.

It causes a growl to build in my throat which I need to swallow down not wanting to startle her within my turmoil.

Then the words change and smoothly transition me into new lyrics which I don't associate with Jessaleia at all.

Not even a little bit.

The emotion, the foundation. It's like my soul has been built upon it.

My gaze zeros in on Adisen as she slathers some kind of sauce on a gigantic rack of ribs, slowly swaying her hips back and forth. So subtly, that I hardly notice she's doing it.

But every time she winces because it seems to pain her, I can't help but see it, feel it too…

The words spoken about being parted from whoever it is the singer seems greatly anguished by, has my chest restricting when I think about the thought of being parted from Adisen.

I cant my head, studying her closely as I try to picture such a scenario. The task is impossible as every outcome that I could possibly envision ends with the world in ruins and me kicking up a storm within the ash to bring her back to me.

Right where she belongs.

Everything bad in me wanted to riot back in my realm when that demon had its poison running through her veins. I'm grateful she blacked out before she got to see the monster I truly hide.

I know I'm in the mundane world, and according to her, that comes with some secrecy to what I can do, but devil help them if I witness anyone treating Adisen less than a queen.

My queen.

Because I'd destroy it all for her.

I almost destroyed my kingdom for her.

Something she can never know.

Because I may not know why she is of great importance to me and my creatures, but I know that I am helpless to fight this bond any longer.

Darkness encroaches on my vision as a red-hot anger bleeds into my gaze. I collar Adisen by the throat, peering into the eyes of crimson as the demon stares back at me. I roar, my chest opening as the army of The Accursed bursts from their cells and stands sentinel upon the lands around me. A dark brewing storm that winds amongst the gray silhouette of the creatures. A collective cry is bellowed to the void, like the sound of a siren, as the wicked screech readies for war. The demon knows its odds, relinquishing its vicious hold on my woman, and like the sun appearing over the horizon, the anger fades and concern creeps into its place as I catch her in my arms. The darkness of my powers that kiss against the earth erupt into flames, burning everything to ruin in my anguish.

"I know you could probably whiz something up right? I mean the food, with your powers," she begins to babble, not looking at me as she moves around with fluidity. Some kind of uncertainty in her tone. "You'll probably think I'm fat after seeing me eat all of this, but after everything we have been through, my body can't take it anymore." She sighs, refusing to look at me as I grunt, an unfamiliar anger burning in the back of my throat at her having such an idea in her pretty, innocent mind. There is this raw possessiveness inside of me that has me seeing red at her thinking of herself as anything other than slender and perfect.

In all my years I've never seen a woman as regal and as magnificent as Adisen. Her beauty is like the sun being kissed by the moon and creating an image the entire world has to look up at because of its wondrous beauty, helpless to look away even when you know you should because such radiance is surely blinding.

Her eyes widen at my sullen response as if I just said, *'Yeah baby. Fatter than an ogre sat under a bridge sniffing its own waste.'*

I push back my seat, the sound shrill as it scrapes across the ground. I move with such force, it skids halfway across the floor before toppling over. The noise is an echoing thud that makes Adisen jump in shock before narrowing her eyes and watching me warily as I approach her with warning burning in her emerald gaze.

A warning that flares to life in the eyes of a gazelle that stares down the lion even though it knows it's hopeless, already the prey of a predator which never loses.

Invading her personal space, I bend down chasing her head with my own until she is forced to look back up at me. Rough hands settle on her hips as I lift her without care and wrap her legs around my waist, holding her close as I back her into the counter and smack the rounded globes of her ass against the blood red and silken black marble countertop.

She yelps, clinging to me tighter as her breathing becomes ragged and brittle.

My nose tickles against the curve of her throat as I growl, inhaling deeply and taking my fill of her exotic scent, sweet like sugar and spicy like brimstone. I don't know what those two scents together create exactly, only that I want to bottle it and keep it forever.

So nobody can smell it but me.

"I'm sorry," she whispers, taking me by surprise. "I'm sorry that I let you down again. That I pulled you from your home. I'm so sorry."

"Adisen, you have nothing to be sorry about. What you went through is enough to shock anyone. You need to give yourself a break. A moment to let yourself accept that you were afraid so you can move past it. You did it once, I know you can do it again."

"Can I ask you something? And please don't lie to me," she utters, taking a deep breath before looking up at me. "Were you forgetting? After you had that memory, that look… I can never forget it. I can't forget it. Were you forgetting?"

I sigh, clenching my eyes shut tightly as I smooth out the ache between my brows and pinch the bridge of my nose.

"No, I wasn't forgetting. I was just a little… disoriented after the memory is all. I could never forget you." She doesn't seem convinced, but she nods either way.

"Maybe I can help you? Piece together the memories?" she asks hopefully and I smirk, raising a taunting brow.

"We can try, but first, pretty girl, I have a lesson to teach." I groan at the thought, gripping the back of her head, I thread my fingers through her cold strands and tug. "Smooth like satin," I rasp against her, groaning when I feel the tip of my nose against her skin that feels so damn good and silky. "Woven like darkened gold," I whisper into her ear, wrapping the ends of her brown and golden hair around my fist more tightly, making her gasp as she arches her back into my touch as I assess her ombre strands.

"Delicate like the petals of a rose," I breathe, trailing my warm tongue over the swell of her breasts, risen under her bra and down onto the fabric of her shirt as I close my mouth around her hardening buds and bite at her nipples teasingly. I smooth my way down her body, placing feathering kisses along her abdomen as I go on. "Slender like the steel of a fine blade, ready for war." Unhooking her legs from my waist, I squat, adding more fiery kisses down the length of her inner thigh making her moan and her hips flex. "As tanned as the golden warriors on the horizon, cast off from the stolen lands." I part her thighs, wrapping her legs around my head and placing an open mouth kiss on her feverish core, through the fabric of her sweats. She shudders, rocking her hips and I pull back. "And this? This treasure is finer than all the honey coated in the dust of the fae, Adisen. I covet your body, your scent, *and* your sounds. You're not fat, and if you say such things again, I'll punish you by withholding the one thing you want most... To come."

"You wouldn't," she pants, head rolling on her shoulders as she drops it forwards to glare down at me.

"I would, and I think I will... I'm rather curious to see what a good girl you can be. Maybe I'll tease you while you cook for me. Would you like that, witch?"

"Erm..." She gulps, her throat bobbing with the excretion as I manage to steal the words lingering on her swollen lips.

I pull back, standing to my feet and stepping away to create some space between us staring down at the wet patch covering her pussy. Still holding both of her thighs in my large hands, I spread them further. I whisper to the wind, watching as her sweats flutter away from her body and she's left exposed to me in royal blue, lace panties.

She inhales rapidly, looking down at her covered core a

moment before they disappear too and her glistening, pink cunt weeps for me.

I smirk, lifting my nose to the air and taking it all in with a deep inhale, capturing it in my lungs in the hopes it will forever linger there, a reminder of how sweet my woman is.

My shadows swirl and gather in the air, bleeding through the kitchen until they come to a hovering stance in the space between us. They twist and twirl, knitting together with woven ink as it takes the shape of a small, rounded egg.

"W-what are you doing?" Adisen stutters through a dry throat. I can hear the words scratch against her as she struggles to get them out.

The question was for me, but she has yet to make eye contact, too busy staring at the entity forming before us. It moves lower to the ground, making room for me and her curious eyes follow it as I close the gap and crash my lips down on hers.

She purrs, her body becoming pliant under my demands as she opens for me. My tongue sweeps inside to dance a battle with her own as I savor every second of it. The tension of the unknown drains from her and I use that moment to push back my hips and send my essence into her tight, clenching cunt.

She cries out, whimpering into my neck as she breaks the kiss and tries to regain her fractured breathing, as she splutters and gasps.

My shadows grow inside of her, filling her completely as she rocks her hips and tries to adjust to the ever-changing size. Sweat beads along her brow, tracing the curve of her features before dropping away and splattering against her heaving chest, silken with moisture. I didn't prepare her with my fingers, I saw no need when I gazed upon how slick and ready my good girl already was.

A little burn never hurt anyone, in fact it can feel damn good.

And watching the way her eyes glaze over with a lustful haze, her lips part and tears well as sensual whimpers pass her thick lips, I'd say she agrees.

And besides, if I played with her beforehand I would have finished before I was ready and I don't want that.

I want her to learn.

To watch her heed my warning and speak no such hate against herself again.

I want her to come undone because of me. To fall weak and sated with how good I can make her feel and to cry for me as she does it so I take away everything that plagues her.

I want everything from this woman.

I want her to break just so I can piece her back together again. To learn what she hides deep inside by making sure there are no walls in place to keep me out.

But most importantly, I want to watch her dance so beautifully for me.

Just like she is now.

I kiss her once more, claiming any protest she may have spoken before I remove myself from her presence altogether. Her underwear and sweats are back in place, covering her from my greedy sight.

Precautions for my withering restraint.

I pull her from the counter, spin her and spank her ass as she staggers forward before heading back to claim my seat from the ground. I set it upright and then make myself comfortable as I lean my elbows on the island, chin in hand as I stare at her with a heat that I can feel licking against my skin, like a taunting caress.

"Now cook for me baby, and do not come unless I say so."

She spins to face me again, a slack look on her soft face as she stares at me, eyes wider than saucers. "I don-" Her words are cut off as she yelps, jumping in the air and rubbing her thighs together as she squirms at the vibrations I send rushing through her.

The small egg made from my shadows moves at my will, caressing her in all the right places. She writhes on the spot looking at me with reddening cheeks as she turns around again and gives me her back. "Fine. If my king wants to play, we shall play," she states with conviction, sounding a little better in herself and it brings a smirk to my lips.

Those words falling from her glorious mouth send a shudder through me, my cock hardening to the point of pain as it chafes against my own sweats. As the egg thrusts in and out of her tight, clenching channel, I can feel it like a livewire in my swollen shaft.

The sensation is greater than anything one could experience by touch.

It burrows under the skin so you don't feel the sensations… you *become* the sensations.

I throw my head back, refusing to take my eyes away from her as she returns to slathering those ribs that look nowhere near as appetizing as she does right now.

Chopping potatoes, she cuts them into thick slices of wedges and tosses them into a bowl full of mixed seasoning before shaking them with more force than I'm sure is actually required.

My beast growls, the sound infusing the power behind the vibrations I'm assaulting her with.

I notice the sweat that beads along her nape before traveling down her back.

She's rigid, holding herself tightly so that I can see the strain in her muscles and she minimizes her movements, trying to not give the feeling I'm forcing upon her any more merit than it already has.

"Can you feel me, baby? That's me stretching you, filling you... and who knows? Maybe my very essence is claiming you at this very moment in a way that can never be undone. Would you like that?" I growl, holding on with fragile restraint from throwing myself at her and devouring her like the monstrous beast that I am.

Savage and greedy howls echo within my mind, The Accursed in my chest rioting in glory at how satisfied I am right now at watching her become tormented with my actions.

"Only you would turn your powers into a sex toy, Elijah. I'm fighting here, but if you speak, if I hear that sensual rasp, I may just lose this game we're playing," Adisen wheezes her words as her entire body trembles.

A wicked smirk curves my lips and my eyes grow hooded as I fight to stay in my seat.

"It's a lesson you need, sweet girl, and I'm all too happy to give it." I clench my fist, digging the nails into my palms until I can feel the tiny wounds open.

I sigh, relishing the feeling as I relax a tiny bit, the sting heightening our pleasure.

Because what is good for me is definitely good for her.

She quivers, crossing her legs at the ankles as she doubles over, falling slack against the counter as she whimpers. "Fuck. *Fuck*!" she curses, wringing out her arms and slowly pushing herself back up to her feet, trying to regain her composure. Resting against the counter before she moves quickly to reach into the kitchen cabinets, she pulls out more seasoning and sauces.

Hastily, she tosses everything into a clean bowl and then retrieves the wings from the fridge.

Everything happens within seconds and before I know it, the contents are shoved into the heated stove and she spins on me. "Okay, done. Lesson learned. I will never speak badly of myself again. I was your good girl, your *best* girl! Now *please,* make me come!"

"How badly do you want it, love? How badly do you want me?" I inquire, still unmoving as my eyes darken. Not showing her just how badly I need to hear her say it. How badly I want to be the reason she smiles and the earth spins.

I can feel the gold draining away from my gaze and favoring obsidian shadows in its wake. My teeth elongate, pointed into sharpened spikes as my canines brutalize my gums and I swallow back the copper in my mouth.

She's never seen the beast. Not enough for her to fear him anyway.

That night in the woods, all she had was the feeling that something sinister lingered.

When she saw me hovering above her, all she noticed was the outline of something far greater and evidently something much more meaner than she ever could have imagined. Then the beast was upon her, teeth sunk into the hollow of her throat making her purr for us both.

I don't want to show her my beast, not yet anyway.

I fear how she will respond when she has no shadows to hide behind. When the truth of what I am towers above her taller than the greatest wave. Demons have already terrified her and I know it's vastly different when those demons possessed her and stole away her will.

I remember what that felt like when I had the flashback. When I fight with whatever is being kept from me.

I banish the thoughts and hold back the monster.

I want her in a way my body seizes from with desire.

I won't risk her repulsion. The burn of a deep rejection—I don't think either of us will walk away unscathed.

So I bite back the beast and let loose a growl of frustration. I won't let him ruin this.

Not now.

Not when I need her so deeply, it rips me apart inside with open wounds and I find the masochist in me itching to pour salt on them.

"I need you, Elijah, more than the stars need to light up the night sky. More than the sun is needed to cast light upon our shivering skins in winter. I need you like my first and my last breath. *Please*, don't make me wait anymore." The sensuality in her voice is like a low humming that kisses against me like an enchantress.

I can feel her so viscerally, it's like she is living inside of me.

That each time my heart beats, it bellows her name.

I work my shadows inside her still, teasing and taunting as I try to gather some kind of control at her declaration. Some kind of control as I watch her come undone for me with a need as brutal as my own.

I've never been one to make my lady wait.

Last time I did this though, I forgot she died by orgasm.

"Bring her to me," I demand.

Adisen shrieks as my shadows lift her by the egg in her pulsating pussy, thickening and pushing inside her that much deeper.

I can feel her clenching around my inky essence, seated further and further until it pushes against sacred parts of her core.

Drawing me in further begging me to never let her go.

Never, Love.

"You writhe for me so beautifully. Tell me, baby… How deep am I?"

"Deep! So fucking deep, Elijah. I can't! It hurts, it hurts so fucking beautifully!"

I use my powers to lay her down on the kitchen island, her back arching as I move myself to the end of the counter, placing myself between her open thighs.

I move forward but she stops me, lifting a weak foot pushing against my chest to hold me in place. "You always make me feel so good. Let me make you feel good too. Use me, Elijah, use me like I'm your good little slut."

I gulp, muscles tense as my entire body erupts. I can only imagine how she sees me right now as the space around us blackens and I know the look in my eyes burns with carnal savagery. "Careful what you wish for, witch."

"I know what I'm asking for, Elijah. Make me feel it, make me feel it all."

"As you wish, love." Like the thrashing of a leash, my shadows whip around her, coiling around her ankles and legs, stretching her wide and tying her to the kitchen island.

I blink, staring down at the darkened cunt which flutters, her silken white desire slipping past my shadows and dripping down her tanned thighs in her slick arousal.

My cock jumps, my stomach tightens and a feral growl is torn from my throat.

I glare at her with wickedness in my gaze, lost to the violent need to consume her, to taste her. Learning forward slowly, so slowly, it's a taunt to her, I breathe her in. My eyes never stray as I capture her in my depravity.

She's helpless but to obey, to follow, our sights locked.

Languidly, I run my tongue along the length of her, lapping up everything she exudes. The flavors of her sweet pussy exploding in my mouth are wrapping around my very essence like she has a power of her own. Licking my lips, I pull back wild with adrenaline.

Craving another high.

Moving around the counter, I come to a standstill behind her head. She arches her back, large doe-like eyes blinking back at me with so much trust, I can feel it flutter inside my chest. Freeing myself from my sweats, I eradicate myself from my clothing and stand before her flexed, tatted and utterly naked. The sight steals a broken gasp from her lips as she dampens them with her tongue, looking back at me as if it's her that wish to eat me alive.

The beast on my chest growls, angry I'm keeping him from his delicate little toy.

"Oh, love, you have no idea what you have asked for." Stroking my thick cock, it's hot and heavy in my hand. Throbbing with a need that ripples throughout my entire body.

Her mouth opens, with the positioning of my hand on her chin, allowing me to ease inside her warm tunnel slowly. She flattens her tongue against my undershaft, and I grip her hair tighter, curling it around my fist. "All of me, Adisen. Swallow it all," I demand as I hold her head still, with brittle restraint, and glide all the way to the back of her throat, tender at first, slow easy strokes as her mouth forms around me, stretching wide as her cheeks hollow and her emerald eyes blaze with molten lava. Her throat bobs, as her head hangs over the edge.

I watch the pulse that flickers in the column of her throat with the strain as she is forced to yield to me. Her arms are flexed wide, as she's tied spread eagle to the tabletop by my inky black essence, vining around her, imprisoning her exactly how I want her.

Adisen's hips lift from the counter, pumping the air as she searches for some kind of friction, her only option is to rub together her soft thighs and immediately open them when she remembers the shadowy egg.

She looks magnificent like this.

A phantom of a man's greatest desire, leading him unexpectedly to his doom, deep into the woods under the watchful eye of a deceitful moon.

A siren serenading a sailor before she sucks the life right out of him and keeps him forever at the bottomless depths of a sea, because let's face it, the things that are the most euphoric to us our often the most dangerous and this woman is pure fucking bliss.

That is Adisen.

My Adisen.

"To use you anyway that I wish, hmm?" I ask, my voice raw from holding back not only my beast, but The Accursed imprisoned within my chest who seeks a taste of her delicate flesh too. I thrust my hips brutally, quickly, taking away all of her air as I close my fingers around her nose. I let go as quickly as I pinched and slow my thrusts once more.

I expected shock, protest, but my girl just whimpers. Eyes wide and encouraging.

My cock vibrates when she grunts a *yes*, eager to see just how much I can use her perfect body. The egg in her sweet, aching pussy elongates. Shaping into a carbon copy of the cock which is finding paradise within her silken throat. *My* cock. She's only taken half of me so far, I've held back. My cock grows with my arousal, aided by my powers. I don't want to hurt her, use her, see her cry for me, yes. But I want her to enjoy this too.

I sink a little deeper, fucking her throat and her tight little cunt before I whisper a tendril of my darkness around her puckered star.

Her ass tightens, her cheeks close but that means little to my shadows.

They can get inside anything I want them too and right now, I want them in her ass.

Thin like string, I ease her into it, thickening my essence the further that I get. "You see this, beautiful? You see what a good little slut you're being for me? I know you can feel it, how hard you make me. Such a shame you can't take it all." I thrust a little deeper, quickening my pace as I begin to fuck her harder with my shadow cock. It wells in her core and with how her legs are pulled apart, I watch in hunger as it seeps in and out of her tight, glistening cunt.

Defiance burns in her gaze, and suddenly, I'm falling forward, sinking to the hilt, and sliding so fucking blissfully to the back of her throat. My eyes widen in shock when I expect her to choke but she just swallows around me, holding me in place and sucking me off like I've never before experienced. It's a suction like a vacuum pack, drawing my balls up tight as the sensation feels like there is a vibration not skating across my skin but living inside of it.

"Fuck!" I lose all of my control and begin to fuck her face forcefully, her eyes well with tears and when she blinks, they trickle down her cheeks. I thicken the shadows in her ass, the shape of a small butt plug as I fuck all three holes with equal force.

I can feel the pressure in my core, it's heady and sends tingles across my lower back and down my legs. I pull out abruptly, moving once again between her thighs and entering her without pause. My shadow cock dissipates inside of her but only inch by inch until I'm fully seated. So for a moment, she is filled so completely, she bucks against her restraints.

I fuck her hard, fast, and fucking wild. I give her everything I have, my fingers biting into her tender flesh as I jolt forward and suck a nipple into my mouth. Her naked body twinkles like the stars against her heated skin, and I bite down around her with a feral growl, driven by the need to see my bruises, my bite marks glistening on her skin. I paw at her, a treasure I cannot believe I have found as I fill all three of her holes, thickening my essence with my power.

She cries out, panting and pleading, "Fucking hell, Elijah! I can feel you baby, every monstrous inch of you! Deeper, harder, mark me and make me yours!"

She has no idea what she's asking and neither do I until the beast sinks his teeth into her throat again, over the scar we first created on the night that we met her beauty, alone and surrounded within the woods.

I howl, rearing back and letting every entity which resides within my chest, bellow to the void above us. It's a shrill sound full of grievance. It's dark and harrowing and it roars with the voice of a million monsters. "Don't be afraid of me," I plead. Unaware my lips are to her ear, whispering pleadingly.

"Never!" she swears, nails dragging down my back and shoulders, drawing blood and embedding in deep and together we shatter.

The orgasm destroying us both as my shadows close around us, no longer in my control and protecting myself and my woman when I'm too fucked and sated to do it myself.

Together we lay there, her head on my chest, my arms wrapped around her and for the first time in a long time, home no longer calls to me.

"How are we supposed to pretend like everything is normal? Like you didn't whiz me away to neverland?" she whispers, her warm breath feathering across my chest.

"One day at a time," I reply. I have complete faith in her.

When the time is right, we'll return back to the kingdom. The more I think about it, the more I realize it is tarnishing everything she once thought beautiful about dark fantasies.

Twenty-Five

Adisen

"Why are you always in pain?" Elijah whispers into my ear, making my heart gallop in my chest when I don't expect it. We have been through so much together, I've learned so much about him and yet I still feel like I'm shutting him out.

I don't want to do that anymore.

Not after he gave me something magnificent and I fucking destroyed it like I destroy everything. I chickened out. I begged for a world of darkness, and had the nerve to cry when it consumed me.

I'd never felt anything like it, being helpless and left without a voice. It stole something from me that I wasn't willing to give

My will, my choice. My body moved without my mind commanding it. Those few seconds felt like grueling hours and I still carry that violation with me in my soul.

How are we supposed to go back to reality? To everything being normal. We took ten steps forward and then twenty steps back.

All because of me.

All because I can't seem to get my shit together and because of it, I'm making Elijah suffer for it.

I try to calm my breathing, allowing our bodies to cool and the sweat to dry but for as long as I remain in his arms I don't think the heat will ever dwindle. There's only blissful heaven when I'm with him, bathed in a silence of eternal content.

I've never wanted to share with him my weakness, to show him just how deeply I suffer.

Every time he gives himself to me a little bit more though, my resolve turns to ruin.

"I have a condition. Something called fibromyalgia," I utter with numb lips, staring at a bead of sweat which shines like a rain drop on his left pec, my fingers deftly running across his smooth chest.

"What's that?"

"A burden which writes its name in bold with the jaded edges of a blade, across the very soul it makes so brittle," I whisper, more to myself than to him because for somebody who doesn't have it, it won't make any sense. Fibromyalgia is a test of the mind, a battle of wills. It's something that affects the whole body, and at this point in our story seems so insignificant. My mind has other things to contend with as I battle the pain. "It's a condition which causes full bodily pain. I could go into detail, but it will be pointless. All that matters at the end of it is that I can't escape it, and the twinges you pick up on are nothing compared to when I can't move at all." I feel his eyes narrow like that displeases him, it's evident when his body pulls tight, but I still refuse to meet his gaze head on. "What's the time? I have a few errands to run before I head into my shift." I try to change the subject, lifting from his chest, but he pulls me back into him, hugging me tighter as if he's afraid to let me go. I scoff, thinking how insane today will be, after walking through an illusion which quite literally dropped my world wrong-side-up. "Do I really have to go in?"

"Yes. For as long as we are here, you need to keep your routine. You need to remember why it is that you so badly crave my world and why we should go back."

"What if it was you?" I offer, thinking it through in my mind.

"What if what I truly craved was you and now that you're here? None of the rest of it seems to matter to me as much?"

"Adisen," he growls, eyes darkening as they stare into mine. "I'm not made for this world. How am I supposed to stay here? Every day, with a power that I fight to keep caged? You may see this gentle side of me but flip the coin and there is nothing but brutality."

I sigh, knowing that he is right. That it's unfair to keep a lion caged and withheld from the wild. "True," I mutter as he smirks at me.

He grips my jaw, turning me to face him as that wicked thumb once again teases my lips.

"How did you take all of me?" he asks, reminding me of what just happened between us.

My shame quickly fades away, replaced with rosy, red cheeks. Not that the ache in my body that is the blissful, ecstasy kind could ever let me forget. I can feel his smirk, defenseless other than to gaze into those eyes and lose myself within this man of sin.

"I don't know, I just wanted too so bad, then you kinda fell in," I reply, meekly. Shrugging a shoulder, his gruff laugh bounces me up and down and I stare up at him in awe. He rims my mouth, before pushing his thumb inside and the look gleams has me thinking of him picturing it all over again as his gaze focuses on the action.

"You laughed," I utter, dumbly, completely transfixed on such a deeply sinful and glorious sound.

"So I did, sweet girl. The visionary in you do that?" he questions with a hike of a taunting brow and I narrow my withering gaze.

I hadn't thought about that, only how good he felt. How badly I wanted him, needed him, like I need the pain meds to make it through another day. I became dependent on his touch, on his kiss, on the way he made me feel so fucking good. Free and weightless, without burden only pleasure. Then I remember when I conjured the sundae, and how it was desperation that motivated me then too. A motivation to please the man looming above me.

"I guess so," I reply and then a gust of wind smacks me in the face and a chill tickles against my naked skin. One moment, I'm there, relaxed and the next, I'm falling harshly and like the snap of a band, I'm pulled taunt before I hit the floor. The ends of my hair kisses against the ground, my back arches as my mouth slacks, agape and I stare at the monstrous sized man hovering above me. It takes me a split second to draw an unfractured breath into my startled lungs and then I notice the kitchen island has given way beneath us.

But mine is solid fucking marble. The same blood red and

silken black design that's all over my damn kitchen. It's basically a thick, unmovable slab in the centre of the room and it's just blown out the sides like a small bomb was sat in the center of it.

Literally, nothing but four sides and a shattered countertop.

It's just another unexplainable event that plays tricks on my senses.

Tears water in my eyes at my abrupt fall, the pain radiates throughout my entire body and I begin to choke on it, clearing my throat as to downplay just how badly it fucking hurts. My fingers swell and tingle as I struggle to clench and unclench my aching hand.

Something feels wrong about this and that same acute awareness which prickles at the back of my neck strings again as I glance around putting two and two together. Seeking throughout the patio doors and into the backyard, I then turn back to Elijah.

This was not an accident and I find myself wanting to know what the hell caused it.

Elijah stands, towering above me as he lowers and pulls me into his arms, his power's the only reason my head hasn't smacked off the ground yet. Softly and without words, he brings his index finger to my jaw, tilting my head until I'm forced to stare back at him. I'm grateful for the silence, and a little stricken with the concern in his worryful eyes.

You can't fake validity and soul capturing horror. You can't dress it up and paint it pretty and expect someone to believe in you or your sweetly spoken lies that say you care when you don't, not really… Because everyone in this world is only ever out for themselves.

But that look?

The one shining like glowing embers in his golden obsidian-veined eyes, a picture of the man and the beast, showcasing his fear, sits like a vulnerability demon on his shoulder, wearing his heart on his tiny sleeve.

I've never mattered. Not to anyone but myself, fighting for another day.

And here he is, a man not of this world looking back at me like I gave him the constellations and painted his world in the colors of my universe.

And what do I offer him?

Nothing but weakness.

He carries me into my room, settling me on the edge of the bed before clothes materialize onto my body.

Soft and easily movable loungewear. Black leggings, a matching cami and a long cardigan that brushes against the floor enveloping me, then the first tear falls.

A large finger wipes it away and caresses my cheek before I even have the chance to process that it's even slipped free at all "You're hurting?" he rasps on a gruff sounding whisper in my ear as he kneels before me, and I nod mutely.

His hand glows green and purple, stroking softly against my forehead and the ache reseeds a little. Breathing a little easier, it flees from me on a tiny gasp. I can't express my gratitude, I don't know how, so instead I turn into him and lean forward, burying my face into his chest, wrapping my arms around his thick waist, and clinging to him like a child with a favorite teddy.

"Pain isn't weakness, Adisen. It's fortitude. It's the stripes of a warrior."

Swallowing thickly, I savor the moment. My heart opening and allowing that little bit of trust I've been holding onto to breathe a little. Coughing, I laugh weakly and pull back, staring up at him with a small smile. "You're good at this, you know that?"

"At what?"

"Comfort."

"Only for you, witch. Ask anyone from my realm and they'll tell you this isn't who I am. I don't know how to be soft or gentle. I'm mean and vicious. Yet when I'm with you it comes so easily, it's like the air I breathe." Rough lips lock with mine as he kisses me deeply. I inhale, trying to devour the man's very essence because it's the only thing in this world worth becoming addicted too. "I'm a different version of myself when I'm with you. One that is learning to enjoy the peace."

"Peace?" I scoff, rolling my eyes at him. "There seems to only be mayhem. I can't complain when it does seem to keep pushing us together though." I smirk, standing to my feet. "Come on, let's go and try to get back to your realm." I sigh, taking his hand in mine.

"Are you ready for that?"

"I have to at least try. It all feels too strange. Like something has set this path for us. Somethings... they just aren't making sense and despite whatever this block is inside of me, I don't like being anyone's pawn," I insist, staring at him with unyielding certainty.

The more I think about it, the more I begin to question everything that has got us to this point.

Most women want to be considered. For the ones around us to notice something is wrong or hard and to try and fix it. Even if it's with something as easy as cleaning the dishes or running a bubble bath. But finding someone who thinks with their emotions is scarce.

Yet here this man stands, wrapping me in clothing because he knew dressing would be too hard.

Every step of the way, he's given me purpose, shown me

greatness and every step of the way, I have given into the obstacles that seem to be standing in our way. Most of them are all my fault.

I'm done hiding and the more I feel that awareness, the one that comes with a chilling foreboding, the more I'm convinced that there is something behind everything that has happened to us this far. Something I vow to figure out.

"Something like what? The same something?" he asks darkly.

"No. I can't explain it. I feel like there are different energies surrounding us. Different kinds of power."

"Hmm. I feel it too. But I could never determine if it was from my powers, tainting this mundane world." He looks back at me with mischief in his eyes as he adds, "Let's try. We have to figure this out. I don't like being taken by surprise. But I got to ask, does the furniture have a habit of breaking like that in your world?"

"No, I cannot explain why the hell that just happened. Listen, when we were walking through that village I felt something. Something that didn't belong solely to the demon. I felt it again back in the kitchen and now it's starting to feel familiar to me. I don't think that everything that has happened is solely a coincidence or because I have this block up. Which, I also don't think is completely natural either. There are so many different things at play, I can feel it."

The room darkens as he growls, growing in height. "You think something is here? That something is watching us? In this realm too?"

"Maybe. I don't know. All I'm saying is, I don't think everything is the fates, Elijah. Something else is at play and we need to figure it out. Maybe Jessaleia sent that demon back in the realm?

Maybe us showing up set off something on their radar. After all, I shouldn't have been there. I'm not a character. I was never written into the story."

He chuckles, staring at me intently with wild need burning in his amber gaze, need for violence, need for lust? I don't know until he speaks next. "That bitch. Oh what fun I'm going to have when I disembowel the poison from her very core. I felt her too. That's why I cloaked you, just before the attack."

"We aren't giving up and we aren't giving in. I'll try and get you home before my shift. If it works, great, if not. Then I guess you get to see more of my world." I shrug, at a loss as to form any other kind of plan. I don't want to go back. Not so soon after an attack that defiled my very soul. But now we think something else is behind this, that Jessaleia could be behind this, I find myself more pissed off than afraid. More infuriated that she thought she had the right to do that to me. To Elijah.

"I'd rather stay and kiss you…" I rasp in a sultry tone, leaning into his hold and spinning to remove myself from his arms when he growls and lunges forward to capture me. "But we don't want to be late. Worlds to save and all that jazz." I chuckle and he sneers, bringing a large hand down across the globes of my ass.

I thought I had won this little game, all until I'm pulled out of the doorway and shoved against the wall, the shadows closing in all around us. "Pretty, pretty girl… Don't think that there is anything in this world that will stop me from claiming what's mine, the second I want it. Even if it's right…" he leans down, feathering a kiss to my heaving chest. "… in the middle of…" He moves up, licking against the curve of my throat, a warm heat following in the wake of his tongue. "… your job, right there in front of every single person surrounding us." His large hand cups my pussy, the egg which I thought had dissipated is now once again moving in a rhythm that has me gasping and grinding against his thigh. As soon as it starts it all too quickly again stops "I'm the beast, sweet girl, and when I'm hungry, I eat."

Did I say a softness has grown inside of him?

Yeah, no. The beast is always just there, right under the surface waiting to pounce.

And fuck if I don't want to be devoured.

This is my story, it's about time I start fighting for it. Creating it. *Believing* in it. I can't promise that it will be instant, but I can promise it will be soon.

It's time I start kicking some ass. It's time I become a warrior.

To do that, I finally need to reveal my fear. Even if it will take me a hot second to do it.

I fucking will.

I *have* too.

Twenty-Six

Adisen

The rough and sensual images of what happened between us is still teasing my mind with a slideshow that hums a soft caress in my mind. We decided to eat before I tried to will anything into existence. I'm bone-tired and sore as fuck, so I was grateful for the fuel.

I suck my fingers clean, daydreaming as I stare past Elijah, licking my lips as the feeling spreads through me, settling in my aching core that clenches from the memory.

I'm looking forward to seeing the grouchy granny when I head into work, providing that is still the cause of action for the day. It feels like it's been weeks since I've had any sense of normality in my life. Dottie has always been like a second nana to me with a soft spot for my flaky ass. I wouldn't have kept my job for more than a week if it hadn't been for her seeing right through me. She says I work too hard, then berates me with I need the break.

I think she does it to make me feel normal.

My mundane thoughts run away from me until a deep rumble snaps back my focus. "You have absolutely no idea do you, woman?" The growl echoes in my ears and I blink, turning my head slightly to stare wide-eyed at Elijah.

"What?"

"How fucking glorious you are. I've never burned before, pretty girl. Never in the way you set me alight."

I smile softly, staring down at the table and sighing to myself. A quick glance at the clock on the wall, and it reminds me I have forty-five minutes before my shift.

"And you have absolutely no idea," he muses, the devil dancing in his amber eyes and I straighten, preparing myself in case he decides to jump over the damn table.

The way he clenches the edges tightly, I say it's obvious it's a pretty clear possibility.

"Do you think I could ever fear you? You and your beast?" I ask, abruptly. Remembering the plea in his voice when he whispered for me to never fear him. It was strange to me, how this man of dominance seemed so afraid that I would reject him.

Cower from him.

It's something that has plagued my mind since it happened and now I'm no longer pussy-footing around and deciding to take my will back, to not hide. I won't let him hide either. Because it has now only just occurred to me that I'm still yet to see his beast.

He stares at me blankly, the stoic look in his eyes a tell that he's shutting down.

Jaw flickering as his eyes tighten, darkening before me as he reverts back into the alpha-hole he was when he landed here.

"I couldn't. I wouldn't know how."

"That's easily said when you haven't seen him," Elijah grunts, refusing to look away from me. His gaze, penetrating mine like he expects to catch me in a lie.

"I have seen him, that first night we were together. Right before I passed out." I remember it like it had only just happened. The way the air had shifted and the sinister feel tickling against my silken flesh was more of a thrilling sensation than it was a daunting one. The way shadow entities danced and wailed, pulled from his skin like a conductor maneuvering his harrowing puppets.

It was terrifying, yes.

That was the first true taste of a monster I have ever before kissed. But instead of malice surrounding me, it was a tortured beauty that seeped onto my tongue instead.

It was a fine taste of sweet, sinful evil, that I craved to devour.

"Oh darling, that wasn't my beast. It was The Accursed." His dark chuckle pulls at the corners of his lips, and those depraved eyes of his glow amber once again, finding me funny.

"The Accursed?" My mind twists and a million words painted in ink rush through my memory. "The forbidden creatures of your realm? The ones inside the prison inside your chest?"

"The very ones. I can usually control them. Never once have they broken free before, not until that night… that very moment, when I forgot everything that I thought was important and gave myself to the sounds of your pleasurable cries. You brought them out in me, Adisen. The monsters within me wants you too."

My breathing quickens, shallow pants that swell the hollowness of my heaving chest as I stare transfixed on his sinner's lips. The thought of that, the dark and dirty thought of everything vile and depraved consuming me from the inside out, sends tingles down my spine. Something dark, gritty, and dangerous writhes beneath the surface. A slithering sensation that feeds into my core and right down into my clenching pussy.

The man is darkness personified, and I've never been afraid of the dark.

In fact, I've loved the dark for as long as I can fucking remember.

Rubbing my thighs together, I lick my lips envisioning the taste of him and just like that, with one thought alone, I can.

Here's there, branding me with a taste stronger than the oldest whiskey.

I can feel him just as if his lips were pressed against mine right now. I bring the tips of my shaky fingers to my mouth and a low moan rips out, my eyes flutter closed.

"What did you think when you saw them, sweet girl?"

"I thought I was in hell and there wasn't anywhere else I'd rather be."

"You dream of hell, little troublemaker?"

"I dream of freedom. I dream of sin and flames. If I don't feel the heat caress my skin and the wrongness of desire feathering down my chest, I don't want to be there. I don't want to be numb." Glancing toward him, my brows furrow. "I don't want to be numb." Panic seizes my chest as realization hits me and I can feel my eyes widen in horror. My heart begins to ache and that tingle that was moments ago pleasurable becomes a heavy numbness as if my fears are solidifying within my very bones. I read not for a different reality, I read for a new personality. One that lives a thousand adventures and never leaves me alone in the loneliness.

Numb. That's the feeling I run from.

I realize now that is how I've always felt. So utterly detached. I've never truly felt anything at all. Emptiness, coldness, loneliness, and complete soul-sucking numbness have been my only friends for all of these sad, trivial mundane years.

And for the first time, I'm alive.

I'm feeling something that sparks a wildfire in my heart and sends gushes of air beneath my wings. It's as if I'm the ink on a page and the words are my emotions, brought to life.

Elijah brings it all out in me, everything I thought only possible in a book, sits right here like a crown of jewels within my chest.

I'm living and I understand now I've only ever been existing.

The air leaves me in a rush and when I blink, I find Elijah kneeling right before me, as if my fear alone had summoned him and he'd moved just as swiftly as the air around me.

"No worries, pretty girl. I'll never allow you to go numb," he vows, the rough timber in his voice vibrating through me and heating my chilling skin.

"Promise?"

"May the hounds devour me if I break it, but yes... I promise, Adisen. I'll be your fire through the storm." He leans in, kissing me softly, sealing his sacred words with a promise just as sacred as the tender brush of his lips. "I'll protect you, no matter the cost. However great the burden. I've tasted you, Adisen, I've tasted you and it's consumed me."

"Elijah?"

"Yes, love?"

"I think I'm starting to learn why I've been so afraid. But... what do you fear? This is your story just as much as mine. How can a king who fears nothing fear rejection from a mundane, like me?" I whisper, needing the answer as it gnaws away at me with desperation.

I'm finally breaking from my shell. Shaking off my depression. But this is Elijah-Fucking-Braxton's story. Isn't it? So what fears does he hide? Allow to dwell within the abyss?

"You aren't just any woman, Adisen. You're a reason. A purpose. A vital part of my story I just haven't figured out why yet. I'm with you and it's easy. I'm without and I want to riot. You're of great importance. An obsession I crave to sink my teeth into. I feel like there is a reason for it, a reason why your opinion matters above all the rest, I just haven't figured it out yet. I haven't figured out just why my parents spoke of tales of a woman so beautifully described as you."

I won't live in a world where he fears rejection. Especially not from me. I think it's time he allowed that darkness to break free. Time I got to see the beast and The Accursed creatures which call to me.

Just as I swallow past the lump in my throat, my Alexa starts screeching "Lilith" By Elise and this time he is more intrigued by the words than he is at the abrupt sound breaking through the tender silence.

Hiking a brow, he leans back and stares at me mockingly, almost quizzically. "Are you a Lilith? A little minx who does as she pleases?"

"When the mood strikes." I wink, pushing him back a step and creating enough space between us that I can stand to my feet.

"Do you feel invisible, Adisen?" he asks somberly, eyes penetrating as the mood changes.

"All the time."

"Am I the monster under your bed?"

"Most definitely, but I love that you are," I whisper, before plastering a smile on my face and shaking my ass right toward the backdoor. My hand grasps the handle when I'm about to turn the knob, then suddenly darkness envelops me.

Twenty-Seven

Elija

"**M**agic is a beautiful thing, witch. You might be human but you have traces of it in you. Just use it. Practice it and wield it like a sword," I whisper into her ear as I teleport us into the backyard. I spin her around and point her toward a tree. "Do you know what I've noticed about you?"

"That I get teleport-sick?" she breathes, before clearing her throat, unsteady on her feet.

"No. That you do better when you're desperate. That's what you were feeling, right? When you pulled me from the pages. When you conjured that sundae? When you thought that demon was killing you? I could feel it. *Have* felt it, this entire time. I just wasn't sure what it meant. I'm not one to feel desperation in a land that was written for me to conquer it."

So much has happened. So much has changed.

I no longer feel the same about my world as I should. I know that I don't belong here in hers, that it is impossible for me to fit in, but now I'm beginning to question that maybe I belong with her instead. I don't know how that will work. If she will fit into my world or even if she wants too. But I know that I have to keep trying, that I have to keep trying to get back to my realm even if it's so we can create a new story for ourselves within the pages.

I don't know if that's even possible. But we can deal with that later. We can deal with the consequences. I can give her everything she has ever dreamed about, if only she tells me what it is that her heart truly desires.

All I know at the moment is, the longer I'm here, the more this unrelenting power inside of me builds. It was never built for this world. I don't wish to destroy a realm that has never lifted a hand against me but I fear the longer that I am here, the harder it will be to suppress.

The beast won't settle. I am in a constant fight with him. Locked with a battle of wills that is draining my very resolve. He has turned almost into an untamed savage inside of me.

He has this craving for Adisen's blood that runs deeper than even I'm able to understand.

Every time we get that little bit too close. Every time I lose myself that little bit too much, he sinks our teeth into her throat and I wonder how much restraint I have left—

if I'll end up ripping out the very same throat I find so appealing.

She wants to see the beast, but the truth is. I have no idea what will happen if I ever allow him out. She's right. This isn't just my story… it's our story. But yet I still hide the parts of myself that she fantasized about. The demon that possessed her terrified her.

Would I have terrified her? If she had seen The Accursed, which I allowed, free to raze the very lands even now I still fight to get back to?

And why am I fighting?

Is it because I feel like it's expected of me?

Is it because that even though I know in my black heart, my realm is no longer my own, but the only place I can be free to be the monster that I am?

I'm fighting to go back to a world that doesn't exist. To fight a war that was written for me. Would this even be our fate if the author had not made us all so villainous?

"Elijah," she whispers, sighing in defeat but this time I don't give her the chance to run from herself.

One hand coils around her waist, trailing up her core until I can collar her by the throat. My other hand flies out, fire shooting from my palm as the tiny embers attach themselves to the greenery surrounding us. The trees catch alight, burning with orange embers that riot into the sky and become ablaze, burning the trees beside them, consuming them in a cloud of crimson and black smoke.

Adisen gasps, jolting forward but is held in place by my unforgiving hold. "No more running, pretty girl. Your will is strong enough to pull a monster like me from the pages? Make it strong enough to stop this whole town going up in flames."

"Elijah, no! Elijah, stop! You have no idea how bad forest fires can be. How quickly they can spread. We'll destroy everything!" she cries, writhing against me, pleading with me to let her go but I refuse.

"I think you have seen too much of the man who has become compliant to your beauty, witch. Too much of the man that somehow seems to care for your soul. After all, it was the beast you fell in love with right? Maybe it's the beast you need to once again fight for?" I whisper into her ear, allowing The Accursed room to bleed from the iron bars of their cells and taint the air around us. She searches her surroundings, noticing the patterns but unable to see their faces. She knows something has changed, that a darkness dwells here.

And she bucks against it. She can do this.

I know she can. She just has to be motivated to do so.

I let her go, stepping back as she spins on me. "Elijah. I can't stop this. How the hell am I supposed to stop this? I don't know how to use my will!" I can feel her panic and I smirk. I know a fire alone won't be enough to make her feel that desperation she needs to call upon, so there is more to my plan than watching my love's heart race.

"Do me a favor, love? Don't let me burn." And then I teleport. Right alongside the treeline, stopping just before the flames of Hell. I glance back over my shoulder, watching her as she rushes forward. "I'm not fireproof." Then I wink.

She was right. The fire is spreading quickly. It's burning half of the terrain and it becomes almost impossible to see beyond the flames. I turn around, keeping my focus on her as I step backward and into the heart of the fire. Heat licks against my skin with an inferno I'm all too familiar with. The last thing I hear is her screaming my name before the thick, black cloud of smoke engulfs me.

"Elijah! No!"

Then like the rewind of time, the flames retreat. Being sucked along the ground, they kiss against the earth and coil into one big ball of fire that hovers high in the sky before it just *poof,* disappears and I'm left standing in the ruins of wilted trees and charred soil. The ash rains down from the sky, falling around me and I glance up, marveling at the ashes like stars as they fall. I'm too distracted watching the fire recced, that I don't notice Adisen run right at me, punching me in the shoulder making me chuckle darkly as I catch her wrists in my hold.

"What the hell is wrong with you? Did your mama deprive you of any damn sense or something? Why the hell would you do that? What if I couldn't control it? What if I couldn't stop it?" she seethes, as I pull her into me. Hands firm on her hips as she tries to ward me off. "You crazy motherfucker."

"Sorry, love. I needed you to become desperate. Want to know what else I've learned?" I tease, finally feeling like we're making some kind of progress.

"That you're thick when it comes to pissing off a woman?" she huffs.

"No, pretty girl. I learned that I'm the key. The desperation? It is always fuelled by your need to protect me or to give me something you think I am missing. You're more willing to fight for me than you are to fight for yourself. Why is that?"

"Do you know how conceited that sounds?" she asks, leaning back to peer at me in narrowed-eyed annoyance. "How would you even know that? How could you possibly know that?"

"Because, I've been paying attention. Every Time you have made something happen you have felt desperation, but you have also felt devotion. You have felt driven by impulse. Tell me I'm wrong? It may have taken me a while, but I finally made sense of all of the foreign emotions."

She pushes away from me and turns her back, stalking through the ruins before once again turning to face me. "No, you're not wrong. It still doesn't mean you get to try and burn down my world though. I was terrified."

"I never would have allowed you to get hurt, Adisen. But I needed you to look at yourself. To find that feeling again if only to confirm that I was right."

"Fine. You're right. I want to be perfect for you. I want to give you everything you want and I want more than anything to go back to your realm. The realm that created you. The realm that I dreamed about. But I can't, okay? I can't be everything you need me to be because I don't know how!" she screams, hands fisting her hair as she spins in a circle and lets out her pent-up frustration. "I thought this was everything I have ever wanted, so what is it? What is holding me back? What makes me able to give you everything else you desire but not this? Not your realm?" she mutters, almost to herself.

"I have never asked you to be anything other than who you are, love. This insidious notion that you're no good, that you're worthless is all inside your head. It is the depression you allow to seep into your bones. You won't ever get us to where we need to be if you continue to be afraid. We can't keep hopping back and forth every time something makes you jump. You need to figure out who you are, what you want and then you need to control it. Stop letting everything around you, control you!" I stalk forward, a growl to my tone as frustration builds in my bones. "You want me to expose myself? To lay myself bare? Then you better do the goddam same, woman. If you want my demons and everything I house, then earn it. Give me something in return."

"I'm afraid!" she bellows, a wild fury sparking in her emerald eyes as they glisten under the dwindling sun. "I'm afraid! Because let's just look at this objectively, shall we? What the hell do we know? Honestly... What the fuck do we know?

This whole thing has been chaos. From the very fucking beginning. You shouldn't be here, Elijah. A power like yours does not belong in a dull world like this and don't even get me started on your world. I am not a character! I am not a queen. I am not supposed to be there no matter how much I wish it was different. What happens if I come with you? If I stay for longer than I already have?" she speaks with a passion that is as infuriating as it is impactful. She's letting it all out and some of it actually makes sense. "So yes, yes, I have been afraid because as much as I want to give you my everything, as much as I want to give you my all and run with this fantasy I can't help but fear what will happen if I give in. What will happen if a world like yours consumes me. Consumes you. I'm a weakness in your world, Elijah. I'm a weakness to you and I have no idea what will happen the longer our worlds mix. You were already starting to forget me. What would have happened if you had? If I was trapped in that world alone and without you?"

"Hold your tongue for the fear, make feast upon it," a British voice sings behind me and I groan, rolling my eyes as I turn toward her damn consciousness. "Hey ya, gang. How we hanging?"

"Really?" I drawl. "You had to bring back this pompous ass?"

"Oh!" he gasps. Hands flying toward his heart as he feigns insult. "I am wounded. Your ruckus caused quite a stir. Though I could lend a hand."

"By not telling us anything?" Adisen screeches, marching toward him. "You're the reason I am so damn afraid! The reason I have so many damn questions."

A knowing gleam glistens in his eyes and I narrow mine, curious as to his true intentions and if maybe he is this other entity that we feel is at play. I brush off the thought, not knowing how he could possibly connect to all of this and growl. Clenching shut my eyes as I pinch the bridge of my nose in frustration.

"What vague nonsense are you going to spew now?" I sneer, lip peeling back.

I glance toward Adisen, my features soften.

"Well, not much. I'm just here to look pretty. But I gotta say, the more you fight each other the more the ripple will part the waves of an ocean that will drown you." He shrugs indifferently. Thick lips pouting as the scar around his eye flares, looking seemingly irritated. My scar only irritates me when something drastic and dangerous is about to occur.

I frown, clenching my teeth as I study him more closely. How is a manifestation so accurately depicted to my character? And why have we never questioned him before? In more depth.

Because he drops his bombs and disappears before we get the damn chance.

I notice the way Adisen is staring at him too. It's no longer in awe but evident annoyance.

"If you keep dropping stupid riddles, I'm so going to will your ass into Timbuktu. You got that? My patience is wearing thin."

"Oh the wounds. How my pretty little tormentor pains me. Maybe if you gave your fear a face, answers will be had. Maybe if you read between the lines, you'll find a conclusion to the reality you so seek… Maybe, if you both stopped being so goddamn oblivious to your internal emotions something magic will happen… Like, I don't know? You'll know how the fuck to wrap up this mess in a pretty pink bow?"

"What the fuck does that mean?" Adisen snarls, face contorting in her anger.

I'd feel bad for pushing into something she wasn't ready to acknowledge if it wasn't needed.

Maybe I'm being a hypocrite. Putting too much on her when I don't even have answers myself about these damn memories. But at least I'm trying to piece them together. Maybe I should give her a chance to help me. A chance for us to finally take down these walls between us and lay it all out on the line. Maybe I've become too comfortable. Too complacent in this gentle peace we have found between us. Too dependent on her tender skin and sweet kisses. Maybe I had given myself to the fact that I was more invested in her and exploring this bond between us than anything else. Maybe we both have, and that's why we're where we are at.

"Hmm, ding ding. The king may just win." The ass winks at me, liking that he can see into my soul and read all of my thoughts. I growl, towering in height as I stalk closer toward him. "Woah, woah there, beastly. Calm now. You know what you gotta do, peace out! Give the bitch a face!" he rushes before he *poofs*, fading from my grasp as I sling out my hands and try to catch him by the shoulders.

"Goddam," I utter. Shaking my head as my temper rises.

"That made sense to you?" Adisen asks, drawing my focus.

"No, but I may have finally realized something else."

"Yeah, what's that?"

"We have to stop running from each other if we ever want out of this limbo."

Twenty-Eight

Elijah

"And how do we do that? Because I'm pretty sure we can't become any more closer," she huffs, hands on her hips as she hangs her head.

I step to her side, knocking away her hands and pulling her into me. Using my index finger, I lift her chin, forcing her to peer into my eyes. "Tell me what you're really afraid of, Adisen. All of it. The underlying panic that pulls at your heart more than anything else."

"If I do that, if I acknowledge it, I make it real, Elijah. I'm not sure I'm ready to make it real." Sadly, her eyes become glossy as she looks into mine, pleading with me to understand.

"I'll catch you if you fall. You're fire through the storm, remember? Just tell me. Trust me."

"Have you ever seen somebody with a quality you have envied but never acquired?" she asks slowly, like she's trying to work through the murkiness of her thoughts.

"There was an oracle. Back in my realm. She was called an old crone. She was a frail and weak old woman. Harrowing to look at and couldn't put up much of a fight if she was ever attacked. Yet, she was the most feared woman in the realm. Because she had something that nobody else ever had. Foresight. She had the ability to see into the future, the good and the bad. She had the ability to take it into her soul, without it ever becoming a burden." I could never forget her. Even if I tried. On the days the crown became too heavy, her ominous wisdom was what kept me humble. "She was the handler of the realm's fate, and she never let it consume her. All of that weight, that sorrow and depression, she never let it take her. She used it as a weapon and do you know why she was the most feared? Because she had the power to make those afraid, see what they forever wished to hide. She could undo you with your future and kill you with your fear. I had always envied her. Always wished I could see what she saw and handle it the way she handled it. But alas, I never had that power. Mine was to destroy, not to prevent and without her, the realm would have fallen into ruin long ago."

"Exactly," she breathes with a little more energy as her eyes flicker toward mine before becoming lost once again in her thoughts. "If you cut me, Elijah, I'll bleed. I'm human. I have dreamed about a dark fantasy - about a world I wanted to lose myself within for years. But right now? Given the chance? I don't fear not being worthy, I know that I'm not. Because this is reality. My fortitude won't make me a victor in a battle of magic. I can't become a queen to a kingdom that could smite me amidst my reign. That's why I'm terrified. Not because of the possibility of losing you, but accepting the fact that I *will*, lose you." She pulls away from me, pacing back and forth as she worries her bottom lip. "Wanting something, and being cut out for it, are two very different things. I want this, *fuck me,* do I want this. If I could trade my human soul to the devil for a soul of a warrior encased in magic, I would. But you can't make me magical and you can't protect me from a kingdom of power. I'd resent it. Being surrounded by it and never being able to have it. Who I want to be and who I am, are very different things, Elijah. I can read about a character facing brutality and plunging the world into ruin as she rises from the ashes and razes the land with her magic, but that can never be me. Because I'm not magical. I'm not a creature and I could not survive," she emphasizes each word with hurried movements of her fluttering hands. "You want to know what I'm most afraid of? I'm afraid of admitting that you can't stay with me in this world and that I can't come with you back to yours."

Her revelation startles me, pressurizing me to my core. I blink at her as a torrent of emotions twirl and gather inside of me like a hurricane in my gut as panic seizes my heart. I can't deny any of her truths. Don't know how to address it or move past it, either. It leaves something rotten and sour in my chest and I find that I struggle to breathe.

"Are you kidding me?" I ask, on a harsh breath. "Adisen, you are the fucking magic. You conjured me from the realm of a world that does not exist. You took a fiction character and you brought him to life. You brought *me* to life and then you literally projected yourself back into that book. Into that world of magic. Don't you remember what fake me said? The magic chose you, love. It *chose* you!" Something shifts in my core as I struggle to keep an even breath. I try to reassure her, to talk her around this absurd fear, but I find myself fighting the beast.

The hound becomes unhinged, thrashing within its confinements as it shreds my soul in a savage need to break free. To claim her. To keep her.

I double over, the pain tearing through my chest unlike anything I have ever felt before.

Ours.

Ours.

OURS.

It bellows our fury. Our brutal and unrelenting need echoes around the clearing. A searing pain consumes my mind, while The Accursed begin to wail and I struggle to fight the current which is crocodile spinning me into a pit of dark demise.

A new memory flashes behind my eyes. One that finally makes sense and I can't believe just how fucking stupid I've been all of this time. How even now… Jessaleia controls me.

"When the fire burns in your soul and a lone flame becomes two, you realize, the one standing beside you is the one destined, Elijah.

"When the ink dries, and the oceans wash away. When the sun dims and the moon crumbles.

When the darkness comes and the light is scarce, it is on that day, your darkness shall bloom.

It will finally find a home and all of those burdens will become grains of sand swallowed by the sea, long forgotten, my child.

"Because, my son, even if the world was to end, and ash blew at your feet and all you could see were the ruins, your mate would still find you standing tall within them." My father tells me, wisdom, and love, thick in his ancient tone. Whenever my

father speaks to me, it reminds me of the old narrators. Deep and captivating, a sound I've come to love.

A sound I've forever needed for my seven-year-old self to fall asleep to at night.

The way he looks at my mother, so deeply romanticized, has forever changed my perspective of this otherwise dark and cruel king. I couldn't understand how a man so beautifully monstrous could be that way inclined to be tender and warm toward his family.

Toward his mate.

He had once told me, that when you set eyes on a queen true to your soul, the rest of the world will never look anything other than black and white again. When an alpha who has only ever known control finds his mate, he also finds a softness within his stone-cold heart that she will draw from in order to bloom and to nest, preparing for a new generation. Because like ying and yang, when trust is involved, we're all just equal parts submissive and dominant.

It's just about finding the right person to give your vulnerabilities too.

He had told me all of that, as I laid my head down one night. Soon after, he stormed into battle and viciously tore the hearts out of his enemies.

When my daddy spoke, hope soon followed. I believed I could do anything, become anything. If only I just believed. If only I was as viscous and unrelenting.

As open and as willing.

"How will I know, Daddy, how will I truly know?"

"Because the thought of living without her is simply an impossibility, my son. You would sooner perish within the lake of the forgotten, erase all that you are and walk the void for all

eternity with a death unbecoming to a warrior, than to ever *lose her."*

"Elijah! Elijah, for fuck's sake, snap out of it! Come back to me! Elijah!" That same voice, the very one that started all of this in the first place reaches me once again in the unreachable.

Her angelic voice bellows around me, consuming me and as my darkness recedes and the pain fades. I blink open dazed eyes as I truly see her for the first time. As I truly and utterly see her.

"It's you…" I breathe. How the hell could I have been so stupid? So blind? "It's always been you."

"What, Elijah? What has always been me?" she asks, frantic, trying to hold me up from being doubled over from the assault.

"My mate."

She stands upright, drawn back as she stares at me in utter confusion. "What now? Don't talk like that. Don't talk to me about things that can't be true, Elijah. It's cruel," she chokes, brokenly. Taking a step back, her brows furrow staring at me in acute awareness.

"I'm not trying to be cruel, Adisen. I'm being honest. I can finally see things clearly. It all makes sense and it only hadn't before because of that fucking bitch. That vile, insidious bitch who poisoned me. Took away all of my memories and made me forget what a true mate should be! How it would feel when I finally found her." I chuckle in disbelief. It's a dark and foreboding sound. "My beast didn't want to kill you. He wanted to fucking claim you! Every time he bit you, he was trying to cement the damn bond!"

"H-how is any of this even possible?"

"I don't know. How did you get me here? How did any of this happen?"

"I-Impossible."

"And yet possible. You're mine, Adisen. You have always been mine." I step forward, everything finally centering within me as my world rights itself on its axis. I pull her into my arms, hand cupping her jaw as I move her head back to look up at me. This is why I fell, why I could never get this little witch out of my head. Because she was always destined to be mine. Destined to be ours. My thumb traces the seam of her lips as I stare at her with new eyes. "I'm sorry, pretty girl. I'm sorry that I was too stuck up my own ass to know what was standing right in front of me. I should have known. Spelled or not, I should have known." She turns her head, sinking into my hold as she inhales deeply. Wrapping her hand around my wrist as she holds herself to me, savoring my touch like a weight has been lifted from her shoulders. "It's a crime y'know? To reject a mate in my realm. I never should have spoken those words to you. I never should have insulted you by claiming Jessaleia was my mate. You never should have had to read that scene where I had her in-in my…" I shake my head. "Rejection-" I choke on the rotten word. "Rejection of a mate is punishable by death, Adisen. Can you ever forgive me, pretty girl? Can you ever forgive me for such a thing?"

Her eyes widen and for a moment, time stands still. She just stares at me, unmoving, unblinking and I can see it like a physical thing as everything comes rushing back and she blinks, staring at me like she's seeing me for the first time.

"There's nothing to forgive. You were never mine until you bled from the ink, Elijah. I wanted you to be. I wanted you like I wanted every other character I ever read about. Well… Not exactly. You were always the one who hit differently. But it wasn't until I met the man that I fell in love all over again. That I knew what it was my heart truly desired. I can't forgive you because there is nothing to forgive." She kisses my wrist, stepping into me until her head lays upon my chest and I engulf her, clutching her tightly. "Is that why you would never show me the beast?"

"Yes. I couldn't understand. I couldn't understand why he kept biting you. I feared that I'd lose control and hurt you. It twisted me up inside. Not having control on one of the creatures that I have always been one with. I was taught to brutalize the land, but to never hurt a woman. Yet…" I lean back, tracing a finger along the curve of her throat. "He kept hurting you. Branding you with a mark, on your neck just like a collar. Making sure the world knew you were ours."

"That's what all of that was about? The fact that he scarred my neck?" she asks in a heavy sigh, shaking her head as the tips of her finger unintentionally trace the risen skin at the column of her throat. "Elijah." she sighs again, trying to find the words. "I don't regret this scar. I don't wake up in the morning fearing that you, The Accursed or the beast, will *ever* hurt me. In fact, I wake up, head to the bathroom and stare at this very same scar with pride in my heart and a smile on my face. I don't regret this bite because it's yours. It's his. And when this is all said and done, no matter our fates, even if I'm left with nothing but memories, I'll also have this. The scar that will forever remind me that the man between the lines was real and for a time… he was mine."

"He's yours alright, and you're mine."

Twenty-Nine

Elijah

I became a man, the one that stands by Adisen's side, when the script changed and I was rewritten within the ink.

She brought me to life. A fictional character with no life nor direction. She gave me depth and purpose and gifted me with this thing called emotion.

Emotion that allows me to feel her so viscerally, as I do right now. I lift her into my arms, hands tangled within her hair as her legs bound themselves round my waist. I stare into her eyes, losing myself in the sea of emeralds.

"I'm not going anywhere, baby. Not now, not ever. I'm going to do what I should have done the moment I fell at your feet. What my beast has been urging me to do since I first laid eyes on you. My wicked enchantress, I'm going to claim what's ours, darling. What has long since been written in the stars." Kissing her feverishly, I give her everything I should have given her from that very first night.

My heart, my love, the soul which now entwines with hers.

The sweat glistens along my skin, my thick cock springing free from my pants and they disappear from my thighs with a whisper of magic. Hard like steel, throbbing with angry veins, it pulsates between us.

My dick knows who it belongs to.

My little witch.

I bring down my left hand to cup her ass, caressing her silky-smooth thighs as I magic away her clothing too. She groans into my mouth, I capture it with my growl, teleporting us back into her bedroom.

"This time love, we're going to do it right." I bend back down, to stand tall on my knees still keeping her clutched to me. With my grip on her hips, my fingers coil into them.

Kissing her slowly, I make sure she feels every inch of passion bleeding from my pores.

Ravished with a need to make this more, to make this matter.

I line myself up with her slick core, my pretty girl already wet for me as I sink inside, sheathing myself to the hilt and groaning at the way she flutters around me.

I gasp on a growl when her pussy walls constrict and she squeezes me tight, drawing me deeper. She encloses around me, clenching me so tightly, the pressure sits heavy in my balls.

I thrust slow and deep, rocking my hips and gliding deeper and deeper still, hitting every part of her I can reach.

Adisen throws back her head, long hair swaying in the breeze as she arches her back and pushes herself further onto me, my balls getting ready to join my cock on the ride. She moans, the sound so sensual, it elicits a shiver from me as it skates down my spine.

"Elijah, oh fuck, Elijah," her sinful whisper disperses into the wind, so I grip her by the nape, gently bringing her head back up, to face me. I gaze into her eyes, intently, emotionally, as I finally give her everything I was unable to do before.

All of me.

"You're my mate, Adisen. Do you know what that means?" I rasp, voice low so as to not disturb the moment as she rocks against me. She shakes her head, eyes refusing to leave mine. "It means, we get to claim you. Do you know what *that* means?" She shakes her head no, once again. "It means the beast wants you too, baby, *needs* you too. Do you think you can handle it? Handle us?"

"Yes," she answers without hesitation. "Everything that you house, all that you are… I want it all, Elijah. I want you."

A wicked smirk spreads across my face, my eyes soft as I can feel the change.

"He wants to say hi, baby. Don't be scared, okay?" I thrust again and again, small pumps which are long and drawn out, so I can truly feel every inch of her. So I can savor every caress that a stroke brings to my senses.

My eyes close, I heave a deep breath and when I open them again, the beast stares back at her.

Complete, and utter black orbs, quick like ink, tainted with the darkest hint of crimson that leaves them looking monstrous, blink their curious gaze down at our dainty mate.

Adisen just smiles softly, tracing my cheek with her delicate hand, the soft contrast to my rough stubble, making me quake.

Her eyes fill with acceptance, love and I wonder how I never saw it before now.

This is how she's always looked at me.

Like I'm her everything and she'd give up all the books in the world, just to keep me.

For her... that's the equivalent to giving up all of the jewels the world has to offer.

Her eyes widen, a shocked gasp stolen from her kiss-swollen lips as my hands change from smooth flesh in favor of sprouting fur as the long and wicked talons extend.

But that isn't the only part of the beast which takes over the man.

I can feel my cock swell and curve, knotting inside of her, lodging within her walls, and holding her steady, fiercely, refusing to let her go. We grow thicker, filling her so completely, I can feel the ache in her core, strong through our bond.

My talons pierce her delicate flesh, drawing tiny beads of blood that I bring to her lips, painting them pretty and red.

She doesn't display any sign of discomfort or pain. Instead, looking awestruck and euphoric. It only cements the fact that she's so fucking perfect for me.

Nobody else, other than a mate, would be able to withstand a mating.

It's impossible.

This cements the fates. This isn't something that can be faked.

Something that can be coerced with a potion or an iron will.

This is a magic that can't be touched and the fact that I'm experiencing it with Adisen proves that I'm right.

There is magic inside of her.

Using my grip in her hair, I tilt her head back. "Keep those eyes on me, pretty girl." Exposing her neck, the strain is prominent and the bite is perfection. She arches her back, creating space between us so I can peer down at the blood running down her tanned thighs and soaking her glorious pussy. "So, fucking perfect," I rumble, using my free hand to trace the crimson river, smearing it over her thighs and using it as lotion to knead her tension filled muscles. She shakes above me, her orgasm closing in, while she pants like a good little bitch in heat.

She may not be magical, but she is in every sense of the word fucking power.

I should have known. Should have realized the hold she had over me.

She continues the tiny, almost missable movements as she feels that pull in her channel, that ache in her core, that high that she chases, and fling her hands forward, nails raking down my back, drawing blood of her own.

She claws at me, peeling the flesh from my shoulders as the carnal energy begins to take root.

Nothing changes, not our tempo, not our slow exploration of one another, not the love we exude. Nothing other than our savage need for one another as it consumes us.

"Do you know what this is, love? What's happening?" I bring my bloody hand between us, showing her the beautiful mess we're making.

It's the bond taking place. Entwining together and cementing us as one.

"Only that it feels so damn right," she moans, making me smirk while she throws back her head.

"It's me… it's us, writing our name in your womb, pretty girl. Claiming you inside and out, leaving absolutely no doubt to creatures of my realm, or the men in yours, that you are so fucking taken."

Her angelic smile chips away my once hardened soul, leaving

only her and her essence in its wake. "It's our vows, little witch. No turning back now. You really are my queen, whether you like it or not."

We stay locked together, the knotting making it difficult to move as it does what it needs too.

"But I didn't write any vows," is her only response before she blinks, left hand clasping the back of my neck for stability as she pulsates around me. "But I can. I can tell you exactly how I feel and I don't even have to think about it." The beast blinks back at her, waiting, expecting, unsure how to process the sensations running wild throughout our body. Coiled tight, I grip her hips bruisingly, loving the purple fingerprints which mar her pretty flesh. "The Accursed act on instinct. Not for a reason. I vow today to act on instinct too. To make room for the darkness, so I can cherish the damned ensuring you never feel alone." Leaning forward, she places a soft kiss to my jaw. "I will love you like all dark creations are to be loved. In my heart, out here within the world and written within the ink of a scripture that can never be refuted. I will love you like my moon, my blood on a rose and my thorns. I will always allow you to make me bleed, Elijah. So that when my heart whispers, it will whisper a secret only you can understand. No matter where in the world you are."

"Oh love, such pretty and dark words spoken from such succulent lips," I groan, running my tongue along her throat, circling her pulse before trailing down to nip around her nipple. "Any girl can play Mrs. Innocent. But it takes a special kind of wild to play with the demons. You didn't just play with them, Adisen, you taunted them. Called them from their prison. Your pain. Your secrets. Your envy and your imagination. That light that teases the shadows. That is what made us love you. That is why we will always love you."

Pulling back, my thumb finds her clit as her eyes widen and her entire body shudders, tightening. "You have bewitched me, love. I knew it the moment I saw you. I once thought I'd have to kill you, cut off your pretty little head because it was the only way I could resist you. But I couldn't do it. Not when I thought you were an enemy and not when you showed me the lies. I couldn't do it because I've always known, in here, I've finally come home. To you. My now and always. My wicked queen." I place my hand over my heart, drawing in a deep breath and I thrust one last time. Deeply seating myself inside of her as I unknot and fill her with my seed, painting her pretty walls white.

Conjuring a hot washcloth and cleaning her swollen and wet flesh, I make sure I'm light handed, cleaning her thoroughly and adding a salve which will help with the burn, although she seems to like it. Coyly smiling at me like I just handed her the stars.

Dressing once again, I pull her into me. My lips finding hers as I kiss her violently, breathing her in. "What a fool I've been. Thank you for helping me read between the lines." We smirk at one another, and my cold heart finally no longer feels such an endless void in my chest. "You know that I have more than one form right?" I ask her, raising a brow. She wants to see the beast, The Accursed are something entirely different. But did she ever read about how I can change between one and all in that book of hers?

"Okay, what?" She laughs and I chuckle darkly.

"I turn into the beast. A gnarly fucker that looks like a cross between a hellhound and a wolf. I have my king form, where I grow wings and a tail and then I have my merged form."

Her mouth hangs open as she gapes at me. "A merged form?"

"I fuse with some of The Accursed and the beast."

"Ooo, I need to see that."

"Impatient little thing, aren't you?" I tease.

"Oh like I haven't waited long enough."

"We need to go back into the clearing." I offer her my hand, pulling her into my hold.

Once we are back outside, the beast howls like a deviant to the skies above and I stand to my feet, stepping back as I put space between us. The Accursed pull taunt from my skin, shadowy silhouettes that stand sentinel around in the shadows of the clearing as my flesh gives way to fur and the beast appears.

We stand black as night, nine feet tall with silver and red-hot lava streaked through our fur and as gnarly as the hounds from hell.

"Oh my lanta! In a DJ Tanner!" she gasps, referencing an old tv show called *Full House,* looking at me with eyes wider than saucers.

A massive smile spreads across her face, lighting up all of her features. "Now you guys I've seen before!" she gushes, running to our side to embed her fingers through our fur. The beast purrs, butting her hand with his head. She turns to the warriors of The Accursed, stoking against their onyx essence as she singsongs, "You kept me safe through the fever, didn't you?" She shakes her head, bringing her eyes back to lock with mine. "When I was sick and I told you about the dreamscape? I was with them," she informs me, a wild spark of pride in her beautiful eyes.

I scoff, nose butting along the ground.

Of course they were.

I don't know what happens from here, but I know that wherever we end up, it will be together.

"What in the fuck-nut on the tits of a hooker is that?" a female voice exclaims, in shock-horror. I whip my head around, bounding full circle to place myself in front of Adisen and sneering in the direction of the brunette struck-wild in the back door.

"Maria?" Adisen asks in small confusion before firmness returns to her tone. "Wait! Elijah, don't! She's my sister."

I howl, then remember myself. Just as I'm about to speak inside Adisen's mind and change back into the man, the earth quivers in a quake that cracks the earth and opens a glowing portal within the mouth of the woods.

Standing there, staring back at us, is the bane of my existence. The treacherous whore I wish to slaughter and standing at Jessaleia's side... is my brother Bradon.

Thirty

Elijah

Instinct takes over and the beast sneers, growing in height, towering above everything else. I trot forward, head low to the ground as I chase the scent of slut and deceit and frown in distaste.

That scent used to make me feel indifferent. Something I should have craved.

Now, I feel fucking repulsed.

I call more of The Accursed from purgatory to the forefront of my flesh, allowing them free for a short time while we surround Adisen. They stand around us in utter darkness, thick and featureless silhouettes that hide their identity from those they do not trust.

Jessaleia and Bradon on the very top of that list.

Placing myself in front of her and her new friend, shielding them both from poisonous eyes, the growl which echoes from my chest reverberates throughout the land, rattling the treetops that enclose around us, the ones that remain unburnt and bathe us in the fallen leaves which dislodge from their branches.

Jessaleia smiles sickly-sweet, those same lips painted red, mocking me. "Now, love. Is that anyway to treat your queen? I missed you when you ran from me, you returned home and didn't even come to say hello?" she purrs as Bradon tenses at her side. "Did you really think you could run from me forever?"

Bradon glares back at me, withdrawn and emptier than I've ever seen him before right now. "I'm sorry, brother, but I'm told a man in love would do anything for his queen," he utters dejectedly, soulless and almost deadpanned.

How he can speak of love in a flattened tone is beyond me. Even the mere thought of love and Adisen within the same sentence burns with a passion that bleeds into my voice.

It isn't flat. It's everything wild within your veins.

I scoff, nose butting the ground as I try to scratch away the offending scent of them entwined as one.

Nothing else matters within this moment other than making sure Adisen is safe. Even if I have to raise Hell itself to make sure of it.

Her love is the rightest thing I've ever felt before in this world, and any other like it.

A feminine growl sounds beside me, and I whip around, eyes searing into Adisen as I growl again, warning her to stay behind me.

"She doesn't love you Bradon, she loves nobody but herself," Adisen hisses, the look in her eye untamed as she struggles to hold her tongue.

Jessaleia clicks hers, tilting her dusty blonde head to stare past me, eyes turning into callus flints as they assess Adisen. "What did the Pegasus drag in this time? I'm sure the livestock are supposed to be kept chained and beaten within the keep, is this not correct, my love?"

I shift, returning to the man so I can communicate with this bitch. I've never been able to project inside her mind the way I can project inside of Adisen's, the reason for that now so painstakingly obvious. As my fur retreats, clothing gives chase, molding to my skin and covering me, with a shirt and gray lounge pants.

"Refer to her as feed again, Jessaleia. I dare you to test the wrath you have created."

"Temper, temper. Come now, love, you have to understand why we want you dead. It's the only way for us to take the throne," she chimes, a false angelic smile on her ruby reds.

"The Kingdom would revolt, brother. Your demise is the only way to remove the realm from its rightful heir," Bradon offers, a moment of sadness flickering in his quick-silver eyes. It passes long before it can plant a seed of regret within my cold heart.

"So you drug me? Lie to me? Have me sleep with the woman you claim to love?" I roar, the words sour in my mouth as I flick my remorseful eyes toward Adisen. She's the only one who gets to see my regret and know the meaning behind it.

She's the only one that matters.

I never thought they would ever be here. But I did question once what would happen if they were to somehow end up here like I did, if it would change the course of their written path. That like me, could they grow and adapt to becoming their own creation instead of a character created *for* them.

But I had asked Adisen the night I had returned back here,

the night she got possessed, what she thought would happen if our worlds were to ever cross. I recall the memory.

Mayhem and grotesque destruction, my love. If those characters were to bleed from the page, only poison would follow. Unlike you, they were not written to have any redeemable qualities.

"We had no other choice," Bradon grits, jaw flexing and showing real emotion for the first time. Contempt and disgust are thickening within the air from us both. "It was the only way we could take the throne and finally be happy."

"You stupid, naive little boy," Adisen spits vehemently, features pinched tight as she shakes her head, grinding her jaw with anger I've never seen her wear before. It bleeds through, reddening her tanned cheeks scarlet. "She never intended to keep you around. The very night he left was the same night Jessaleia tried to convince him you were a threat. The same night she wanted him to kill you."

I narrow my eyes, now remembering such a moment. It was seconds before an enchantress bellowed my name to the void and stole my soul from the vicious grip of an ice queen's brittle fingers.

"Whore! She would never do such a thing!" Power erupts within the clearing as Adisen is yanked from her feet, suspended within the air. She cries out from the shock, my demons flying beside her, wrapping her within their essence and bringing her back to the ground as I throw out a hand, wielding an unforgivable power of my own as I thrash Bradon with the strike of an unrelenting whip. I lift him by the throat, yanking down my arm forcefully and embedding into the ground, denting the earth and forcing it to cave around the slumped form of his body, knocking him out cold.

"Never!" I growl inhumanly. Savagely. "Touch. What. Is. Mine."

"You never spoke such a way about me, Elijah. I should be offended that this harlot has stolen you so easily from my grasp," Jessaleia utters with forlorn in her lowered voice. It all changes when a demented fire sparks within her gaze and her entire body hardens as her eyes brighten. "So you're the mate I've been searching for all of these moons."

My stomach bottoms out at those words, my powers darken within the air, becoming stifling and stealing all of the oxygen around us.

I didn't know that Adisen existed. There is no way Jessaleia could have known it either.

"This is over for you, Jessaleia. Over for the both of you. You'll die here for your treachery."

Bradon groans, rolling onto his side with an evident ache from my assault. "See, brother. The utter lack of concern she holds for you?" I tell him, finding it a pity I have to slaughter my flesh and blood.

The thought of my father in his grave, hating what we have become sickens me. Then I remember I don't have a father. Not really.

When life hands you poison, shove it down the throats of your fucking enemies.

"Seriously, Addy. How did I walk into wonderland on acid? What's happening right now?" Maria whispers, clutching Adisen's arm tightly as she gazes around at the scene unfolding before her.

"Stay quiet and stay behind me," Adisen whispers in reply, shoving Maria behind her and squaring her shoulders, looking back at me with determination. But I can feel the gut-wrenching fear weighing down her core.

The feeling makes me murderous, the thought that anything could scare my pretty girl at all leaves me with fire in my veins, blood rushing between my ears and a brutalizing power that could destroy it all kissing against the earth.

"So you finally found her, your mate? Hmm, that will do. That will do nicely."

"Enough! Enough of your games, you cruel bitch." The roar creates a gail force of wind that picks up within the clearing. A tiny tornado that twists precariously between us.

"I'll kill her, Elijah. I'll kill her just because I can." Disgust is like an acid in the spittle of her sneer. Her cheeks reddening in her outrage at my lack of shits to give about this bitch.

"Listen to her, Bradon, listen to how little she cares about you," I implore, not for any other reason than I want him to feel the stupidity of his actions.

"Don't listen to him, my love, it's you. It's always been you. I could never betray that." Her whole demeanor changes, coy innocents beaming from her like a lighthouse in the storm. A taunt to the safety you know you'll never find within the unforgiving waters as the light flashes up ahead mockingly, just before the waves swallow you whole. "Remember, love? Remember our plan?"

I can feel Adisen's rage, her fury as it burns within her blood at the insult, but she manages to bite her tongue and stand there in stoic silence.

But I can still feel the hurricane beneath her skin.

The riot brewing within her core.

"Times up, bitch. Think of me - the king you thought you could beat - when the void feeds from your rotten flesh for all of eternity. Forcing you to relive the moment I took your fucking life." My lip curls in disgust as I pull the darkness around me, harboring my powers like a capsule, the shell of a bullet waiting to detonate and shatter all those close to me with its shrapnel.

"Oh, darling. You think we came alone and without a plan? I would have thought you would have thought better of your mate," she sings songs, staring down at her nails with disinterest and a whimsical attitude.

"He is not your fucking mate!" Adisen yells, the need to defend us an impulse neither of us can deny when our bond is called into question. It's like razors shredding our senses, turning into liquid metal within our veins. Thickening and solidifying within our throats, making it hard to breathe at all.

She lunges forward, making Maria squeak.

I jerk forward myself, just in time to catch her around the waist and haul her back into my chest. "Patience, pretty girl," I whisper into her ear, only to have the side of her head smack me dead in the mouth when it thrashes to the side like she's just been bitch slapped. The force of it has my lip throbbing, blood pooling along the seams. Her head thrashes to the left, another quick strike from an invisible hand that has Adisen's hair whipping back and forth making her gasp and sputter.

Jessaleia's powers are a rotten scent, potent in the air around us.

My back arches as my shoulders pull toward the ground, my chest opens, letting free an enormous howl filled with grief and vengeance. The harrowing sound ripples like a bomb that has just exploded and uproots every single tree that lines the perimeter, knocking into the second line further into the woods and wiping them clean out.

Hesitation stares me in the eyes for a split second and then arrogance fills Jessaleia's gaze once again and the force of my howl has her swaying on her feet. She stumbles into Brandon's arms, who catches her as my wrath pushes them further toward the cracks in the earth, leading to a black hole I hope will swallow them whole.

Lighting cracks through the skies, blue and blood red as the sky rains crimson tears. Red covers the ground as we become soaked in the color of my vengeance and wicked wrath.

Adisen's hair slicks back in soft curls that cling to her face, the outfit she's wearing blending with the burgundy that clings to her slender frame. I don't need to move my hand or offer any command for my powers to redress her in black leathers that cling to her ass in a specific kind of fabric which allows her to move. It's built as armor but is flexible and allows you to feel like you aren't wearing anything at all.

It will protect her from any kind of penetration. But evidently not from Jessaleia's sickening cackle.

"Red looks good on her, not as good on me, granted. But it will definitely be her color match when we attend her wake." She moves back toward the portal and as much as she fronts the confidence, I can still smell the trepidation on her.

Her wary eyes find mine once more as the Accursed circle Adisen, removing her from my arms and ushering her toward the backdoor with her friend.

She thrashes within their power, arms reaching through the shadows as she fights for me. "No! Elijah, no! Please don't do this. We fight them together. We fight them together!"

A soft smile places on my lips as I look at her sadly, her strength and fortitude a balm to my soul. I know she's terrified, I know she knows in her heart she is defenseless against powers which don't belong in her world.

But still, she'd risk it all for me.

For us.

It's why I'll allow her to watch from behind the glass while I obliterate everything that tries to destroy us. It's why I'll allow her to see me bare, giving it my all, as I unleash my worst on those who are deserving of my wrath.

But I will not allow her to fight these battles for me.

I will not watch her die.

"Don't worry about me, love. Magic and mayhem, remember?" Vicious contempt curls my lips as my smile turns cruel. All aimed at the people I once would have died for and now, want nothing more than to brutalize.

"Elijah, Elijah, please!" she screams, and it cuts me deep. She fights harder, thrashing wildly and I know how agonizing that will be for her.

I blink, and when I open them again the entity of my gaze is a deep and dark, petrifying blue, speckled with black obsidian. It's like a marble that has captured the storm. Crimson bleeds through the cloudy look, mixing with the two-tone colors as little dots. Adisen stops struggling, watching me wide-eyed as she takes in the change with heavy breathing.

"Stay safe, my love. The only thing that can kill me, is losing you. Remember that." Then The Accursed lift her, carrying her and Maria through the doorway and into the kitchen before sealing it shut and becoming a gas-like smoke which seals the glass doors closed permanently, while tinting the glass with a black, translucent hue.

She stares at me through the darkness with such desperation within her eyes, that it rips me open from core to throat, leaving my essence bare to bleed into the earth, hoping it may one day be reunited with her.

I'm about to destroy it all in the name of love and when I'm done, I'll write my declaration to Adisen within the ruins.

"The void will be too good for you. I think the Netherland would be more fitting," I sneer slowly, turning my darkening eyes toward Bradon and Jessaleia who are backed up against the portal, cuddling into one another as the storm I have created picks up force, dropping buckets of blood-like water onto our chilling heads.

Jessaleia sputters and coughs, fighting to see me through the storm clouds which drop from the heavens to filter as a mist that coils around our ankles, rising higher still.

My powers are linked to my emotions, and each time the land is stricken with a bolt of lightning or the roar of thunder, the turmoil shows within the black-blue of my eyes and even I know, the look is damn right frightful.

A thing made of horrors.

A thing made of sorrows.

I'm the regret you live with and the demons you try to fight.

I'm the embodiment of your worst deeds and the holder of your retribution.

In my realm, I am the fucking devil.

Adisen's just never knew it before now.

My tail elongates from the bottom of my spine, my massive leathered and lethal wings unfurl from my shoulder blades, pointed to the tips of razors as my fingernails protrude into claws and my hands become those of my hound. Covered in fur and looking like a Lycans.

My mouth opens, splintering around the jaw as the beast's head emerges and exposes himself as I become half of my creature, half of my hound and a lot of The Accursed.

My features become stronger, more prominent and defined. My ears stretch, my face hardens and my magic intensifies.

Inhaling a deep breath, I pull from everything around me, feeding into my core, into my blood. As I scream, punching down into the ground and uprooting even more trees as I shake up our surroundings and make the terrain uneven in my rage.

I summon my fire and the shards of my ice together. Weapons that coil like steady pistols, levitating at my sides just as the first creature steps through the portal with an ear-shattering screech.

Thirty-One

Adisen

Everything in me revolts at the scene unfolding. At the harrowing beasts which escape the portal and soar off into the skies disappearing into the thickness of the abyss. But that is nothing compared to the man who grows the human shaped head of a bestial hound.

Elijah told me about his different forms. Seeing it however is something that has fractured my mind in a way which I will never unsee it.

I should be there, at his side, even if it means my demise. Elijah stands tall in the face of our enemies, an unmovable and untameable force which threatens to tear to shreds the very existence of this realm. And I might be half his size and a human dud, but I do yoga.

I can stand tall with him.

Because he's right. Desperation is my trigger. So consider me fucking triggered because he's alone and outnumbered by the very people who were able to trick him into tales of delusions for all of this time.

It was the will of the author, I know. And I also know that now, for all intents and purposes, he's a real boy, but it still makes me wonder what the hell will happen now that fiction is crossing with reality and just how much power they still hold over him.

How can he lock me away in a glass tower and ask me to sit back and watch him in battle?

How dare he wage a war and not have me bellowing a war cry standing tall at his side.

I get it.

I'm mundane.

I did this. I fucked up and gave into my fears and told him that the reason we have been such in this pain forsaken limbo is because I felt defenseless against this world of magic.

But he's also right, too. I do have power in my heart. Even if it is miniscule and the most I've done is brew a coffee. I also pulled his ass here too. I just need to find the part inside of me that can face my fear.

I can't wield any kind of power, uproot the earth or bring the darkest creatures known to man to their knees.

Compared to him… to them, I'm nothing.

But still there is a heaviness in my core, trepidation in my veins and an impulse in my naive little heart that has me bursting at the seams to insert myself into the action.

To help in any way that I can, because the longer we're apart, with anything between us, the more I feel like something horrendous and irreversible shall happen.

"Seriously, Addy. What the fuck is going on. What's happening right now because I am freaking the fuck out!" Maria grabs my arm, trying to yank me to attention but my eyes are glued to the back shimmering door. The souls of the damned staring back at me with sorrow within their dangerous eyes.

I can't tear them away, in fear if I do, I'll never see my beast again.

"Adisen!" she bellows and I shrug off her relentless grip.

"What the hell are you doing here? You shouldn't be here," I whisper, a new panic fresh in my heart as I look back at the woman who has always been more like a sister to me than a friend.

Someone who has been my constant and my wall between insanity. We may not see each other all the time, but if I've ever needed her, she'd be there.

In a heartbeat.

Just like now.

"It's Thursday, Adisen. I was supposed to come last week, remember? And I couldn't. I was supposed to come tomorrow night," her eyes flicker back and forth between mine, searching for any kind of recollection. "For two damn weeks, I couldn't fucking reach you and I was worried sick!" she screams in my face, terror clear in her rich and silky brown eyes. "I was this close to sending out a search party, this fucking close but I thought maybe you were having a bad pain day. Maybe just maybe, you'd get back to me in a day or two and you hadn't."

"I thought you had to work tonight?" I utter absently, my mind not catching up to the horrors unfolding.

"I did, he wouldn't let me go. So I fucking quit. Nothing comes before you, you know that. Now please tell me what in the ever-loving-fuck-a-suck is happening." Her tone softens when she sees the tears welling within my eyes.

I never wanted to bring her into this mess, but I'm grateful I don't have to leave her behind either.

"You wouldn't believe me even if I told you."

"If you told me, probably not. But I have two eyes and right now they're watching as some kind of creature with a dangling spinal cord is currently beating the fuck out of some four headed lizards. Tell me I'm not crazy!" Her eyes are huge, jaw slack, as it swings above the ground. She looks awed, horrified and confused all at the same time.

"You're not crazy. I kind of... maybe, a little accidentally... summoned the guy from the book I was reading. And I was apparently able to do such a thing because I'm, I don't know? Lucky. Have a strong will? It's all still kinda a blur."

"Right. Blur. Erm, Addy? Your man has a tail!"

I spin back toward the door, watching Elijah in all of his dark and depraved glory.

It eerie, utterly unnatural and ominously fucking spectacular.

I catch the look in Jessaleia's devious eyes, glowing through the darkness as she steps away from Bradon and onto the other side of the portal so he's left standing by himself. Together they stand, like two frightful sentinels. There is something too smug and something too cruel about the look on the pinched and milky features of her beautifully ugly face which makes my chest itch with the wrongness of it all. My hands swell as I clench them at my sides and makes my heart beat a million miles a minute as it burns within the fires of Hell, caged within my chest.

I run toward the door, my hands slapping against the black force field. The damned begin to wail, heart-wrenching sounds that pierce the veil of the realm around us making everything blink in and out of existence like the frequencies are throwing off the molecules which make the earth. The repetition is strong enough to slowly dismantle the land by peeling it back layer by layer. The lights are flickering on and off, like the world is an old TV losing color.

"Unholy hell, fucking a clit with a vibrator!" Maria exclaims, and she becomes unsteady on her feet, swaying until she eases herself onto her ass and brings her knees to her chest to starve away the nausea.

I don't give in so easily though, vengeance burns in my eyes as I pound on the door even harder, somehow just knowing what the souls of The Accursed are trying to communicate.

They're just as grief-stricken as I am.

Torn between their master and their love.

I'm not making them choose between us, or maybe I am. Maybe it's unfair, selfish of my mundane ass to act like a little brat that fights to help instead of fighting to stay alive.

But my entire life has consisted of just existing, and never truly living.

Every day was a battle to survive just one more fucking day.

Now, my whole entire world has purpose.

It matters and I finally feel like *I* matter.

My *entire* life I've had to fight tooth and fucking nail to keep pushing on. To not let my pain consume me. Debts, betrayal, heartache, grief, sorrow.

Live it long enough, and it will soon become a depression that gains a face.

A demon which taunts you from the dark.

Don't get me wrong, humans have good days.

We can feel joy, love, and remorse. We can feel regret, burdens, and anxiety.

But we share this world with monsters and just watching the morning news is enough to leave you with a heavy heart, the sadness of what happens in this world drowning you with the knowledge.

To us, to everything around us.

It all becomes too much, year after year.

Being bullied, losing my family, dealing with a body that hates me, feeling so utterly alone.

I won't ever go back to a world where *that* is all that I know.

I fucking refuse.

You want to see power from a mortal, baby? Just fucking watch me now.

"Let me out! He needs me, Elijah needs me!" I scream, frantic.

The Accursed screech back.

Fuck me in the ass and paint me pretty because I can actually understand them.

"Don't, don't you dare. You're a part of him and I love you and much as I love them. The king of it all. So don't you dare ask me to stand back while he fights this alone. He's always been alone and you aren't even there to protect him!"

They wail again as the first tears fall freely from my welling eyes.

He has the army of my brother's, Adisen. And you have us. We vow to protect you. To be your steel in battle and the sword which pierces the skin of your enemies.

Trust us and trust him.
We'd destroy it all, sacrifice it all…
For you, Adisen. All for you.

The Accursed screech in unison. Each soul speaks to me as one, settling in the hollow depths of my cold, chilling core.

"But I'm not worth it," I quietly sob, leaning against the glass and feeling their essence kissing against my skin in comfort.

I blink open my tear-riddled eyes and stare back at Elijah. He soars high in the sky, now adorned in an armor much like my own.

I haven't paid attention to it before now. How he dressed me in an effort to save me.

I look down, noticing the thin black fabric which clings to me like scales of a dragon and has me feeling like I'm standing here naked. I run my fingers over the black scales and shiver, feeling just how hard they are under my touch. The beast, surrounded by an army of The Accursed, sketched into my chest palate and I smile softly, looking back at Elijah and noticing he's wearing the same.

The armor of a king honoring his warriors with.

He flies in a loop, circling overhead like a vulture on the prowl and he releases bolt after bolt of fire and ice. It balls in rounded globes of flames that stitch together within the palms of his hands and as soon as he throws it, a shard of ice follows in its wake. Piercing through the flames once it makes contact with the skin and begins to burn the leather-like welted flesh of the monsters he fights, then embedding the enchanted ice into their flesh straight after, finishing the job.

It's a cruel punishment. One that forces them to feel the pain of a magical fire before ending it all in the ultimate taunt.

Ending them for what I can only assume is all eternity.

Something, that I can only describe as the angel of death with tits, hovers in the baleful sky opposite Elijah, with an ill-boding, looking whip made of razors and spikes in the shapes of stars, constructed with whitened-bones that gathers into a sharp-tipped wrecking ball on the end, which swings recklessly.

I had always assumed an angel, even an angel of death would be beautiful, but I was wrong. So far from fucking wrong.

This creature looks gnarly. She's bald with a white/red leather-like skull that pulls all her features taunt like Voldemort. She hisses and screeches, flailing the whip through the night with a crack, aiming for Elijah's throat. He counters the blows, using the vines of his darkness to coil around her ankles, anchoring her in place. She thrashes and wails, issuing strike after strike which is missing him by mere inches.

He's smirking at her with a mocking look in his obsidian eyes. It's clear he is taunting her, having fun with her and finding her extremely lacking. Yet something sours in my core, a thick trepidation which claws at the back of my throat as he seems to bounce in the sky, seemingly becoming unsteady.

But he's too lost to his ignorance to notice.

The whip edges closer and closer still, until it strikes him, tearing apart his flesh in a wound so deep, it curdles and all I can see is crimson tissue.

The scream which tears from my throat is agonizing and seems to last for as long as it takes him to fall from the sky and land with a thud. Distorted in a mess of broken wings.

The vines snap from around the creature's leg, and she pulls back her wings, woven like a bat and descends on him with a cry of a crow. Just before she makes impact, the heavens ignite in a wild blue light—with thunder that roars as loudly as a lion howling for his lioness—which bellows around the abused earth. Elijah's tail licks along the ground before it rises high into the air, slicing across the throat of the creature that falls freely into a tail-spin, obliterating into an ashen dust, long forgotten before even hitting the ground at all.

She just dissipates.

Gone.

Just essence now, the gas of the wind which spirals into tiny tornadoes in Elijah's wrath.

Something's wrong though. Very wrong. He's weakened and Elijah should never be weakened.

Panic holds me in its vice and that all too familiar feeling of a panic attack rushes to the surface. My limbs become heavy, my mouth numb as my face tingles and all air leaves me in a rush. My mind distorts as does the scene around me as I begin to lose all sense of the world.

Breathe, Adisen. Breathe.

The Accursed command and it's the alien voice which feels like my kind of heaven that penetrates the darkness.

I focus my breathing, counting to ten as I draw in lungfuls of air and then I start to sing, Yeah Yeah Yeahs "Sacrilegious".

It's a trick I learned as a teenager, that when the panic attacks get bad, or even when my asthma plays up and attacks me in the dead of night, that signing helps to regulate your breathing.

So I sing, opening my eyes slowly as a deadly kind of resolve takes hold of my bones. Everything becomes eerily still as determination chases away the dread and infuses within me the refusal of discouragement.

The utter tenaciousness tastes like cherries on my tongue, sweet and savory, as I can almost feel the will in my core becoming an entity all on its own.

With sinister-filled eyes, I place my open palms onto The Accursed, pushing hard onto the glass, just as the portal shimmers and a fifteen-foot stone man walks through, the sound of the solid rock-like joints giving off a chilling creak that echoes like grinding gravel, as he lumbers toward an ashen looking Elijah.

Holding his chest, blood bleeds through his fingers like a crimson crying waterfall. He sways where he kneels, turning to look at me over his shoulder with terror and confusion in his amber eyes. I can feel him, beating within the center of my heart. He's uncertain as to what is happening and as to what kind of monstrous creature has the power to drain him, but even through it all, one emotion seeps through stronger than all else.

Desperation.

He has no idea what's about to happen but he's still begging me to stay put with the power of his eyes.

But I've never been one to listen.

Breathing deeply, I pull back and slam my hands down once more, the power of my scream adding strength to the action as it shatters the essence of The Accursed, sending them screeching back into the confinements of Elijah's chest.

He heaves in a cold breath, drawing a tiny bit of strength from the souls I just returned to him. The glass to the patio doors shatters alongside it, the shards of glass flying outward and littering the lawn as I charge into the night.

I run with everything I have toward Elijah, sucking my gut into my spine when I breathe in, drawing high onto my tippy toes while I try to avoid a thrashing from Jessaleia's powers as she chars the earth around my feet in the fire of her outrage.

But it doesn't stop me. I duck, dive and weave through her

wrath before I skid along the crimson covered grass on my knees, coming to a stop beside Elijah.

He grips me instantly, using the last of his strength to turn us until he's towering above me, caging me in with his humongous frame and deadly wings as he encloses all around my tiny body with a roar in his voice. "What are you doing, pretty girl? Do you have a death wish?" I can feel the sneer of his anger like knives against my skin, and had I not been high on the power of will alone, of utter 'I'm an unmovable fucking mountain' will of determination, the sound of his voice would have bothered me.

But right now, everything within me is alight like the burning coals of the stars that fall from the skies as comets.

I'm a comet burning within the night and as I stare back up at him, so empowered with a rush that is so wild, I can't help but steal a taste that adds to my resolve.

Our bodies crash together as our lips wage a war. The taste of him detonating like a quake in the ocean on the tip of my senses that I savor with everything that I have.

It's quick, brutal, and under the tears of crimson rain. In a way, it couldn't be more of a fucked-up kind of perfect.

Something crashes against Elijah's back, sizzling through his wings as the tanned complexion of his skin begins to glow an inky, translucent, onyx kind of black with a deep burgundy tone. He stutters and chokes, unable to communicate through wide eyes as he clutches at his chest.

I can hear the harrowing screams of The Accursed and I know instantly, through the agonizing pain in their cries - the feel of a ripple crawling through my chest - that they're being pulled from him. Savagely.

Shifting at the waist, I reposition ourselves so I'm hovering above him, arms splayed wide across his chest as I put myself in the sights of the cunt I wish I could flay.

Elijah weakly clutches at my arms in an attempt to pull me back into him.

Brandon looks horrified. Like the consequences of his actions may be too much to handle, but Jessaleia just looks fucking proud.

It's her I focus on when I set my face and settle my breathing.

It's her I focus on when I pull every ounce of strength and fortitude from my core and instil it within my iron will.

And just like the warble in the air on a heated summer's day - the one that looks like the shimmering of glass - is the very same essence that bleeds from my skin and acts like a force shield around us.

The night distorts, the lightest pearl of silver from my iron will the only thing other than the wild blue soaring overhead in the ominous sky, is the only bit of color to be seen.

"What-What are you doing?" Jessaleia hisses, face wild like a slithering snake ready to lose its shit. She looks around frantically, turning to face the stone man that is towering above us unmoving, huge head canted to the side as he studies Elijah through chiseled eyes.

It's now that I notice the runes etched into his stone skin.

The same runes weaved within the ink of Elijah's tattoos.

I narrow my eyes, steeling my features and daring this fucker to make a move.

He'd crush and crumble me like the brittle edges of a cliff, obliterating me like dust.

But I'd go down with a fight.

Not much of one, but I'd still fucking fight.

If there's one thing us humans know how to do, it's fight against all the odds stacked against us.

"Try it, stone man. This is my beast," I sneer in warning, turning my sights back to Jessaleia. "You can't have him!"

She bellows a scream of frustration, coming undone at the seams as she assaults us with the viciousness of her magic, but it just clashes against the shield before hissing away into the night.

"No! No! This can't be. Not after all this time, all this work," she charges toward the stone man, thumping her dainty fists against his unyielding back. "You're The Vessel Of Corruption. His *only* weakness. We have spent countless moons crafting you! Drain him, bleed him fucking dry and kill him!" Her screams, the shrill sound of her voice, barbing to my tender ears as I smile at her cruelly, confident in my love for this man, that I know even death itself couldn't get to him.

I can't explain why I'm this way.

Why my impulsive will is so strong, right now, that it can contort the world?

But right now, I'm grateful for it.

A face peeks at me from the shadows, hidden behind the trees which have been left untouched by Elijah's power.

First, I see Elijah himself, the British version before his features flash and change with each bolt of lightning that strikes, showing me the men from the diner, the bullies of my past, my deceased family, and even Maria, bloodied and bruised.

I choke on the air within my lungs, the dryness that burns like acid scratches against my walls and it captures a scream within my throat. Then just as fast as the daunting images appeared, they fade and I'm left swinging my head back to check on Maria as she stands in the doorway in horror. I turn back, once I know she is safe, and stare at an unhinged Jessaleia once again, knowing to never turn my back on a backstabber.

"Kill him! Kill them all!" she thunders and my patience wears thin. I just stare numbly at the royal-blue, silken gown she wears, my eyes catching on the jewels which glisten around her neck, in chunks of emerald diamonds.

All the fine clothes and expensive jewels Elijah had once given her and she had never appreciated. It leaves me with a rage unlike anything I have ever experienced before. My skin flushes, burning red as the fires of hell kiss against my skin and my humanity closes down. The images of fire rising from the ground, catching the ends of her skirt, and sending her up in flames plays a beautiful image within my mind and when a shrilling cry penetrates the fuzziness within my head, I blink back into focus and notice that she is in fact, on fucking fire.

I gasp, drawing back as she becomes consumed within the orange and yellow flames that dance like the demons of hell around her.

Elijah grunts, pulling himself onto his elbows, finally regaining some of his strength from the protection I've been able to give him. Savage eyes bore into Bradon's as he rushes to his mate's side and utters a spell which douses the flames.

"This isn't over, bitch," Jessaleia wails. Her skin is welted and blistered as it peels from her tissue, exposing bone in certain places while her flesh begins to knit back together in a gruesome display. She burrows into Bradon's loving arms, whose only focus is on her. I shudder internally, biting down on my inner cheek to keep from wincing at the sight.

Elijah growls and it moves the heavens, shaking the earth and obliterating the trees. "Oh how painfully you will die, whore. This Vessel Of Corruption, I can promise you, will not harm me the way you think it will. You not only threatened Adisen, but you used your powers against her. Run, Jessaleia. Run, because I am coming for you." Then a bomb explodes, the portal screams before more monsters escape just as the roar from Elijah devastates it all, burns the land and sends out a darkness that must travel like the plague, blanketing the world in an abyss.

Then all sound dissipates and I'm left with nothing but the feeling of The Accursed surrounding me in darkness, enveloped by the thick arms of my man holding me tightly.

Thirty-Two

Adisen

The world is on fire and the heat torments my chilling skin. I'm cold all over, despite my temperature rising at the scene left before me.

The power showdown has destroyed the terrain and left us in the dawn of the apocalypse.

Charred earth surrounds us as the dirt and rubble turn brittle in the orange hue of the flames.

I stumble forward on unsteady feet, in a state of shock as I realize how utterly fucking bad this is.

How utterly fucking devastating.

Power unlike anything I could have ever imagined has been unleashed on the world and it's all my fault.

All because I wanted what I knew I could never truly have.

The destruction, the depredation, it's all broken, left before me, leaving me unable to deny the feeling of just how fucked we are standing in the ruins.

It's finally hitting me, just how real all of this madness really is. How real Elijah and everything he stands for is.

Satan apocalypse. We're dicked-fucked real damn bad.

I've always wanted to be that character, that bad bitch in the middle of the book that finally gets her shit together and charges into a battle with a war cry which is fierce enough to send your enemies running in the other direction before we even step foot on the battlefield and for a hot minute, I convince myself I'll never get that moment.

We read to escape, to crave things that we do not have thinking that if given the chance we'd carpe diem the shit of a scenario we're determined we'd do better in. Only right now, I don't know what better is. I'm afraid. I'm afraid of the purgatory I've brought to a realm I've never loved but also never wanted to suffer.

For all the evil in this world, innocent little lights dwell here too. Tiny little souls who deserve to never know anguish and brutality.

I feel another panic attack coming on. So overwhelmed and terrified of everything spiraling around me. My mind becomes fuzzy, a thick haze clouding my judgment and pushing away all other senses and sound. My breathing becomes erratic, palms sweaty and tingly as I heave every fractured breath with a heady struggle. I spin in a circle, my eyes roaming over the burning greenery as my head aches and my heart begins to hurt.

I stop dead in my tracks when my eyes catch on Elijah before my brain catches up and I hear the snarl vibrating like the sounded embodiment of venom from his voice.

Only he looks different.

So far from my Elijah as his tanned skin bleeds into black obsidian. His taloned hands extend further into sharpened nails of wicked spikes. Rounded horns protrude from the top of his head, a second set of horns curving from his skull curve out in the opposite direction. Eyes flame in the colors of Hell as they stare viciously into space. He's breathing heavy, freezing the air around him in a cold cloud of smoke. His muscles grow muscles as the thick ink of his tattoos crack and glow like runes of vibrant orange. A mixture of the burning sun and liquid lava. The tail thrashing back and forth like a wicked whip from the bottom of his spine in a dark onyx, almost burning in an undertone of deep, deep burgundy fire.

I saw him before, but it's only now that it's all really sinking in while I pay attention.

It's that damn wolf head, I can't seem to blink my watery eyes past it.

This isn't the man merged with his beast and a few warriors of The Accursed.

This is a creature born of dread and sorrow.

Of nightmares and torment.

This is a man born of purgatory.

This isn't a merging, no it's an infusion.

They no longer share aspects of one another, instead becoming one whole being untouched.

With *one* vengeful mind.

Seeing his downward spiral is enough to make my breathing reset as it stills for a moment within the back of my throat, burning throughout my chest.

I can see the darkness that spins like a halo of evil around his head, taking away his humanity and leaving him with wicked wrath.

Maria is panting, tears streaming down her cheeks, flowing from her dark eyes as she rocks back and forth on her knees in the bloody rain, hands fisting her hair as she shakes in disbelief, staring at Elijah in terror. Gawking at him, like he's insanity in the flesh and I get it, I do.

But when the hero's spiral, who's left to save the world?

I know Elijah is a ticking time bomb. An entity powerful enough to wipe us all out in a black cloud of destruction and leave not even ruins in his wake.

I did this and now, it's my turn to fix it.

It's my turn to rise.

"Maria, stand up," I order, rushing to her side and trying my hardest to ignore the pains shooting down my neck like the shot of anguish in the form of a prickly needle.

I help her to her feet, setting her steady and pushing her wet strands out of her face. "You gotta keep it together, okay? Because I fucked up. I fucked up bad and I can't fix it and save you in the process. I need you Maria, we need each other right now." Her befuddled gaze seems to penetrate the layer of numbness as her watery eyes find mine and she nods mutely. "Elijah isn't a threat, but those people. Those creations, they don't belong in this world, Maria. I have to find a way to send them back. I have to before Elijah flips and ends it all." I'm rushing through my words, imploring her to hear my truth. Needing her to snap out of it so I can get Elijah on track, to try and keep him stable enough to fight this fight with a clear head and win.

"O-okay. I'm okay, Addy. I'm okay. But those things... those things are gone, flown into the sky, and gone. This is bad, really really bad."

"I know."

"What do we do? How do we fix it?"

"I don't know," I whisper, not thinking that far ahead.

I turn back, facing Elijah as the ground now begins to shake from his rage, from the fury which sets aflame his ebony skin and burns wild in his onyx eyes. "Elijah?" I utter cautiously, taking a wary step forward. "Elijah?" Demonic eyes fly toward mine, it's then I notice the rows of layered and razor teeth in his mouth. It cuts into his gums, having little rivulets of blood dripping from the corner of his mouth down onto his chin. He tilts his head ominously, terrifyingly, like a creature just hatched and taking in the warped and curious world before him. He's damn right frightful, but I refuse to cower from the one man, the one entity I know would never hurt me. " Elijah, you need to breathe." Firm and tender hands find his chest, as I run my fingers over his ink, soothing away the burn I know is flaming deep inside of him. "Just breathe and come back to me. *Please*, Elijah. I need you."

"Dead. Die. Dead. They have to be dead," he grits, the sound coming out like a frequency of a poltergeist that screeches and riots with the wind, mixing together like pieces of multiple realms.

"And they will be, as soon as we figure out how. But you have to calm down, calm down before you kill us all."

Aggrieved and animalistic, he sneers, blinking those black orbs before he shakes his head, dropping it back down to stare at me with a baleful and almost sorrow-filled accusation glaring back at me. Just an intoxicating blend of everything deep and dark.

"Never could I hurt something so pretty. But if I don't find them soon, I don't know if I'll be able to contain this darkness,

Adisen. It's a poison in my veins begging to be fed back to the earth," he growls, closer to his normal voice now but it's still strained.

Slowly he returns to me.

"Something happened, some creatures escaped the portal and took off into the sky. Then those cunt waffles followed when you went all Hulk-in-black on us. But dude, I'm pretty sure they're going to destroy the world," Maria chimes in, breaking through the moment as I'm still transfixed on those dark and harrowing eyes of his that have a way of drawing me in and never letting me go.

"The town," he grunts, one of his fur-razored hands tangling within my hair as he brings me closer to him, still searching my eyes like I'm his anchor in the mayhem.

"Devil say what now?" Maria and I ask in unison. Sparing a quick eye roll at one another.

"I didn't beat my fury into the world for the fun of it. I cast a spell, a shield on the town. They can't get out and nobody can get in. It saves the world, but Adisen..." He grips me tighter, pulling at my hair until my head curves back softly, a better angle to see him in as he continues, "If we don't act soon, they will destroy this town. The things that escaped? They're the spines of the furies. A damaged race of a species that punishes wrongdoers. They will punish you for anything, feeding on any sin, even something as simple as a white lie. They're vicious, insidious, hungry little bastards and right now, I'm sure they have already fed on half the town." Authoritative and commanding is his tone as that husky voice envelopes me.

He feeds me the violence and I can feel it in my core, then as a flutter in the depraved pussy that wants more of this dark dark man.

"Furies. But a rouge demented version? Right. Okay. So… what's the plan Batman with a crack like Pac-Man?" Maria mumbles, swaying on her feet like she's toying on the edge of tucking tail and running for the hills.

I look up into the sky, my heart sinking when I see the beautiful green which glistens and glows, shimmering like emerald stars that resemble the stunningly specular northern lights that I've never been able to see before.

It must be the force field.

But it's strange, because despite the emerald vibrancy, such a consuming inky, darkness encompasses it, woven like liquid marble.

Panic sizes my chest, constricts my heart, and brings on the feeling of a damn heartache when I think about Dottie.

Defenseless and alone, then I look back at Maria and remember the strange faces in the woods, when I saw her all bloody and bruised.

I can't have that happen. I can't watch the only people I have left in this world die.

"We get to the diner, we get to Dottie," I state, convinced of the plan forming in my mind. "Elijah can protect it, just like the veil over the town," he stares at me for a moment in curiosity and intrigue before he nods firmly, agreeing. I turn to Maria, taking her hand in mine. "You'll stay with her, drag anyone fleeing on the streets into the diner. Stay there, do not leave. It will keep you all safe."

"What about you?"

"I'll be with Elijah. I did this. I have a funny feeling I'm the only one who can undo it."

"Its-"

"No, no more. You don't understand this anymore than I do,

Elijah. All we know is that I conjured you. How the fuck that portal opened I don't know, but what if I'm the only one who can put it back? Put it all back? We have to stay together."

Fury ignites in his black eyes and he grits his teeth, the hammering of his jaw prominent and even more wild with how square his jaw is at the moment.

Pulling Maria into me, I burrow myself close into Elijah's creature-form's arms.

We've wasted enough time as it is, we need to get to the diner, to Dottie and just pray we aren't too late.

Thirty-Three

Elijah

She calms me within an instant, a balm to my tortured soul and her worry that I'd kill them without knowing, a knife to my throat. No matter how wild I'd become, it will always be the scent of her which envelops me that keeps me sane.

She burrows into my chest, as Maria huddles into her and I narrow my eyes, "You never told me you had a sister."

"She's my best friend. My only friend. So technically, she's my sister," she mumbles, shrugging a slim shoulder.

"You didn't tell, talk-dark and handsome about me? I'm offended," Maria huffs, an annoyed lilt to her indifferent tone. "Hey, you got a brother?" she asks, eyes widening when she realizes what she's said. "Erm, never mind. Addy gave me the rundown."

"No I didn't tell him about you, I didn't tell him much about anything because it's been a whirlwind of magic, dick, mayhem, and mermaids. I never thought any of this was real. That It couldn't be. Yet here we stand in my backyard that's burned to a crisp as will be the rest of the town if we don't get a damn move on." She pulls back, looking up at me with so much emotion in her pensive gaze. "Dottie's out there."

She doesn't need to say anything else before I teleport us in front of the diner. I don't bother hiding my form or morphing into an alley. The world is already plagued with darkness, ominous screeching plays a tune of music overhead. Everyone in this town is already dead,

My mate is right, we're running out of time to save the cesspool of humans, she claims that have the right to be saved.

This part of the town is derelict, thunderous clouds rioting overhead as a storm screams its grievance in the distance, growing closer by the shrill sound of the wind.

"It looks like a ghost town," Maria mumbles, her knuckle-grip hold on Adisen turning white. I place my hand on her back, taking away some of the pain I know she will be feeling right about now from the stress.

Some of the street stores have been shattered, bodies litter the way hidden by the debris which I don't think either of the girls have noticed at the moment, too distracted in getting into the diner.

Cars are upturned, and woodwork splinters along the ground.

The door swings open when Adisen rushes inside, the bell above us dinging just as a strike of lightning hits against the land.

Walking inside, two men sit at a booth closest to the door and smirk when they see Adisen. As she rushes inside, they place their arms out wide, tightening their hold on the booth, fingers turning white as they bite into the fabric of the seats and block her in.

"Just what the doctor ordered. *Man* are we glad to see you. We were fancying something sweet, but now that I think about it? *Nah*, honey. I don't think that it's you we want," the dirty blond one says, recognition sparks in her startled eyes as she glares at the greasy dude opposite him.

"I bet she tastes divine," the other guy chimes in. Leaning forward as he licks his lips, like he is about to taste the sweetness he refers to, makes me see red. How the fuck has he not noticed his surroundings?

The muscle in his arms twitches like he intends to touch her. "I'd be real careful and remember what happened the last time you laid your filthy hands on me. I see your face is still a little blistered. You should really put some cream on that." Then she spins, refusing to give them an inch as she walks forward and breaks his arm from the booth. It slumps down with easy slack but he's swift with the movement as he brings it back up to slap the rounded globes of her ass. The flat of his palm bounces off her, as I send something wicked and electrifying, spiraling around her to cause a push back of pressure against her lower spine making her yelp.

The man cries out, flying back in his seat as he cradles his arm, the flesh boiling from the center of his hand. But instead of being red, the edges are smudged a dark gray and a zigzag shoots through the middle like a lightning bolt. Frantic eyes widen in accusation as they stare back at her, but before she has the chance to process any of what just happened, or to realize that the wind wrapped around her was very much an electric shield, I'm there.

A large and daunting shadow, that falls over them.

Now the nightmare registers and the customers scream, scattering further back into the diner. I lift the blond with an unforgiving grip around his throat before shoving him back into the wall. "W-what are you?" he cries, frantic.

"Your end," is the growl he hears before I punch through his chest and pull out his heart. "Never touch what is mine." I allow it to hit the ground with a wet thud as I turn back to a wide-eyed Adisen. The other guy rushes to his feet and bolts out of the door before the others in the diner begin to cry and huddle together. Screams of fear are piercing through the air, which is cut short as the window crashes, caving in as a spinal fury soars above us, only to go flying through the diner when something rams into it from the side.

"Dottie! Dottie!" Adisen bellows, stopping when something crunches underfoot. She looks down, seeing the obliterated glass amassed together by some tossed over tables, halting her in her tracks.

"Now hear here, creature of all Hell. I ain't ready for you to take my sinner's soul just yet. Now get," Dottie's withered voice hisses, and the sound of something smacking against something wet echoes through the night.

Adisen shrieks, rushing forward, deeper into the darkness of the building until she nears the counter.

The spinal fury screeches, flailing as it tries to bat those brittle, broken wings, and flap into the air, it makes it a few feet from the ground from behind the counter before a wrinkled and leathery old hand reaches out and snatches it by its spinal cord, smacking it against the countertop like a mallet beating against meat.

Pound, pound, pound.

The ol' girl got some bones of bravery in her frail body, I'll give her that, but one swipe from the claws of this creature and she'll be paralyzed while they feed from her flesh.

Huge wings unfurl, smacking Dottie in the face and sending her flying backward, twisting with a raised claw ready to strike.

"Dot!" Adisen screams, before squaring her shoulders and taking on that look of unwavering determination. But she isn't strong enough, quick enough or trained enough to act right away. So I step to her side, taking her hand in mine as I throw a curve ball into the air, sending it sailing across the room before my firebomb embeds into the center of the shoulder blades of the wailing creature as it begins to bleed like trickles of orange ash, burning like hot coals as it feathers across its chest, consuming it from the inside out and making it swell with the need to explode. It looks like a black volcano cracked with lava.

Dotty wobbles back to her feet, bat in hand as she takes a swing and sends the spinal fury into an explosion of guts and gore.

"And stay gone," she pouts, picking off the spine draped across her shoulder and tossing it across the room. The sound of it cracks through the air.

"Fuck me with a cheeseburger, she's insane," Maria breathes, eyes wide.

"Nonsense, girl, need to be tough in these parts. Or the assholes will eat you alive."

"That wasn't a greasy old trucker, Dottie. You know that, right?" Adisen asks her warily, rushing to her side as she pulls the ol' broad into a tight, relief-filled hug.

"And that ain't no normal looking pretty boy. Didn't have you pegged for a bestiality type of girl," she deadpans, staring at me with curious eyes before breaking out into uncomfortable laughter filled with disbelief. "Must have lost it in my old age."

"Erm. Dot? We kinda have the end of the town as we know it type of situation going on and I don't have the time to explain it all over again. You okay?" Adisen asks, pulling back to level Dottie in the eye.

"I'm old, child. Live long enough, you'll convince yourself you'll live for the apocalypse. It may just take a hot minute to be able to say I've made it. You also live long enough, see enough new creations and new age technology that nothing ends up surprising you. That's a fact. Hell on earth is nothing out of the norm for an old girl like me." She waves her hand in their air, but I notice she's trembling. "Besides, I was young once too. You aren't the only one who got lost in books and dreamed of a better life. Dreamed of the beast jumping from the pages and savaging your sinner's soul raw."

Adisen cackles, starstruck, staring at Dottie like they have only just met as she shakes her head.

Sadness etches itself into the corner of Dottie's wrinkled and withered old eyes, and it unsettles something within me.

Has she loved and lost? Has she experienced something like Adisen and me?

Was she robbed of the chance? So many unfamiliar thoughts run through my mind but are overshadowed with the power inside of me, boiling over.

The lights flicker overhead, causing Maria to gasp and rush backward into a table making her cuss when the edges bite into her flesh. "Now, any plan on fixing it?"

I share a look with Adisen who shrugs. "Follow the scent of evil, I guess?" she utters, as we both turn back toward the street noticing how the spinal furies screech and soar, coiled within the night sky feasting. Yet, all seem to be traveling in the same direction.

"Following the yellow-brick-road takes your ass back to Kansas. Where does following the blood-brick-road take you?"

"Into the bowels of hell."

Thirty-Four

Adisen

"What did I do?" I whisper meekly as we walk through the town painted black, completely desolate, and burnt to a crisp. My heart clenches as I scan the area, bringing a shaky hand to my quivering lips. There's nothing left.

Houses stand without roofs, bodies scatter the ground and butchered corpses hang from ridges and broken pieces of various building structures. "I did this. I created the damn plague. No, I started the fucking apocalypse." Tears well in my eyes, as sorrow is the only thing able to make my heart ache. The tears fall numbly down my cheeks as I blink them away in a state of shock. Elijah casted a protection spell on the diner, now we walk the streets on the tail of evil.

"Sure did, darling. Now be a good little witch and help clean up your damn mess," Elijah growls and I gasp, straightening my shoulders as I stop dead in my tracks at the roughness of his voice. When we left the diner, he seemed more tense. More angry. I almost had a heart attack watching him rip the heart out of that man. It was a shock. A dark contrast to the swoon-worthy man I was falling in love with. But I didn't lie when I said I fell in love with the monster too, and I didn't lie when I said I knew his power would be too much for this world.

It's evident now.

The man. Beast. Fictional character or however the fuck you want to refer to him - who could literally obliterate me with a gruff grunt and cocky tilt of his head - clenches his jaw and bores a hole into the ground as tension rides him hard.

"What? Do you think I wanted this? That I wanted to pluck hungry little bastards that need a good spa day from the pages of a book and plop them smack dab in the center of humanity? Who couldn't even defend themselves in a human war let alone one forged with magical monsters?" I demand. Finding my voice, refusing to cave into my fears. My eyes ignite in fury as I take a step closer.

His eyes drop, roaming over my body with the hike of one of his thick brows. "No? Then what did you want?" he rasps, hands landing on my hips as those sharp talons pierce the tender flesh of my skin.

"I wanted you!" I scream, then huff before groaning and going slack in his hold, sighing in defeat. "I wanted you, I only wanted you." A soft smile plays on my lips as I remember how I felt the first time I ever read about Elijah. This man terrifies me and it has nothing to do with the fact he could kill me and everything to do with the fact he is everything I could ever wish for.

Literally.

Feelings are more often like the plague than we like to admit. A disease that riddles our body and curdles our bones, then leaves us aching with the emotions we never asked to experience in the first place.

I never asked for these desires.

I also can't imagine living without them either.

Elijah visibly relaxes, his ebony and burgundy skin blending with the shadows as he towers over me in his beast form. His four horns glisten within the moonlight and make me notice the divots and ridges for the first time.

Everything about this man is frightfully glorious.

"I'm sorry, love, I never meant to be an arse. I just - I don't want anything to happen to you. I know you're safer at my side and the only way we can fix all of this is with your will. I just - I hate it, okay? I hate not being the scariest thing in the world." He bends down, placing a kiss on my awaiting lips.

"Not being scary. Elijah. Is impossible. You're kissing me with the head of a damn wolf." I chuckle, pulling back and watch as he changes back into the man.

"Sorry, love, I forget myself."

"I think we're close, Elijah. I can feel the power in the air as it licks against my skin. I think they are going toward the town hall." We continue on our way, until I'm pretty certain that is where everything ends.

Elijah teleports us, and we end up standing in the shadows outside of the town hall, watching darkness unfold within the wicked deeps of ominous magic.

It's a hard thing to think about death. Maybe it's because there is something in our brain that blocks the magnitude of it.

When I think of suffering or unexpected deaths, it doesn't penetrate. I can't fathom the end. I can't imagine my last days where I take my final breath.

Maybe it's what's making me brave now, what's cementing my determination to stand at Elijah's side and correct my wrongs.

I know I can die, I just can't imagine it and if I can't imagine it, I can't fear it.

"I'll be fine. We'll protect each other, okay? I know humanity is flawed, but not everyone in this town is vile. There are innocent people here. I can't let them all die, Elijah," I tell him, clutching his hand tight as I can feel the worry pulling in his core.

"Such a pretty warrior, love," he muses, rough hands caressing my cheek. "But if I see a drop of crimson bleed from this pretty flesh, I'll destroy this town and everyone in it, understand?" Devotion. Conviction. Not an ounce of wavering uncertainty.

I gulp, nodding as we move deeper into the shadows and up the steps of the town hall, and we were right.

Bloodied roads do lead into the bowels of hell.

The closer we get, the more the air around us changes into something dark but almost sensual. A chill runs down my spine, making me quiver where we stand in the shadows. It's a messy contradiction. Something dark and ominous with something that promises deep pleasure with hefty pain.

It lures me in and has my mind going hazy as my panties grow wet with desire. Something carnal wakes within me and I struggle to fight the urge to claw at Elijah's flesh in desperation with the need to feel him. To have him consume me, rutting against me and making me bleed all over again.

I love bleeding for him, the crimson is my ink on the contract that signed over my soul and the impulse to claim him in the same carnal and brutalizing way is too much to deny. I bite down on my inner cheek, rubbing my thighs together and clenching my hands at my side as the sensation becomes maddening.

Elijah growls and when I turn to face him, I find him sniffing the air, face wild in fury as it contorts to a distasteful kind of rage he utters, "*Lustriel*." A name that has no meaning to me, while my skin begins to burn with desire. "Adisen, he is the demon that feeds from lust and pain. He will drive you so wild with desire, you will claw away your own skin just to reach the core base of that wanton need that is setting alight the very cells of your skin." His black skin tinges red with his rage and I fight through the struggle in my mind.

Pulling me into him, he kisses me deeply, feeding me his power to fight the pull or face tragic desire. "Holy fucking shit I want to ride you until my vagina breaks," I wheeze when my mind begins to clear, my hands roaming all over his seductive skin as the smoothness taunts me. I trace the scar around his eye and lean forward to lick it, running my tongue up the side of his face making him snarl like a beast.

"Later love, you're killing me," he growls against my lips, making me shiver with the vibrations.

A body falls from the sky, unburdened with his flesh as the rack of bones falls at my feet and I scream, the sound echoing through the night and making the furies cackle harrowing laugher, that mocks me.

Rage burns into fury and fury burns into a wrath that has my mind in full control of what it wants to do. I stare at three of the creatures right above me, taunting me as my face becomes a stone-cold mask and all of my energy is pushed into my will making their heads grow in size. Bigger and bigger they grow like a balloon with a little too much helium before they go *bang*, splattering the gunky musk-like black slime - which I assume was their rendition of a brain - into the sky. Their wicked wings and spinal cords fall in a heap on the ground beside us.

"You're sexy when you're mad," Elijah growls, before those huge wings of his carry him into the sky. He circles overhead, laughing like a maniac as he soars through the sky like a phoenix rising from the ashes. Huge wings, wider than life, with a tail as wicked as a whip. The sky which was already an abyss becomes an endless chasm of absolutely nothing. His shadows steal everything from sight and I fall to the ground, cowering as I bring my knees into my chest and try to make myself as small as possible on instinct.

I can't see anything, so I'm only left with the traumatizing sounds of slaughter.

Something that sounds wet and sloppy smacks together and I have a gut-wrenching fear that is flesh. I can hear it as bones hit the ground, organs following from their hollow chests.

Their wails are horrendous, a sound of terrifying torture and before I know what's happening next, huge arms are wrapping around me and bringing me to my feet.

"Step one of the plan is complete, love. All those beasts are dead," he sneers with pleasure but I'm too afraid to open my eyes. My darkness is a comfort but being trapped within a realm of black is utterly terrifying as well. "Open your eyes, pretty girl," he whispers as soft lips find the top of my head.

"All of them? You killed all of them?" I ask, trembling in his hold.

"All of them. Every last one of them."

Pulling back, his shadows treat slowly wrapping around the both of us like a warm embrace. Creature after creature scattered around us, left in heaps of stomach-churning carnage. I bring my hands to my mouth, hoping to hold at bay any sickness that may try to escape. Heaving heavy breathes, I try desperately not to focus on the strange mutilation in front of me.

"This demon, Loreile?" I try to remember the name, but Elijah corrects me.

"Lustriel."

"Right, this Lustriel, will he be as easy?" I ask hopefully, looking back to lose myself in his otherworldly eyes, needing a break from the sick reality which is all my fault.

"Of course." He pulls me into him, tilting my head back so he can get a better angle to study me. "You need to prepare for what you're about to see in there. It will change you forever and I wish more than anything that I could protect you from that, but I can't. This is what you dreamed about baby, this is your story. I'm starting to think this is all about you. Your desire, your will. You wanted to be the warrior? You wanted to destroy the bad guys? Do it. There are no laws in a lawless realm and right now, I own this town."

Thirty-Five

Adisen

This Moment's "Oh Lord" filters through the speakers spreading throughout the halls. My body seems to heat from the tempo and the closer that we get, the more I burn.

We enter a grand hall and I'm confused when I'm confronted with bloody ball gowns and torn tuxedos. It's eerie and grotesquely beautiful the way their silken flesh writhes against one another. A fluttering of billowing skirts and mesmerizing dresses whiz past us as they dance to the tune of death. Like puppets dancing under the moon of demise, they twist and twirl with fluidity leaving me horrified. Ankle deep blood sloshes along the ground and as soon as I step foot over the threshold, my feet are consumed by the bloody waters. I gasp, dread and heart-seizing horror making it hard to breathe at all.

Welcome to the ball of the dead, Adisen, babe. We've been waiting for you.

The same voice from my dreamscape whispers into my mind, eliciting a foreboding chill to skate across my skin, making me shudder. Elijah grips me tighter as he scans the room with vicious, animalistic eyes. Our two worlds are merging in a way I don't know how to handle. The depravity is one with the darkness I've always seeked yet being confronted with it leaves trepidation in my heart.

I don't think my world can survive a fantasy like this.

The couples on the dance floor paw at one another, gentle at first, and then the nails come out as they begin to shred one another's flesh, drinking the blood of their lovers from open arteries in their necks. Pretty gowns become saturated in liquid crimson and if I didn't think that was horrific enough, they begin to ravage one another sexually. Women snarl like beasts as they bite off the penises of their partners and begin to pleasure themselves with the appendage viciously as the men continue clawing and kissing at their woman's tender flesh. They dance and bend, contorting in ways I never thought the human body capable of moving. It looks painful, it looks hideous and malformed and yet every single person has a demented smile of adrenaline and passion lighting up their sinister faces.

"Oh God." I gag, hand covering my mouth to keep the bile at bay, but it doesn't help.

"I know I lived it, I just can't believe you fantasized about it," Elijah whispers at my side as I turn watery eyes on him.

He's right to some extent. The darker the book, the more in love I fell with it.

I guess it was because the darker it was between the pages, the more gray the skies above me seemed. Like the horrors of our world just aren't as bad and on the day they begin to toe the line, we would have men like Elijah to make it all okay again.

"Please, we can't leave them like this. We have to save them. I never wanted this, I never wanted innocents to suffer. I just - I just wanted an escape!"

Rob Zombie's " Pussy Liquor" begins to play, and the frenzied couples become even more infused to reach what they desperately crave.

"I just wanted an escape." I sob, as Elijah wipes away the tears which fall. They drop like rain pelts onto his long talons, making them shimmer a midnight blue as he becomes the creature once again. It's a reminder, a realization that has the tears drying as quickly as they fall. A realization that this goes beyond the ugly. There is such beauty here too. Beauty that shouldn't exist as I stare back at this magnificent man.

Back at my mate.

"I'm sorry that your fantasies have been ruined. That all of your dreams have been crushed," he whispers again, and I can hear the torment in his voice as it itches against my senses as he places his lips against mine softly as he murmurs, "I'll make it beautiful again. I promise, pretty girl."

Magic is what I dreamed about. The strength of a thousand warriors to send me striving for victory. A man who would destroy it all for me and a monstrous torment to test our devotion.

That's what life is all about, isn't it?

Trials after trials. Days upon days of testing our worth.

That's all this is, another day fighting to survive, only this time, our troubles are standing before us in the shape of demons.

Real entities we can fight and defeat so we no longer feel like we're only fighting ourselves. That's why we, as readers, crave the darkness because in every foe we fight, a depression without our hearts is crushed and one of our worries withers.

This demon, these creatures, they're all just the faces of our torment and we are just handed the metaphorical mallet to beat them off. It doesn't make us wrong or sick.

Dark and depraved.

It means there is a wickedness in our hearts that is trained for those who deserve it.

We know where our wrath belongs and it's never misplaced.

So now? Now I'm going to stop hating myself for craving something so dark and daunting.

Now, I'm going to become the damsel who grows a set of teeth and sets it all on fire.

Every worry I've ever had, every burden, will go up in flames within my story.

I just have to be brave enough to light the match.

"Elijah," I sneer, trying to calm my breathing.

"Yes, love."

"Fucking skin him alive. I think it's only fair, don't you?"

"An eye for an eye makes the whole world blind, pretty girl." He smirks, not at all repulsed. I can see the eagerness burning within his obsidian, two-toned blue eyes.

"Maybe they'll see better in the dark." I smirk in return.

"Wise. Always so wise." He smiles, tucking a loose strand of hair behind my ear. "Stay hidden, no matter what, do not come out." He kisses me again before weaving his way through the crowd. His large wings coiled around him to keep the sweaty flesh of the writhing bodies away from him.

Keeping to the shadows I stalk around the room, getting

deeper into the thickness of it as I try to search out the demon behind this. The demon who thrives on anguish and bloodthirsty sex.

A couple spin and twirl, laughing like maniacs as they bleed into a wine glass and lock arms, clicking them together before knocking them back, then once again throwing themselves at one another.

Then like a blood ocean, the sea parts and the bodies all drop to the floor one by one. I shriek, jumping back to avoid any landing on my feet before bending down and checking the pulse of the woman beside me. It takes me a moment to convince my brain to touch the gory sight of the mutilated body as her nipple lays half off, peeled back and exposing the ribbed tissue of her breast underneath. I gag again, choking on vomit before I sigh in relief when I realize that she's alive, just unconscious. Elijah must have knocked them all out. I flick her bitten off nipple with the tips of my fingers so it files back into place and makes her look seemingly normal again.

I heave a breath and turn up my nose, shuddering as the creeps skate down my spine.

"No!" Something vile slithers over my flesh like the coiling of a snake as the sound of that voice assaults everything inside of me as it booms around the hall. "My babies! My bodies! Dance, dance, and fuck wildly for me, my darlings! Get up!" he shouts with a musical lilt to his tone, and my mind suddenly thinks of the movie *Labyrinth*. "What happened? Who did this?" he sneers, and when the dark edges of the room retreat, I notice he is in the middle of the hall, sitting on a throne higher than six-feet tall, towering above the rest of us. I wonder how we didn't notice it before. Especially when I see what it's made of.

The throne is made from body parts, actual body parts, but

they are metallic and look almost tin-like, silver and shiny as they sparkle under the low lighting.

Elijah shows himself, smirking at the creature before him. It's a man with purple skin. It illuminates and shines like a hidden gem beneath the sea as his eyes flame a wild blue, glowing from within his skull. It's like a siren's call, the one thing you become transfixed on before noticing you're staring at the face of death. But two orbs for eyes is the only thing he has. The rest of his face is featureless and when he speaks, it booms without a source. He glows and pulsates with the lust and agony exuding through the room but the longer everyone remains unconscious the more the skin begins to lose its glow.

I rub my jaw, smoothing away the aches from Jessaleia before tracing the mating mark on my neck, needing it for reassurance that all of this is nothing compared to Elijah, his beast and the horde.

"E-Elijah? King Elijah?" he stammers, lifting from his seat before floating to the ground and taking a knee before his master. "I-I had no idea you were in this strange land. The-they never told me!" he pleads, frantic with horror even more potent than my own bleeding through.

He places his hands out before him, in a calming gesture as he tries to halt Elijah but it doesn't stop him, instead he walks right up to him and places a hand on his forehead. It glows black and the darkness of Elijah's skin begins to shimmer.

"Welcome to the brotherhood, creature. There's less pussy but much more power. Do not disappoint me." Then he absorbs him, taking his essence and banishing it to purgatory to become another Accursed.

"Adisen." He beckons, and something about him changes. I can see the power as it filters through him and his entire aura turns darker, more sinister. Those dark eyes find me and like an unbreakable lure, I stumble over to him. He catches me with those demonic hands and I shiver with the need to feel more of them.

"Everyone who is alive, will remain alive. I'll heal them and make them forget. I'll make *you* forget." His voice is multilayered and sinful.

A shrill cackle echoes around the great hall bouncing off the walls as it encloses in around us.

It's a taunting sound that has my hair on the back of my neck standing on edge. I spin in a frantic circle, looking for the source of the sound but every time I focus on one dark corner from where the sound originated from, it echoes again from the other side of the room. I can feel Jessaleia's oily essence slick against my flesh as it drapes all over me.

I shudder, rubbing at my arms wanting any trace of her gone from my body. Another dark laugh booms with the first and the two-tones of contrasting sounds thunders around me louder than a hurricane.

Elijah growls and my mind begins to swim from all the otherworldly sounds. My eyes blur and I stumble, feeling like I'm drunk. I'm moments away from face planting when a dark fog begins to separate me from him.

The wind is displaced behind me and I shudder, drawing in a deep breath ready to scream when familiar hands land on my hips. "Careful now, love. Wouldn't want to alert them to our presence," The British Elijah coos in my ear, pulling me back into him. "You know how to fix this, Adisen, you just aren't listening to yourself. If they're attached to your will and your will is here with you, how do you think you need to close the portal?"

Only one thing occurs to me and after seeing how dark this world is outside of the pages, I'm convinced now it will be a resort that I won't survive tossed into the very dark depths of it. The wind once again whispers against my neck and I know that he's gone.

Darkness falls like a veil once again and this time I don't think it's from Elijah. I try to find my footing and trip, falling over a mutilated corpse mangled and slick with blood at my feet. My hands slide along the hardwood floors as my face smacks against flesh. I yelp, scurrying, desperate to find my footing but instead falling flat back against the bloodied ground. Closing my eyes, I make the darkness my own, heaving in a deep breath I hold it and center myself.

I won't let this bitch scare me and I sure as all heck won't let her intimidate me.

Digital Daggers' "Razor's Edge" whispers against my skin as the lyrics drown out the vicious taunts from the menacing shadows. I can feel The Accursed as they kiss against me and I find comfort in their presence. The entire hall erupts into horrendous cries of chaos and anguish.

"Elijah!" I scream, as something pulls at my ankle and drags me along the ground. I kick back at the shadows, screaming through the screeching that pierces my ear drums and electrifies my brain.

"Get off me!" the bellow tears from my throat in a frantic cry. "Stop! Get off! Don't touch me!" Something razor sharp slices into my ankle, I can feel the slickness of my blood as it drains out onto the floor beneath me.

The same darkness comes back to say hello, only this time it doesn't offer me its numbness, instead, it leaves me hyper-aware of the brutal assault which tears open my skin and leaves me with gushing wounds that sting like a motherfucker. I sneer, gritting my teeth at the unexpected feeling that comes with each unseeing attack. The Accursed screech around me and I can vaguely make out their demonic faces fighting off whatever it is that is thriving for my blood. Crawling on my hands and knees, I push away the limbs obstructing my path and try my hardest to find any sense of security. My hands seek the structure of a wall and instead become enveloped in someone's vicious hold. Nails dig into my wrist and I gasp as the wicked talons push against my veins.

"Elijah!" I bellow, but all I can hear in return is grunting and a battle fit for the ruthless.

Realization dawns and I gasp, choking on the cold air that scratches against the back of my throat. I thrash wildly, pulling and twisting to dislodge their hold on me but it only results in me lying on my back, being dragged along the ground like I'm nothing but a ragdoll. "Get the fuck off of me!" I scream in vain. I close my eyes and decide to give myself to the pain. Because nothing these creatures can do to me would hurt more than what losing Elijah would do to me.

There's only one reason Elijah would be unable to answer me.

One reason that horrifies me.

The Vessel Of Corruption.

"No," I whisper. "No, no, no." Throwing my head back, I arch into their hold. My chest is drawn toward the ceiling, opening wide as I draw air into my suffering lungs. I let it all go, like a pool of darkness I allow the beads of obsidian water to wash over me like a cold shower and project my will into a scream which detonates likes a bomb. I can feel the strength rushing through me like a tsunami, towering with the wave of destruction. Digging deeper inside of myself, the claws which hold me embed further as I yank my arms free from their grip, not caring if it shreds my veins in the process. The Accursed wail, fighting off the essence but they're too late.

I give my grief to the void and let it all go. "I. Said. Stop!" The words explode from my throat like a grenade. The foundation of the building quakes under my wrath as the dark entities clawing at my flesh explode, combusting like clouds of onyx dust which shimmers in a ruby red and I have a feeling whatever it was that was attacking me belongs solely to Jessaleia. The force of the explosion sends me flying through the air. I sail like a bird gliding with the wind and somehow end up outside the building which is crumbling before me.

I look up, finally able to see the destruction in front of me and my heart sinks. Lumbering to my feet on unsteady legs I stumble forward.

Large arms wrap around me, pulling me back into a hard chest, halting my efforts to get back inside the town hall. "Get the fuck off!" I sneer, writhing in his grip as I wiggle my shoulders in an effort to get loose.

"Don't do this, Adisen. Don't go back in there. Not when you know how to fix this," the British Elijah utters in my ear, desperately. The rough timber of his tone sends a shudder down my spine.

He's unwelcome.

Not my Elijah.

Not my mate.

I stamp on his foot and he grunts, letting me go with a savage sneer as I fall once again to my knees. It takes everything within me to fight against my pain and bleeding wounds to get back to my feet and run toward the town hall. Running up the steps, I throw myself backward when a demonic shadow bleeds from the gray cloud of chaos that is billowing within the crumbling structure. I stalk backward slowly, not wanting to make any sudden moves as I stare down the face of wild danger.

A creature with the body of a man, the head of a skull with fiery red eyes and the pointed tongue of a lizard, crawls toward me with webbed hands embedding into the earth like a hiker stabbing into the side of a cliff. The earth cracks and the sound is deafening.

Wired teeth smile at me as the creature hisses, his skull peeling off from the side of his head into skinned spikes like a posturing peacock. With a long tail, thick like a dragon, and heavier than stone sends my heart bottoming out and somersaulting away from me.

Scurrying backward, I focus on the need to not want to trip. The creature stalks me slowly, a twisted gleam in the hell-fire eyes that tells me I'm his prey and he's the predator salivating to pounce.

Staring beyond the creature, into the yawning-mouth of darkness, my chest aches as I shake my head in denial. I don't want to leave Elijah, but there's no other way. There is only one way I can think of to save him, a failsafe which will send everything back to whence it came before the unthinkable happens and the possibilities it could arise drowns me in terrorizing anguish.

"Adisen, quick love. We're running out of time," my conscious calls, and I flick my eyes toward the British Elijah, my breathing heavy as I weigh out my options. He holds out his hand, beckoning me with desperation in his emotion-soaked eyes.

I notice the creature twitch and I scream, darting away from it and running with everything I have left inside of me when it pounces from the shadows and lashes out at me with his forked tongue, as his hiss splinters on the wind and follows me on my path.

I throw myself from the fourth step of the town hall and straight into the fake Elijah's arms as he envelops me and the world once again goes black.

Black used to be my favorite color.

So was red.

Now I'd give anything for a wash of midnight blue to lighten up my dark abyss.

Thirty-Six

Adisen

The familiar scent of my home drifts under my nose when my feet once again find the ground. I push away from Elijah, wiping the blood away from my mouth with the back of my hand and glaring at him with the daggers of death.

"Don't look at me like that, witch. You know there was no other option."

I narrow my eyes at him, looking him up and down in assessment. "Do I? Do *you*?"

"Adisen..."

"Don't Adisen me, we're running out of time," I grouse, turning and running back through the yard and into my house. I search for the book, *Elijah's* book and head back out into the clearing.

My conscious is still there, standing by the portal. Turning, he looks at me with emotion in his eyes. "Adisen, in our world… Mates aren't born. They're created. What determines a true mate is the soul they carry. It's the strength they exude and the fortitude they build themselves armor with. A soul like Elijah's, it didn't exist in his world and a soul like yours didn't exist here either. The unthinkable happened and you pulled that soul, the one that recognised yours from the page in a book, which you didn't find by chance," he tells me, taking a step forward as I stumble backward, watching him through mere slits of pure accusation.

I don't need the internal dialogue right now.

"You found one another through all the odds. He has been your king and now you have to be his queen. You have to save him, Adisen. You have to send everything back from whence it came. Don't worry about what will happen when you get there. The two of you will always find one another."

The portal is pulsating now, the thundering charge sounding louder and more harrowing as it nears. Darkness snakes along the ground like tendrils of smoke and I flick open the book hurriedly, praying this is the right thing to do. The smoke coils around my ankles and I sigh in relief when the familiarity sinks into my bones. Elijah is okay. He's safe and he's near, searching for me.

Something crashes into my back and I'm sent sailing through the air. My bones grind and churn but, thankfully, I don't think anything is broken. I cry out, rolling to my back to see Jessaleia standing tall above me. Coated in blood and looking crueller and more demented than Cruella herself.

The Accursed soar through the sky, rushing around her in a

torrent so wicked it knocks her off her feet. The demonic faces circling in the wind, stare back at me, knowingly.

I weakly climb back to my knees, crawling forward until I'm once again holding Elijah's world in my hands.

"Adisen!" my Elijah roars, and I snap my head up. Seeing him charging toward me but he gets lifted off his feet by Bradon who sends a torrent of flames licking against his tanned skin and he suddenly looks like a phoenix burning within the darkened sky.

"Elijah!" I bellow, the sound grievous as it tears open my chest.

I fall back to my knees, sitting on my legs as the dark outfit Elijah had conjured for me is stained in ruins of crimson.

A dark and chilling calmness overtakes me as I allow the numbness to creep back in.

I'd never give up on myself to save my soul.

I once thought I could be selfish, but love isn't selfish.

It's selfless.

I'd sacrifice it all for him. I'd burn the world and become a captor of its torment if it meant that Elijah was safe.

"Adisen!" he roars once again, sending a wave of power through the clearing and knocking every whore, creature, and entity on its ass as he rises from the ashes and grips his brother by the throat, lifting him from the ground, talons drawing blood that drips from his neck and bleeds back into the earth.

I have no idea what will happen once I close that portal, but I know that the love I have for Elijah Braxton will surpass the ages and survive the different dimensions of the world.

It has too. I'll carry it with me always.

So I grip the book, flipping it open to the part before the first blank page and close my eyes. Allowing the ink to rise from the chapter and circle me like a storm, wrapping me in its embrace and sucking my essence into the pages of the book. His book. His world.

I open my eyes, peering through the tendrils of darkness and catch the wild look on his face as he stares back at me, animalistic and raw.

I smile, feeling it too, burning in my core as the fears fall like silken tears from my eyes. Glancing down, I notice my blood is dripping onto the rose bed I had planted around the perimeter of my property. The white petals turning crimson as the song from Everybody Loves An Outlaw "Blood On A Rose" Comes to mind.

My will must manifest because it begins to dance on the wind, the lyrics playing around us and wrapping me in warm comfort. I close my eyes as I get pulled into another world.

My heart stops when I see the shadows from the Vessel Of Corruption sneaking up behind Elijah.

I love you falls from my lips as darkness descends for the final time and I hope more than anything that on the other side, he'll be safe.

I swirl with the ink as I'm left not knowing if I'll survive the portal, or if I'll ever find any way home again if I do.

Thirty-Seven

Adisen

Is it gallant to sacrifice yourself to the evil when you know the evil will be the thing to destroy you?

I'm debating that now. As I swirl into oblivion with sinister creatures chasing my heels.

I knew that the only way to save Elijah and the town was to throw myself into the book. I didn't have time to learn my will and everything that would come with controlling it. I had no other option. I was terrified back in that town hall and not because of what I saw, but because of what I felt. An entire chasm between me and the one I love, and I was helpless to do anything about it.

To help him, to fight against the darkness and to be the one to make sure he was safe.

Instead, I did the only thing that I could and I allowed his world to consume me.

I gave myself to the void, a sacrificial lamb to the slaughter.

Something twists in my core when I'm spit out of the void and I tumble toward the harsh ground. Debris, rocks, and twigs cutting into my already savaged skin as I tuck and roll, coming to a halt when my back smacks against a giant rock. I heave a broken breath and it takes three inhales before I finally catch a steady one. I'm able to ride it like a wave.

My entire body riots against me. The agony is too much to bear as I turn my head and vomit all over the shiny green texture of the rock I'm plastered against, as it tangles within my hair. "Oh, God," I groan, the ache in my neck tortuous. The rock mumbles, splitting across the center as it blinks open one huge and judgemental eye which has me screaming and almost paralyzed... or not. I'm on my feet in the next instant running. "Fuck green fairies on a tortoise's bulging neck!" I screech, then shake my head when the absurdity of my panicked outburst rings in my ears.

I was spat out in some kind of desolate and barren desert. The skies are a raging emerald green and blood red. Brittle gravel and lifeless twigs are the only other things around me for miles, but as I start to run, I find myself in a tall-standing and soul sucking forest. Tiny orbs of orange dance high in the sky, the only source of a very scarce light that does nothing to heighten my shadows. Trees are shaped like hanging corpses, the darkness is a hue of blue that allows me just enough light to show me the dead swinging in the breeze. Only I can't tell if they are actually dead beings or just the harrowing shapes of the trees themselves.

The deeper I go, the more the wind around me whispers. At first I think I'm going crazy, that I'm hearing ghosts on the breeze until The Calling's "Wherever You Will Go" starts humming around me. The sound is theoretical and somehow wickedly morbid, as it promises sweet demise and a brilliant show all at once.

Plant creatures bounce from their stems, yapping at the air. Little demon creatures that look like jesters as they lick the air, like they're craving something like blood.

I fist my hands through my matted hair, pulling at the strands and trying to smack away the torment that's plaguing me. The shadows start dancing, ever-growing essences of spirits that guide my way deeper into the dark unknown. Evanescence's "Bring Me To Life" starts bellowing next and I scream, sure this is the lands way to drive me fucking insane. I spin in a circle, dispelling all the confusion and fury from my aching lungs as I finally let myself fall apart. I knew this world would chew me up and spit me the fuck back out again.

It's all too much. Too far displaced from reality and all too much at once.

But I can do this. I just have to breathe.

"Ahhhh!" I roar, throwing my hands out and wishing more than anything I had the power to make it all stop. A gust of wind dispels from my palms as the taunting wind finally falls mute, kicking up a storm in my anguish as it swirls around me.

Falling to my knees, I rock back and forth, debating if the silence is any better than the tortuous songs.

Think, Adisen. *Think*!

I never expected that I'd be forced to fight for the magic. That it would strip me down to barebones and forge me in the ruins of my own brutalized and broken soul.

I hold my breath, blinking unseeing eyes as that thought dawns on me.

I never expected that I'd be forced to fight for the magic.

Why hadn't I thought that? Isn't that what I read about? Isn't that literally the wings of courage in every book that I've ever read? Embedded in the stripes of every warrior I've ever admired?

I'm no different. I'm nothing special.

I got so caught up wishing for the happy ending that I overlooked the trials needed to get there.

You don't deserve the magic without a fight and I haven't been fighting. Not since I landed here and not even back on earth. No, I didn't fight, I surrendered. I accepted what the fates had handed me and lived every day like it was the same.

I've always prided myself on being a fighter, in being a survivor, but right now, I don't think I know what it is to fight at all.

Looking down at my arms, I take in the cuts and bruises all over my body. I can feel the need to retreat and cower in a bed until my body feels like it can move again clawing away at my bones, but instead, I narrow my eyes on the crimson rivers that glisten like glitter along my skin.

Never look a gift-horse in the mouth.

That's what my momma used to tell me.

I dreamt of this, it's only fair that I see it through to the end. Whether it kills me or not.

Brushing away the crap clinging to my bruising skin, I stand with shaky legs on my feet and take in my surroundings. I'm in a forest, one that depicts wailing corpses and golden lights which now I look up, look more and more like beady little eyes and I pray to Satan that I'm not in the dead man's lands, or forest of the dead, or whatever the hell it was Elijah called it when he was worried about poisonous vines back when I was lost to the fever.

I etch up onto my tiptoes, now suddenly scared to walk along the vined ground in case this is the place he was speaking about.

A burst of fire licks against my back and warms me from the brittle chill and my entire body shakes in refusal to turn around but I force myself too.

Turning slowly, ever so fucking slowly, I come face to face with two back holes that look like giant caves and two orange orbs which blink like eyes, I gulp. Too terrified to move, I shake like a leaf where I stand when the giant dragon rears up and steps into the limited light. I scream inside my head.

This is it. The moment I get my chaotic ass fried.

I tense, my entire body ridged with fear and anticipation as to what was to come, but a loud neighing cuts off the building roar when a passive horse with massive wings swoons overhead in divine light and ushers the dragon back into his cave. Its head was larger than two trees standing together, so I'm grateful for the fact that the body was lost to the darkness or I might have actually fainted at the sight.

I stand looking a little shocked and bewildered as the white horse flies away in an angelic light that has my heart racing.

"You got this," I whisper to myself. "You got this. Amelia Hutchins is our favorite author, right?...Right!" I pace up and down, boring a hole into the dark terrain. "Right. And she is human just like the rest of us. Only she's a human who writes the unthinkable. She writes what we all crave. She writes about women that set your soul on fire and never make you want to give up through the pain. She writes characters like Syn, Lena, Ciara, Aria. She writes the warriors in our souls. I can do this. I can be strong. I can allow my soul to bleed on the paper of a page in a book and I'll make myself worthy to be a character written within the ink. Worthy for a king I'd destroy myself just to save," I rant, walking in circle after circle when all of the words from a woman who saved me in my darkest days rushes through my mind. She's my warrior in the battlefield of doubt and the second I think about her, I draw a strength unlike anything I've ever felt before into my lungs. It feels like actual raw, uncut power. It sizzles within my veins and lights up my withering soul like a beacon for the damned.

But that's the thing about magic. If you feel it, how isn't it true? If you feel it, isn't it enough?

"There you are, witch. I thought I'd lost you," a voice calls out behind me, and I twirl, a smile on my face as I seek that comforting baritone. Only it's the British Elijah that I come face to face with.

My shoulders slump in defeat when I notice it's only my stupid conscious and not the man of my dreams walking toward me. "I've been sucked into purgatory and all I'm left with is my conscience. Fan-freaking-tastic," I groan, rolling my shoulders and crying out at the pain which follows.

"Yeah, about that," he utters, a joker's smile on his face that has me straightening my shoulders and paying attention. The man in the woods, the one with the changing faces flickers before me and I see all the same heartbreaking features that I did before. I stumble back, my brows furrowing in confusion. "I'm not really your conscience, Adisen. I'm your nightmare." Then the veil parts and his true face is revealed. I wheeze a broken cry at the horrific reality standing before me and stumble back, hands up warding away the frightful sight.

The man with crazy hair, wild and stood-tall like horns as it spikes at his temples, thick and straggly, cants his head to the side and peers at me. The man with the scars over his eyes in deep slashes and the anchored nose which hooks over his jester's smile, sneers.

Rows and rows of razor-sharp teeth and eyes as demonic as the soulless, stare back at me.

"Do you remember me, Adisen. Do you remember me now?"

There were things which taunted Elijah Braxton, things which go bump in the night. There were forces at play outside of the betrayal and pretty lies hidden from him within the very walls of his own bedchamber, that he was still yet to uncover. Something wicked, played with the strings of his mind. It created torment, and uncertainty. It created unsettled riots which would become dancing mishaps that would taunt his control. Many things would plague the king, things unseen to those around him. He'd spend his nights wondering if he was going crazy. If the people surrounding him were friends or foes and if he could be trusted to distinguish the difference anymore. One moment, deceit was there with a crooked finger beckoning him near. Then poof, it was gone, fading within the distance with an echoing laugh berating on the wind and Elijah began to wonder… If magic was a kingdom, was the stage within the walls of his mind?

I toss and turn in the sheets. Sweat clinging to my heating flesh. The scene from the last chapter I read in Elijah's book flashing within my mind like the strobe lights of a storm as lightning cracks across the earth. All the unknown pieces of his story cut gashes with jagged edges into my fearing soul and I begin to wonder if the author has written a danger which could kill my beloved.

It's a nightmare, one I can't escape.

The face of a monster follows me everywhere I go. It's a terror, as solid as a pill, one I struggle to swallow. My mind races, unable to shut it off as my brain creates scenarios, writing chaos of its own, filling in the blanks on what could happen before I'm even able to pick up the book once more. My mind conjures the faceless foe, which is after my beloved and here, within the walls of my dream, I find the courage to want to face the darkness for him.

Never trust the demons, created from a nightmare. My momma told me that too.

I stumble back, hands covering my mouth as I recall the nightmare I had months ago. The creature wearing Elijah's face changes into the horrible man from the diner. The first one to ever grab me and my heart riots, shattering in my chest as it struggles to set into a calmness that I desperately need right about now. "Y-you? I don't understand."

"I'm the trickster, babe. That night, after you read that scene and you had that nightmare, your brain needed to create a monster. Something you could fight. So it created me. That chaos? You're looking at it, darling. You needed to face it. You needed to face it so it could get you here. I'm made, to heighten that fear. I'm made, to break you. But I found I wanted to push you to greatness instead." He sighs. "Like a genie in a bottle, babe. I want to be set free."

"B-but that would mean-"

"-That I'm the first thing you ever conjured? Yes. It does." He smirks, stepping closer to me before reverting back to his demonic face which steals my breath away. "It also means I'm independent from this world. I'm tied to you, Adisen. Not Elijah." The smirk on his face has me swinging.

It's probably a stupid move but I need to hit something right about now. He poofs out of existence and I'm left spinning in a circle before rough hands grab me and bring me to a stop. I shrug them off and turn on him with a glare that could scorch the leathery skin from his bones.

"Why? Why would you try to hurt me?"

"Well you kinda made me into a big, bad, and scary thing that goes bump in the night. But I never actually tried to hurt you. You created me as your fear, so I've been making you face it." He folds his arms across his chest, tilting his head back to the sky and blowing out a breath which frosts in front of his face. "I'm not actually bad, babe. I just want you to grow a pair and stop being so afraid all the damn time."

"I can't deal with this," I stammer, my head aching like a jackhammer has been plugged in and has gone rouge on me within my brain. "So you…"

"All I did was push you and Elijah together. I did it so you would learn how not to be afraid of the things you crave. What's the point in running from what you desire because you're afraid? The only thing you lose is the chance to be happy."

"Big words from an ugly motherfucker," I utter as my brain tries to wrap around all of this.

"I'll be sexy again when you stop being so damn scared of everything. This is your world, Adisen, and if you feel like it isn't, then *make* it your world."

I don't even know how to process any of this mayhem and naturally I'm not even given the chance. Vines sneak out from the ground, coiled from the trunks of the corpse trees as they wrap around me and lift me into the air. The corpse inspired twigs and branches contorting until they all look like they're smirking back at me and the harder I stare the more those withered, ashen lips begin to look ruby-fucking-red.

"Trickster!" I scream and he shrugs, back to looking like my handsome Elijah.

"You want this pretty boy face? Find your strength, love. Y'know… become the hero of your own story?" he offers, and I screech, kicking my legs wildly as I thrash within my woodland restraints.

"Ergh! I hate this. I hate this. I hate this," I chant, as I redouble my efforts for escape.

"Well, how fitting, darling. Because I just hate you too. Now, are you ready to help me kill your love?" a sickly-sweet voice singsongs, and it sends the sensation of spider legs crawling all over my skin. "After I play with you first, of course. I have so many painful things planned for such a pretty little thing." Jessaleia tuts her lips as she steps from the darkness below me. Her wild eyes spark demented fury as they bore into mine and I can't help but hold my breath because this is so not my world.

Thirty-Eight

Elijah

Darkness used to be my closest friend. Now it's the foe standing between me and my love.

I tumble through the void, sucked back into the world I haven't thought about since danger came for Adisen.

The script may have changed, but it will still end on a happily ever after.

Fuck me, don't we deserve it? This has been no ordinary love story; an ordinary ending is the very least that we deserve.

It's been grueling, terrifying, and filled with so much of the unknown, that there was not even a thread of peace. I had nothing to hold onto. Nothing that made sense. Not until I met her.

It was as if I had been a man reborn from amnesia. I knew nothing, until I knew her.

I crash through the portal, landing heavily in the unforgiving waters. The tsunami swims around me, pulling me under as I fight the current. There is a sharp pain twisting within my chest and I instantly know something is wrong.

Adisen is here and she's hurt. I look around frantically, wondering if she had been dispelled close by, but she is nowhere to be seen.

Unleashing my beast's inner voice, I howl to the waters surrounding me, using the force as a projectile to push me back to my feet. I rise from the cold, murky depth of the chilling lake. My howl is filled with despair as I break through the surface. Rivulets of beaded water trail down my naked pecs, caressing my ink while the beast paces along my chest in a restless type of agony, pining for his mate. My skin is torn and brutalized from the trial of the battle between myself and my brother. The sting bleeds through the layers of flesh, searing my bones but I hardly feel it. I hardly feel any of it.

I'm too maddened, too consumed with the need to find Adisen.

Being parted from her is like having my heart torn from my chest so it can walk freely around a realm that used to be my responsibility, my burden.

A realm that will be too much for her to handle alone.

There was no hiding anymore, no more keeping the monsters at bay. My back arches as my chest bursts open, freeing The Accursed I had imprisoned there, uncaging them to seek and destroy it all at my will. My shadows bleed from my skin, twirling around me as a ferocious force as harsh as the wind as the screaming faces travel through the realm like a torrent of smoke.

I know they took what's mine.

Stole her from my unforgiving grasp.

Now, I'll see them all dead. My kingdom be damned.

Screeching fills the air as the creatures worse than hell itself riot and coil within the skies, making their distraught anguish heard. The waters glow a crystal blue as the pool of health rejuvenates my powers, feeding me the energy I need for this warpath I have found myself on.

I'm letting it all go.

This world was one that was written for me. Not one I had chosen for myself.

I finally found a slice of heaven and it was hidden between the thighs of an angel.

On the lips of a siren and within the eyes of an enchantress.

Adisen lit up my world and showed me the way home through the darkness.

She showed me what it was like to love and to hope. To want something more than an army without a mind. To rule without a queen. I had once loved this kingdom and all the wonder which came with it. Now I'm ready to watch it all burn to ash while I seek out the one who makes my beastly heart finally stop aching.

I can feel her pain through the bond and it rips a roar of flames from my throat which scorches the earth around me. The ground trembles from my wrath and rocks fall from the mountains standing tall in the kingdom.

I can see my palace in the distance, not too far from where I stand. It's just far enough away that it paints a silhouette full of regrets. I roll my eyes, moving my head on my shoulders when I feel the power in the air. The army that is coming to detain the untameable.

A force field of amethyst explodes around me. The power digging into the earth and finding its root as the collective chants echo within my ears. It takes a moment for the potency of the force field to dwindle and become transparent.

A dark laugh is pulled from me as I turn slowly in a circle, mocking the witches that surround me. The witches with white hair and even whiter eyes, lost to the magic and unable to see who stands before them.

My warriors. My witches.

The witch army under the command of my general, *Jareth*.

"Who dares use unlawful magic without the permission of the king?" his voice booms from in between the thousands of bodies of women standing around me in a triquetra, thinking that will save them from the king of it all.

I laugh again and this time it travels for miles, waking the creatures with the ability to fly, making them shoot into the sky in panic.

"The king," I growl, turning to face him as his golden face turns ashen.

"M-my king? Elijah, is that really you?" he asks with bated breath, staring at me with wide and uncertain eyes. It hasn't gone over my head that he demanded to defend my laws and now Jessaleia's.

"It is," I respond, clapping my hands together and shattering the force field sending the witches flying in an ungraceful arch with cries of shock.

"Man, where the hell did you go? You just disappeared and then before we knew it that bi- I mean, *Jessaleia* disappeared too." His brown eyes shine and his blond hair is slicked back, turning the golden curls into waves with the amount of product he uses. His armor is immaculate as always, dressed in the same armor I dressed Adisen in. Sleek black and scaled with my crest on the breastplate. It curves to him just as well as it curved to her and the more I stare at how put-together he is, the more I begin to question how I never suspected any of this to not be as real as when I'm with her.

"She's more than a bitch, Jareth. She's a fucking whore and I won't stop tearing through this land until I have her head hanging from the castle walls right alongside my brother's. Do you understand?" I roar, stepping from the waters.

"Woah, okay. Seriously what the hell happened, man?" Jareth has always been a close friend to me, in the sense of the written word, but I guess I haven't really known him at all.

I can't think about that right now.

Right now, I need to find my mate.

"Got yanked from the pages of a book by an enchantress I naturally assumed was a witch. Went bowling. Learned my very existence wasn't real and then had an epic showdown with my traitorous brother and his whore of a mate. Shocker. The mate is Jessaleia. They drugged me. Made me believe she was mine. Now I'm back and my true mate is missing and I no longer care for this world as much as I care for her. Now if you'll excuse me. I have my woman to find and corpses to mutilate."

"Wai-" I cut off anything else he is about to say with my shift.

I break free, allowing The Accursed unrestrained reign over this kingdom. It's only fair I give my furry counterpart the same courtesy. This shift isn't as smooth and as flawless as the last. This time I need to feel everything. I need to feel it as my bones break and rearrange. As my beast obliterates my spine, shattering my discs and tearing through the center of my flesh, out of my back shedding the skin of my human form to make way for the monster made from wolves and hell alike. I land on all fours, larger than when Adisen saw me for the first time after being revived within the pool of health. The lava streaking through my fur burns hot, pulsating like flames themselves. My ribs suck inward, my black fur parting to display ribs of fire. Metallic silver shimmers throughout, giving me a moonlit glow and adding an ethereal light to my monstrous form. I snap my rows of razored teeth, snarling like a savage, as rabid saliva hits the ground beneath me burning holes around my taloned paws as I run off into the distance, away from the pool of health and deeper into my kingdom.

I can feel Jareth on my heels, the witches on his.

I never knew where his loyalty would lie, but now I can feel it.

This will be the final battle. The one which will conclude this world and finally set myself and Adisen free.

Keep up, stay out of sight, and make sure they don't see you coming.

The voices of The Accursed carry my message, a smug snarl as Jareth's response is echoed back to me.

I know that Jessaleia and Bradon won't take Adisen back to the palace. They can't be that stupid. They have to be keeping her somewhere I've never been. Somewhere I would never *think* to look.

For all I know she's beneath the ground right now, hidden in some dungeon as she bellows my name waiting for me to save her.

The only way to find out is to tear apart the ground as I go. My fire burns trails which disintegrates the rubble within the earth, splintering it down the middle and leaving nothing but sinkholes in my wake.

I'll find my love. Even if I have to destroy this world to do it.

My paws stop moving for a moment, my spine arches as I tip my nose to the three-colored moon and howl. It's my loudest, harrowing howl ever to be torn from my throat. It travels through the lands, carrying a warning.

A promise.

Adisen, love. I'm coming for you.

Thirty-Nine

Adisen

Terror seizes my entire body and it has nothing to do with the amount of blood that swims in rivers beneath my feet. It has everything to do with the earth that is quaking around me and the horrific howl that travels on the wind torn from my beloved.

I'm hanging from chains, bolted to the ceiling of some kind of dungeon-cave that Jessaleia and Bradon are holding me in.

I've learned three things in the time I've found myself a captive in a world I once found beautiful, and if I'm being honest, I still do. It isn't the realm making me bleed, it's just the realm that accepts the sacrifice.

One, this bitch is cruel just to be cruel. She was written with vile toxicity running in her veins and absolutely nothing redeemable coursing through her blood.

She's evil incarnated wearing a pretty face.

Two, Bradon is a love-sick puppy, struck stupid as a man who will do anything Jessaleia wants just for the sake of her demanding it, even if he knows it's wrong. It's left me observing him, looking for the hidden key because the more I'm watching him, the more I'm sure he holds it.

And three…

I can endure so much fucking more than I've ever given myself credit for.

I hang here, limp and drained of all energy as I stare at the ground with a breaking heart at knowing how much Elijah is suffering right now. His howl rocks my bones and rattles my core as his anguish fills me with his sorrow.

But as I hang here, I also learn that turning it all off and shutting it all down, is really a thing.

I always wondered if it was when I got to the point in a book where the hero is suffering and they find a strength from a core of steel, which only arises from the numbness that infuses their veins and boils in their blood. I used to think it was so wrong, that when you're suffering in so much agony, that it is impossible to ignore it.

I suffer every single day with pain that often has me bound to my bed with useless tears rolling down my cheeks because it didn't matter how much I cried.

My pain never cared.

Now I'm drowning in a different kind of agony. A pain which poisons the blood and hurts so much more than broken bones and pulled fingernails ever could. It's a bone-aching pain that sucks away at your soul and leaves you in a darkness you can't find your way through.

I feel that now, I feel like I'm drowning and my soul is the one holding me under the brutal waters just waiting for me to find my end. I have nothing left in me, nothing but sadness that makes me want to cry, but I have no tears left to give. I miss Elijah, I want him to know that I'm okay and to take away the pain that is eating him from the inside out.

You don't get the magic without fighting for it first.

And I'm fighting. I'm fighting with everything I have until my last dying breath because that is what being an avid reader has taught me. That is what being the mate of a warrior who doesn't know how to lose has taught me. You never give up, you don't cower in the darkness.

You rise in it instead.

I stare at the array of candelabra lining the dungeon walls. Crafted from black fantasies in the shape of ravens and dragons. I focus everything inside of me. Pushing my will to the surface as I intently glare through the darkness, focusing on the unlit wicks. My mind begins to ache, my eyes tight as I struggle to keep them open throughout the pain. But the more I glare - the more I will any kind of light - the more those unlit wicks begin to flicker. "Dammit!" I sneer into the darkness, begging for any kind of progress. "Damn you, light! Just fucking light dammit!" The Orange embers dance, thinking they're taunting me but instead I smirk.

Any light is better than no light and the more I practice, the stronger I'll become.

The dungeon doors open and Bradon steps inside, taking in the blood dripping down my temple and off of my chin.

"Ohh, pretty girl, how beautiful you bleed for me," he whispers as he stalks *across* the chamber, leaning in to smell my hair. The term of endearment has insidious chills skating down my spine, making me shiver in repulsion.

"Don't call me that," I sneer, gritting my teeth as I sway in my chains. A broken chuckle leaves me and once it starts, I just can't stop.

"What's so funny, beautiful, have we finally broken you?" he muses, a wicked smirk on his stupid face and I just laugh even harder. It winds me as I fight for an unpainful breath.

"No, Bradon. You haven't broken me."

"Then what's so funny?"

"I just realized, I'm everything I ever dreamed of being. I'm a character in my favorite book. And, the thing about loving certain kinds of stories is I already know how this one ends." I lick the blood from my lips, focusing on the clothing they couldn't burn from my flesh. They tried, and when the outfit Elijah conjured wouldn't move, they decided to attack the parts of me left exposed. My feet dangle and brush the surface of the puddle beneath my feet. "Oh yeah and how's that?" The condescending look on his face makes me smirk. It's an ignorance the fucked like to hide behind. He trails the tips of his fingers down the column of my throat, over the swell of my breasts and down the center of my core.

"With you dead, and your cunt of a mate gutted and turned into a fixture on the palace wall. *Huh*," I scoff, eyes feeling heavy and I bring them back to lock with his. "I guess this world really does have a way of changing you. Because I find the humanity inside of me is gone and the wicked evil really enjoys the sound of that."

"You think you're strong enough to withstand this world? To withstand us? You're bait to lure in my brother, and trust me when I tell you, that once he sees the state you're in, he'll be so stricken with grief he won't even see the Vessel Of Corruption coming." He leans in, teeth sinking into the lobe of my ear making me wince and instinctively pulling away from him, making the sting worse. "We're only playing with you because my love doesn't like to lose. She wants to see you hurt, Adisen. She wants to mess up the pretty little face you wear so she becomes the fairest of them all."

I think about that, letting it settle in. How could any man, let alone any mate, not care when his woman cares more about being desired by the world than anything else? How would you live in peace knowing that once somebody else gives her attention, how easily she will forget yours. Something just isn't right.

The second he lets go to speak, I turn my head back toward him like a whippet and sink my teeth into his flesh, locking around his nose and drawing blood. He hisses, pulling back but I just sink my teeth in harder, not caring about the copper taste which fills my mouth. I finally let go as he stumbles back, covering his face and trying to replace the skin which has pulled away from bone around the bridge of his nose. I scoff, smiling at him with bloodied teeth. "I can understand that, the fates did lump you with a dog playing dress-up."

"You little bitch!" Jessaleia hisses, rushing from the shadows to strike me around the face. My head snaps to the side, my jaw aching instantly as it adds to the welts already along the sides of my face.

I knew she was there, hiding in the darkness like a self-proclaimed queen pulling the strings of her minions. Only I don't play that way. I won't play into the game which makes her feel like she's in power. Like she's in control and can stand within the shadows regally while the world ushers to do her bidding, like a mindless flock that circles around her, making her feel like she's untouchable. I spit the flesh I was holding between my teeth in her face, widening my smile like a demented shark. I wish I could use my will, that I could do some heroic and badass move which would have me walking out of here like a bad-bitch-warrior, but I can't. The most I've been able to do is small things that easily revert. Setting her aflame seems to be my favorite.

But I'm getting stronger. I'm getting better.

I just can't give up.

My mind won't focus and it's a painful reminder of just how human I am.

I'm taunting the madness and I just can't stop myself.

The trickster told me to face my fears, so I am. I'm looking them in the eye and not feeding them with my terror because that bitch doesn't exist. It's locked away in a box even I can't reach.

"You really think you're something special, don't you? That you won? I never lost, sweetie. I never wanted Elijah in the first place," she hisses, spittle flying from her slithering lips.

"But it kills you that he never pined for you after you were exposed doesn't it? Because bitches like you need to feel wanted, and it barbs that black heart that he can't give two fucks about you now he has me, right?" I'm playing with fire, but right now I don't care if I end up burned. Outrage sparks in her menacing eyes as her pencil-thin brows draw together. Her ruby red's quiver and her pale cheek's flame scarlet. She raises her hand and I prepare myself for another strike, only it never comes. When I open my eyes, I see her hand halted within the air, restrained as her entire body shakes with her anger.

When she knows she has my attention, she strikes. Nails shredding the skin of my cheeks causing me to sneer.

She narrows her eyes, before they flicker down to my core and then a sickening smile graces her face. "Oh, how things just became all the more interesting, darling. How did we miss this before? Too sidetracked with your torture, I suppose." She turns toward Bradon, still nursing his bleeding nose and places a hand on his shoulder. "I grow tired of the torture, my love. It's time we use her as bait, but oh how sweet the bait has just become. In two days, we'll lure Elijah into the barracks where his own soldiers will wait to disarm him. It will give my spell time to work. We'll lure him with the sweet scent of his mate and then, we'll watch as the Vessel Of Corruption drains the souls from purgatory and kills him where he stands. The kingdom will finally be ours." A victorious smile lights up her face and once Bradon sets eyes on it, it becomes contagious and they both end up smiling like demented entities, scarier than this realm's monsters.

There is something so much more sinister when it hides behind beautiful faces, harboring the darkness of all evils.

"What spell?" I utter, my arms numb from the pain in my joints, hanging here like livestock.

"This one." She smirks, throwing out her hands as a burst of darkness shoots from her palms and smashes against my core. I gasped, crying out as the pain sears into my flesh, and constricts my entire womb. The pain is unthinkable, everything within me feels like it's moving out of place. My ribs ache, my organs feel heavy and before I have the chance to voice my cries, darkness takes me.

Forty

Elijah

I haven't been able to find her.

Dark magic is at play, concealing my beloved from my senses, from my abilities.

All until she's there, wafting right under my nose as her scent drifts on the breeze.

It's an intoxicating scent, one I can't ignore as she beckons me near, chanting my name like an enchantress. I was standing within the keep belonging to Jessaleia's demonic pets - pets I had no idea the wicked witch even had - and within the next instant, I've flashed to the other side of the realm, stalking through the old barren barracks that were once used for our warriors. Now it's just a plot of destroyed and uneven terrain sat upon the graveled ground.

The clouds of hell trail like smoke through the skies darkening all that encloses us as the heavens riot and the thunder roars like pissed off lions. A thick and potent fog wavers down from above and a vicious storm brews evident with my wrath as it kisses upon the realm which cowers from the power that cackles within the air.

Jessaleia and Bradon stand tall within the clearing. My shadowed demons come to stand at my side, scattered by the thousands across the realm as The Accursed take on their shadowed forms. All the rotten and satanic creatures stood tall in all their wicked glory staring back at the ruins that wrecked this kingdom. Jessaleia gulps, only now for the first time seeing The Accursed freed.

The first time seeing how raw my power is when it is my mate that I fight for.

Trust me, it's a harrowing sight to be seen.

Everything unleashes in a brutal torrent, my emotions, a conductor for my powers as it thrashes wildly around our feet.

"And so the king has come to save his queen. How very romantic," Jessaleia shrills, her voice like sirens to my ears.

"Is it still romantic when I bathe the realm within your blood and dance with my mate under the veil of your innards, bitch?" I sneer, towering in height as the shadows grow around me, darkening my silhouette.

"Honestly, Elijah. What has become of you since you have left here? You never would have addressed a woman in such a way before meeting this harlot!" She gasps, eyes wide as they feign actual insult, bringing her hand to cover her heart.

A hell-flamed fury burns through me at the disrespectful venom in her voice when addressing my mate. "I became a man, Jessaleia. Not a character. I grew a heart and became a beast with a purpose instead of your mindless puppet. Now, where is she? Where is my mate!" I'm done playing games. Done fucking around. Everything within me becomes an impulse to have Adisen in my arms once again.

"Oh, you mean her?" she singsongs, turning at the hip to beckon behind her as an army steps from the abyss.

A soldier drags a limp Adisen forward, the black armor I conjured for her a color that blends in with the raging storm. It isn't until she is yanked from her feet, that I first notice the blood pouring from her face and then the rounded stomach which protrudes from her core. I swallow wickedly when I see something inside of her move. Like a still wave disturbed with a pebble, her stomach dances.

"What in-the-ever-loving seed planted that?" I ask, flabbergasted. Apparently taking on a lilt of my mate's witty outbursts. A moment of shock steals away the dread infused wrath burning in my veins.

Time stands still as the world seems to spin around me, every other entity fading away as if life itself has been suctioned into a void. I stare back at my bone-weary mate and my heart cracks wide open seeing what they have done to her. The shock of seeing such a crazy sight almost slips away in my horror, all until her stomach moves again.

I feel like I'm losing my mind and wonder if this is all another kind of warped spell.

Another sick and twisted trick.

Because she certainly wasn't pregnant before we came back to this godforsaken land.

Wasn't she?

I throw out a hand, gathering my shadows and allowing them to coil around the throat of the warrior who holds her, snapping his neck and tossing his lifeless body through the air to wipe out another ten soldiers standing sentinel behind Jessaleia and

Bradon. Noticing this is not *my* army. The one that was always in service to the king.

"Adisen, love!" I breathe, hurrying to her side. I help her stand on unstable feet and bring her into my arms. "Are you okay? What happened to you? Talk to me, pretty. Tell me you are okay," I ask, frantic. A cackle has my eyes swinging back to Jessaleia. Gritting my jaw, I prepare to smite her ass, burning her where she stands.

"Oh, how very cute. It will be such a sight seeing two lovers brutalized where they stand in a kingdom they think will come to their aid. In a kingdom which no longer belongs to you. How does it feel, Elijah? How does it feel to be powerless and without a throne?" she taunts, walking in a wide circle as if she's on some kind of power trip. Like this realm and everything it has to offer kneels at her insidious feet.

I'm about to answer, to unleash all kinds of hell and raze this land when something occurs to me. A long-lost memory on what happens during a mating. The other half of all that was lost to me finally unlocked.

A memory that had been stolen like the rest of them.

I stare down at Adisen, my hands covering her stomach as the baby kicks and something inside of me twists with warmth.

With uncertainty.

The shocking revolution has me lifting my head toward my stoic brother, only now noticing he stands as still as a statue at Jessaleia's side. "Where is he, brother?" I ask, placing myself in front of a beaten Adisen, while I use my powers to take away some of her pain. She sighs, sagging in my hold as I can feel her resolve building through the bond.

"Elijah," she whispers brokenly.

"Hush now, love. I'm here."

"Where is who?" Bradon asks in confusion, brows furrowing as he takes a step forward, causing Jessaleia to tense.

"My nephew. Or perhaps the two of you birthed a daughter?" The color visibly drains from Jessaleia's ashen face. Guilt is bright in her dull and soulless eyes before it is replaced by something cruel and calculating.

"What the hell are you talking about?" he sneers, for the first time showing true emotion as she stares hurriedly between the two of us.

"Jessaleia is your mate, is she not? I forgot, when she cursed me. Forgot what it was to be blessed with a true mate. When twin flames find one another, brother, a child is conceived during the first ever mating. I'm presuming this is why my mate is so heavily pregnant with the aid of some of Jessaleia's dark magic, when she wasn't showing even a little before we got here? Go on, brother. Tell me I'm wrong. Tell me you and this vile whore have a child together."

He pauses for a fraction of a second at my words, not long enough to disrupt the cadence of our knowing banter but long enough for me to catch the hesitation. "The only thing I need to tell you, Elijah, is that you will be the destruction of everything you love. Your powers are unrelenting, are they not? Tell *me* I'm wrong, brother," he says, volleying my words back in my direction as the fury, the uncertainty, all boils into a wild storm inside of my aching core.

They hurt what's mine. They hurt my mate, the wrath that comes with the knowledge is almost blinding and as each second passes, the harder it becomes to control.

"I can't," I concede. "But that is love, is it not? Finding someone whose chaos compliments your own, then destroying each other in the most primal, brutal ways possible so that you may use the ruins of both of you to create a kingdom that you shall rule together? I love my mate enough that I would destroy it all for her. Can you say the same?"

"We prefer liberating a kingdom whose throne has been held back under the weight of a weak sack of idiocy that dares think himself worthy of the crown, brother. My love and I see it as a service to our people."

"Perhaps, but once she has *her* crown - what then? What use is there for a steppingstone who has already provided what aid you could beneath her wicked heels? What use shall she have for you? A man who could never become king unless I gave up my throne?" I see his eyes flicker to the bitch in question and I know my efforts are starting to chip away at his blind loyalty. The fool. "At what point did her blasphemous crusade become yours? And when, dear brother, did you truly turn your back on me? Do you remember?"

"The moment I pulled him from the shadows and made him realize that you forced him to remain subdued and weak while you absorbed all the power from this realm and The Accursed for yourself and enslaved any who dared object, I showed him the way. I showed him the power he could wield if only he took it," Jessaleia chimed in. "Consider this my formal objection, love," she adds with a sardonic smile, before turning her head slightly to the side to address the hordes waiting in harrowing silence. "Kill him," she whispered. Those two words burst the fallacious civility of the moment - gone was time for words of reason as the metallic ringing of blades was heard sliding free of the sheaths holding them captive, their almost musical tones rising into the night sky above and creating a harmony that was laughably at odds with the scene unfolding in their dissonance.

Relentlessly they swarm around me, so quick to forget that it is me to whom they truly answer. Endlessly I strike them down with every weapon at my disposal, making generous headway with my shadows as minions around me and thinning the continuous onslaught. But still they come, and farther still do I find myself from my Adisen. My gaze flicks back to her every spare chance I carve out, my eyes never failing to land on her swollen belly that burns my mind as if it has been asleep and refuses to truly awaken. To *see*.

Fuck me, I'm going to be a father.

Adisen uses her will, small little pops of magic as she staves away the creatures trying to get to her.

Laughter floats all around us as Jessaleia starts making rhythmic movements and chanting something much too low for me to hear. The skies begin to darken slightly and everything mutes only to return at deafening volumes as she sets whatever witchcraft she weaves into motion.

The earth beneath us all rattles as if it's angry about all the disturbance. Stones increasingly larger in size shake loose of the dirt burying them, many bearing symbols that I am unable to place until I strike down another warrior standing against The Accursed and the same symbols stare back at me from my very own skin.

"You may not believe that she is my true mate, brother, but you really should have believed me when I said you'd be the source of destruction of everything you truly love." The stones cling to and build upon one another, morphing into something humanoid and erect.

"Another puppet of your dastardly creation, I presume? This wicked vessel," I deadpan, tired of the games and insulted they think such a thing can defeat me.

"Not of mine, Elijah. Yours," Jessaleia taunts with a cruel

smile that lays her fangs bare. Pointed and gleaming ominously within the storm of vicious blood clouds. "You once boasted that the only being powerful enough to kill you was yourself. I thought that was a marvelous idea, though I did add my special touches. All those times I dutifully cleaned up after your training and battles, you were too ignorant to realize that I was collecting your blood and infusing it into what would become your downfall. Horde King, I present to you the Vessel of Corruption. You had hardly any time to become acquainted when that bitch set me alight and ruined my efforts. May he do you proud. A reminder of your reign," she says with mock grandeur, as the beast begins to mobilize.

My shadows attack the Vessel, testing its mettle yet having absolutely no effect. I dodge a blow aimed for my face and respond in kind with one of my own to its torso. It would stand to reason that if this creature is the only one that possesses the power to kill me, that I, in turn, might be the only one who can kill this monstrosity. How poetic of Jessaleia, to force two versions of me to duel it out until the more desperate of the two is the only one that remains. Foolish, even, considering she also created the desperation that renders my victory an inevitability.

With Jessaleia's attention fully on the fresh entertainment, I see Adisen bolt from her position at Bradon's side, only for him to give chase. But he quickly finds that his prey is not as meek as he presumes, with her fighting violently when he ensnares her once more in his unyielding clutches. The hands that clasp her firmly become aflame when she burns away his poisonous touch and takes off once more. My next strike to the creature - this Vessel Of Corruption - throws him off balance and has him stumbling backward into the structure where Adisen and Bradon struggle vehemently. A roar is clawing its way out of my throat as everything unfolds in slow motion in front of me - the creature's arm flailing and about to crush my mate and the precious babe she carries.

Just as I am sure Jessaleia's prediction is about to fulfill itself, the limb's careless descent halts and I watch Bradon scramble out of its reach with my world cradled to his chest. Once in relative safety I can see they're having a very heated discussion, but when Adisen takes Bradon's hands in her own and guides them to encircle her swollen belly, I can practically hear what she's saying. *Listen, to me. Everything she has ever told you has been a lie. Everything she's ever shown you, nothing more than magic to make you believe in her lies. But this, Elijah's child in my womb, this is real. Can you not feel that? Your brother doesn't want to kill you. But if someone is threatening his mate - his* true *mate - and his offspring, he will not hesitate to relieve their shoulders of the weight of their head - even if it is yours. Help us, Bradon, before there's nothing left of your home to save. Before there's nothing left of* you *to save.*

I see Bradon's head nod once and they start making their way to me, my breaths coming a little easier as they do.

"Well it's about time you found a way to remove your head from your ass, brother," I say nonchalantly.

"Thank your mate. Her will is one that cannot be disobeyed," he says with a wink in her direction.

"Tell me about it," I concur with a grin. "Now as for our other problem…"

"Which one? We have so many at the moment," he says, jokingly.

Adisen interjects before I can find the right flavor of sarcasm to respond with. "Um, guys? How about focusing on the one that's looking at us like he's about to give us an up close and personal example of the 'ant-meet-boot' scenario? Because the pregnant one votes for that one."

"Your wish is my command," I tell her, simply happy to have her within my reach again. Turning my gaze to my brother, we clasp forearms. "Bradon - you better guard her life and that of my child as if it were your own," I say warningly, squeezing a little bit to add emphasis to my words.

"With my dying breath," he vows. Our eyes lock for a moment before I break the contact and abandon them to face the monstrosity.

I'm proud of Adisen. For having the strength to break Bradon's curse as thoroughly as she broke my own.

I leap into the air and come crashing down onto the creature's head with enough force that would have made a crater in the ground beneath us. Yet it only made him stagger back a single step, and I have an accompanying pain in the exact spot I connected with the creature. Again and again, I come after him, with little more success than that first blow. The only thing I manage to achieve is an assortment of injuries coinciding with my blows to the creature and my dwindling energy supply but every time I think I have run out, I catch a glimpse of Jessaleia and my anger revives me. But the dance seems endless and I am more than aware of the fact that I cannot continue this for eternity.

I make my way back to where Adisen and Bradon stand observing the entire display, my breaths coming out in hot pants and sweat dripping over every inch of exposed flesh. My brother's expression is more pensive than I have seen it in a long time.

"These marks on your body correspond to the matching marks on the Vessel. That's how she created him. Blood of the black. Blood of your blood. Destroy the mark, and you might just break the connection between the two corresponding parts," Bradon explains. "You can always be rebranded, brother," he said apologetically, with an easy shrug.

"Fuck, you might just be right," I respond, knowing what I have to do but hating it all the same. I have to at least try. This dance grows tiresome.

"Our world truly is coming to an end then, isn't it?" Bradon quips with a chuckle, before unsheathing his blade. "Now let's hope I make prettier work out of skinning you than I always did with our prize after a hunting trip, yeah?"

"Shut up and get to work," I spit, his attempts at humor only adding to my growing dread. "But we'll need protection from the ongoing attacks." I add. They are relentless. They won't stop just so my brother can carve away at my flesh.

I want this over and I want Adisen and my baby safe.

"I've got this," Adisen sneers, straightening her shoulders and using her will to create a force field.

I grit my teeth almost to the point of breaking but I bear it in silence as one by one I watch my markings fall to the ground at my feet, feeling emptier as the pile grows. How strange, I think, that in order to save my kingdom I must forsake it. Forsake myself.

These cursive inks painted on my flesh I gained as a youth, which once added to my character, now lay flayed from my skin. With each one I can feel the ties that bind me to the creature coming undone, some snapping altogether like a band that has been stretched beyond its limitations. Jessaleia is much too enraptured by her chaotic orchestra to notice that we have gone off-script, too wrapped up in her perceived success to see that it is as much a lie to herself as those she told to the rest of us.

"That's the last one."

"You're done?"

"Yes. Go!" he screeches, and for the first time in this whole godforsaken venture, I don't doubt him or his plan.

Again, I aim a lethal blow to this creature's shoulder as I burst from the force field Adisen had created, mostly expecting the same results as before. Instead of meeting resistance, the stone I connect with implodes and crumbles to gravel that falls to his feet as he roars his fury into the night sky. Seeing that my brother's endeavors were a success, I gather my strength for a kill shot directly to the heart. I break through the layers of rock as easily as if I had just swan dived into the lake, latching onto a black gem deep within its center and yanking it out, watching the towering corpse crash lifelessly to the ground and shatter into nothing more than a pile of rock as inanimate as every other pile of rubble here. I crush the dark crystal in my hands, the blackened blood covering my palms as I spill its putrid contents.

"Pity, I thought that would have been more exciting," trills a monotone voice that grates against my frayed nerves.

"And I was hoping you'd be dead by now."

"Boredom is many things, love, but lethal isn't one of them. The Vessel was meant to crack you open for me to steal your powers of Purgatory, but you just couldn't go along with the plan now, could you? Always making things difficult for the poor little peasant girl," she pouts, but her slip catches my attention. "Oh well - that just means I get to torture you until you're almost dead and take it from you myself." As she speaks her armies surround Adisen and Bradon, and I abandon my position to help them keep her minions at bay.

"We're going about this all wrong," I say to Adisen and Bradon as we form a circle, back-to-back. Keeping our guard and reading our powers. Everything in me revolts. Adisen shouldn't be here. She should be somewhere safe and not lost to the battle. SVRCINA'S "Battlefield" begins to bellow around us, manifested by Adisen's will as she picks up on the emotion of our bond. "We don't need to stop her - we need to give her exactly what she wants," I say, the expressions on their faces blatantly asking me if I've lost my damn mind. Well the answering smile on my face tells them that yes, I have in fact lost my damn mind. But that might be why this works.

If Adisen has taught me anything, it's to be whacky.

"Elijah, I love you, but I really need you to listen to me right now - read my lips if you have to. What the actual fuck?"

"Don't you see? Jessaleia was a peasant girl - not a witch or an immortal. She was *gifted* dark magic, not born with it. She was nothing before us brothers. She was never meant to wield a power like it. That means her body isn't built to sustain dark forces, let alone a force as dark and powerful as she is demanding. So I vote we give it to her - and I mean *all* of it - it will be too much and will kill her. It will kill her beautifully."

"What the hell, right?" Adisen chirps. "I got impregnated by my favorite book character and sucked into his fantasy world to slay his bitchy ex, so why wouldn't this work?"

Still covered in my own blood, I roll my shoulders as I take a more secure stance. One by one, I dissolve every layer of control I built within myself to shield everyone around me from the darkness I carry inside me. That consumes me. That *is* me. It resists me at first, conditioned to the absolute control I forced it to submit to ages ago, not trusting the door I just swung wide open for it. It gingerly begins to slither across my skin, testing the boundaries and the truth behind what I am now offering it:

freedom. Pure, unrestricted freedom. That one taste is enough for it to run loose.

Inky black surrounds me in cottony layers, looking like when a drop of blood lands in water and separates into webbing delicately tethered together, floating carelessly, and tainting anything it can touch.

"What the hell is all this?" Jessaleia gasps.

"You wanted purgatory..." I begin, letting my power flood the atmosphere with the souls desperate to escape their endless lingering existence. "This is me giving it to you." I look over at Adisen, weary and battle worn, and the most ethereally beautiful I have ever seen her. "I can't do this on my own, love," I tell her.

"What? I can't! I'm not as strong as you, Elijah. Setting bitches aflame and creating force fields I think is my limit."

"No - that's because you're stronger. You always have been, just like you were always meant to be my queen and rule beside me. They are your subjects just as they are mine. Now give them a reason to bow to you and kill this bitch. The power chose you because you fought for it. Now unleash it, Adisen," I order her.

A determined look covers her face, her brows knitting together in concentration. At first only one or two souls start being dragged in Jessaleia's direction, beads of sweat forming on Adisen's forehead. *Come on, baby girl,* I chant in my head as if I'm trying to add my will to her own.

"Isn't this sweet - the two of you fighting side by side. You know what will be even sweeter? After I've won and you're clinging to life by the thinnest of threads, not alive enough to fight me but just alive enough to watch me carve the unborn bastard from your womb and end your legacy before it ever pulls breath into its filthy little lungs." She grins as she licks away the beads of blood dripping from her claws. "Can't have a semen demon running around with a legitimate claim to the throne now, can I? That would be in very poor taste."

The ground quakes as the threat feeds the ire fueling my shadows desecrating her army, but that pales in comparison to the wrath storming in Adisen's eyes. Something demented and unfeeling passed there. A soulless demon consuming her irises. Letting out a scream that only a mother can unleash, she throws out her hands and unleashes a torrent of brutality and ruin. Every being on the battlefield feels the cry rattle them down to their bones mere moments before all of purgatory begins swarming about, the chaos purposeful as it descends upon Jessaleia like a baleful storm of demise. The power is evident as it shimmers like a snake within the air around us.

Jessaleia tries to scream but the second she opens her mouth souls start pouring into it, drowning the sounds of her horror and anguish as she forcibly consumes the very thing she had spent so long hunting. But that wasn't enough to appease the angry torrents. Every opening of her body now becomes a gateway for them to infiltrate. Tears of blood run in rivulets down her face as she struggles to contain that much raw darkness. But it's too much for her body to bear. Her skin bubbles on the surface as it forces its way into her veins, replacing all that was once bright red with a lifeless black, and deeper inside to her marrow, eating away at every cell, consuming and corrupting everything in its path. Her once creamy white flesh, that she boasted to be the envy of every maiden in the kingdom, now looked grotesque and rotted, bursting open like wounds overrun with infections too far gone to fight, wretched black slime oozing down the surface. It bubbles sickenly out of her mouth, streaming from her eyes, nose, and ears, until her body ruptures and her corpse splatters across the ground like a plump frog stomped on by a merciless boot.

With her innards laid before me and still steaming, I call the souls back to me and rein them inside once more, locking away The Accursed. Another battle won.

∼

The battle armor I dressed Adisen in begins to turn into a princess gown that pinches at her waist and turns out at the bottom. Sky blue and almost electrified. Nothing about this dress is mundane, the color shimmers like lightning twirled with metallic ink, and the corset wrapped around her torso almost melds to her skin. She brings a shaky hand to her heart, stunned at the beauty gracing her body. Her hair falls from its messy bun, hanging in waves around her shoulders and falling down her back before ballerina pumps entwined with forest twine wrap around her feet, all without becoming uncomfortable. She looks like a princess and it isn't until the stain of ink shows itself splattered all throughout the dress, mixing with the otherworldly blue do I see the look in her eyes that makes her start to feel like a queen.

"I took something beautiful and my world destroyed it. I don't ever want to destroy you, Adisen. I don't want the light to fade in your eyes and all of your fantasies to break because they're something darker than you ever could have imagined," I murmur, dressed in a fine tux that makes the look of heartbreak shine within the beauty of her eyes. "There will always be darkness, but for as long as we believe, there will always be light too. Believe in me, Adisen, don't ever leave me," I implore, my hands fall to her hips as I step into her, moving her to the tune of Bebe Rexha's "Sacrifice".

"In my world, love. We dance amongst the dead, if for no other reason than to honor their lives." We had won the battle and I had renounced my throne.

My brother Bradon is now the king and to celebrate, we hold a ball amongst the dead and we dance until our feet become numb and our bones forever ache. We haven't had time to discuss much else, not with everything going on. But I did make the decision that I no longer belong as this realm's king.

Adisen blinks, taking those words in as it finally catches up to her idling brain that we're dancing like a king and queen amongst bloody corpses. I see her panic for a second, thinking for a moment how awful this is. But then my words penetrate and she realizes that in nearly all of her fantasy books there is some kind of scene with the dead. It's always been something I know she has found disturbingly hot. She's told me in the past, under the veil of night and hidden between the sheets.

But what I just said finally puts the wrongness of it into some kind of warped perspective.

I spin her out, only to twirl her back into my arms and I laugh lowly. A strange kind of shyness coloring her cheeks red as she buries her face into my chest. I chuckle with her, lifting her head by the chin to stare into her eyes, "I'll make everything dark, beautiful again, Adisen. I'll always turn tragedies into happiness. Into these pretty coy smiles, I'll chase with my lips and make my own."

"Hmmm, you have to be a powerful man to keep to that promise." She smiles, lost to disbelief that she truly has found herself a savior.

I cling her to me tighter, not needing anything sexual to feel like I'm falling into a blanket of a warmth that I associate with home.

She's my home. My forever. We dance to a tune as old as time, and for the first time in a long time, everything feels right.

"Now, you're mine. Forever and always, without compromises. You. Are. Mine. Adisen," I whisper, kissing her as it lifts her dark soul from her quivering body. I can feel it through the bond. How she suddenly feels like her essence is what's moving around this bloody ballroom, dancing, and twisting with my beastly essence too.

As everyone around us parties in celebration of the new king, my brother, Bradon.

He was a victim to a wicked witch.

Everything settles and I finally start to believe again.

To believe in magic and to believe in us.

Under the lights of purgatory, surrounded by the souls awaiting their reaper.

It should feel wrong, but it doesn't. I give myself to Adisen and the music. I close my eyes and allow myself to feel everything around me. Dancing with the shadows.

Kelsea Ballerini's "Peter Pan" begins to play next and it sparks a deep awareness in my heart as we dance to the tune, lifting me with bliss. Swaying back and forth as the words wrap themselves around me.

I'm Adisen's lost boy. One who came to be, not knowing where he belongs.

Then I became a real boy because she gave me a life.

She's my queen and together, we're about to become parents. I was handed my dreams on a skull platter and it would take the end of the world to rip that all away from me now.

We fought for the magic. I'm going to fucking keep it.

"Your world wasn't made for me, Adisen. I can't be the Horde King there. These powers, my beasts, will forever live inside of me. You saved that when you saved me, but they have no place in that world either. I'd give them all up for you, I'd suppress them all and live my life as a human just to have you as mine. You're my heart's desire, Adisen. You, I'd give it all up for you. So if you want to find a way home, I'm willing to follow you. I'll follow you anywhere, pretty girl. Just say the word."

She shakes her head, stepping away from me to wipe her eyes. Looking down at her dress and back at me, something passes within her two-toned eyes. "You're too great for that world, Elijah, too great for this one and I was misplaced when I was born in it. I can't live through something like what we just have and go back to everything being normal. I don't want to. I love you, Elijah, I love our son, enough that I would never ask you to give up who you are. You have saved me enough. You saved us both the moment you fell from the sky and taught me exactly how the world should be. Let me do something for us. Allow me the gift of being yours, within the pages of our own story." I stare down at her with curious eyes as a beaming smile spreads across her angelic face. Our story has been one of harrowing anguish and unwavering fortitude. We have survived through blood and war, trial, and error and yet here we stand, the victors of it all. What more could this woman give me? "I know you don't understand yet. But you will. We just need to collect a few tag-alongs first. I think I finally know how…"

Epilogue

DRIED IN INK- A ROMANCE NOVEL WRITTEN BY ADISEN AND ELIJAH BRAXTON.

Adisen

The thing that makes your world perfect, is the people you center it around.

Maria had always lived inside of Adisen's world. So had Dottie.

It wasn't until Elijah consumed that world that she figured it out.

The age-old question that everyone has forever asked themselves in the dead of night when that demonic depression crept back in.

How can I be happy?

You can be happy by never giving up the fight. By embracing the anguish and forging it down into a steel blade you carry with you into war.

If you were to live in ignorance, you'd know a moment of bliss.

But if you were to live in knowledge, you'd forever live in power, in happiness.

Because you'd have the key to it all.

The key to life.

And what is that key?

Knowing how to appreciate everything you have and savor the moment.

Because that is what is overlooked as humans, appreciating what you have no matter how small it may be.

Adisen had suffered much sorrow in the human realm. Too much anguish as a confused little girl who just didn't have the answers her soul was desperately looking for.

Elijah had also left behind all of his torment in a realm that had never really belonged to him.

They were born into the biggest trial of their life.

A trial in finding one another.

Adisen didn't want to compromise anymore and how predictable the ending would have been if it was as simple as living in one of their worlds and expecting a happily ever after from a place that had set the course of their trials.

So instead, once they had entered through the portal and back into the human world, Adisen headed back to the diner and picked up Maria and Dottie. After making sure the town was turned back to normal and the dead were honored and memories were wiped, Adisen then headed downtown to the nearest bookstore. Found the isle which displayed beautiful, old, and expensive bound novels with blank pages she brought one, returned home and asked those that she loved most to go on one, final adventure with her.

They all agreed, so instead of reading between the lines, Adisen and Elijah now live between them.

Using the power of her will, Adisen projected them into their own world, one a little less chaotic and a whole lot more wholesome.

Adisen stares out of the kitchen window from her family home. The one she recreated when they once again got sucked into a book of their own creation. She watches as Elijah chases around the twins, Theo and Theola. Her little beasts laugh and cry with their father, beaming with so much joy that it makes her heart happy and warm. Dottie sits on the grass in the backyard, readying the picnic as Maria pours out lemonade and blood orange gin.

Adisen never thought she could have everything she ever wanted. She guessed miracles did happen, just never in the way they would have thought. She never dreamed she'd be sucked into a never-ending story, tortured, and tormented only to have the realization that absolutely every second was worth it. That every second of the heartache was needed to bleed out onto the earth in order to make something beautiful.

Adisen gasps when the wind changes and a man appears in her kitchen. He's tall, handsome and has eyes that shine brighter than mischief. That smile though?... that smile is one she knows she's seen before.

"No... No, you can't be here. I'm not afraid anymore. I'm not afraid," Adisen hisses, placing her hand out in front of her with the wet dish cloth as it drips onto the floor.

"No, love. You aren't. But I told you you'd get to see me again being all sexy and shit." The trickster smirks, making Adisen's brows furrow. "I'm an entity you created, and one you don't know how to get rid of. I fulfilled my purpose, I taught you to face your fear, so I have no idea why I'm still here." He shrugs, leaning over to snag an apple from the counter. She whips him with the cloth, making him chuckle as he backs away.

After everything had happened, Adisen had told Elijah everything after the aftermath of the barracks. Including about the Trickster. Together they had assumed he had gone, since they had yet to see him since.

"So, you have what? Just been lurking for all of this time like a creeper?" she asks, folding her arms and narrowing her eyes.

"Sure have. Been watching that babe out there, want to introduce me?" He winks, before heading for the door. She hurries after him as they both halt when Elijah is already in the doorway, dark eyes boring into the Tricksters.

Elijah stalks forward, carrying his shadows with him. "Friend or foe? It's been a while since I've played with some dead man's bones." He smirks, hiking a brow as he pouts his lips with such a thought.

The trickster backs away, bumping into the wall with both hands before him like a shield. "Woah, hey. Definitely friend. I helped save her, remember?"

Elijah's shadows wrap around the man's throat, already having sensed who this man is. He finds great humor in toying with him, playing with his emotions and bleeding dry his fear. Allowing the shadows to circle his throat, they stroke against his skin in warning before disappearing in the blink of an eye. "Guess so, but I'm watching you, pretty boy," Elijah growls, stepping aside so that the trickster can pass.

"Aww, you think I'm pretty?" he teases, stumbling away from them and toward Maria.

"Who's the fox?" she asks, knocking over her glass of gin when the trickster appears out of nowhere.

"Maria, meet Triks. Triks, meet Maria." Adisen wave's a

hand, turning her back and pushing her husband back into the kitchen.

"Something you need, love?" the cocky bastard taunts, and before Adisen even has a chance to huff, she's lifted in the air by his shadows and brought to him, like a juicy bit of pussy on a platter. She can't help herself but arch into him, eying those tendrils as she imagines all of the places they could be, just like our first time together.

"Are you ready for forever, love?" he whispers against her lips.

"Always." She smiles, sinking her teeth into his lower lip making him growl as he carries her back through the house.

"I have a surprise for you, pretty girl."

"You do?" Adisen asks meekly, pulling back to stare at her beloved in heartfelt awe.

"I do."

Elijah teleports them into the forest bordering their home. Using his powers, he makes darkness fall so the sky twinkles with the beauty of the stars. Elijah then steals those very same stars from the night sky and scatters them throughout the forest.

They are blinding like the brightest fairy lights Adisen has ever seen. The entwine with fiery rocks and multi-colors of otherworldly blues and golden tones that float around her, capturing her in their angelic beauty, they refuse to let her go. Silver orbs that conform like an ocean wave, parting like a metallic sea, mixed with vibrant strokes of colors twinkle as she walks through them, trailing her hands softly against the constellations which stoke against her inner palm like the caress of smooth satin.

He's given her the world and all that surrounds it, placing it at her feet.

A tender slice of heaven that has left the kiss of addition within Adisen's veins.

She's awestruck, twirling within the stars as they wrap around her like vines of silk, leaving Elijah mesmerized as he stares in awe at his mate. His beastly heart is utterly content and wholesome at the sight of his beloved so completely happy and safe.

"Elijah, what did you do?" she breathes, unable to look at anything else other than the unbelievable magnificence before her. "It's nothing like I expected. Stars up close are just as beautiful as they are strange." She giggles, dancing in a circle, lost in a wonderland that she twists and twirls within, with a huge smile on her beautiful face.

"You have always looked at me like I've handed you the stars, Adisen. I want to be worthy of that look. So here they are. Here's the stars, pretty girl," he whispers, as he steps into her space and takes her into his arms.

Together, they dance amidst the beauty of the galaxies. Twirling her under his arm, he spins her out and smirks wickedly at her beauty as she beams back at him.

Hovering Adisen in the air with his magic, Elijah lies her down on a bed of stars.

A bed of roses is seriously overrated in his opinion.

A broken gasp whispers past her lips as she arches her back, crying to the sky as the quick action draws a sensual response from her needy body.

"You're so pretty when you whimper for me, baby girl. Did you know that?"

She shakes her head, rolling it from side to side as she tells him that no, she didn't know that.

It's a damn right shame that this woman doesn't even begin

to comprehend just what she does to him, so he begins to think it's only fair that he shows her.

Folding his large arms, Elijah taps a finger rhythmically against his chin as he eyes her through narrowed eyes of scorching lust, that devil's smirk becoming all the more deviant on his thick lips.

"I think I'm about to play with you, love. Really and truly show you what you do to me. Would you like that?" Elijah taunts as he uses his powers to peel the clothing from her tender flesh. He tears it away, layer by layer, achingly slow as he teases himself with the reveal of the sweet and succulent body that he craves to devour.

Her thighs snap open harshly, held apart by the vines of Elijah's magic as he binds her wrists the same way. Rosy, hardened buds pebble under the cool night air and she shivers, teeth chatting for a split second as the heat of her arousal adjusts to the coldness that surrounds us. The tips of his magical vines feather across her skin, tickling her in a delicate caress that has her breathing increasing and her heart rate spiking.

Elijah's cock is hard and heavy, aching in his pants begging for attention as he fights the urge to abuse it, wanting to watch her just a moment more. The moon casts a silver glow along the length of her shins and forearms, making her look like a goddess dipped in silvery-angelical paint.

So fucking glorious.

The definition of temptation and perfection.

The definition of sin and need.

Because, fuck if he doesn't need her, like he need the darkness that runs in her veins.

Reaching down, Elijah takes his cock in hand, stroking it with a brutal grip knowing it will draw a small scream from the back of her throat. Adisen jolts forward, pulling on the restraints of his magic as her entire body shudders and quivers with the sensation of how it feels when Elijah pleases himself.

He had taunted her with the subtle stroke of his magic around her most naughty parts, but he is yet to actually show those wicked parts of her the attentiveness she so desires.

In fact, he hasn't touched her or her swollen cunt at all.

"What the fuck is that?" she breathes, the shocked question trailing off into a sultry moan and she feels exactly what it is Elijah is feeling in that very moment as he jerks himself into an orgasm he is eager for her to experience.

He has connected their souls through the link they share with the mating bond. He has pulled on that thread and entwined it within his nervous system.

So right now, she feels firsthand just how good it is to have a dick and how good it feels to use it.

Granted it will never feel as good as when Elijah slips inside her tight heat.

That, nobody can never recreate. The feeling of ecstasy he can only feel when she uses those pussy walls to hold him hostage as she wages war on his dick elicits a shiver from him.

A man's orgasm is greatly different to a woman's and if Elijah is going to give his little witch the world, he's going to give her all the sensations that come with it too.

He groans, fighting to stay upright. Elijah straightens his back and squares his shoulders forcing his hand to move faster as heat runs throughout Elijah's stomach and sends tingles that shoot straight down his spine.

Elijah's balls draw tight, ready to shoot his load over the most spectacular creature he's ever seen.

Delirious and drowning in the sweetness of her pussy juices, high off the natural scent she exudes, Elijah is unable to give her his undivided attention as he watches her unravel like a pretty little bow.

"Can you feel that, my good girl? Can you feel what you do to me?" he growls, circling his beauty on her bed of stars, the beauty of that which is nothing compared to the stunning enchantress lying before him.

"Yes, yes…W-What is it?" she stutters, clenching her eyes closed as tight as she can while she thrashes back and forth, unsure as to how to handle the sensations she's never been accustomed to before now.

She knows what she knows.

Her body.

Her lust.

She doesn't have a clue as to what it feels like when it's his own, but she's about to.

"That's me, love. That's what you do to me, how you make me feel. Tell me, pretty girl. Tell me how you feel right now," Elijah commands through his heavy breathing, stalking his prey as he settles between her thighs.

He leans forward, running his tongue up the length of her throat and shuddering when the taste of her detonates like a bomb to his senses. "So sweet, pretty girl."

"I'm hot. All over… Everywhere," she wheezes, arching her back and fighting against the decision to open her legs wider or shut them and starve away the sensitivity plaguing her. "I feel powerless, without control. I can't fight it, I can't stop it. My heart is wild. I can't tell if I'm coming or going. I'm chasing something, something so close but so far and I don't know what. It's too much and nowhere near enough, Elijah. It's nowhere *near* enough! I feel like I could die if I don't get to touch you!"

Sweat gathers across her chest, dripping between her ample tits as they shine for him, drawing the eye and making her all that more alluring.

"That's the point, love. To show you exactly what you do to me. To show you how I have felt every single second, since the very first moment I met you. Powerless and at your mercy." Elijah leans down, lining up his heavy cock with Adisen's slick and ready apex. "And something else? I want you to feel what I feel each and every time I get to steal your innocence." Thrusting his hips, Elijah once again breaks through that oh-so-sweet barrier he was all too eager to set back into place. It made the beast in him roar each time he got to become her first once again, painting those glorious thighs red.

Writing his name within it all.

"I love you, love. Fuck, do I love you. Thank you for being my pretty girl. For giving me our beautiful children and for giving us this world. You made the character a man. Every day it makes my dark heart happy to write this story with you."

There was still magic in this world. Still creatures that flew through the skies.

Only now, none of them wanted those who lived here dead.

"You gave me everything I'd ever dreamt off, Elijah, and you did it all with a growl of the devil and the love of a saint. Thank you for this life, for always being my fantasy. I love you."

Heaven?

It's left in the place you make it and Adisen and Elijah decide to make it every day, with the person that they love.

"Thank you, thank you for everything, Elijah. Thank you for saving me." She choked, the emotion too much for her to bear.

"I didn't have to do anything, Adisen I chose to fight for you because you're worth fighting for," he reposed with utter conviction.

I'm Adisen.

I'm Elijah.

And the ink has just dried within the pages of our story.

The End

Prologue

DEATH'S WISH

Aviya

Darkness gathered around me in a heavy abundance. Unable to move my arms or open my eyes, I fought desperately to find stable ground for one breath, that I'm unable to obtain. There's a hollowness here. An endless depth of nothing as I struggle through the enclosure, wrapped around me in a relentless grip. I'm being suffocated, my lungs burned.

I wiggled, shifting within the harshness of whatever rubbed against me.

Whatever it was, it rubbed me raw and the harder that I fought, the more my skin chafed.

I fought my way through the bleak abyss, like a warrior fighting away the hand beckoning you to the afterlife. It resonated with me. But my purpose was here. On earth. So I fought for the right to be blessed by the ancient necromantic gods.

Fuck the promise of a promised land. In that moment, all I wanted was freedom.

Redoubling my efforts, I'm able to coil tight my hand as I use it to punch through the surface of something solid, which broke easily under my scorching wrath.

My fist punched through the earth as it shattered like a detonation of a dirt bomb. An opening was made like the wave of the sea parting.

I crawled from my grave, still gripped by the darkness, stumbling on unsteady feet as I stared around me and tried to find any surroundings. Soil thick on my tongue.

There was nothing around me. Nothing other than *nothing*... Not even a moon.

With dread in my heart and a weight bottoming out within my stomach, I walked through the shadows, lost to the numbness - lost to everything around me and lost to any and all sense that one should have when awakening to a scene as sinister as this one.

But I was entranced. Unfeeling as I strolled further into the night.

I was a ball of unwavering emptiness and when I spotted lights in the distance, I still felt nothing other than a cold kind of stoicness. Lumbering my way toward a noisy bar, I sneaked through the back door after shouldering it open. Seeking out the restroom in the back, through the buzz of mind-rattling noise, I carried on my way. Yet, I hardly heard the noise at all, it was all a faint distortion around me.

I kept to the walls, not drawing attention my way as I moved like a wraith through the low lights and murky air.

The door slammed shut with a clap of thunder behind me while I made my way to the sinks.

Standing like a vessel in the process of awakening, I stared back at myself, trying to piece it all together.

But there was nothing there.

Nothing other than a frozen and welcoming *nothing*.

Nothing?

Can there be so much of nothing at all? All at once as it consumed you? All as once as it left you emptied inside?

I zoned out, waiting…

Knowing.

Something led me here.

I'm pushed against the bathroom sink, the porcelain bit into the bone of my hips but the pain was void. Unfeelable as I tried to turn around but I'm shoved again. My head slammed into the glass, shattering the shards that sliced into my cheek, drawing blood, while I felt something being pulled from my body.

With heavy limbs and a coldness that bled into the warmth of once heated skin, I finally spun around to glare at the feral beast of a nightmare that stood behind me, pulling at my clothes, like a possessed barbarian hunkering for a bone.

"I saw you walk in, dirty girl. From the very corner of the bar. You seemed a little lost so I thought I'd come and say hi," he uttered with a smile from ear to ear. He leered at me with eyes that roamed all over my broken and torn skin as he stared at the dirt which hid the flesh beneath.

I'm covered. Brittle and broken, yet this man is relentless in his pursuit.

"What do you say, sunshine? Want me to help clean you up a bit? A little shower of pearly white will wash away all of this black, my sweet bitch," He beamed, eyes alight in something sick and twisted as he tore the ragged shirt from my shoulder. "After all, who's going to stop me? And who's going to know? Looks like you've already met one man that made your night tonight, princess. Where is he and will he share?" The taunt fell flat.

Calculating eyes stared back at him as I remained unmoving, only accessing.

I wasn't afraid. I was curious. With immoral thoughts of death running through my mind.

The man gripped me by the jaw, forcing my head back to stare at him, but I had no emotion to share, no tear to shed. "What's up, dirty girl? Nothing to say? Nothing to offer? Oh, me and my friend are going to love you. But I have to admit, we love a little bit of a fight as well. What do you think? Can you do it, dirty girl? Can you fight us?"

My stoic face contorted with a dehumanising smirk as I showed him my teeth, the first hint of emotion that seeped through and it left him dumbstruck before he quickly recovered from the demented gleam that gazed back at him, promising everything cold and wicked.

The numbness held hands with the new awareness that echoed within my mind and I knew what I had to do.

One, two, three.

The voice chanted inside of my mind. The voice of many bellowed back at me.

We call the four elements to thee. Take this man, brutalize him be. End him now. Gut him like swine and feed the power of death to the bone witch necromancer, the last of our line.

Accept this offering, Adda! Awaken the last.

Allow the descendent free, to toy with the dead and bury the weak.

The world blinked and darkness was the only thing to be seen. Wind kissed against me, chilling me into a seduction of sensual chills.

Light snapped back into the abyss as I stared at myself in the mirror, horrified beyond belief at what stared back at me, laced with utter curiosity at the warped kind of beauty of it all. My raven hair turned pure white, falling down my back to brush against the curve of my ass. My face turned pale and ashen, as the perplexing and foreboding-looking designs contoured to my face. White markings lined my cheekbones, under-eyes, jaw, nose, forehead, and lips until it feathered down my throat and across my skin. It was shadowed to look like a skeleton. A creepily beautiful skeleton as small white pearls glistened against my skin. The color of my gaze bled into a remarkable gray, as the sudden and unexpected change left my mouth agape in confusion. My heart beat wildly in my chest as I felt the pulse thump against my taut skin. My hand trembled as I stared down at the ground, at the dead man laid at my feet.

The same pearls, somehow stuck to my skin, entwine within the left side of my head like a jeweled hairpiece and I was left shaking where I stand.

What's happening? What the fuck is happening?

I panicked, my voice frantic in my mind. As the coldness began to fade and my conscious began to fight back for control.

This man tried to hurt me. He tried to take what wasn't his to take and I did everything I could just to survive. To keep myself untainted from a man born of everything vile.

I threw my hands out and I screamed. I screamed with everything I had with no other thought other than I wanted this monster dead.

I wanted him un-alived and stone-cold at my feet.

I wanted him to feel the anguish of a life about to end and to feel the ice-brittle hands of death as they choked him, forcing him to stare at the abyss without any hope of escape.

I wanted him to feel it all. To be tormented with the promise of a painful demise.

I wanted him to die. To die and to never be able to try and take another woman's voice again.

But more importantly, I wanted him to see how rotten his bones were.

So I tore the skeleton from his flesh. It now laid beside him, next to the husked meat-suit of the earth's bitter-scum. Deflated and like a blow-up doll gone bang, socketless eyes flicker to the side as he stared at the insidious and black rotten bones laid alongside him. Poisonous as they hissed like acid. All before he took his last breath. That was the final thing he saw. The truest thing he would have ever had the chance to have seen in his miserable little life.

It just happened. The son of a bitch keeled over with my malicious thoughts, and I was left looking like a beauty of the dead - ethereal and utterly chilling.

To look into my eyes, was to see the land of death itself blinking back at you.

A cold and barren place where lost souls roam. Alone and without a voice unless I decided to give them one.

I felt that I had that kind of power.

This was my land; the ruined realm only holds one soul at the moment.

The soul I just murdered.

A coldness crept into my bones, infusing me with a brutal resolve as I stared back down at the boneless man and smirked.

I smirked something wicked and depraved, as the knowledge

that I did that set fire to my veins. I had power. A power greater than life and death and I had to learn how to use it.

The door to the bathroom in Ronnie's Bar swung open and Mr. Cold, Dead and Blue's pal walked in with a slimy smile on his twisted lips as he rubbed his hands together, like he was about to dig into something devastatingly sweet.

Ooo, this will be fun. Cal always picks the best bitches.

His voice whispered into my mind and I tilted my head, staring at him through the eyes of the otherworld, and knowing what I had to do. Knowing what power it was that I held deep inside.

He stopped short, looking at the body on the ground in shock, before a set of dark green and largely wild eyes flicked back to me.

They had picked their prey, unaware what a bittersweet predator she truly was.

I threw out my hand, wind gathered around me as a tiny, movable storm drifted through the woman's bathroom and offered me the power of the elements. Red, blue, green, and yellow swirled around me like the dance of ominous darkened-hued fairy lights.

I called forth what felt right.

What felt natural and I watched as the earth filtered through his veins, causing black-pebble-like tendrils to slither under his skin like dirt. His eyes became inflamed with balls of fire as his mouth filled with water. He spluttered and choked, mouth fused shut and unable to dispel what assaulted him. The air swirled around him, lifting him from his feet as the elements spread through him like the plague. Blood bled from his eyes. Organs bulged under his flesh. Taking a moment to appreciate the vile being I was about to cleanse from this earth, I allowed the moment of appreciation to pass as I blinked, allowing the teasing elements to consume him thoroughly and quit playing the game of *when,* as they drained the life from him and fed it back into the earth. A sacrifice for the wrongdoings of heartless men. An offering.

It gathered within the soil beneath the very earth before burning against the soles of my feet and rushing back through me like a livewire. It lifted me. Lighting me from the inside out with the electrical waves of blue lightning.

Empowering me.

Encouraging me.

I was gifted with the hand of death and I had every intention of using it.

Tonight, I entered this bar a terrified, underage fifteen-year-old girl who had crawled from her own grave without any idea as to what the fuck was happening or how I ended up there at all.

I was led here by a knowing. By the voices of the dead.

Tonight, I'll leave this bar as a creature empowered, dedicated to growth.

Tonight, I learned what I am and tomorrow… I would show the world what I could do.

Just before I claimed my consciousness once more, another voice drifted through my mind. A darkened and sinful voice of brutality and lust.

Finally, wicked love. How beautifully, you have awoken. Careful now, the games have begun and so has the hunt.

About the Author

Emmaleigh Loader is a stay-at-home mum of three - her two boys and her brother-in-law - and a wife, who lives in the UK.

Her favorite things are storms, the sea, and anything witchy! She finds winter beautiful and enjoys the beauty of the sun. She loves anything dark and adores loving alphas and strong women. She's an avid reader, and despite living with disabilities, pushes herself to be someone who her family, husband and sons are proud of.

Follow my socials:

https://linktr.ee/EmmaleighLoader

Also by Emmaleigh Wynters

Fantasy/Paranormal

Standalone:

Don't Read Between The Line's

Death's Wish - TBA

Devoured By The Lines TBA

Also By Emmaleigh Loader

Kings Wolves MC Standalone series:

Savage

Ouija

Straightjacket

Stitch

Toothpick- TBA

Novellas:

Who I Crave To Be

Daddy's Calling- TBA

Paranormal Novellas:

Rising From The Ashes- Imperfectly Beautiful

Are you a fan of notebooks?

Emmaleigh also has a series of notebooks.

The Witches series.

The Fantasy series.

(All Can Be Found Under Emmaleigh Loader On Amazon)

Merchandise:

Open Book: The Villains That Feed Our Soul Quoted Notebook.

Knife And Blood: The Villains We Need Notebook.

Girl In The Mind Library: Don't Read Between The Lines Quoted Notebook.

Black Unicorn: Savage Quoted Notebook.

Skull And Butterfly: Ouija Quoted Notebook.

Skeleton Couple: Stitch Quoted Notebook.

<u>All notebooks will be live March 2022 on amazon. Other products with the merchandise designs will be available soon as well.</u>

Printed in Great Britain
by Amazon

39636435R00253